Needle at the Bottom of the Sea

Bengali merchant ship from a *pīr pat,* scroll painting, Murshidabad ca. 1780–1800.

Needle at the Bottom of the Sea

Bengali Tales from the Land of the Eighteen Tides

Translated by

Tony K. Stewart

with contributions by Ayesha A. Irani

UNIVERSITY OF CALIFORNIA PRESS

University of California Press
Oakland, California

Cataloging-in-Publication Data is on file at the Library of Congress.

ISBN 978-0-520-38893-2 (pbk. : alk. paper)
ISBN 978-0-520-38894-9 (ebook)

Manufactured in the United States of America

32 31 30 29 28 27 26 25 24 23
10 9 8 7 6 5 4 3 2 1

for their gracious guidance

Momtazur Rahman Tarafdar (d. 1997)
Anisuzzaman (d. 2020)
Perween Hasan
Abdul Momin Chowdhury

CONTENTS

Introduction

Introduction

BENGALI TALES FROM THE LAND OF THE EIGHTEEN TIDES

What would you do if that white fly buzzing around your head landed on the wall and started giving you marriage advice? Or what could possibly be your response if the mendicant Sufi you often see at prayers should in the blink of an eye shape-shift into a giant ogre, enormous fangs bulging from a bloody maw? These events, and many more like them are not uncommon in the stories (*kathā*s) of miracle-working Sufi saints (*pīr*s) that have circulated in the Bangla-speaking world for most of the past millennium. The stories are romances filled with wondrous marvels, where tigers talk, rocks float and waters part, and færies carry a sleeping Sufi holy man into the bedroom of a Hindu princess with whom the god of fate, Bidhātā, has ordained his marriage. Each of the five stories in this anthology features unlikely heroes and heroines, intrepid oceangoing traders, fickle gods and goddesses, prophets and holy men, and the royal whimsy of kings and wealthy landowning zamindars. The protagonists encounter predicaments faced by every human being, but the presence of marvels beyond the ordinary signals creative solutions on a heroic scale. Characters revel in the skillful navigation of the quirks of everyday life, adroitly maneuvering through the obligations of pressing kinship, juggling the tensions of conflicting allegiances, and cleverly satisfying competing social and religious demands, which are inevitably political. While the protagonists, both male and female, are nominally religious, Sufi saints, the texts are in no way sectarian statements or theology. They are literature, adventure stories of survival that underscore the need for people of all social and religious ranks to work together in hostile environments. They explore ways to overcome the physical challenges of living in the Sundarban mangrove swamps of southern Bengal, which both abound in natural resources and teem with myriad tigers, crocodiles, and dread diseases; and to ameliorate the occasional hostilities born of social differences of caste and economic class.

In addition to their timeless marvels, familiar from all great storytelling traditions, these tales have a historically conditioned cultural import for South Asia. While they entertain with their convoluted plots—very much in the vein of *A Thousand and One Nights*, or when the animals take center stage, as we find in the parables of *Kalīla wa-Dimna*—they subtly introduce an Islamic perspective into a Bengali world that was initially in this early modern period traditionally Indic. Whether read or sung, or staged in often raucous theatrical productions still today, they do not intone theological propositions, apart from the simple injunction to worship God, who is the God of all. They never propose anything resembling an imposition of *sharī 'ah* law or any other legislative code than to conduct oneself with dignity and respect for others. In their inviting tone, they translate a generic Islamic history and cosmology so that it comes to seem natural to a Bengali imagination. It is readily intuitive that the heaven fashioned by the Hindu god Kṛṣṇa, widely recognized as *vaikuṇṭha*, is understood to mean *bihisht*, the Islamic paradise found in Persian poetry, or that the *masjid* (mosque) and *mandir* (temple) are somehow functionally equivalent, but not fungible.[1] But contra the all-too-common narrative that today charts Islam's entry into Bengal as a series of military and political events—although, make no mistake, military politics were involved—the long-term transformation of the Bangla-speaking world into a Muslim-majority society

1. For the dynamics of this translation process, see Tony K. Stewart, "In Search of Equivalence: Conceiving Muslim-Hindu Encounter through Translation Theory." *History of Religions* 40, no. 3 (Winter 2001): 261–88; anthologized in *India's Islamic Traditions: 711–1750*, edited by Richard M. Eaton, 363–92 (Delhi: Oxford University Press, 2003); and in *Figuring Religions: Comparing Ideas, Images, and Activities*, edited by Subha Pathak, 229–62 (Albany: State University of New York Press, 2013).

was more subtle. These tales demonstrate how wondrous stories undertook the work of adding a natural Islamic substrate to local culture. Of equal import, these romances performed a cultural work that ran in the opposite direction, gently writing Bengal into the larger realms of Islamic literature, finding a place for it in the vast early modern Islamic world that Shahab Ahmed calls the "Balkans to Bengal" complex.[2]

The ethical issue that binds all of the narratives together is how to balance living honorably and morally in a world fraught with checkered allegiances, while somehow not allowing its vagaries to blind one to a larger reality—that is, how to be in it without being of it. It is a restless, often frustrating search to achieve the impossible, like finding a needle at the bottom of the sea, a feat that one of the stories attests could only be performed by the ageless and perfected ideal Sufi al-Khiḍr (in these stories, Khoyāj Khijir) to help the hero Gāji Pīr survive the horrible ordeals inflicted on him by his disgruntled father. The search for love and acceptance lies at the heart of those odysseys, but the elastic relationship between divine love and its worldly forms generates a constant, shifting tension. These concerns lie at the forefront in the north Indian allegorical romances created by Sufi authors, and although these Bangla tales adopt some of the form and spirit of those allegories, they eschew their analytical formality of aesthetics to explore in more ordinary terms how the indigenous Bengali construction of pure love (*prem*) equated to the Islamic world's equivalent (*ʿishq*). They reimagine, over and over again, the higher reaches of the sublime as fundamental to everyday Bengali life. To experience such love, whether in human terms or divine, was to embrace a larger moral universe whose quirks were routinely, but usually indirectly, explored in the situation creativity demonstrated by the stories' characters. They capture real-life situations their audiences recognize, thrown into sharp relief by the fantastic, which is the reason for much of the tales' appeal and makes them classics of Bangla literature.

The tales' heroes and heroines take their places beside, indeed, interact with, the gods and goddesses of Bengali Hindu mythology. Blurring the distinctions between heroic romance and mythology, they appropriate those myths. Dating from the early fifteenth century,

2. Shahab Ahmed, *What Is Islam? The Importance of Being Islamic* (Princeton, NJ: Princeton University Press, 2016).

the first of these extraordinary Bengali Sufis to emerge was the holy man Satya Pīr. In his narrative beginnings, he was understood to be a composite form of the popular *hinduyāni* deity Nārāyaṇ fused either with the *musalmāni* God, Khodā, or Allāh (Āllā, as it is spelled in Bangla), or with the Prophet Muhāmmad. He always appears in the tattered mantle of the itinerant Sufi mendicant, but with the social markers of both a *brāhmaṇ* priest and various ascetic practitioners. As Kṛṣṇahari Dās describes him:[3]

He wears the dress of a *phakir*,
the hair on his head smeared the color of mud,
    the Prophet's patched scarf cinched at his neck.
His lotus body shimmers brilliantly,
four times more effulgent than a full moon
    perched above dark clouds thick with rain.
The sacred thread drapes his shoulder,
a chain belt hangs at his waist,
    in his hands trembles the staff of one's aspirations.
A short string of anklets jingle
in time with his dagger's clink
        to each clopping step of his wooden sandals.

Kṛṣṇahari Dās, *Baḍa satya pīr o sandhyāvatī kanyār punthi*, 214

This sartorial image signals a new religious orientation. As all of his tales attest, to worship Satya Pīr was to alleviate one of the most pressing issues of this early modern society: penury. The tales make clear that poverty makes it virtually impossible to lead an ethically sound life, and such a life is made even harder in an environment of conflict. Satya Pīr encourages people to recognize that all humans share in this existential predicament, and that sharing can be the foundation of a genuine amity and the basis for good government.[4] This impulse

3. Kṛṣṇahari Dās, *Baḍa satya pīr o sandhyāvatī kanyār punthi* (Kalikātā: Nurūddin Āhmād at Gāosiya Lāibreri, n.d.). There is an earlier translation found in Tony K. Stewart, "Alternate Structures of Authority: Satya Pīr on the Frontiers of Bengal," in *Beyond Turk and Hindu: Rethinking Religious Identities in Islamicate South Asia*, edited by David Gilmartin and Bruce B. Lawrence (Gainesville: University of Florida Press, 2000), 25.

4. On Satya Pīr's mission, see Stewart, "Alternate Structures of Authority," passim, and Tony K. Stewart, *Witness to Marvels: Sufism and Literary Imagination* (Oakland: University of California Press, 2019), ch. 6.

embodies the concept of a properly settled, well-functioning community, described as *ābādī*, that is, "cultivated." Today, many might regard the combination of Hindu and Muslim as unthinkable, but that stark binary is largely a product of the late nineteenth and early twentieth centuries, when religious affiliations had become political identities based on exclusion. In these early modern stories, orientations are better understood as markers of difference that are malleable and porous. Religion is more a matter of what one does than of what one believes; it is enacted, gender is enacted, social standing is enacted, all driven by the push for a universal morality and a well-fashioned society.

The heroes and heroines of these tales are indigenous to Bengal, and they cross-populate from one story to another in a closed set, hence the choice to translate them together. Although several of the characters and events repeat, the tales do not constitute a cycle. Literary historians have somewhat mistakenly characterized them as fairy tales or folktales, but those labels impose expectations on the reader that imply in the South Asian context that the tales lack literary merit. While they are certainly akin to those genres in spirit, the stories involve a kind of timelessness, taking place in an indeterminate age, long before the present, though not without occasional allusions to historical events. That timelessness draws in readers without restriction. Yet unlike most fairy and folktales which tend to be as nonspecific in their geographic locales as in their temporality, the action in these stories tends to take place largely in, or while passing through, a very real part of the landscape of the Bangla-speaking world, the Sundarbans, the southern mangrove swamps of the Āṭhārobhāṭī, the "low-lying lands of the eighteen tides," as the territory is locally known. Place-names that we do not recognize today sometimes occur in them, but the region's rivers are always precisely identified, its cities and ports, mosques and temples, are precisely situated, and the vagaries of its intense climate, tides and currents, and oppressive heat ring true. And when a trader's adventure carries his ship further south, down the east coast of India and back again, the authors extend their reach, accurately depicting significant landmarks and pilgrimage sites, such as the temple of Jagannāth in the city of Nilācal (Puri) in Odisha, while locating their stories in the ancient legendary landscapes of past epics, including the Isle of Laṅkā (generally assumed to be modern Sri

Lanka), as depicted in the *Rāmāyaṇ*. But most of these tales take place in the wild jungly islands of the Sundarbans.

Defined by the braided distributaries of two of the largest rivers in the world, the Gāṅgā and Brahmāputra, the Sundarbans form the planet's largest river delta. Many of the stretches and diversions of Gāṅgā and Brahmāputra have different local names—notably, the Bhāgīrathī, or Padmā, and the Jamunā, which combine to form the Meghnā.[5] The Royal Bengal tigers of the Āṭhārobhāṭī are legendary, magnificent beasts, whose exploits under the tutelage of Sufi masters loom large in a number of these narratives. The region is, of course, also home to several species of crocodiles—the mugger, the giant saltwater, and the ghariyal, whose tapered snout ends in a distinctive cartilaginous boss—denizens of a different sort, who often provide ready opponents to face off against the tigers, but can also aid and abet the *phakir* or *bibī*, once enlisted in their cause. And of course there are different species of cobras, most commonly king and speckled cobras, as well as a variety of kraits and vipers, and non-venomous keelbacks and pythons, to name only a few of the better-known snakes, though in these stories they tend to play only bit parts. The Sundarbans are densely rich in natural resources. The mix of fresh and brackish waters of the mangroves have made the region a prime source of hearty timber—the primary tree locally called *sundarī*[6]—but also of honey and wax collection, salt extraction, and, most recently, a locus of shrimp farming, accelerating the destruction of the fragile environment, a natural buffer between the powerful typhoons blowing in from the Bay of Bengal and the alluvial floodplains that constitute most of Bangladesh and the Indian state of West Bengal. Unsurprisingly, the natural riches of the mangrove biome attract humans, who intrude in these tales on the habitats of tigers, serpents, and crocodiles.

5. The waterways of the delta are constantly migrating, carving new straits and passages to the Indian Ocean, piling up silt to create new islands, engulfing others, sometimes shifting riverbeds scores of miles. The places named in these stories are specific and often consistent from one story to the next, but it is impossible to derive a map of any accuracy from them; many of the river settlements the stories name that can be found today are landlocked, miles from the rivers that once fed them.

6. The most common is the species *H. fomes* of the genus *Heritiera* in the Malvacae family, but conservationists report that nearly half of the world's species of mangrove trees can be found there.

Just as they do in real life, humans and beasts inevitably threaten one another in the stories, and negotiating those encounters plays a major role in them. Invariably, it involves the mediation of a Sufi master, who preaches a balance both among the peoples of the Sundarbans and between them and the delta's nonhuman fauna.

Completed in 1686 CE, the second oldest tale in this anthology, Kṛṣṇarām's *Rāy maṅgal*—the auspicious narrative of Dakṣiṇ Rāy, Lord of the South[7]— perhaps first sounded the alarm about the fragility of the Sundarbans' environment, what with too-greedy humans' laying waste to the mangrove swamps' rich resources. God Himself had delivered a dire warning about the future of the land, Kṛṣṇarām writes. After a short opening tale involving woodcutters, the bulk of the first half of his story has two protagonists, who become mutual antagonists—the Sufi warrior saint Baḍa Khān Gāji and Dakṣiṇ Rāy, a demigod in the lineage of the Hindu god Śiv. Fighting over issues of public humiliation, of pride and prestige—but notably not of religion, as we understand it today—they slay one another in battle, which would seem to put an end to the quarrel. In the magical manner of romances everywhere, however, Baḍa Khān springs back to life. He sheds his old body and assumes a new one, a special boon from the Prophet Muhāmmad. It takes God to intervene and resuscitate his opponent, Dakṣiṇ Rāy. After both are revivified, they stand humbly before the divine presence, chastened by his scathing indictment of their petty hostility, a not-so-subtle message about the hollowness of apparent differences in social standing and religious affiliation. The two enemies become brothers, an eventuality that was reexamined as the story was told and replayed over the next several centuries, yet always ending in a delicate balance between them.

Significantly, Kṛṣṇarām tells us that God chose to appear before them as Satya Pīr, whose popularity was already well attested. After chastising his two recalcitrant devotees for their small-minded antagonism, Satya Pīr turns his attention to the hecatombs of tigers they have slain, whose corpses litter the field around him. First, he revives the lot of them through the power of his glance, then he dramatically pauses to warn the top tiger, Khān Dāudā, of the danger of humans,

7. Kavi Kṛṣṇarām Dās, "Rāymaṅgal," in *Kavi kṛṣṇarām dāser granthāvalī,* edited by Satyanārāyaṇ Bhaṭṭācārya (Kalikātā: Calcutta University, 1958), 165–248.

the hazards of tangling with the aboriginals who populate the region, and the need to be wary of any other people who might venture into the Sundarbans:

> The vile savages of these wilds are unpredictable animals. Should you encounter them, they will break your necks, and for this reason you should avoid them. Should you hunt them to eat, you should be no less wary than when you meet ordinary human beings. After twelve years or so, the cubs in your streak may not always find the hunting successful.
>
> Kṛṣṇarām Dās, *Rāy maṅgal*, vv. 424–25

Setting aside for the moment the author's characterization of the indigenous inhabitants of the region—the so-called aboriginals, *ādibāsīs*, here called *bāḍ*—as somehow subhuman and fit for tigers' eating, his warning is prescient: the tigers' cubs may starve because of human harvesting of the Sundarbans' flora and fauna at an alarming rate. The message could hardly be clearer: animals and humans must get along, find a balance, just as aboriginal and exploiter must, just as *hinduyāni* and *musalmāni* peoples must. That seemingly simple refrain ripples through all the tales. Balance is engineered and maintained only through the intervention of the Sufi *pīr*, a holy mendicant who repeatedly orchestrates an alliance between the two sets of apex predators—kings, their merchants, and aboriginals, on the human side, and tigers, representing the animal half of the equation. Yet the tales' heroes tend to advocate for and defend those caught in the middle: farmers, woodcutters, honey collectors, salt workers, and fishermen, those most intimately bound to the land and most familiar with its dangers.

An old Bangla saw stresses the unremitting danger lurking in the landscape—*ḍāṅgāy bāgh, jale kumir* ("tiger on dry land, crocodile in the water"). Though the cobra on occasion interlopes into the equation, the tiger would seem to have been the most feared of the many zoological threats, hence the increasing pressure on its dwindling populations as clashes with humans increased. The already fearsome tiger was widely believed to possess a shape-shifting power in addition to its terrifying stealth, and in these tales the tigers seem to stand in for all forms of existential precariousness, dangers both seen and unseen. These majestic creatures are, moreover, often mocked in the stories, with their individual idiosyncrasies presented in comic relief, perhaps a way of somewhat nervously coping with their extreme danger. The litany of complaints that one hears from the tigers once they are persuaded to vent their frustrations to the *pīr* is like a mirror held up to the human inhabitants of the islands, who recognize in them reflections of their own fixations on their appetites—territorial, culinary, and sexual—as well as their woes—broken teeth, arthritis, and a slower gait as they grow older. The message seems to be twofold: the frustrations and ailments that afflict people generate a knowing response, but Kṛṣṇarām makes clear to the reader that animals suffer too, like humans.

Diseases such as smallpox and cholera, were endemic to the region, so driven by the desire to protect themselves, Bengalis have historically sought a way of peacefully co-existing by anthropomorphizing those threats. Centuries before Kṛṣṇarām composed his *Rāy maṅgal*, Manasā was recognized as the goddess of all serpents, her favorite being the cobra. A little later, the goddess Śitalā was understood to have extended her domain to the control of smallpox and other diseases of the skin, ranging from cowpox and measles to warts and wens. Kṛṣṇarām also composed a *maṅgal kāvya* depicting Śitalā's exploits along with her henchman, Jvar or Jvarāsur, the fever demon, which suggests that in the eyes of many, these pestilential threats were very much all of a piece. A little later, Śitalā acquired a cousin-sister, Olābibī, also known as Olādevī or Olāicaṇḍī, who was soon recognized as the *musalmāni* matron and *hinduyāni* goddess of cholera and, by extension, of water-borne ailments such as hepatitis and dysentery. Leprosy and elephantiasis make cameo appearances in these tales, but they fall to deities less central to the narratives. To tame the most towering threat of all, the tigers, tales stretching over several centuries tell how people turned to the extraordinary powers of the trio of Dakṣiṇ Rāy, Baḍa Khān Gāji, and Bonibibī, who gradually come to team together. Their stories are instructive for their listeners, few of whom would have entered the mangrove forests without invoking their powers of protection.[8]

8. Among the several ethnographic portrayals in English, with a focus on the strategies utilizing Bonbibī, see Annu Jalais, *Forest of Tigers: People, Politics and Environment in the Sundarbans* (London: Routledge, 2010); in Bangla, see for a nearly comprehensive survey of all the region's prominent gods and goddesses, *pīrs* and *bibīs*, and their tales in popular performance, Debabrata Naskar, *Cabbiśparganār laukik debdebī: Pālāgān o lok saṃskṛti jijñāsā* (Kalakātā: De'j Pābiliśiṃ, 1406 BS [ca. 1999]).

These allied *hinduyāni* deities and *musalmāni* miracle-working saints are still individually and collectively honored and worshipped by the inhabitants of the Sundarbans and other parts of Bengal, Odisha, and Jharkhand today, without regard to sectarian distinctions—just as Satya Pīr argues they should. Over the past few centuries, the local communities that call the Sundarbans home have pragmatically turned to whatever works to protect them. Just how this current state of inter- and intra-sectarian cooperation and collaboration eventually came about is part of the cultural work of the stories in this anthology; it is a celebration made possible by the rejection of sectarian exclusion and the promotion of common kinship ties. Differences among communities are recognized, but given the precariousness of life in the littoral, antagonisms weaken the population as a whole and cannot be tolerated. That their protagonists are mainly Sufi *pīr*s and *bibī*s, holy men and women of extraordinary power, makes the tales nominally religious, but the religious perspectives, both *musalmāni* and *hinduyāni*, tend to be generic in tone, projecting only simulacra of sectarian specifics. Save in the broadest strokes, theological these tales most definitely are not. What they are first and foremost is narrative literature about the necessity of having a helping hand to survive in a hostile environment, whether the trader's precarious oceangoing voyages to lands unknown, the plundering of the wilds of the jungle, or simply the unpredictability of encountering powerful individuals adamant about the importance of their different social and religious backgrounds. One should not expect lectures or overt didacticism from any of these authors, apart from an occasional aside or a framing dedicatory passage.

Miraculous happenings are not the exclusive province of these fictional romances, however, and it is important to distinguish them from similar stories found in the historical record in the Bangla-speaking world that depict the marvelous exploits of Sufis. Take, for example, the well-documented life of the warrior-saint Ismāil Gājī, who flourished in the reign of Ruknuddin Bārbak Shāh (r. 1459–1474 CE) and was martyred in battle with the Rājā of Mandāran in northern Odisha. Eyewitness and later accounts report that Ismāil's decapitated head carries on the fight in one direction across the land of Bengal, while his body did the same in a different direction, the latter declared to have further dismembered itself in order to multiply its fighting presence; today different tombs are said to house his arms, legs, torso, and head.[9] In the early modern period, the stories of Ismāil Gājī and other famous historical Sufis, such as Shāh Jālāl of Sylhet (ca. 1271–1346 CE), Baḍa Khān Murid Miñā aka Shāykh Nūruddīn Quṭb-i ʿĀlam (d. 1415 CE), were composed in Persian, eventually some in Urdu, and few in Arabic. The genres signify "biographical acts," "hagiographies," "histories," "diaries," and so forth. The Bangla tales of the *pīrs* and *bibīs* in this anthology, however, are generally called *kathās*, stories or fictions. Not until the late nineteenth and early twentieth centuries do the legends of the historical *musalmāni* saints find expression in Bangla, but even then the genre markers do not overlap with the *kathās*, preferring instead *itihās* (history), *carit* (biography), and *caritāmṛta* (hagiography, lit. the nectar or essence of actions). As a result, none of the fictional characters are mentioned in those historical accounts, nor are those historical figures ever invoked in the fictional *kathās*. They operate in discrete discourses, with virtually no crossover, though it would be hard to imagine that today a reader of the latter would not be familiar with the former.

This "in-between" story literature of Sufi saints—that is "not folktale or fairy tale" and "not history or hagiography"—constitutes a corpus generated by more than a hundred authors in the early modern period. Taken collectively, the surviving hand-written manuscripts number a fraction under eight hundred and account for the second largest body of early modern Bangla writings; only the *vaiṣṇav* compositions exceed them in number. The earliest surviving manuscripts in this corpus date from the mid-1600s and include the very oldest Bangla books to survive the rains and floods, the mold, the white ants, and human neglect, all of which ravage the old hand-made paper.[10] That survival attests to a widespread popularity, but the shape these writings took was very much conditioned by the symbiotic

9. The sources of these stories are scattered, but are mostly summarized, although not completely, in Girīndranāth Dās, *Bāṃlā pīr sāhityer kathā,* 1st ed. Kājipāḍā, Bārāsat, Cabbiś Pargaṇa: Śehid Lāibrerī, 1383 BS [ca. 1976].

10. For a comprehensive list of these earliest manuscripts, see Stewart, *Witness to Marvels,* 203, n. 17 .

relationship they had with another genre of early modern Bangla tales, the *maṅgal kāvya,* semi-epic poems extolling the auspicious appearances and interventions of various gods and goddesses. Goddesses—Manasā, Caṇḍī, Annadā, Śītalā, Ṣaṣṭhī, Kālikā, Sāradā, Subacanī, and Gaṅgā—dominate that genre, but gods—Śiv, Dharma, Pañcānan, and Dakṣiṇ Rāy—are sometimes favored, too.[11] They tell of the harrowing adventures of merchants, of cities being carved out of the jungly wilderness, and the plagues of disease and wild animals.

The very earliest of the extant *pīr kathā*s follow the general structure of the *maṅgal kāvya* adventures in extolling the exploits of Satya Pīr. Appearing a little more than a century after the initial tales about Satya Pīr, Kṛṣṇarām's *Rāy maṅgal* would seem to be one of the first crossover tales of the genre to introduce and promote the prominence of the Sufi saint, indeed, to elevate the *musalmāni* Baḍa Khān Gāji to a status equal to that of the *hinduyāni* demi-god Dakṣiṇ Rāy. It is from this point in the literary history that the stories of the *pīrs* take on a life of their own. In these new *kathā*s, which constitute the bulk of the stories in this anthology, Sufi saints came routinely to be promoted as the equals of any god or goddess in the Bengali *hinduyāni* pantheon. New forms of divinity were required to right the wreckage of the Kali Age, the last era of a debased humanity, and the solution found in the composite image of Satya Pīr soon stretched to include all *phakir*s: *musalmāni* saints were promoted as the solution to the problems that ailed the *hinduyāni* world, who should be recognized for their positive interventions.

In their initial symbiosis, the *pīr kathā*s parodied the *maṅgal kāvya*s in the sense of positive mimicry, but eventually the parodies began to turn the *maṅgal kāvya* genre on its head. The *pīr kathā*s began to challenge the *maṅgal*s or auspicious manifestations of the god or goddess with the stories of the descent of their own *pīr*s and *bibī*s, who could be counted on to domesticate the wilds, impose order, and promote

11. For the most comprehensive literary history of the *maṅgāl kāvya* genre, see Āśutoṣ Bhaṭṭācāryya, *Bāṅglā maṅgalkāvyer itihās*, 6th ed. (Kalikātā: E. Mukhārji āyāṇḍ Koṃ Prāibheṭ Limiṭeḍ, 1381 BS [1975]).

the general weal of the population.[12] The stories spread their fame and glory, their *jahur or jahurā*, and the titles of the books that served that function style them as *jahurā nāmā*, "chronicles of majestic fame," a clear equivalent to, if not direct translation of, the literary genre of *maṅgal kāvya*. In this functional sense, as parodies, the stories should be seen as complementary to the *maṅgal kāvya*s rather than in direct competition, because a parody also preserves that which it parodies.[13] The *pīr kathā*s began to expand their scope in works such as Śekh Khodā Bakhś's *Gāji kālu o cāmpāvatī*, composed about 1750 CE, whose approximately 18,000 lines of poetry[14] make it equivalent in size to many of the *maṅgal kāvya*s, and it emerged just when the production of the latter began to wane. *Pīr kathā*s, on the other hand, continued to be composed up to the cusp of the twentieth century. Mohāmmad Khater's late nineteenth-century retelling of the *Bonbibī jahurā nāmā* is the newest composition in this anthology.[15] Sent by Khodā Himself, the female Sufi, Bonbibī, consolidated the whole of society within the mangrove swamps and became Mother to all the inhabitants of the Āṭhārobhāṭī. That tale brings the anthology up to the present. The honey gatherers, salt workers, and woodcutters who populate the mangroves depend even today on her beneficence, a manifestation of her *kerāmat*, the famous miracle-making power wielded by Sufis, and bask in the righteous well-being that emanates from her *baraka*, that divinely bestowed charisma that signals God's blessing and which envelopes those fortunate enough to fall within its orbit.

The adventures of the *pīr*s and *bibī*s evidently struck a chord somewhere in the Bengali psyche, establishing an equivalence of characters and cosmology that normalized the Sufi world in the Bengali cultural

12. Domesticating the frontier for habitation is central to the thesis proposed by Richard M. Eaton in *The Rise of Islam and the Bengal Frontier, 1204–1760* (Berkeley: University of California Press, 1993).

13. Linda Hutcheon, *A Theory of Parody: The Teachings of Twentieth-Century Art Forms* (Urbana: University of Illinois Press, 1985, repr., 2000), 72–74, 93.

14. Khodā Bakhś, *Gāji kālu o cāmpāvatī*, in *Bāṅglā sāhitye gāji kālu o cāmpāvatī upākhyān*, edited by Ābul Kālam Mohāmmad Jākāriyā (Ḍhākā: Bāṃlā Ekāḍemī, 1396 BS [1989]), 1–307.

15. Munsī Mohāmmad Khater Sāheb, *Bonbibī jahurā nāmā* (Kalikātā: Śrī Rāmlāl Śīl at Niu-Bhikṭoriyā Pres, 1325 BS [?] [ca. 1918?]); the original date of composition was 1880.

landscape. The *pīrs* and *phakirs*, the *bibīs*, the *gājis* became the equivalents of *vaiṣṇav* mendicant *vairāgīs*, of *nāth siddhas*, of ascetic *sannyāsīs*. And this is certainly a large part of the cultural work these tales performed, for they did not seek to impose a new religion imported from outside, but to locate their holy figures in the traditional Indic cosmology of Bengal. These stories are not just commemorative of how Islam came to Bengal, but of how they served to naturalize, to insinuate Bengal into Islam. Writing Bengal and Bengalis into the literature of the wider Muslim world, they give us a glimpse of the way Bengal made Islam its own.

THE TENSIONS IN THE TALES

While the alleviation of hardship provides a sustained and consistent undercurrent to all the stories, the large, existential issues of social organization and religious reconciliation constitute the very stuff of the "big romance," the kind of tale that chronicles adventures reminiscent of hero mythology around the world. But in these stories, a frequent twist transforms protagonist and antagonist into allies.

"THE AUSPICIOUS TALE OF THE LORD OF THE SOUTHERN REGIONS": THE *RĀY MAṄGAL* OF KṚṢṆARĀM DĀS

The first story in the anthology extols the virtues and benefits of worshipping Dakṣiṇ Rāy, a Hindu godling in the lineage of Śiv, who is master of the Sundarbans.[16] In the initial episode, Rāy is presented as a jealous, vengeful deity who demands human sacrifice, but once appeased, restores his victims. The second episode is the most famous; as noted above, it testifies to a confrontation with the Sufi warrior-saint Baḍa Khān Gāji over social slights and insults. Both field large armies of tigers, but ultimately the confrontation is reduced to the two fighting solo in a pitched battle. Both die, both are revived, and Satya Pīr brokers a lasting peace by insisting that these two miracle-working leaders function as brothers of equal stature, for honor and respect are prerequisites for any kind of social recognition and rapprochement. The somewhat unexpected resolution subtly implies that Hindu and

16. Kṛṣṇarām Dās, "*Rāymaṅgal*," in *Kavi kṛṣṇarām dāser granthāvalī*.

Muslim communities both have standing in Bengal and must learn to co-exist. In the final installment, Rāy demonstrates his protection and benevolence to his devotees by rescuing the son of a merchant who has gone on a trading voyage in search of his father.

"SCOURING THE WORLD FOR CĀMPĀVATĪ": THE *GĀJI KĀLU O CĀMPĀVATĪ KANYĀR PUTHI* OF ĀBDUL OHĀB

The second tale complicates this uneasiness between Hindu and Muslim by seeking to resolve their seemingly irreconcilable positions through explorations of the nature of love, or the "little romance," though that diminutive hardly does justice to its compelling power.[17] Composed a few years after the *Rāy maṅgal,* the same Baḍa Khān Gāji renounces his royal upbringing and eschews his designated kingship to pursue the life of a mendicant Sufi *fakir*. His half-brother renounces with him. But soon the tensions that had previously erupted into battle between Baḍa Khān Gāji and Dakṣiṇ Rāy are now displaced onto a new set of tensions that pits the Sufi ascetic's love for God against the amorous love Gāji bears for a Hindu woman. After a trick played by færies that results in Gāji's midnight betrothal to the princess Cāmpāvatī, followed by their pre-dawn separation, the well-known trope of *viraha*, "love in separation," dominates the narrative. This recurring theme is easily the most prominent in the literary and religious world of Bengal. The search for re/union—spiritual and carnal—ends up with Baḍa Khān having to fight Dakṣiṇ Rāy, his betrothed princess's hired protector. Gāji again prevails, this time enlisting Dakṣiṇ Rāy into service, after which the Muslim Sufi is united with the Hindu princess and properly married. The tension of worldly human love pulling against the spiritual love for God impels the action: the oldest brother, Julhās, absent from most of the narrative, embodies a traditional married love; Gāji's half brother, Kālu, embodies the Sufi's ascetic renunciation, which favors divine love; while Gāji, also a Sufi, but married, seems to argue it is possible to enjoy both.

17. Sāyeb Munsī Ābdul Ohāb, *Gāji kālu o cāmpāvatī kanyār puthi* (Kalikātā: Munsī Ābdul Hāmād Khān; repr., Kalikātā: Śrīmahāmmad Rabiullā at Hāmidīyā Pres, Es Rahmān aṇḍ San Printer, 1315 BS [ca. 1908]).

"GLORIFYING THE PROTECTIVE MATRON OF THE JUNGLE": THE *BONBIBĪ JAHURĀ NĀMĀ* OF MOHĀMMAD KHĀTER

The third tale, composed more than a century later, obliquely reconfigures the two sets of tensions—Hindu versus Muslim; human love versus divine love—into a struggle between a benevolent, compassionate justice and rapacious greed.[18] That biting commentary on just rule in the face of entrepreneurial excess reverses expectations when a new character, a female Sufi mendicant named Bonbibī, becomes the champion of the Sundarbans and everything in them. In his willingness to trade the life of his young nephew to Dakṣiṇ Rāy for fabulous boatloads of honey and wax, a venal merchant pillaging the Sundarbans' natural resources shows himself devoid of morality. Dakṣiṇ Rāy, now reduced to controlling just a small area of the Sundarbans, shape-shifts into a tiger to receive the boy as a blood sacrifice, reminiscent of the opening episode of Kṛṣṇarām's *Rāy maṅgal*. The boy appeals to Bonbibī, now the ruling matron of the entire forest and Mother to all, who flies to his aid. In the ensuing scrap, the boy is saved, but Dakṣiṇ Rāy is shielded from Bonbibī's wrath by the same Baḍa Khān Gāji, who this time is the one to counsel rapprochement. Bonbibī acquiesces to his wisdom. The boy is sent home, laden with riches, and, rather than punishing the uncle who tried to sacrifice him, treats him benevolently, marries his daughter, and becomes the kind of ruler of whom all subjects dream. His just rule, based on public-spirited generosity, brings back to the fore the trope of ameliorating widespread destitution as the foundation for an ethical life, underscoring the need for humans to manage the vulnerable Sundarbans better, according to the ideal of *ābādī*, noted above. Many readers will recognize Bonbibī's story from Amitav Ghosh's retelling in his novel *The Hungry Tide*.[19]

"WAYWARD WIVES AND THEIR MAGICAL FLYING TREE": THE *SATYANĀRĀYAṆER PUTHI* OF KAVI VALLABH

The fourth tale, the earliest tale of the lot, is considerably shorter than the previous three, and chronicles one of the many mad adventures of

18. Khater, *Bonbibī jahurā nāmā*.
19. Amitav Ghosh, *The Hungry Tide* (London: Harper Collins, 2004).

Satya Pīr, relating various permutations of the popular themes.[20] In this particular tale, the activities of good merchants are sabotaged by the machinations of their shameless, selfish wives until the men's virtuous younger brother and his equally virtuous wife set things right by spreading the worship of Satya Pīr, which ensures an ideal world. The author depicts the divinity of Satya Pīr as consonant with Nārāyaṇ, Kṛṣṇa, Śiv, Śaktī, and, of course, Khodā, while invoking a range of popular stories and far-flung ritual practices that humorously skewer virtually every community in Bengal.

"CURBING THE HUBRIS OF MOSES": THE STORY OF KHOYĀJ KHIJIR

The anthology concludes with the earliest Bangla rendition of the story of Khoyāj Khijir (Arabic al-Khiḍr, Persian Khwaja Khizr). Taken from Saiyad Sultān's *Nabīvaṃśa*, a monumental seventeenth-century rendering of the life of Muhāmmad, it retells the famous Qur'ānic story of God turning to Khijir to curb Musā's (Moses's) hubris.[21] Khijir is touted in Islamic literature as the teacher of all the great Sufi saints, which these stories tell us includes the Bengali figure of Satya Pīr. Khijir figures in several of the tales, not only intermittently popping into the various narratives of Satya Pīr, but also interjecting himself into the life of Baḍa Khān Gāji, always to give timely instruction and assistance. Khijir helps Gāji find the needle at the bottom of the sea, the final test of his status as a *jindā pīr*—the highest recognition any *pīr* can hope for, a level of accomplishment universally recognized, but never self-proclaimed. Tying the Qur'ānic figure of Khijir directly to the tales' protagonists enfolds these new Bangla stories directly into a larger Islamic literature and history, equating these *pīr*s with the pantheon of Sufis known throughout the Islamic world.

20. Śrī Kavi Vallabh, *Satyanārāyaṇer puthi*, edited by Ābdul Karim, Sāhitya pariṣad granthāvalī no. 49 (Kalikātā: Rām Kamal Siṃha at Baṅgīya Sāhitya Pariṣat Mandir, 1322 BS [ca. 1915]).

21. Saiyad Sultān, *Nabīvaṃśa*, edited by Āhmād Śariph, 2 vols. (Ḍhākā: Bāṃlā Ekāḍemī, 1978), 1:670–87.

THE LANGUAGE OF THE TRANSLATIONS

All of the translations in the anthology are from printed editions, though wherever possible, manuscripts have been consulted for confirmation or to resolve the occasional questionable reading. Differences in readings often reflect editors having adopted modern synonyms for older terms, with little, if any, significant shift in meaning. No traditional manuscript of the *Bonbibī jahurā nāmā* is registered in any of the repositories in India, Bangladesh, or the United Kingdom where most Bangla manuscripts are found, and it is not clear whether an older-style handwritten *puthi* was ever generated. Mohāmmad Khater, the author/editor, states that the text is based on oral versions of the story circulating in the Sundarbans

The other texts in this volume have much more robust print histories, and rigorously edited scholastic editions are readily available for several of them. The interested reader should consult the brief introduction that prefaces each translation for its circulation, printing history, and the details of the edition used for translation.

The transliteration of Bangla into English vexes every translator, because orthography does not automatically follow pronunciation. Many of the words are derivatives of Sanskrit and several closely allied north Indian vernaculars, which retain characters that are not pronounced, or that in Bangla generate euphonic combinations one would never imagine simply from the orthography. For example, */vaiṣṇav/* (the term for a religious follower of the god Kṛṣṇa) would be pronounced */boishnɔb/* or */boishnɔbo/*, inasmuch as */b/* and */v/* are not distinguished in pronunciation (both being pronounced like English */b/*). The language seldom differentiates among the sibilants */ṣ/*, */ś/*, or */s/* (all being pronounced as English "*sh*"). The inherent vowel */a/*, when pronounced is */ɔ/* (similar to the sound "awe" in English), unless it is followed by a high vowel or follows conjunct consonants, where it is pronounced */o/*. The inherent vowel in this example can follow apocope or not, a flexible feature of vowel epenthesis in compound words on which poets frequently rely for metrical purposes. For popular words, many translators of Bangla texts follow contemporary English spellings or simplify the transliteration with approximations of the sound using no diacritics. These issues are hard enough, never mind words approximated or transliterated from Persian or Arabic into

Bangla. Because the Bangla unvoiced fricatives /ṣ/, /ś/, or /s/ are all pronounced as the English "*sh*," in these texts authors will often write /*ch*/ to signify the sound of "*s*" in the English word "miss," hence one finds both *muchalmān* and *musalmān*. Those seeking the Persian or Arabic equivalent of such terms should note that in Bangla /*j*/ represents the voiced alveolar fricative /*z*/. The familiar transcription of Allah or Allāh, becomes Āllā in Bangla, which comes closer to approximating the sound (otherwise Allāh would be pronounced Olā), though to Persian and Arabic speakers Āllā itself is something akin to an abomination. But to render a Bangla term that clearly derives from Persian or Arabic back into some transliteration of the imagined source is to make historical and theological judgements regarding the semantic content of those terms which may not be appropriate. As I have read these texts over the years, I can attest that, in this example, the semantic field of the Bangla proper name Āllā is simply not the same as its Arabic or Persian counterpart, in spite of the obvious connection. No attempt has therefore been made to "re-transliterate" the Bangla forms of loan words back into imagined Persian or Arabic sources. *I have transliterated terms as they appear in the text, and those who know Persian, Arabic, and Sanskrit will be able to hear their equivalents*. Hopefully the slight dissonance will signal to those readers not to assume that the referents are the same, underscoring how religious ideas do sometimes change as they move from region to region. There are of course many other variables, but it should be clear that every transliteration strategy has glaring weaknesses, and consistency remains an impossibility, because the language itself is very much still developing during this early modern period, which is to say that no one will ever be fully satisfied with the conventions adopted, myself included.

Choosing to render the Bangla as it is spelled in the text means the consistency expected in English publications as dictated by the likes of *The Chicago Manual of Style* is to misrepresent the dynamic and changing nature of early modern Bangla, where scribal *in*consistency was the norm. The reasons for this inconsistency are several. No doubt it derives in part from pronunciation, especially of conjunct consonants and homophones, but it is also a matter of scribal choice, education, and skill, and a result of techniques of copying often generated by an individual reading out the text to copyists, which made it difficult for the scribe to stop and query. As a result, we find both *phakir* and *phakīr* (rather than Persian *faqīr* or Arabic *fakīr*—there is no voiced labiodental fricative */f/* in Bangla, though */ph/* is generally pronounced like that). Whether Bangla meanings correspond to their Arabic or Persian equivalents, I leave it to the reader to decide, but there should be enough contextual clues to ascertain this one way or other. Multiple spellings for the same figure or concept are not unusual, for instance, one author will write about Dakṣiṇ Rāy and another of Dakṣiṇā Rāy, and Gāji's father is variously named Sekandar, Sekāndar, Śekandar, or Śekāndar; similarly for author's names, such as Khater and Khāter, which is spelled both ways even in the same publication. For a considerably more detailed explanation of these and related problems of nomenclature and transliteration, I refer the reader to the appropriate section of my monograph *Witness to Marvels*, whose conventions hold in the current translations.[22] In the translations, I have rendered the terms as they appear in the texts, including multiple spellings in the same verse. The reader will find each of the spellings clearly indicated in the Glossary.

The second group of challenges to the translator are even more elusive, for Bangla in general, and especially the forms found in the early modern period of these tales, tends toward an extreme economy of expression. But economy of expression with respect to implied meanings, cultural assumptions, and notions of causality (frequently not spelled out, but intimated through the syntax of events, often appearing to be agentless) is not the same as in modern English, conditioned over the past few centuries by the prose of the novel, which eschews repetition and strives for concision. The Bengali authors assume the auditor or reader of the text can supply the culturally relevant context for a scene, so expressions are often shorthand indexes to very complex cultural assumptions. When I have felt it necessary, I have spelled out those situations in the briefest manner by incorporating them directly into the translation without doing violence to the original. If the meaning is too technical or the explanation too long, I have acknowledged the failure of the translation and included a footnote. In the story of Bonbibī, for instance, the young man Dukhe's mother expresses her need to assuage her anguish over his absence, saying, "I long to immerse

22. Stewart, "Conventions Regarding Transliteration and Nomenclature," in *Witness to Marvels*, xxv–xxx.

the kebab of my liver in the cooling waters of your presence."[23] We can stretch our imaginations to guess the meaning, but our guess is likely to come up short. Emotions, especially painful ones, are understood to be seated in the liver, which in its affliction is roasted like a kebab, graphically suggestive of just how painful it is, or the author might be alluding to a liver that has turned black, an expression used to indicate a poisoned or necrotic liver, with emotions to match. Clearly, if we retain the expression—and I have endeavored to include all of these unique idioms—that kind of cultural reference requires intervention to make sense to an English speaker, hence the note, which may interrupt the flow of the narrative, but helps to retain the text's Bangla flavor, hopefully making the bitter taste of that liver more palatable. This kind of challenge is a true pleasure of the translator's art.

The translations are entirely unabridged: I have chosen to translate every word in every line, including what might be considered unnecessarily repetitive descriptors in English. This expression of a single meaning by serial synonyms or similarly descriptive words connected with "and" is, of course, known in English as hendiadys. Including the Bangla word for technical terms, such as official government titles or theological positions, with their English translations or glosses, for instance, in effect produces what we might consider a bilingual hendiadys, so that general readers are not slowed and forced to consult the glossary (though they will find each of the Bangla words defined there), while adding precision for the specialist interpreter. For some readers this may appear on occasion to be pleonastic, but it is a small price to pay for precision. In some instances, capturing the semantic field of a single word requires two or three words or a phrase, and in other cases an entire Bangla phrase may be expressed in a single English word. Early modern Bangla favors the use of a small stable of verbs, which serve as the workhorses of the narrative; when translated literally, the monotony tends to create an impression in English readers that the author was not particularly gifted. Where English loads tone and nuance into the choice of different verbs—and the range is remarkable—Bangla accomplishes those same subtleties through the use of adverbs and adjectives, and through causal syntax, so that what the Bangla speaker hears is indeed the same rich variety of modulation, of

23. Muhāmmad Khater, *Bonbibī jahurānāmā*, 32; see also p. 311 below.

shading fine distinctions, that one finds in English. Capturing the graded tones of those distinctions pushes the translator to enter imaginatively into that early modern world in ways that inevitably make it intimate and the translation more satisfying if not natural.

The standard *payār* meter—the couplet of two fourteen-syllable lines, with caesura after eight syllables and at the end of each line—is the narrative mode, which I have translated as prose; it is not unusual for the author to employ redundant adjectives or nouns for the sake of meter. When the author shifts to the three-footed *tripadī* or triplet—two sets of lines composed in a variety of syllabic combinations, such as 6–6–8 or 8–8–10, and so forth—I have translated as blank verse, though for reasons of syntax, sometimes one foot will be transposed with another in the same verse. When the text shifts to the triplet, the reader should expect a pause in narration as the author goes into riotous detail to enumerate the opulence of prepared foods or wedding gifts or the various armaments and soldiery a king brandishes or commands. But more often the triplet sections are used to slow down the narrative, to probe emotionally charged issues. The explorations of these interior worlds can range from a sense of awe and humility when addressing divinity, or elation at the good turn of events, to intimations of the exquisite agony of lovers' separation, *viraha*, perhaps the quintessential poetic experience. At times the expressions will seem excessive to English readers, but it is important to understand how culturally significant the exaggerated emotional expressions of these odysseys can be when we try to interpret characters who are reported regularly to act in ways with which we are unfamiliar, for instance, to beat one's own head and fall to the ground senseless because of the extremity of anguish; translated thoughtlessly, a phrase of that sort could trivialize the emotion and transform its characters into caricatures. It is typical of early modern Bengali culture to elevate the lament to an art form, and that practice can still be observed.[24] While the authors routinely explore the interior landscapes of their primary characters, we should note that just as Northrop Frye predicted of the

24. Early modern literature attests to scores of *bāramās* lyrics, the "twelve months" of lament. For a modern analysis of the use of the lament, see James M. Wilce, *Eloquence in Trouble: The Poetics and Politics of Complaint in Rural Bangladesh* (New York: Oxford University Press, 1998).

genre of romance as a whole and Georg Lukács argued was typical of the nature of the Western epic prior to the novel, this exploration does not include character development.[25] Heroes and heroines and their antagonists have a fixed character, which the story never changes, but only confirms. There is precious little psychological development; the characters are simply given the opportunity to prove over and over again who they are.

I have also noted the technical classification of most flora and fauna, because the authors are highly knowledgeable about their environment and frequently chose those references with care.[26] There are, of course, ancient, culturally coded expressions conveying features such as winsomeness as lotus-faced or moon-faced, but when the author invokes a specific bird or flower that is not one of the time-worn images, that specificity calls for a closer look. In some cases, it indicates the precision of geographic locale, but at other times it serves to alert the reader as to how to interpret a particular passage. Here is where I feel the general tenor of these tales frequently exceeds what one expects of fairy tales or folktales. For instance, toward the end of the *Rāy maṅgal*, when the young merchant Puṣpadatta has secured Princess Ratnāvatī as his bride, and they begin the journey north, Ratnāvatī is carried alone in her palanquin. She pulls the curtains back for one last look at the places of her now-ended youth. As she peers out and her eyes flit from one place to the next, she is compared to the white-browed wagtail, the *khañjan* (*Motacilla maderaspatensis*). Considered an especially attractive bird, the *khañjan* is distinguished by white bands that set off its darting black eyes, not only a comparison for women of singular beauty, but precisely mimicking Ratnāvatī's glances as she greedily soaks up the sites of her father's kingdom one last time. But the image is more complex, for the *khañjan* is highly prized and kept in cages, trapped just as is the beautiful Ratnāvatī,

25. Northrop Frye, *The Secular Scripture: A Study of the Structure of Romance* (Cambridge, MA: Harvard University Press, 1976), esp. ch. 3; and Georg Lukács, *The Theory of the Novel: A Historico-philosophical Essay on the Forms of Great Epic Literature*, translated by Anna Bostock (Cambridge, MA: MIT Press, 1971), esp. ch. 3.

26. It should be noted that the technical information for the flora and fauna has been gathered and cross-checked from more than two dozen Bangla dictionaries, no fewer than a dozen print encyclopedias, and approximately fifty websites, both technical and popular. It would unduly burden the production to append an exhaustive list.

who, framed in the opening of her palanquin, looks out from it as if from a cage—and, perhaps, as if from the new cage of her recent marriage.[27] Not every author will be so sophisticated, but overall there is considerable high literary quality, perhaps more than one would expect from such popular tales. Sometimes the literary quality seeps through in a simple image, as in Ābdul Ohāb's tale of Gāji, Kālu, and the young princess Cāmpāvatī. Gāji is engaged in battle with Dakṣiṇā Rāy, whom the goddess Caṇḍī aids with invisible ghosts and goblins. Pummeled by rocks that seem to rain down indiscriminately from the heavens, Gāji's tigers turn to their master, who divines the source of the attack and the remedy through meditation:

> When Gāji recited and blew the *bichmillā* to the winds,
> the heads of the invisible ghosts and goblins were set alight.
> Shocked and disoriented, the ghosts could not escape,
> for the inferno raged catastrophically in all directions.
> What appeared to be stars twinkling in the sky were actually
> the heads of the ghosts igniting brightly and bursting into flames.[28]
>
> Ābdul Ohāb, *Gāji kālu o cāmpāvatī kanyār puthi*, 64

It is but one of many elegant touches to be found in the stories.

Since these were popular tales meant to be told and retold in public, a wealth of contextual and emotional information is conveyed through allusions to and direct invocations of traditional Indic mythology, such as the epic *Rāmāyaṇ* and *Mahābhārat*, the love play of the god Kṛṣṇa with the cowherd girls, or to episodes found in the Qur'ān and later Muslim hagiographical material. In some instances the litany of references may seem unwarranted, but in their excess the author guaranteed that each member of the audience would likely find at least one allusion to be able to grasp the point; those who picked up more than one would more fully intuit the point. Because these tales were sometimes intended for oral recitation, there are recurrent markers indicating the direction of the action and who is speaking to whom. The performative nature of the text frequently required the author to identify direct speech with expressions like "Saying this . . ." or "She said . . .", nearly always with the same verb /*bole*/ "to speak," but which in Eng-

27. Kṛṣṇarām, *Rāy maṅgal*, p. 242; see also p. 121 below.
28. See also p. 219 below.

lish would require different verbs depending on context, as I have noted above. I have followed the English inclination in these cases; so the expression "she said" /*se bole*/ has been rendered with at least a dozen or more different English expressions depending on context. The oral impulse that drives these tales also includes recapitulations of the narrative, convenient for anyone who arrived late, or was not paying attention earlier—nearly all of the performances of these texts occurred at night, and they often lasted till the wee hours, so coming and going or simply falling asleep were to be expected.[29] But those recapitulations also serve to control the content by guarding against midstream emendations by scribes, editors, or other writers, and also allow the performer to truncate a performance by simply summarizing those missing parts. That orality can incline the author to make asides as a personal commentary on the situation, or pose a rhetorical question to the audience, for example, "*What do you suppose the king did then?*" I have rendered in italics all of those asides, including the interjection of the author's voice in the closing lines of each section, the so-called signature line, or *bhaṇitā*. The *bhaṇitā*s sometimes include autobiographical information about the author, which roots the composition of the tales temporally and geographically. And, finally, the texts are rife with multiple honorifics, all of which I have chosen to translate. Some might argue that these frequent invocations—for instance, of the perfect wife, the *sati* (a direct invocation of purāṇic mythology), or of her husband as *prāṇ nāth*, "lord of my life"—make for a certain tedium and over-formality for English speakers used to contemporary expressions, but the diction lends a quaint flavor to the narratives, hopefully helping to transport the reader seamlessly to times past.

29. The rich performative dimension falls outside the scope of this current essay, and unfortunately for the English speaker, the bulk of the studies tend to be in Bangla, but interested readers should look at the works of Syed Jamil Ahmed, who has examined the popular performance and function of *jātrā* and other forms of dramatic presentations; see Syed Jamil Ahmed, *Acinpakhi Infinity: Indigenous Theatre of Bangladesh* (Dhaka: University Press Limited, 2000); Syed Jamil Ahmed, *In Praise of Nirañjan: Islam, Theatre and Bangladesh* (Dhaka: Pathak Samabesh, Losauk, 2001); see also Saymon Zakaria, *Pronomohi Bongomata: Indigenous Cultural Forms of Bangladesh*, with a foreword by Tony K. Stewart (Dhaka: Nymphea Publications, 2011).

The Auspicious Tale of the Lord of the Southern Regions

The Auspicious Tale of the Lord of the Southern Regions

Introduction to the Rāy Maṅgal of Kṛṣṇarām Dās

Kṛṣṇarām Dās, the author of the *Rāy maṅgal*,[1] wrote that the god Dakṣiṇ Rāy, Lord of the Southern Regions, visited him in a dream and commissioned him—if threatening to kill him and everyone in his family if he did not comply constituted a commission—to write his story properly, because a previous author had made it into a farce, and he was displeased. Understandably terrified, and not knowing Rāy's story, Kṛṣṇarām hesitated, but Rāy promised to tell him everything he needed to know:

> Do write my auspicious tale using the theatrical style of *pāñcālī* so that it will be broadcast far and wide through the Āṭhārobhāṭī, the Land of the Eighteen Tides. Previously, one Mādhav Ācārya composed such a song, but it did not suit me and failed to do its proper job as a work of art. Merchants never gamed with dice on any cremation ground as he claimed—he bamboozled rustic farmers, misled them, and now his song is widely and popularly recited. Nearly all singers are ignorant of my story and so repeat the familiar, but end up performing songs that extol others in their all-night vigils. The salt workers and honey collectors are reduced to hysterics when they hear his farcical comedy, with all its jokes and banter. But no longer. Should any person fail to appreciate your poem in the proper manner, my tigers will slay every member of his lineage.

Kṛṣṇarām Dās, *Rāy maṅgal*, vv. 17–22

1. Kavi Kṛṣṇarām Dās, *Rāymaṅgal* in *Kavi kṛṣṇarāmdāser granthāvalī*, edited by Satyanārāyaṇ Bhaṭṭācārya (Kalikātā: Calcutta University, 1958), 165–203.

Rāy's grievance was about his public image, a move to save face and a desire to be widely known and respected, a not uncommon theme in the early modern literatures of the region. His humiliation here was that other gods and goddesses were receiving accolades and respect, while he had become the butt of jokes—it would seem that the parody discussed in the general Introduction above had already slipped into humiliating satire. His rationale for commissioning the text gives us an opening into the workings of the Bangla genre of *maṅgal kāvya*.

A *maṅgal kāvya* was a poetic form dating back perhaps as early as the fourteenth century, but which expanded rapidly in the following centuries. The genre marker signified a composition that described the auspicious appearance of divinity, but forms that tended to be regional to Bengal, deities that were not universally attested in the ancient Vedic, epic, or purāṇic mythologies.[2] The literary record points to a poem in praise of Manasā, goddess of serpents, as probably the first in the genre, though the text is known only by attribution. With her connection to the serpent *nāgā* deities, Manasā had the most ancient roots of the new forms of gods and goddesses celebrated in this emerging genre. The goddess Caṇḍī and the god Dharma Ṭhākur soon rivaled Manasā in popularity, with significant numbers of authors eulogizing their exploits. But the seventeenth-century author of the *Rāy maṅgal*, Kṛṣṇarām Dās, who was a prolific exponent of the *maṅgal kāvya*, focused on somewhat less-celebrated deities. Among his writings that have survived are works in praise of the goddesses Kālikā, Ṣaṣṭhī, Śitalā, Kamalā, and the *Rāy maṅgal* translated here, each of which was significantly shorter in length than his predecessors' signal compositions. Whereas the massive texts of Manasā, Caṇḍī, and Dharma Ṭhākur were given over to large ritual recitations, often lasting several nights (*jāgaraṇ*), these shorter tales lent themselves to less grandiose ritual processes, many of them eventually ending up in the cycle of *vrat*s, the domestic rituals performed largely by women in the household to ensure the general health, welfare, and general weal of the family, whose stories are today called *vrat kathā*s. The double move toward greater economy of expression and the domestic environment seems to have anticipated the direction later tales would take. The *Rāy maṅgal*

2. For a comprehensive survey of the genre, see Āśutoṣ Bhaṭṭācāryya, *Baṃlā maṅgal kāvyer itihās*, 6th ed. (Kalikātā: E. Mukhārjī ayāṇḍ Koṃ Prāibheṭ Limiṭeḍ, 1975).

translated in this anthology is approximately the same length as the attenuated tales of Gāji and of Bonbibī, and their circulation seems largely designed for the home and hearth, unlike the longer temple- or court-oriented productions.

Kṛṣṇarām's *Rāy maṅgal*, the second-oldest work translated in our anthology, is dated 1686 CE and has three distinct narratives. The first is the short tale of Ratāi, a woodcutter who inadvertently fells a tree considered sacred by Dakṣiṇ Rāy, who then demands that Ratāi sacrifice his son in appeasement. Horrified, Ratāi reluctantly complies and is richly rewarded for his devotion.

The second tale is the story of the conflict between Dakṣiṇ Rāy and Baḍa Khān Gāji, which is nested within a longer narrative about a young merchant named Puṣpadatta, who sails south in search of his father. When Puṣpadatta was born, his father was away on a trading voyage, and many years later, he has yet to return. Having come of age, Puṣpadatta asks the local ruler to allow him to go on a trading expedition like his father's, not only to generate the kind of sustaining wealth such ventures accrued when successful, much needed because he is now the sole adult male provider in the family, but with the not-so-secret intention of searching for his long-lost father. With divine help building his fleet, Puṣpadatta assembles experienced crews, loads the ships with various trade goods, and shoves off. As they are sailing south, the inexperienced Puṣpadatta noticed onshore people performing *pūjā*, the traditional act of ritual devotion, to some strangely shaped aniconic images, which were but smooth mounds of earth. He asks his seasoned helmsman about them, who launches into an explanation of their origin and worship, telling Puṣpadatta about the conflict between Dakṣiṇ Rāy and the Sufi warrior saint Baḍa Khān Gāji. Even though this portion of the *Rāy maṅgal* constitutes only about a third of the text, it is the most celebrated and original of the three tales found in it and would be taken up again and again by subsequent authors. The remainder of the story, more than half of the narrative, concerns Puṣpadatta's further adventures south to rescue his father and establish his own claim as a successful merchant.

The story of the conflict between Rāy and Gāji as told by the pilot—an aside of 268 couplets and triplets out of the text's total of 976— is significant for several reasons, for this part of the tale has become the primary focal point of the Rāy narrative retold and refashioned by later *maṅgal kāvyas* and Sufi *pīr kathās*. The helmsman explains that many years earlier, an unwitting merchant passing through the Sundarbans had paid his respects to Dakṣiṇ Rāy, but out of ignorance failed at the same time to honor Baḍa Khān as Rāy's equal. Humiliated, Baḍa Khān blames Dakṣiṇ Rāy for what he sees as a deliberate slight, for it is clear that the merchant is a devotee of the latter and probably simply ignorant of Khān's rights. He perceives this as an affront, and tempers are quickly aroused. (As Dakṣiṇ Rāy's command to Kṛṣṇarām to compose the text makes clear, Bengali culture is especially sensitive to such snubs and insults, the commonest terms for them perhaps being *mān, abhimān,* or *apamān.*) Baḍa Khān and Dakṣiṇ Rāy are soon locked in a struggle to the death. As noted in the general Introduction above, it takes God, who appears in the form of Satya Pīr, to mediate the outcome. The cultural significance here is that following the growing popularity of Satya Pīr in *kathā* and *pāñcālī* compositions, Baḍa Khān was the first *musalmāni pīr* to be elevated in a major *hinduyāni maṅgal kāvya* to a status equivalent to that of a traditional Indic deity. By the turn of the eighteenth century, Islam was thus clearly not considered an alien intrusion (as it is often portrayed as having been today), but had begun fully to insinuate itself into local culture in a way that was natural to the Bengali character; the *pīr* and his cohort were becoming truly Bengali, caught here perhaps just in the moment of transition.

Versions of the Text. We find variants of this unwitting merchant's adventure rehearsed again and again in both the *maṅgal kāvyas* and the *pīr kathās*. Later poets, however, took a somewhat different approach to the story of Baḍa Khān Gāji. Haridev's lengthy *Rāy maṅgal,*[3] for instance, composed in the early decades of the eighteenth century, chooses to elaborate Rāy's divine lineage in a manner reminiscent of the complicated purāṇic accounts of the affairs of a multitude of gods and goddesses, situating Rāy in the midst of a stream of divine exploits; other authors, such as Kavikaṅkan or Mukundarām Cakravartī always preface their stories with succinct purāṇic-style genealogies, but for Haridev that seems to be the tale's raison d'être. He does not go into

3. Haridev, *Rāymaṅgal* in *Haridever racanāvalī: Rāy maṅgal o śītalā maṅgal*, edited by Pañcānan Maṇḍal, Sāhitya prakāśikā, vol. 4 (Śāntiniketan: Viśvabhāratī [1366 BS (ca. 1959)]), 1–172.

detail about the conflict between Dakṣiṇ Rāy and Baḍa Khān but focuses on their kinship after their conflict as "brothers" who jointly manage the affairs of the inhabitants of the Sundarbans, a temporal shift suggesting that Haridev was in some sense expanding the fuller story of Dakṣiṇ Rāy and Baḍa Khān, contextualizing their relationship in a larger nexus of Bengali divinities.

The other extant published *Rāy maṅgal* is by Rudradev. Like Kṛṣṇarām's, this is only a few verses shy of a complete manuscript, but considerably shorter than its predecessors.[4] Rudradev includes condensed versions of all three major stories told by Kṛṣṇarām: the sacrifice of the son of the woodcutter Ratāi, the conflict of Dakṣiṇ Rāy and Baḍakhān Gāji, and Puṣpadatta's adventure rescuing his father. Like Kṛṣṇarām, Rudradev documents the pitiful complaints of each of Dakṣiṇ Rāy's tigers about how difficult life has become in the Āṭhārobhāṭī, how run-ins with humans have become even more dangerous than before, and how internecine conflicts with other tigers allied to Baḍa Khān Gāji have taken a toll. Unlike other authors, Rudradev names another half-dozen or so Sufi *pīr*s and *gājis* reported to have joined the fray on the side of Baḍa Khān Gāji, including Mānik Pīr, Gorcānd, Dāyānā Gāji, Śalemānā Badar, and Daphar Khān. Rather than God himself intervening, the end of their struggle and subsequent peace is brokered by the classical Indic sage Nārada, a celestial gadfly who arrives riding his traditional vehicle, the husking pedal. Two more known authors attest to the popularity of the themes: only small fragments of the *Rāy maṅgal* by Dayāl Dās have survived, but the version told by Balarām exists in one complete manuscript, dated 1130 BS (ca. 1723), and there are several fragments that have unfortunately not been published.[5] Of all these, Kṛṣṇarām's text set the standard narrative and remains the most popular.

The language of Kṛṣṇarām's *Rāy maṅgal* is learned, not only in his extensive vocabulary and sophisticated expressions, but in his measured use of metaphors and a very studied use of intertextual allusions,

4. Rudradev, *Rāymaṅgal* in *Dvādaś maṅgal*, edited by Pañcānan Maṇḍal, Sāhitya prakāśikā vol. 5 (Śāntiniketan: Viśvabhāratī, 1373 BS [1966]), 121–48.

5. Jatindra Mohan Bhattacharjee, comp. and ed., *Catalogus Catalogorum of Bengali Manuscripts*, vol. 1 (Calcutta: Asiatic Society, 1978), p. 268. There are eighteen manuscripts attested by the five authors.

which demonstrate more than a passing familiarity with the Indic classics. Significantly, when conveying direct speech, he can be counted on to code-switch, adjusting for the background and status of the speaker. For instance, the diction of the ruler's strongman, Dakṣiṇ Rāy, and, in one passage, that of his emissary, the judicious, prudent tiger Lohājaṅga, tends to be elevated and elegant, adopting courtly expressions and tact, while Baḍa Khān's reported speech would have struck his audience as much cruder, a colorful mishmash, or *kichaḍi,* of local Sundarban dialects, mixed with Awadhī and Hindavī and Urdu (what used to be indiscriminately called old Hindustani) expressions, especially vile abominations for curses, with a steady dose of Persian and even a touch of Arabic imported, but reconfigured, sometimes awkwardly, with Bangla pronunciations and spellings. That switch signals that Baḍa Khān Gāji was not originally from the Bangla-speaking regions, but was a *jāban*, a foreigner and *musalmān* who was in the process of becoming properly native. The tigers, too, adopt certain expressions that lend a distinctive flavor to their litany of complaints, with a somewhat lower-order lexicon and a delivery that is much more declarative, in the voice of the uneducated, though not that of the bumpkin, which the tigers make clear is reserved for the local villagers they encounter, on whom they play pranks. I have tried to retain some of the flavor of this code-switching, which not only adds to the distinctions of class tension, but also the humor—and that humor percolates through the text, revealing Kṛṣṇarām's very practiced eye in recording the idiosyncrasies of his fellow Bengalis and, of course, the plight of the tigers, who we might easily imagine stand in metonymically for all the other animals of the mangroves that struggle as the region is increasingly subject to human intrusion.

PRIMARY ACTORS, HUMAN AND DIVINE

Baḍa Khān Gāji, Baḍakhā̃, Gāji, Gāji Pīr, Khān – Sufi warrior-saint

Dakṣiṇ Rāy, Dakṣiṇ Īśvar, Rāy Ṭhākur – Lord of the Southern Regions and master of tigers

Devdatta – merchant from Baḍadaha, incarcerated by Surath

Dhānukī – chief of police and armed forces for King Surath

Hānumān – the great monkey god, general of Lord Rām's army, and construction genius

Kālu Rāy – close companion of Dakṣiṇ Rāy, resident of Hijali or Hijuli

Khodā, Īśvar, Dev, Bhagavān, Nārāyaṇ – God

Līlāvatī – queen of Dakṣiṇ Rāy, daughter of Dharmaketu

Madan – ruler of Baḍadaha or Baradānagar, who commissions both Devdatta and Puṣpadatta to trade

Mādhav Ācārya – author of the first attested, but now lost, *Rāy maṅgal* in praise of Dakṣiṇ Rāy

Prabhākar – sage-king, father of Dakṣiṇ Rāy

Puṣpadatta – son of Devdatta, who rescues his father and marries the daughter of Surath, Ratnāvatī

Ratāi – *bāulyā,* or woodcutter, eldest of seven brothers

Ratnāvatī – daughter of King Surath

Surath – king of Turaṅga Pāṭan who incarcerates Devdatta, father of Ratnāvatī

Suśīlā – wife of Devdatta and mother of Puṣpadatta

Viśvakarmmā – chief celestial architect and builder

OTHER CELESTIAL AND EPIC FIGURES

Ananta Mādhav – form of Kṛṣṇa-Nārāyaṇ at Gaṅgāsagar

Aṅgad – monkey king who aids Rām in finding Sītā in the *Rāmāyaṇ*

Balarām – older brother of Kṛṣṇa or Jagannāth

Bharat – brother of Rām who rules as regent when Rām is in exile in the *Rāmāyaṇ*

Bidhātā – god who inscribes fate on one's forehead

Biśalakṣī – alternative form of Biśalakṣmī, a form of the goddess Gaurī

Brahmā – the four-faced creator god of the celestial triumvirate, with Viṣṇu as preserver and Śiv as destroyer

Damayantī – Nala's sorely tested wife who never abandons him in the epic *Mahābhārat*

Daśarath – king of Ayodhyā and father of Rāmcandra, Bharat, Lakṣmaṇ, and Śatrughna in the *Rāmāyaṇ*

Draupadī – wife of the five Pāṇḍav brothers who joins them in exile in the *Mahābhārat*

Garuḍa, Khagendra – Nārāyaṇ's gigantic bird-mount

Har, Maheś – Lord Śiv

Indra – king of the Gods

Jagannāth, Svayambhū – presiding form of Nārāyaṇ in the city of Puri or Nīlācal

Kaikeyī, Kauśalyā, and Sumitrā – wives of Daśarath in *Rāmāyaṇ*

Kalyāṇamādhav – a form of Kṛṣṇa local to the Kalyāṇa region

Lakṣmaṇ – brother of Rām who accompanies him to the forest in exile

Madan – Kāma, the god of love,

Mahāprabhu – the deity Jagannāth and the sixteenth-century god-man Kṛṣṇa Caitanya

Mārīc – *rākṣas* demon who tricks Rām by shape-shifting into a mesmerizing deer in the *Rāmāyaṇ*

Medinī – a personified form of Earth as mother goddess

Nīlakantha – the blue-throated form of Śiv

Nīlāvatī – the goddess of the Deep Blue Seas, consort of Nārāyaṇ

Padminī – "she who sits on the lotus," the goddess Lakṣmī

Rām, Rāmcandra – hero of the *Rāmāyaṇ*

Rāvaṇ – ten-headed enemy of Rām who captures Rām's wife Sītā in the *Rāmāyaṇ*

Śatrughna – brother of Rām in the *Rāmāyaṇ*

Śaytān – the Devil, Iblis, primordial rebel against Āllā

Sāvitrī -wife of Satyavān whose devotion prevents Yam from taking her husband as described in the *Mahābhārat*

Sītā - daughter of King Janaka and wife of Rām, heroine of the *Rāmāyaṇ*

Skanda - son of the god Śiv, Har, or Maheś

Subhadra - younger sister of Jagannāth in Puri

Sugrīv - younger brother of the monkey king Bali, who becomes ally of Rām in the *Rāmāyaṇ*

Śūrpaṇakhā - night-faring demoness, *rākṣasi*, sister of Rāvaṇ in *Rāmāyaṇ*

Varuṇa - Vedic lord of waters and morality

Vidhudev - the moon god

Yam, Śāman - god of death

TIGERS

Baḍa Khān Gāji's tigers (see esp. §§14–15):

Khān Dāuḍā - Baḍa Khān Gāji's personal mount

Āsinikustā, Baḍabalavantā, Bāgharol, Betarāḍ, Dābāḍyā, Dāriyā, Ḍumbari, Gāmāle, Ghusule, Hisirā, Hogalabuniyā, Hugharyā, Huṭiyāghoḍā, Kachuyā, Kālānal, Kāśuyā, Kāṭapāḍyā, Khān Dauḍyā Rāṅgā, Khoḍā, Mārmmadā, Nādāpeṭā, Nāṭuyā Rāy, Pāṭuyā, Rāḍ, Raṇajay, Sisir, Sisiri, Sugharyā, Sumbaryā, Surmmadyā, Ṭaṅgabhāṅgā, Tātālyā, Timirā, Tuṅgaṣadā, Vajradanta

Dakṣiṇ Rāy's tigers (see esp. §§16–17):

Hirā, Hīrā - Dakṣiṇ Rāy's personal mount

Lohājaṅga - Dakṣiṇ Rāy's emissary and diplomatic advisor

Akhaṇḍa, Bājāl, Balavanta, Bātāl, Bāṭapāḍ, Beḍājāl, Bekāl, Belāki, Berābhāṅgā, Betāl, Bhūtaliyā, Bijani, Budhi, Bulubulyā, Caḍai, Camaki, Cañcalā, Cād , Cātaki, Chākini, Cini, Citi, Dāgar, Dalani, Dāmi, Daṇḍadhar, Dāuḍā, Dhāmalā, Dhani, Dogar, Durbār, Gahani, Gajaskandha, Galagali, Gherini, Ghoghora, Guḍaguḍyā, Guṇḍagulā, Hāmalā, Hiḍimi, Himirā, Huḍā,

Huḍakākhaśāle, Hukī, Jābak, Jāmalā, Jhamaki, Jojhār, Kadamba, Kālā, Kālidhali, Kiḍimiḍi, Kumudā, Kunil, Kusubyā Śuṣabyā, Lākeśvarī/Lākheśvarī, Lokanaki, Loṭākān, Māgurā, Māmudā, Māsuyā, Mātālyā, Maṭukā, Maṭukā Masālyā, Mekamekī, Muḍai, Nāgini, Nāṭuyā, Neuli, Pābakamukhi, Pāhiḍi, Pākharā, Pātā, Pāṭābukā, Phakaphaki, Phaṇī, Pheṭānākā, Pracaṇḍa, Prakharā, Rūp, Rūpcāndā, Sākini, Sāmalā, Sāṭuyā, Sudā/Sudhā, Śumi, Ṭaṅgabhāṅgā, Tibir, Tini, Tiri, Titilyā, Tobali, Tomari, Vajradanta Khān, Udām, Udāmī, Uḍāna Caḍai, Uḍani, Ugracaṇḍa, Ulyādal, Uṭhāni, Vajradanta

The Auspicious Tale of the Lord of the Southern Regions

The Rāy Maṅgal of Kṛṣṇarām Dās

SECTION 1

With palms pressed together in respect,
I praise the lotus feet and magnificent girth of
    the Lord Dakṣiṇ Rāy, Master of the Southern Regions,
together with his queen Līlāvatī,
accompanied by five royal counselors, and
    a spectacular constellation of adoring attendants.
Apart from you, O Lord, who is there to direct and
dispose the inhabitants in your suzerainty over the expanse
    of the low-lying land of the eighteen tides?[1]
You are mounted on a horse named Hīr Rām,[2]
and clad in a tightly fitted tunic,
    bound round with cummerbund and flying scarf.
A golden stud pierces your nose, biceps banded broadly,
a necklace of gold etching the line of your neck,
    and from your ears, baubles dangle, glistening.
Armed with a sure enemy-dispatching cudgel,
hard cannons for forearms,
    and a quiver bursting with arrows,
strapped full across your back a massive metal shield.

1. The Āṭhārobhāṭī, consisting of the eighteen large islands that map and are hence synonymous with the Sundarbans, but technically meaning their western half.

2. Dakṣiṇ Rāy's mount is depicted alternately as a horse or a tiger, both named Hīr or Hīrā. Popular iconography in scroll paintings used by storytellers presents both.

You wield a razor-sharp sword in one hand,
tucked at your waist, billhook and double-edged dagger.
On your sleeves there glitter brightly
brilliant rubies sewn in patches upon patches,
crisscrossed with strings of glimmering pearls.
Your body glows the burnished hue of gold,
a gallant born from a constellation of stars,
a brilliant bolt of lightning cutting across the dark night.
Your eyes are bright and long, their corners
stretched right to your ears, your unrelenting gaze
striking fear in those subsumed by the six passions.[3]
Reeds, stalks of the lotus, and beeswax—
you have dominion over all such products;
and gatherers of honey and salt producers serve you too.
Whatever goods find transport by water,
even the egress of entire fleets of long-haul cargo ships[4]—
who except for you can grant permission?
Showing honor and respect with single-minded attention
untold numbers of people in the region
enter deep into the forest to cut wood,
but they are not eaten when caught,
for tigers turn their faces away—
by your grace and mercy, no one need fear.
Those who construct riverboats or build cargo ships,[5]

3. Viz., sexual passion, anger, greed, infatuation, vanity, and envy.

4. The Bangla word for "cargo ship" is *bhāule*, referring to large vessels with ample room for passenger cabins and cargo. The author at times appears to be a little uncertain about the classification of watercraft, often appearing to substitute names in a generic fashion in the way English speakers will in casual speech fail to differentiate a boat or sailboat from a ship. I note this because in so many areas, Kṛṣṇarām is exacting in his identification of flora and fauna, types of fabrics, and so forth.

5. The Bangla word for "riverboat" is *ḍiṅghā*—a double-ended craft, propelled by sail or pole, that can be as long as thirty-five feet and has an elegant sheer line; this should not be confused with the *ḍiṅghī*, a smaller version of the *ḍiṅghā*, or even a wherry or skiff, hence the English term "dinghy." Today, the term *jaṅga*, or cargo ship refers to considerably larger wide-beamed vessel with substantial holds, though this can also refer to the *jangar*, noted in the historical dictionary of Anglo-Indian words *Hobson-Jobson*, a coast-hugging catamaran made from two skiffs with bamboo placed transversely to create a platform. The generic Bangla term for "boat" is *noukā*, which refers to watercraft of all sizes. Kṛṣṇarām calls oceangoing merchant ships both *noukā*

any foreigner who mans a ship,
    or those slaving in factories scattered here and there—
all thoroughly attest that
as long as one worships your holy feet,
    nothing untoward will ever transpire.
Whether a crocodile attacks in the Gaṅgā's waters,
or one pisses away money out of spite and anger,
    or screams deprecations at one's wayward horse—
no ignoramus would deny, and
everyone else knows fully well, that in the end
    the root of all problems is the fruit of one's *karma.*
Against Baḍa Khān Gāji,[6] the Great Sufi Warrior,
You waged war throughout the territory's canals and channels,
    but in the end you became close, fast friends.
Kālu Rāy, who rides on the back of a stallion,
is your close companion as well;
    untold numbers worship him with single-minded devotion.
Whether at war, or in the forests, or in the fortifications of kings,
one can remain calm and blissful,
    for what misery can befall any servitor of yours?
The poet Kṛṣṇarām earnestly requests that you,
meet the ardent desires of your lowest-ranking soldier:
    grant me the boon of singing and playing your story in song.

SECTION 2

Listen, everyone, to how this strange and wonderful tale came to be composed and made famous in wide circulation. The name signals, the Khāsapur Pargaṇa region is a delight, and Viśvambhar Baḍiṣyā is the eastern portion thereof. I was passing through there on a Monday in the month of Bhādra [August-September] and at night lay down to sleep in the barn of some cowherd. Toward the end of the night I saw in my dream a great man mounted on the back of a tiger! Massive of

---

and *ḍiṅghā*, which suggests that the author was neither a boat builder nor a sailor; on occasion, too, he uses *tarī* or *torī* as a generic term for both "ship" and "boat," but this more technically designates a smaller boat, skiff, or raft.

6. *Gāji*, also spelled *gājī*, is the Bangla spelling of the Persian *ghāzī*, warrior-saint.

girth, he gripped a magnificent bow. He introduced himself as Dakṣiṇ Rāy, the Lord of the South: "Do write my auspicious tale using the theatrical style of *pāñcālī* so that it will be broadcast far and wide through the Āṭhārobhāṭī, the Land of the Eighteen Tides. Previously, one Mādhav Ācārya composed such a song, but it did not suit me and failed to do its proper job as a work of art. Merchants never gamed with dice on any cremation ground as he claimed—he bamboozled rustic farmers, misleading them, and now his song is popularly recited. Nearly all singers are ignorant of my story and so repeat the familiar while they perform songs that extol others in their all-night vigils. The salt workers and honey collectors are reduced to hysterics when they hear his farcical comedy, with all its jokes and banter. But no longer. Should any person fail to appreciate your poem in the proper manner, my tigers will slay every member of his lineage."

When I heard this grave pronouncement, I grew apprehensive in the extreme, and quickly placed my hands together in the sign of humility and spoke, bringing to his attention that "I know virtually nothing of your feats, your character. How can I, ignorant as a child, properly compose your tale in song?"

Rāy smiled and spoke in gentle reassuring words, "By my grace the song will be unsurpassed and complete. If you are diligent and mindful, you will discern it all. Listen carefully. I will tell you everything you need to compose my tale. One day, carefully following the words of a sage, the brilliant sun king Prabhākar performed the ritual service of Lord Sadāśiv, who granted him the boon of a son. It was I who became his son, and it was I who cleared the forests and established a viable kingdom. I married the daughter of Dharmaketu; then, and by the power of *yoga*, my mother and father left behind their bodies and took themselves as a couple to Kailās. So by virtue of that boon granted by Hara, I became Lord of the Southern Regions. At first the food offerings of *pūjā* from the settled areas were offered insincerely, half-heartedly. Then I dispatched Kālu Rāy to the city of Hijali, for there the king, that man-lion among men, failed to recognize and honor me. I slew his son and then restored him to life, whereupon the king dutifully lavished me with honor and respect by making the requisite sacrifices of offering.

"There was a merchant, Devdatta by name, who hailed from Baḍadaha, but for many long days he had been held prisoner in Turaṅga, the City of Horses. Paying heed to my words of guidance, his son Puṣpadatta made ready seven sturdy ships and pushed off in search of him. He insisted to the king, Surath, that the mirage he had seen on the way was real, but it did not register on that lord of men, so when he could not see it, he did not believe it; as a result the king ordered Puṣpadatta's execution. As he was about to die, that merchant's son focused his thoughts on me; at the crucial moment I went to protect him. With a tiger in tow, I attacked, raining down mighty blows. I slew King Surath and all of his many soldiers. The queen then appeared and importuned me with solemn hymns of praise, and suffused with feelings of compassion, I gave her back his life. Afterwards they married their daughter Ratnāvatī to the young merchant Puṣpadatta, and so the father and son returned to their own land. Puṣpadatta was one valiant hero: he constructed a citadel for me, and within it a palatial dwelling, and then routinely performed my worship with due diligence. So do make known all such escapades in my auspicious *maṅgal* composition."

And so Kṛṣṇarām has composed the maṅgal *of Rāy in the* śaka *year 1608.*[7]

SECTION 3

The young merchant Puṣpadatta had concluded, "I need to construct oceangoing ships in order to trade by sea," and so he gave the orders to start cutting and hauling the timber. As soon as the order landed on his head, Ratāi of the *bāulyā*[8] woodcutters rounded up his six younger brothers and his eldest son. Each of the seven picked his preferred axe and honed it to exquisite sharpness. Their ships were fitted out and stocked with plenty of food and other necessities. One by one the ships sprang forward in good order to the rhythmic rowing chant, and in rapid order they headed straight for their destination. They laid up the

7. *Śaka* 1608 is approximately 1686 CE. The editor of the text notes that the *śaka* date is embedded in a riddle called *hēyālīmūlaka śloka*, frequently based on astrological signs, but sometimes on other known "sets" of things (e.g., *kar* = hand = 2), decoding 1608 inversely as *vasu* = demigods [8]; *śūnya* = null or void [0]; *ṛtu* = seasons [6]; and *candra* = moon [1].

8. The text reads *bāulyā*, which is *bāoyāli*, in this early modern text, the traditional class of timber-cutters, haulers of wood, and sometimes collectors of honey unique to the Sundarbans. The term can also signify the individual who accompanies a work gang to help ward off tigers.

ships in a convenient landing and moored them fast. After carefully choosing different species of wood, they picked up their axes and in a flurry of activity began systematically to log black mangrove and tulip or looking-glass mangrove,[9] and so forth. They lost track of how many days and nights they labored, logging until they had meticulously ricked a veritable mountain of wood. Ratāi calculated their take and pronounced that there was no more work to be done. The entire clan of woodcutters trilled their joyful success. "There is enough here to construct seven or eight ships. The sons of the merchant will be recognized among the most fortunate." When the woodcutters heard this pronouncement, they swung their axes in an excess of mindless jubilation.

There was one tree venerated as special to Dakṣiṇ Rāy, that Lord of the Southern Regions, but no one was aware which in this forest it was. They espied one especially mature tree and together felled it. In the split second of this misjudgment, disaster struck. Dakṣiṇ Rāy's anger welled when he realized what they had done, so he summoned six of his tigers to him. Māmudā, Kumudā, Sudā, Ṭaṅgabhāṅgā, Vajradanta Khān, and Dāuḍā—these six quickly scurried around. Presenting themselves before him, they made their obeisance.

Now Kṛṣṇarām tells of the command Rāy gave them.

SECTION 4

"Woodcutter Ratāi *bāulyā* and his son
must not be put to death,
  but do slay his six brothers.
Do not mangle or rip their bodies to shreds, for
I will later restore the lives of those six men."

9. The black mangrove, or *kirāpāpuśuri*, is *Lumnitzera racemosa* in the Combretaceae family. It is a massive evergreen, growing to a height of thirty-seven meters and highly prized as construction timber. The *sundarī* is the tulip or looking-glass mangrove, *Heritiera littoralis*, in either the Malvaceae or Sterculiaceae family, usually identified as the tree that gave rise to the name Sundarban and is the most common tree in the region. The buttressing roots are shallow, spread horizontally, and send up aerial roots, or pneumatophores. At the time of Kṛṣṇarām's text, trees between two and one-half and three meters girth were not uncommon, each sprouting three or four major branches. With tight grain and good elasticity, they were and are still valuable in general construction, especially ship-building.

And off the six foot soldiers flew.
Those tigers were giants, royal Bengals,
each of whom broke his man's neck,
but only lapped the blood spewing from his gut.
They abandoned the bodies there and scampered away,
reassembling deep in the forest, while
Rāy watched perched on his celestial chariot.
When his six brothers were brutally slain by the tigers,
Ratāi could only wail in his grief,
"What has happened? What did we do wrong?
I will cut my own throat with my axe,
and abandon my own life!
I have no more desire for this life!
Were I to remarry, my wife
could bear many more children, but
I will never have brothers from our common mother.[10]
At one fell swoop all six of my brothers
vanished—was this misfortune
etched on my forehead from time immemorial?
The beloved wives of these men
we left in wait back home,
and now their lot has fallen to me.
Is there any way to explain something like this?
I issued strict, disciplined orders without fail,
nor have I had the slightest lapse in devotion.
But now what end is served by going home?
What excuses can I possibly make to their wives?
How will I ever show my face for the shame?
My son, you go back to our home
and there tell everyone that
'my six brothers have perished in the forest.'"
Weeping, overcome with grief, the *bāulyā*
picked up the axe with his hand
in order to decapitate himself.
Just out of sight in the sky above,
Dakṣiṇ Īśvar hovered in his chariot
and called out to him loudly:
"You stupid man, you failed to recognize me properly

10. This is a traditional Bengali saying that sons can be replaced, but not brothers, a proposition that plays a deciding role in a number of early modern tales.

and your axe felled that
special tree so beloved of me.
Incensed and in a raging anger over the offense,
I summoned six tigers who
gathered to slaughter your brothers six.
I am Dakṣiṇ Rāy, Lord of the Southern Regions—
all peoples sing of my greatness, and
in the Āṭhārobhāṭī, everyone performs my worship.
If you make a blood sacrifice of your son
and worship me with due propriety and care—
then will I bring your brothers back to life."
As soon as he heard this command
Ratāi was exceedingly grateful,
relieved of his anxiety and stress.
He gathered *kusum* flowers,[11]
climbed up the special tree to the perch,
the special place of the Lord of the Southern Regions.
With a supreme devotion permeating his heart,
He bathed his son and brought him forward,
and executed the worship with great resolve.
I beg you to fulfil the hopes of this poor foot soldier—
this is my hope and that of your servant,
sings the poet Kṛṣṇarām with profound emotion.

SECTION 5

Pressing his hands together in respect, Ratāi's son said to his father: "I took birth in this world at a particularly auspicious moment. I will effect the work of our lord, making it a fortunate event. I will revive my uncles, my father's six younger brothers, and my fame will spread throughout the world. If this gratifies and appeases Lord Rāy, what more can I say? There is no great misfortune in this for me."

When he heard his son's generous words, Ratāi wept uncontrollably. His heart so overflowed with emotion he could scarcely keep hold

11. The *kusum*, a favorite of Dakṣiṇ Rāy's, is *Schleichera oleosa* in the Sapindaceae (Soapberry) family. The tree, whose leaves are bright red in spring, grows as high as thirty meters. The oil of its fruit is used for both grooming and cooking, and its bark is used as an astringent for treating various skin diseases.

the boy. Somehow, he struggled up to the crotch of the tree,[12] then, gripping his machete tightly, he grabbed his son by the hair. "I fathom nothing at all," he cried out, "while you alone Lord understand the reason for everything." With one swift slashing cut, he severed his son's torso in two. So with his son as the sacrificial beast, Ratāi performed the requisite act of worship—and at that moment of consummation, Rāy manifested himself right before his eyes. The woodcutter stretched himself in obeisance fully prostrate on the ground. Right then and there Rāy revived his son. He sprinkled water from the pool of immortality and up sprang all six brothers, hugging one another in jubilation. Listening intently to their brother describe the Lord Rāy's wonderful qualities, all eight men together sang songs of praise.

Rāy is an ocean of qualities who possesses a great nurturing love for his devotees, and he took immense pleasure in receiving the worship of those woodcutters. Having granted the desired boon, the Lord God of the Southern Regions did the needful and then magically vanished. The wild jubilation of the men itself erupted like a lion's roar, and they soon boarded their ships and pointed them toward home. Rehearsing Rāy's many praiseworthy qualities over and over, in no time at all, they reached Baḍadaha. They all went together to the merchant to tell their story of how the Lord of the Tidelands dispensed his boons. When he heard this, the merchant Puṣpadatta was filled with a great joy and satisfaction; it was as if he had reached up and grasped the moon itself.[13] He knew in his heart that any undertaking would now meet with success, and with great generosity and pleasure, he bestowed on those woodcutting men untold numbers of gifts. The men fell to organizing the building of the new ships. The command was given to circulate the announcement that a gold bar would be the reward for successful construction.

Making obeisance at the holy feet of Rāy,
Kṛṣṇarām Kavi has composed this mellifluous tale.

12. Since attested in the Vedas, the sacrificial post is shaped from the crotch of a tree to hold fast the neck of the victim (Skt. *yūpa*); the Bangla word *yūp* is not, however, used here; the image is simply invoked.

13. There is popular conceit that babies are attracted to the moon, reach up to grab it, and are consequently frustrated because what they desire remains out of their reach. But Puṣpadatta got what he wanted this time.

SECTION 6

Overflowing with a profound happiness,
the son of that oceangoing merchant
    was sent to proclaim a reward in gold publicly:
"He who is able to build seaworthy ships,
come forward and claim the gold bar!"
    This was the word circulated through the town.
Sitting on Mt. Kailās, the lord Bhagavān
issued a command to the two gods
    Viśvakarmmā and Hānumān.[14]
The pair quickly disguised themselves as humans,
then availed themselves of the power of the wind,
    materializing instantly to lay claim to the gold brick.
As soon as they appeared, the helmsman and pilot
proffered betel nut to this pair
    and escorted them into the presence of the merchant.
After everyone properly greeted the two new arrivals,
that experienced oceangoing merchant asked them:
    "Just how many days will it take to build the ships?"
Hānumān, of enormous heroic vitality, and
Viśvakarmmā, of equivalent stature, carefully deliberated—
    but no mere mortal had a clue as to who they were.
"Were there seven hundred shipwrights available
building day and night, the entire project
    would take two or more likely three months.
The wage you would rightfully pay,
and the special reward you posted,
    we do not want to claim right now.
First we shall construct all the ships
and only afterwards take our due,
    at which point we will head for home."
After proposing their conditions,
they bade farewell
    pretending to return to their own homes.
Calculating the precise point of midnight,
they meditated on Śiv—He who Holds the Pināka Bow—

14. The architect of the gods and the monkey god, the latter the general of Rām's army in the *Rāmāyaṇ* epic and renowned as an engineer.

boarded their ships and sped away.
Hānumān with his magnificent strength
simply milled all the timber with his fingernails;
what need had he of a saw blade?
Viśvakarmmā fashioned ribs and wales, fitting them to
the keel and chine, affixing the strakes with iron fasteners.[15]
In seven turns of the watch, they produced seven ships.[16]
They fashioned a total of forty-two anchors,
and ran the pennants up high,
so they could be seen well in the distance.
They outfitted each with a poop deck,
set up jewel-encrusted biminis, or sun tarps, and
worked beeswax into the seams of all seven ships.
They fabricated six cannons, each restrained
with iron chains of untold numbers of links.
Everything was completed in the twinkling of an eye.
Then the mighty Hanumān
picked up the seven ships and
with great fanfare plopped them in the water.
Calculating that the night was coming to an end,
each of the two assumed human form
and then spoke to the merchant in his dreams.
"You have been blessed beyond measure, for
The Lord of Creatures, Paśupati, is merciful.
Travel now to the city of Turaṅga.
You will encounter no obstacles along your journey;
everything you set out to do will be accomplished,
and you will return with all seven ships intact.
You will marry the daughter of the king,
and fill your ships with all manner of jewels and treasures,
all under the protection of the Lord of the Southern Regions."
Resident in the village of Nimiti,
born from the clan of kāyestas
of one Bhagavatī Dās,

15. It is not clear whether the strakes were attached by strip-plank, clinker (lapstrake), reverse clinker, or carvel methods; all four techniques were employed by shipwrights in the region at the time, the first two being most common.

16. A "turn of the watch," *daṇḍa*, is twenty-four minutes, so this is just a fraction under three hours.

with mind singularly focused,
Kṛṣṇarām composed the Song of the Lord,
whose praises he sings.

SECTION 7

When dawn finally broke
and the merchant finished washing his face,
he looked up and gazed at the seven splendid ships.
The merchant was a man of great virtue and propriety,
so he performed the appropriate rituals to award each a name;
most elaborately decked out was the flagship, Madhukar.[17]
The local king, Madan, a man
imbued with a treasury of qualities,
sat in full regal splendor in his royal chambers.
Taking care to leave his wooden sandals outside,
two scarves knotted around his neck in humility,
the young merchant bowed in obeisance.
The young boy's beauty was itself enchanting,
so the king was inclined to benevolent favor
and seated him affectionately by his side.
The king sized up the boy's physique, which
shone with a beauty that surpassed the Lord of Love himself;
he then asked, "What brings you here?"
His face more brilliant that the moon,
Puṣpadatta the young merchant said,
"I beg you, with all your greatness, pay heed.
My misery knows no limit,
my mind is continually tormented,
in great matters Fate has turned its face away from me.
In order to fetch a variety of precious jewels
and arrange their transport home,
you sent my father far, far away.
I have not seen him since I was born;
unbidden, my eyes fill with tears,
yet I reside in my home seemingly without a care.
There is only my mother,

17. The term *madhukar*, lit., "maker of honey," i.e., a bee, and is also a euphemism for a male paramour; it is the traditional proper name of the merchant's flagship in many of these early modern narratives, with both senses intimated.

who has known nothing but misery, and
has effectively given up all food and water.
Affected by her austere condition,
it came to me that I must go to seek him out.
Grant me your permission, O Jewel of Virtue."
Hearing him out, that great protector of the earth replied,
"You are still a small child,
how can you propose such a thing?
Do not feel anguished in your heart,
for your father is sure to return.
Calm yourself and stay at home.
I repeat: I expressly forbid you!
Should you make that journey, you will suffer untold miseries;
your lot will be a poison-filled serpent if you launch the ships.
Your mouth still smells of your mother's milk, you are not ready.
It will be impossible to cross the seas to distant lands
without undergoing numerous trials and tribulations."
The merchant pressed on, "Still I am determined to go.
Please, O king, pay heed, for
I will manage it, if you but grant your support.
If not, then day and night will I undergo penance
and kill myself by eating poison;
then I am sure to die."[18]
When he heard the merchant's earnest declaration,
that most accomplished man grew deeply agitated,
but summoned the astrologer to bring the divining chalk.
He worked his calculations, then summarized their essential points:
"Thursday, the day of the Danujas,[19] is auspicious,
the third lunar day in *hastā nakṣatra*, thirteenth asterism of the ecliptic.
The journey will be filled with success."
There was nothing else to say;
the merchant was grateful and appeased.
Then the merchant took his leave from there
and returned to his own home—
that is the saga Kṛṣṇarām sings.

18. . . . and your prediction of my demise will come true.

19. Lit., born of Danu, the daughter of Dakṣa, and mother of the *dānavas* who revolted against Bali.

SECTION 8

The young merchant had the helmsman brought and bestowed on him the turban of honor as captain, furnished him with expense money for his home, and gave him assorted other treasures. To each hand and mate the merchant generously offered one hundred rupees' salary. Precisely at the auspicious moment, all seven ships were launched into the waters, with untold numbers of deckhands weighing the heavy iron anchors, allowing them to slip their moorings into the downstream current. All manner and varieties of unhusked rice, split peas and lentils, and assorted other legumes, sugar, honey, crystal sugar, sweetmeats, and oils had been loaded. There were great quantities of jute, hemp, flax, sesame seeds, peanuts, betel nuts—transported from the storehouse and loaded into the holds of the ships. Medicinal plants, such as prickly chaff-flower,[20] opium, and a full inventory of precious and semi-precious stones, and turmeric and ginger accounted for fully half of the ship's freight. Many different varieties of betel nut, yellow-dyed loincloths, delicately embroidered fine cloth—everything was carefully sealed in casks. Common mynahs,[21] rose-ringed parakeets,[22] and other caged birds for pets were stowed. The chatter of the rarer talking hill mynahs[23] mingled with the whistling of the magpie-robin,[24] while the

20. *Āpāṅga*, or *Achyranthes aspera*, in the family Amaranthaceae, found in scrubland and used in traditional Ayurvedic medicines, including for migraine; its seeds are rich in protein.

21. The common mynah, or *śālika* in Bangla, is *Acridotheres tristis*, a member of the Sturmidae, or starling, family. Sometimes called the Bengali grackle, it is an energetic bird, ten to eighteen inches long, with a dark brown-black body, an orange-yellow bill, yellow feet and legs, and yellow around its restless eyes. It makes a *chake chake* sound, especially in pairs, chattering, whistling, and gurgling.

22. The rose-ringed parakeet, *Psittacula krameri*, found throughout South Asia, is prized for its ability to mimic human speech.

23. The much less common hill mynah, *Gracula religiosa*, is famous for its vocalizing, especially its abilities as a mimic, including human speech, making it highly entertaining. Valued in classical India, hill mynahs were given epithets that variously meant the "one with stunning eyes," "fond of argument," and "delightful or fun-loving."

24. The Oriental magpie-robin *(Copsychus saularis)*, is called the *dayel* or *doyel* in Bangla. The national bird of Bangladesh, it has the same black-and-white markings as the Eurasian magpie, but is much smaller, more like a European robin. Classified as an Old-World flycatcher, it is easily recognized by its loud singing during mating season.

various kites,[25] were pleasing to the eye, as were the swans, peacocks, and other magnificent species. Goat and sheep wethers and deer were loaded with much jostling. All these and many other different items that could be found in the markets were systematically loaded for one could never predict what strange things from this miscellany might be needed or come in handy.

Amidst it all, the dignified matron, Suśīlā, felt deeply agitated, unable to check her tears when she had heard that her son was heading off by sea to trade. So she performed the worship of Dakṣiṇ Rāy and sang his praises. With her hands pressed together in submission, she intoned, "Nothing transpires without your mediation. May you be pleased to extricate him from any grievous threat! Your countenance puts the moon to shame, your physical beauty exceeds that of Madan, god of love. Apart from you, there is no one to pretend to be Lord of the Southern Regions. I do not have seven or even five sons, I have but one. Please extend the shadow of your feet to protect him."

At the lavish praise of this female devotee and servant, the Lord Himself, filled with all good qualities, extended to her the garland of his graciousness. "I shall protect your son from all forms of danger. By virtue of my favor, you should not trouble yourself, not even for a moment." When she heard this promise, the distinguished matron's heart rippled with pleasure. She then gave Rāy's leftover offerings of *prasād* to her son. "Safeguard this and suffer no worries; not even the protective amulet from Lord Rām is its equal. Whenever you encounter any travail or have some doubt about your life, concentrate your heart on the feet of Dakṣiṇ Rāy, that Lord of the Southern Regions. Because you are true and honorable and I am a perfectly devoted wife, a *satī*, then at no time will you suffer any misfortune." She took great care to impart this instruction, then fetched a letter that vouched for her prior pregnancy, and placed it in the hands of her son.[26] Then she

25. Kites, raptors in the family Accipitridae, are sometimes mistakenly called hawks, birds to which they bear a strong resemblance. The black kite *(Milvus migrans)* is the commonest species. Its specific name probably conflates the black kite, the black-shouldered kite (smaller and mostly gray), and the brahminy kite *(Haliastur indus)*, which is chestnut-colored with a white head and breast. All are abundant along the rivers of the Sundarbans.

26. This *garbhapatra*, or letter of attestation, was issued by a merchant or traveler to protect the honor of his family by certifying that his wife was pregnant before he left on

performed a worship for the flagship named Madhukar so that it would escape danger: "I entrust my son to you. Whatever threats he encounters in those vast and endless seas, may you rescue him at the moment of critical danger!" Then she placed the hand of her son into the hands of the helmsman. Once she had delivered her son to the ship, this woman took an oath on her own fidelity as *satī*. "Should he commit some mistake, or exhibit some fault, please do not be angry. Always bear in mind the strength of my resolve generated from my practiced austerities." Everyone then agreed, "It is nine o'clock in the morning. Now is the time, O son of the merchant, for your departure."

Concentrating on the feet of the Lord, and making obeisance, Kṛṣṇa-rām has composed this in the sweet bhāratī *recitational form reminiscent of the goddess of speech.*

SECTION 9

The merchant grew somber as he studied the movement of the pigeons,[27] and meditated on Dakṣiṇ Rāy as he departed for the greater world. The ululating trill of victory reverberated around the city and the blaring sound of a pair of conchs was pleasing in the extreme. The blessings of the great gods of the Veda were invoked, then the son of the merchant embarked on his auspicious journey. As he made his way out of the settlement, he offered seven plates of rice cakes and a bowl filled with seven clusters of *kadamba* flowers,[28] then with a ripple of delight looked to his left and took quick steps. On his right he paused to gaze at images of local deities indigenous to the subterranean world, serpents, their hoods flared. All manner of instruments sounded

---

his voyage. The wording here suggests a triple guarantee: to reassure the husband about his wife's condition, to the wife to safeguard her status with him and with others, and to a son born after his father's departure; beyond that there might also be an unexpected fourth guarantee for the father if a son used it to convince him of his paternity.

27. The movement of pigeons is a form of augury.

28. The *kadamba* (previously classified as *Nauclea kadamba*, but now *Neolamarckia cadamba*), is a fast-growing fir tree with distinctive highly aromatic orange globular flowers, long associated with Kṛṣṇa, who plays his flute beneath it; it is sometimes called *haripriyā* or "beloved of Hari [Kṛṣṇa]." There are four other flowering trees that go by the name *kadamba*, but this is the variety most often described in older texts. It can reach a height of forty-five meters.

through the town, the raucous noise portending success. He caught a glimpse of a cow that ran quickly to catch up to a cowherd girl, who sauntered along with a basket filled with pots of curd on her head. He witnessed these auspicious things as he walked along and realized with full conviction, "I am certain to meet my father and recover everything."

At the precise auspicious moment, he boarded the flagship Madhukar, and rigged up its bimini, studded with sparkling gems. The mustered oarsmen were chained together and the merchant gave the order to set all seven ships to sail at the auspicious moment.[29] The seamen and the armed garrison created a din as they beat the stroke of the oars, while resounding double-headed drums, large and small, regulated the time. High-pitched single-belled trumpets and low-pitched horns amplified the cacophony. After the anchors were raised, a thousand hands pulled the ships. With cymbals crashing and bass and kettledrums booming, the Madhukar took the lead. In perfect order the garland of boats lined up in a pattern reminiscent of decorative embroidery. Stringed lutes or *rabāb*s, kettledrums, and tambourines sounded mellifluously. Four cannons were loaded, their fuses were lit and their retort boomed louder than a storm-cloud's thunder. One by one the seven ships joined formation with the grace of Dakṣiṇ Rāy, Lord of the Southern Regions, looking upon them with favor. That virtuous merchant beheld the scene and, giving approval, ordered them to set sail. Leaving Baḍadaha behind, they ventured into the sea. Gradually, they were lost to sight in the distance.

Kṛṣṇarām pleads, O Rāy, may you fulfil their hopes!

SECTION 10

The winds blew the treasure-laden ships past vast expanses of uninhabited land, until they finally ended up at Kalyāṇapur, where they went ashore and paid homage to Lord Balarām. Following a deep, continuous racket emanating from the village, they soon came to Ḍihi Medanamal. They dutifully kept their minds fixed on the lotus feet of the Lord Rāy, and shortly left the stone landings of Hogalā far behind.

29. The large number of oarsmen suggest this could be a *koś* or *koṣ*, a hundred-oared cargo ship or barge, but as noted *supra* n. 4, the *bhāule* may be indicated.

To starboard lay a settlement thriving with inhabitants, the city of Bārāsat, as rich and expansive as Vaikuṇṭha heaven itself. They offered humble obeisance at the feet of the primordial Śiv. They heard that the Lord of the Southern Regions, Dakṣiṇ Rāy himself, had a dwelling in Khaniyā. There the ships hove to and dropped anchor. Ashore, they carefully bowed, fully prostrate in obeisance, and performed a proper worship, a devotion reinforced with the offering of many precious gems. Some distance away from there they espied the dwelling of a Sufi *pīr*. Crowding around the *phakir*, they offered the prescribed obeisance of salaams. Observing Islamic *hālāl* custom, they ritually slaughtered a chicken and a wether,[30] offered elegant *kusum* leaves,[31] and mounds and mounds of *sandeś* sweetmeats. This sovereign merchant made copious offerings of *śirṇi*.[32] Then the merchant inquired of the helmsman, "Why does this particular offering have to be so elaborate when there is no professionally crafted icon, but only a mound of earth? How can these *phakir*s be worshiping gods and goddesses?"

"The Lord who reigns over the southern regions does not appear sitting on his tiger, rather he is invoked only in the form of a smooth unadorned water pot, which signifies his head."

"Why is the worship here performed in this particular manner? If you know, please explain. I'm intrigued." And so the two began their conversation.

The helmsman began, "Brother, there is most definitely a reason. Since you are not aware of it, I will tell you, but you must pay attention. You must have already heard of Baḍakhān Gājī, a *pīr* who appeared in the flesh, and the Lord Dakṣiṇ Rāy of the Land of the Eighteen Tides. Previously, those two had been fast friends, then a conflict between them escalated into an all-out war. Each of the two lords wanted complete suzerainty over the same vast domain, so the two brothers pursued their dispute on all fronts. The Gājī struck Dakṣiṇ Rāy's expansive chest, and he was felled, but just as promptly sprang back up, his body

30. The "ritual slaughter" is *jabāi*, from the Persian *zabḥ*.

31. See n. 11 above.

32. *Śirṇi* (also *śirṇī*, *śinni*, etc.) is an offering of rice flour mixed with sugar, milk, and banana, and sometimes augmented by various spices, a common offering to *pīrs* and their tombs and to locally powerful figures. The offering can be made by anyone regardless of religious affiliation.

a trick of the illusory nature of creation, *māyā*. Then Baḍa Khān hacked through his now-raised neck and that phantom head bounced to the ground. And so it went. Finally, God, Īśvar himself, broke the stalemate and these two giant figures afterwards became fast friends. Since that event, worship has been directed toward the water pot, representing Rāy's severed head; but in some places, his arresting image sits astride a tiger. Wherever a settlement is associated with the name of Baḍa Khān, the established practice is to erect a mound of earth.[33] No image is fabricated for worship; only contemplation will impel him to fulfil the supplications of his devotees. The jurisdiction of all Āṭhārobhāṭī lies with Dakṣiṇ Rāy; and Gājī's dominion lies therein by virtue of his being the Lord's close friend. The two are truly satisfied by joint worship. One sees them appear together in the same place as brothers."

Puṣpadatta urged him, "Go on, tell me; I have not heard the whole story. Why did the two fight? And where did it happen? How did God come to grant the boon whereby their conflict was dissipated and reversed and they became fast friends?"

The helmsman then began to recount the convolutions of that tale. The poet Kṛṣṇarām says, "Listen carefully."

SECTION 11

While Dhanapati the merchant was pursuing his sea-faring trade, by the intervention of Fate, he laid up at one particular landing. He had spotted the special water pot of Dakṣiṇ Rāy on the shore and, knowing he was the special boon-born son of Har, Śiv, he made a generous offering of fragrant flowers and varieties of ornaments studded with gems. Who else could lavish so much? Finishing his service of worship, he begged leave with his hands pressed together in respect. But he unwittingly failed to pay his respects to Baḍa Khān Gājī, and soon he was surround by great hosts of *phakir*s. The naïve merchant felt he was being had and grew angry, driving them away from the premises. He boarded his ship and set sail for Siṃhala, while the *phakir*s went together to complain to Gājī Pīr.

33. That is, in the shape of a commemorative tomb, a *dargā* (though it is not named as such), homologous with God's court in heaven.

Situated in that particular village was a sanctum for Gājī, and the city and its markets were appropriately resplendent. All the *phakir*s arrived, disgruntled and complaining, "Respected sir, you no longer seem to give proper attention to the administration of the region and are now overlooked. Some no-good merchant fellow paid his respects in worship of Dakṣiṇ Rāy and departed, but he ignored you altogether. We consider this an egregious offense. The bumpkin Bāṅgālī does not know how to fear. He attacked us and drove us from our rightful place. We cannot show our faces to the people out of our shame. We will no longer consider ourselves *phakir*s; we spit on that title."

Right then a tiger by the name of Kālānal spoke up, "When I went out to hunt, I received none of the usual deference, or the run of the territory. The tigers of Dakṣiṇ Rāy always deferred to us so that we could snatch the prized head, the delicacy of the slain beast, but now when they hear your name, Gājī, everyone simply casts knowing looks. The honey harvesters, the salt manufacturers, and the woodcutters recognize no one else save Dakṣiṇ Rāy. I had just eaten one nobody of a salt worker, when in a rage three streaks of twenty tigers each came roaring after me. Seeing the situation, I began to calculate just how important this lordly Baḍa Khān really was, for the *pīr* is no longer recognized or revered in Āṭhārobhāṭī, the Land of the Eighteen Tides. This anger festers, because everyone had previously acknowledged your authority."

The order was quickly delivered: "Cut off his ears and shave his head."

"I am the only relative who looks after my dear Lokalaki, the aunt of my wife's brother," said Kālānal, who then fell at the feet of Rāy begging a reprieve. "Grant me bail so that I may take care of her! I only came to you Sāheb to inform you. Hearing all these tales, I knew that you, O Gājī Khān, would be deeply angered."

In the presence all gathered there, Gājī cursed the merchant. "This daughter-fucker has fled! Now what are you going to do? The bastard will be totally lost. Can't you just hear Dakṣiṇ Ray wail when he is bound and hauled back here? Only then shall I again be considered a true warrior-saint, a *gājī*." Thus Khān instructed them to crush the ears of Rāy's servants. "I have to see for myself quickly what kind of devil, Śaytān, he is. Every day his bare fists pummel people into bloody submission. He seizes their land and with a flourish produces a document that testifies to his ownership, that claims it as his property." Then he ordered them, "Be quick, go to Rāy's house, search him out. It will take all of you together to corral him and pound that enormous body to a pulp!" With these words he exhorted and aroused the *phakīr*s gathered there. In a breathless, unruly mob they sped off to start the quarrel. They destroyed everything in Rāy's dwelling, then hurled what was left into the brackish waters. With the help of the tigers, they destroyed the carefully crafted icons. Someone laid hold of the *brāhmaṇ* priest, ripping off his sacred thread. They jostled him to the ground and with a swarm of fists battered him senseless. This army of *phakīr*s deliberately polluted his food: "Your social standing, your *jāti*,[34] like your body, is stripped, and now all you can wear is a beard, you daughter-fucker!"

Rāy Ṭhākur had there one particularly devoted follower. When he saw what the *phakir* disciples were doing, he jumped up and scampered away. Rāy had settled his family in a bamboo dwelling along an estuary, and there the one known by the women as Baṭe—she who was bestowed by Ṣaṣṭhī at the foot of the banyan tree—arrived to report the news. Listening to Rāy after he had heard the report made even those inclined to perfect virtue tremble: it was as if copious quantities of ghee had been poured onto an already burning fire. "What incredible audacity to destroy my home! I will cut all those participating *phakir*s into tiny pieces and feed them to my tigers!" He brandished an exquisitely sharpened sword, swinging it menacingly. He called out to his scattered tigers, summoning them from wherever they happened to be. "Make yourselves ready," he ordered, and had the war drums struck savagely.

Kavi Kṛṣṇarām observes that there was great method in his madness.

SECTION 12

The chief advisor put his hands together in respect and spoke,
"O Lord of the Land of the Eighteen Tides,
    please pay close attention, O great refuge.
Whether this report be true or false,

34. *Jāti* is "birth" or station, often wrongly translated as "caste," which is an imported construction from the Portuguese "casta." The language implies that now that he is symbolically and literally stripped, only a beard—that is, becoming a *musalmān*—can cover his shame. But the motivating factor for this forced change of status is significantly not ideological, and therefore not a religious "conversion" as the term is understood today, but about honor, social standing, and pollution.

I believe you should send
someone in person to find out.
If he truly be your friend, then
he will be at pains to conduct himself properly,
so speak to him affectionately and mollify him;
you should be friendly and offer pardon.
Now rein in your assembled tigers, for your goal
is not achieved by hooliganism in the service of vanity.
Even as you acknowledge him as a *pīr*,
only punish Baḍa Khān Gājī
should he indulge in some kind of treachery.
In an instant he will realize that
you will return incensed, aflame with rage, and
personally do physical battle with the *phakir*."
The lordly Dakṣiṇ Rāy
recognized the wisdom of this, so he sent
the seasoned and savvy tiger Lohājaṅga.
"You are truly intelligent, so suss this out
and return quickly. What you fathom
determines whether I subsequently attack."
Ever so swift, he bounded through the skies,
and came into the presence of the Gājī,
a guard standing vigil, holding a sword.
As if he were Indra in the heavens,
the visage of Baḍa Khān Gājī's dress and
accoutrements soothed the eyes.
His body was in repose, leaning against a pillow,
a peacock tail fan spread above,
a manservant tendering a betel quid.
The hair on his head black and oiled,
a *phakir*'s *chilimili* rosary firmly in his hand,
Gājī sat reading the Korān.
Understanding the protocols of timing, the emissary
introduced himself at the proper moment,
"The Lord Rāy has dispatched me to speak to you.
Knowing that you are his dear friend,
then why was his house destroyed
and the wreckage thrown into the river?
The *phakir*s destroyed all the icons,
after which they swarmed around
and beat the *brāhmaṇ* priest nearly to death.

Do you know about this? Or do you not?
I have come to ascertain that fact.
    As soon as I know, I will leave.
As yet no one has openly broken from the other.
What is the point of this treachery, this rivalry?
    Should conciliatory words be uttered, all will be well."
Kavi Kṛṣṇarām sings,
O Master, Lord of the Southern Regions, may you
    extend protection to your chosen foot-soldier.

SECTION 13

The Gājī spewed his words in anger,
"Who the hell is this imbecile?
    He is a bumpkin with a pretentious attitude.
Every day it's vegetarian fare: unhusked rice and banana,
five and one-half bushels wolfed down.
    Would you honor him with the title *gosā̃ī*?
A share of his largesse comes back to you;
you do not even have to search to get it,
    for his honor and his wife enjoy an abundance.
That sister-fucker has freed me from all promises.
When he comes around, I will shave the bastard's head
    before severing it, lopping it off into his lap.
I have received no jurisdiction of my own,
my name is not as well respected as his,
    nor do I have under my control his kind of wealth.
I've not constructed elaborate bamboo dwellings,
replete with flashy lamps and other accoutrements,
    nor do I have courtiers, male and female, to keep me company.
I suffer no friendship with anyone
who revels in such an evil state of affairs—
    so take care to stand down and keep your mouth shut.
You watch to your own good welfare, and
take steps to protect your own royal consignment.
    Now go quickly and break the news to him."
His entire body shaking with anger,
the tiger Lohājaṅga retorted,
    "You are the one who must be on your guard, Bābā.
You have not seen much of the Lord Rāy,
but in battle he appears before you as Yam, god of death.

You will reap the fruits of your action in no time.
Just as Rāvaṇ deluded himself with insolent pride,
then suffered Aṅgad's prowess—
there is no one in the triple world to match Rāy!
When you are destroyed in that same way,
won't I remember this very conversation?
Do not treat all of this as some kind of ruse."
Having said his piece, the emissary departed.
Now the Gājī grew apprehensive, while
his unruly pack of followers remained safely inside.
A final meal was served to each and everyone.
"Let the destruction begin when the kettledrums
and small double-headed *dundubhi* drums signal!"
Gājī dispatched formal summons to tigers' lairs,
everywhere they were scattered about the area and beyond,
each called from the roll of a master registry.
"In addition to the Lord of the Southern Regions,
we must lay hold of all the timber cutters there as well!
Move it! There isn't a moment to waste!"
When they heard what had happened,
two particular tigers called out, one to the other,
each sick with fear.
"We cannot possibly go and engage that one, for
we shall surely lose our lives in return.
He is the most formidable enemy we've ever met."
Kavi Kṛṣṇarām sings,
Why are you so afraid?
Whoever is mustered first
should simply go and commit to skirmish,
for afterwards it will all work out.
That strikes me as a liberating solution.

SECTION 14

Baḍa Khān Gājī, warrior-saint,
cloaked himself in his magical powers.[35]

35. Magical powers are *bhaḍakā* (Arabic *baraka*), spiritual power that is a blessing from God and manifests as inherent virtue. In this genre there is often a conflation of *kerāmat* (Arabic *karāmāt*) or miracle-working, usually deployed to convince an unbeliever, and *bhaḍakā*, the effulgent charismatic power of a religious life well-lived.

In response, a great many tigers came running,
appearing no less than *avatār*s of Śaman, god of death.[36]
Their fluid movements manifested such an irresistible force,
not even the wind itself could keep up.
The tigers from Bālāṇḍa Bāliyā
had already arrived,
those from Pāighāṭi came along as well.
Baḍa Khān was bursting with magnificent strength;
should someone not arrive, he would be deeply insulted,
and none could escape that wrath.
All of Gājī's tigers
found in Madanamal
assembled in orderly fashion before him.
From Baridahāṭi and from Mayadā—
to him they came in such large numbers, that
one grows uneasy trying to call out their names.
From Beyalā and Māguarā,
his tigers had come straight to their master,
rippling with power and strength.
At the summons issued by Gājī,
any stray tigers that remained
trickled in gradually.
Consumed with worry about this change of events,
how could he concentrate on the recitation of the qualities of God?
The two great figures were inexorably drawn together.
When two giant bull-elephants square off to do battle,
the tender shoots of reeds and grass inevitably get trampled—
of this everyone was all too aware.
Upon receiving Gājī's commission,
Hogalabuniyā—"He Who Lurks in a Clump of Reeds"—showed up,
beyond which there is not much else to write.
Kāśuyā and Bāgharol
arrived with a pack,
along with Ghusule and Gāmāle.
Next came Sisiri and Hisirā,
Raṇajay and Timirā,
followed by Khān Dauḍyā Rāṅgā.
There was Āsinikustā

36. *Śaman*, an epithet for Yam, god of death, means calming, tranquilizing, soothing, allaying, extinguishing, destroying, killing, slaying.

and the very senior Baḍabalavantā; then
  Ṭaṅgabhāṅgā angrily arrived in a wild scamper.
Tātālyā, Tuṅgaṣadā
Mārmmadā, Surmmadyā, and
  the regal Pāṭuyā and Nāṭuyā Rāy,
Hugharyā, Sugharyā, and
the giant man-eater Sumbaryā—
  all charged in as soon as they heard of the conflict.
One very old tiger, Rāḍ,
loped along with his son, Betarāḍ,
  dreadfully menacing in their stealth.
Dābāḍyā galloped in like a horse,
while Kachuyā scampered helter-skelter; then
  Kāṭapāḍyā appeared, slyly like a wicked thief.
Arching his thick brows to accentuate his eyes,
gleaming like two flaming torches,
  their luminescence blurred like falling stars.
Huṭiyāghoḍā loped along,
his tail whipping this way and that,
  as if he were painting flames along Laṅkā.[37]
The entire forest reverberated
with the prodding sounds of *hula hula*,
  even flushing the reclusive Huḍā out into the open.
His head was hugely out of proportion
to his scrawny body which was bereft of all fur—
  he was an ancient one, a full eighty-two years old.
The massive tiger Dāriyā or "Slasher"
could knock down an elephant with but a slap,
  his massive paws the size of winnowing fans.
Small animals in pairs never stand a chance,
for he strikes like lightning, ripping their heads apart
  with his shiny white teeth like neat rows of puffed rice.
Ḍumbari came along, and

37. This is another allusion to the epic *Rāmāyaṇ*, wherein Hanumān sets fire to Laṅkā with his burning tail. The image is perhaps even more complex than a simple allusion; *sundariyā*, here translated as "whipping this way and that" (following Jñānendramohan Dās, *Bāṅgālā bhāṣār abhidhān*, from *sundari*) is read by Sukumar Sen (*Etymological Dictionary of Bengali*) as the *sundariyā* tree, and he cites this line explicitly as "his tail is like a *sundari* sapling," which sticking up on the back of the tiger would not undercut the connection to Hanumān.

any number of female tigers roamed about.
    Altogether seven and one-half thousand tigers appeared.
Vicious striped hyenas, scavengers by nature,[38]
ran pell-mell through the thickets in small packs,
    no one could possibly keep count of them.
Picking up the tigers' scent in the distance,
dogs, in one dwelling after another,
    barked and whined, agitated with fear.
At this parade of tigers tramping through
with unparalleled strength on display—
    who dared to make the slightest peep?
After two nights had passed, with
incessant arrivals in their town, the locals
    desired to know nothing more.
Baḍa Khān Gājī
welcomed all with kind affection,
    and stroked their bodies lovingly.
Amidst the jostling, and roaring back and forth
among those boasting their power,
    he began to impose order.
Kavi Kṛṣṇarām
makes deep obeisance,
    O Lord, please hear my song!

SECTION 15

First to speak was Khān Dāuḍā, "It is so obvious,
it is hardly worth the bother for me to speak,
    like sucking water is to the brain of an elephant.
What I mean is that I have devoured hundreds of thousands
of water buffaloes for their meat,

38. Sen glosses *kāchuyā* as a noun, a type of hyena, literally "residing in thickets," but I am inclined to read it adjectively with the additional meaning of scavenger or stealer; Jñānendramohan Dās notes that the term designated a form of marriage by capture. Because zoologists have documented only the striped hyena (*bāgharola*) in South Asia, it seems more likely that only one species of hyena is indicated by a very observant Kṛṣṇarām. It is also notable that the striped hyena bears a certain resemblance to the tiger in its markings; and all hyenas can be found in competition with tigers and lions, which will mark their territories against one another, each scavenging off the other.

from herds in cowsheds, in open fields, and in forest."
Then Sisir spoke up,
"You must understand that in all this,
I, Sisir, have double the strength in my body.
I have stalked men by the hundreds in the forest,
then strike and maul them from my hiding place.
Is there any other who can match my footspeed?
"When I crouch and ball up my body,
tighter and smaller than a cat, I slink undetected,
with my chest pressing the ground.
Herds of cows or groups of humans,
the fates decree when it is their time of death;
if not, I simply leap and snatch birds on the wing."
His eyes thoroughly bloodshot,
the tiger Taṅgabhāṅgā—"Loft-Destroyer"—spoke,
"I am extraordinarily ingenious at stealing.
Whatever a stupid farmer manages to harvest,
I simply lie down in the top of the hut in wait,
and in the end, everything is destined for my stomach.
The destruction is worthy of Yam, god of death.
I plan the trap very carefully.
After I ransack the hut's loft and destroy what's in it,
I rejig the bamboo with flimsy straps, thin as hair.
At the appropriate moment, everything collapses and
the victim tumbles into the pit and breaks his neck."
The tiger Khoḍā—"The Lame One"—spoke up,
"When I run, I streak like one insane,
though I have only three legs.
The moment I bring a rhinoceros down on his belly,
that triggers all my voraciousness, and
soon my body swells to the size of a mountain."
Vajradanta—"Diamond Teeth"—
spoke deliberately, "Listen Sāheb Pīr,
though I have grown oh-so-old,
my teeth are still pristine rows, harder than diamonds,
I can sink them deep into stone,
I can grind bones into powder.
To satisfy the stomach's cravings is always a priority.
Whatever number of ripe young
succulent women I can find, I simply eat.
I never eat women who are suckling their young,

for their dugs are sucked dry, like two radishes without blood;
    but the little boys in their laps are a delicacy I favor."
The tiger named Nādāpeṭā— "Potbelly"—
said to his son the tiger Dāriyā,
    "I cannot always fill my own belly, but
my wife is constantly on the hunt
for walking catfish and small leopards,[39]
    bits and pieces of which she gives me to eat."
One by one each of those remaining
let it be known in the most serious terms
    what particular prowess and capacity he possessed.
As he listened to this litany, the Gājī was pleased.
Every single one turned and faced south, anticipating the moment
    when the tyrant Rāy would spring forth out of hiding.
Lohājaṅga had returned there
and reported the words of the *pīr*,
    the hearing of which sent Dakṣiṇ Rāy into a rage.
Kavi Kṛṣṇarām says,
The summons for his own tigers he roared,
    as he twirled the ends of his mustache.

SECTION 16

First to arrive to meet Rāy was the tiger named Rūpcāndā, his mouth resplendent with flashing teeth mounted in gold. He routinely kills wild elephants to feed his family; and flesh-eating *rākṣas* ghouls flee in alarm, even the demon Dakṣa himself. The thicket-haunting panther Māsuyā was colored jet black all, his eyes glowing like two stars in the distant night sky. Beḍājāl, Bekāl, and Bājāl moved with a dark deadly stealth, while the svelte bodies of Bātāl and Betāl advanced like a raging forest fire. Ugracaṇḍa, Pracaṇḍa, Akhaṇḍa, and Daṇḍadhar arrived, then the triplets Nāṭuyā, Sāṭuyā, and Huḍā. Kusubyā's maternal uncle

39. *Māgumor* is *māgur*, the walking catfish (*Clarias batrachus*). Sukumar Sen notes that the *maṅgal kāvya* texts attest to *kālaciti* as either a spotted black snake or a kind of leopard (he says "tiger," but a spotted tiger can only be a leopard, though they do interbreed), possibly the clouded leopard (*Neofelis nebulosa*), which ranged freely through the Sundarbans at the time of this text and is notable because of its diminutive size, an adult body only two to three feet long and weighing thirty to fifty pounds.

was the tiger named Ulyādal; his brother-in-law was Balavanta, appearing like the flickering of flames. Bulubulyā ran with blinding speed, his roar booming across the entire region. The large-bodied tiger of Māgurā was a sight to behold, and with Loṭākān and Uṭhāni, they were three brothers—voracious, their three stomachs routinely required to share at least five forest deer. There came Pākharā, Prakharā, Citi, Cañcalā, Dhāmalā, then Bijani, Neuli, Pātā, Hāmalā, and Sāmalā. Next were Guṇḍagulā, Guḍaguḍyā, Uḍani, Caḍai, Pheṭānākā, Pāṭābukā, Maṭukā, and Muḍai. With the tigers Jāmalā and Jojhār, came the young and able-bodied Hīrā, who would hunker down to rest after sinking his teeth firmly into a rhinoceros. Berābhāṅgā, Bāṭapāḍ, Huḍakākhaśāle, Mātālyā, Titilyā, Kālā, and Maṭukā Masālyā were there. The lumbering bodies of these streaks of tigers raised massive clouds of dust; one by one they arrived there, a full eleven thousand in number. It was like the ocean's roiling surge at the deluge of Doomsday, signaled by the incessant howling and barking of jackals all around. All the assembled wild beasts had mouths full of teeth like steel blades. But then, there were so many flights of tigresses prowling on the hunt. Untold numbers of tigers had gathered, each displaying his might; but now hear the names of all of the tigresses.

Tomari, Tobali, Tiri, and Tibir came along, but it was Sākini, Chākini, and Hukī who spelled certain death to humans. Jhamaki, Camaki, Cini, Tini, Lokanaki, Nāgini, Gahani, Dhani, Phaṇī, Phakaphaki, Udāmī, Udām, Dāmi, Cātaki, Dalani, Jābak, Pābakamukhi, Ghoghora, Gherini, Kiḍimiḍi, Pāhiḍi, Hiḍimi, Kālidhali, Śumi, Budhi, Dāgar, Dogar, and Galagali were all there. Lākheśvarī, though looking youthful and slender bodied, scampered so fast that her feet never touched the ground. Even when the hyenas would rally themselves into packs, they would back off and crouch together to conserve their numbers when they encountered the tigress Khaṭāsa; even otters and other wild beasts fled, retreating into packs, and fish-preying hyenas similarly slinked back to their lairs.

All the many tigers named here at the beginning of the conflict could be heard to brag and bloviate, advertising their self importance. Listen, for instance, to the creeping boasts of prowess by the tiger Bijani: "I don't really care for elephants, so I eat large numbers of cows. And the flesh of humans doesn't really suit my taste, they are bitter; nevertheless all the beasts of the jungle are frightened at the sound of my name!" The paternal aunt of the tiger Himirā is Uḍāna Caḍai. *Lis-*

ten carefully as I describe her story next. "Culling a solitary ox from a herd, I kill it, then hoist it on my back as easily as humans carry the weight of a palanquin on their shoulders. When I give chase, beating the wind itself, hunters send out the alarm, 'Who is there? Is that a tiger?' I jump on the husking machine pushing the pedals round in a whirl making such a racket that the householders pour outside shouting, 'Kill! Kill!' But in those houses where I suspect people are present, like a thief, I move undetected, then fall on the back of someone's neck as he screams to be saved."

"That is frightfully wicked of you," observed the wizened old Vajradanta, whose head was enormous, about the size that would fit in a five-bushel basket. "Once I could, with a single leap, bound more than ten *kāṭhā*s— half a *bighā* of land[40]—but now, in the ebb tide of my years, I am no longer able to do such things." This decidedly striking one continued, "When I move lithely, camouflaged with dust, is there anyone on earth who can spot me? Then, when I shake the dust from my body primed to kill, I become still as the temple on the mountain top. When I crouch to kill from ambush, I shrink to the size of a mongoose. When my name is uttered anywhere in the vicinity, the rice-pot cracks.[41] Yet when I stand erect on some pretext, I seem like a dagger cleaving the earth. But should some cow or human fall into my clutches, what fear should they have if they are under the protection of your grace, Lord Rāy?" Hīrā spoke just then with hands pressed together in respect, "When I have eaten a whole leg of water buffalo and drunk my fill of water, and then devour more meat till I am stuffed up to my neck, I need only belch deeply and it is all digested.

Kavi Kṛṣṇarām says, This is clearly the essence of good humor. Then more tigers broke in, wanting to speak their minds.

SECTION 17

Rūpcāndā then spoke, "Listen with the attention of a devoted parent. My power can only be understood when compared to a lion's. I eat a

40. Twenty *kāṭhās* (Indian Eng. *cottah*) is a square measure equaling one *bighā*, approximately one-third of an acre.

41. This is an old Bengali proverb that saying aloud the name of a particularly obnoxious, dangerous, or evil person can cause your pots to crack.

rhinoceros as if it were nothing at all, while elephants are beneath my dignity; I approach the wild forest boar as little more than a blade of grass." Lākeśvarī, whose majesty and spirit are indomitable, burst out in a rage, "I am able to jump over a mountain with a single leap. Every tree and temple lies beneath my outstretched body; just tell me what ocean to cross, what land to traverse." Then Kuṣabyā Śuṣabyā spoke next with a big grin, "I float over the waters, bobbing along like some clay cooking pot. When I spot the biggest boat, one that is loaded to the brim, I spring onto it. I exact the toll of an arm or leg, but spare the life of anyone who advances toward me. But one day I had a scare, O Lord Rāy, when I had jumped back into the waters, a lurking crocodile suddenly clamped down and tried to subdue me from behind. I was able to sink my claws deep into both of his eyes. We disengaged and he slipped away blowing a mighty ballast of bubbles." Then the tiger Huḍakākhaśāla spoke next, "Generally, in the thick of the night I, Huḍakākhaśāla, move with practiced stealth. I am particularly savage, so when I slip into the house, one by one I deliberately break the necks of each and everyone there. I am the inevitable victor; of that no one has ever harbored any doubt. Among all those attacks, only one honey gatherer managed to strike me. One day a young chump came at me swinging a cudgel, and he managed to deliver a low blow, which shattered my spine below the waist." As his eager eyes lapped up Rāy's visage, the tiger Bhūtaliyā added, "Some young women had gone to the market. I pounced on one little slut who was alone, all by herself in the middle of the market. Then a gaggle of bitches appeared out of nowhere and squeezed and crushed my nuts. I sprang up and fled, but now my hunting is pure vanity—since then my scrotum and testicles have done nothing but swell and ache."

Listening to this tale of woe, the tiger Durbār spoke up, "I bow in deep salutation to that class of women blessed with leaking nipples! One time there was a particular woman who had just given birth in a small hut deep in the forest, but it was encircled by a protective fence of woven netting. Scoping out the hut, I saw the pitched roof was not fully thatched. So I immediately jumped up there. I ripped open the thatch with my front paws and thrust my head through. Just then, sensing something, the little bitch stood up, fearfully grabbed a smoldering faggot of mangrove wood from the fire, and managed to singe my whiskers! In a mad scramble I leaped out, rolling around on the ground. Both sets of whiskers were charred and the pain was excruciating. And, Lord Rāy, let me tell you about the time I crashed into a cattle pen. I was not paying attention and had stupidly struck without precaution, putting myself in grave danger. I entered the milkman's enclosure in order to eat a scrumptious young calf, but suddenly the latch on the gate of the bamboo fence tripped shut and I was trapped, unable to get free. I could search out no escape, and I quickly concluded that the eating could wait, I wanted only to save my life! My chest heaved in pain as a cow butted me. I realized that that day I was to be killed, the food in my mouth turned to ash. My ribs were crushed as a bull gored my side. I slumped down and lay still, pretending to be a corpse. In the morning the cowherds came and cried out, 'Ah, we have a dead tiger.' Then they dragged me out a safe distance and dumped me. Crows even came and perched on my body. Wild dogs began to gather around, while vultures circled overhead. Then I suddenly jumped up and fled, showing them the banana."[42]

Hearing them out, another said, "Rāy, please give me your full attention. It is by a stroke of good fortune that my dwelling was located on the banks of a particular river. Humans have long brought their corpses there to dispose of them. I lived in a nearby logging forest and they provided my food. I found a tigress by the name of Mekamekī, so I pretended to marry her and adopt her two tiger cubs. Sending her out to hunt in the forest, I gobbled up her delicate cubs with the greatest of pleasure. Another time, she was unable to go out to hunt for us, so I simply ate one of her legs, and now she walks with a decided limp."

The poet Kṛṣṇarām sings his tale, a study in humor,
while Rāy chuckles as he listens to the prowess of these tigers!

SECTION 18

When he mounted his tiger Hīrā, Rāy became a cavalryman, a shield strapped on his back, sword in hand, and double-edged dagger in the folds of his cummerbund. Ceremonially accoutered with two quivers,

42. "Showing them the banana" (*dekhāiyā kalā*), which evokes the image of the backside of a tiger fleeing with tail upraised, expresses disdain. Figuratively, the idiom has the sense of "quickly giving them the slip," but conveys defiance, like "giving someone the finger."

each chock-full of war arrows, Rāy shook with rage and waved a firearm in each hand. Five staunch companions mounted their respective tigers, and off they rode. The night, dark and forbidding, was already halfway through its second watch. Imposing on their tiger mounts, these broad-bodied warriors sped northward, with Dakṣiṇ Rāy, the Lord of the South, taking the lead. They moved with alacrity, arriving at Khania, where they got down. From there, a great commotion ensued, with vigorous jostling. The *pīr*'s tigers were scattered all through the area and as soon as any were detected, Rāy Ṭhākur savagely attacked. Those who had their lairs close by were engaged first, routed, and sent scurrying like a swarm of locusts. As soon as the most prominent of the tigers, six in all, were laid hold of, Rāy gave the order to cut one ear off of each one. Numberless *phakir*s were rounded up and herded together, then their busy patchwork garments were ripped to shreds, rending them scarcely more than tattered handkerchiefs. A fusillade of blows from clenched fists and open palms rained down on them, accompanied by a torrent of taunts: "Why don't you try and go to destroy the dwelling of Dakṣiṇ Rāy now!" With vicious swipes, they knocked loose their pots of opium, which shattered on the ground. The tigers clamped down jaws on necks and lapped the spewing blood. Then the tigers gobbled up as snacks all of the domesticated cocks and hens that had been destined for the kitchen.

Then the master and great king Rāy reined them in and issued a warning to those left, "It is too hard, too much trouble for me to kill off the whole lot of you mendicant beggars. So, repent and reflect! Remember later that you survived this conflict. Send back this message to the Gāji, the great Khān! 'What are you doing sitting still, Gāji? Whose face do you see? You had better settle for the whore-daughter of some toady *brāhmaṇ* in court and flee!'"[43] Then Rāy and his tigers surrounded the Gāji's village. "Understand the real law of this land well, Gāji Baḍa Khān! Where are your tigers now? There are none to be seen. What of your great wonder-working power?[44] What can you possibly do all by yourself?"

43. *Maṭuka* is a shortened, and therefore demeaning, title for a *brāhmaṇ* who sold his services in the court of the Pathans in Bengal.

44. *Kerāmat* is the magical power wielded by Sufis, which depends on extreme devotion and virtue.

They replied, "Whatever plot you hatch now is without substance, for the limits of Gāji's virility have hardly been tested.[45] We are only *phakirs*, yet you have provoked this dispute, so when we track you down, there is no knowing what will transpire."

All this bluster incited the anger of Śāheb Dakṣiṇ Rāy and he looked for any excuse to rain death and destruction down upon them. He seemed to be everywhere, like a broad-winged owl circling around them, screeching menacingly as he hemmed them in. "Is there one among you all who bears the strong sharp blade and commands the throne of a ruler? Who would like their head sliced into worthless slivers like the moon's digits?" The more he spoke, the angrier the *avatār* of Yam got, while Khān Dāuḍā raced to round up the other tigers. Placing his sword and shield into the hands of a fawning lackey, Rāy picked up a crossbow and quiver bristling with arrows. The anger that had been building up suddenly burst out, which sent flying the roaring tigers gathered about. The tigers split into their separate groups, each greeting the other with frantic complaints; they gave voice to their grievances at being judged unfairly. "This struggle has nothing to do with any of us on either side. Understand that only total victory or defeat will determine who is to be deemed lord, Ṭhākur."

When suddenly the two eminent sovereigns appeared, they began to heap abuse on one another. Rāy was first to scream insults at Gājī. "Previously you fell at my feet—do you not remember? But when you started to eat meat, you became high and mighty, so who is that chum to you now? You snatched away the mercenary *brāhmaṇ*'s whore-daughter, and that act makes you little more than a common highwayman.[46] Were there a real *pīr* standing here, he would receive an offering of *śirni* from me; I would have brought proper food for him to eat—but instead this one runs after tits and cunt. If you had managed to take possession of my army of tigers just now, then you would be the master-in-control and I would be like the thief. Just as ants sprout wings only in order to fly into the fire and die, you go and destroy the

45. Virility here is *ras*, the essential energizing force of his enormous physical prowess, associated with semen.

46. The insult seems to refer to the maiden Cāmpāvatī, Gāji's eventual bride in the *Gāji kālu o cāmpāvatī kanyār puthi*, the earliest versions of which predate this *Rāy maṅgal*. See introduction to "Scouring the World for Cāmpāvatī."

sacred room that houses my worshipful image. If you will relent in these despicable actions, I will make nothing more of it. You are not normally considered to be a nasty or particularly evil person, so return to your good standing now. If you take refuge in me, I will be mollified and consent to protect you."

Kṛṣṇarām now relates how the Gāji replied in the rising flush of his anger.

SECTION 19

"What kind of infidel are you, you low-life bastard? Listen carefully to my pronouncements, you dunce, you filthy vulture. What do you do here in the jungly wild besides smoke your hookah and get intoxicated? Are you really such an ignoramus that you can only spew deprecations from your pumpkin chariot?[47] You really have no clue about the *pīr* Baḍa Khān Gāji. Just as Khodā, God Himself, has given the coral tree[48] to this world as proof of the good things in life, has anyone blessed you with such a kingdom with its abundant flowing rivers? Tell me, have you paid no heed to that great opportunity and benefit? If there is no sense of honor or propriety in the gush of big talk you aim in my direction, you will learn to show respect after I have chastised you. All of the prosperity you previously enjoyed as a result of your various offices will disappear like so much wet smoke belching from your water pipe. Are you listening, whoremonger, to this rehearsal of your death? The Lord Gosāñi is the essential reality of all manner of creation, you daughter-fucker. Everyone will ignore your cry for help, Dakṣiṇ Rāy, they will not offer you even the tiniest shriveled teat to suck. If you desire your own well-being, make yourself scarce, scamper away like a scared cat. With power like a raging river, we swept away your icon, utterly dismantling your thatched hut. The tiger Kālānal tried to stop me, but this outrageous and treacherous action has seri-

47. The bowl of the hookah is the pumpkin chariot (*kaduratha*) .

48. In the Bangla-speaking world, the coral tree (*mādāra*) is *Erythrina variegata*, sometimes called the flame tree or the tiger-claw, with its distinctive red claw-like flowers. It is a special favorite for gardens and attracts a variety of nectar-seeking birds. The intertextual reference is likely Qur'ān 55, *Sūra al Raḥmān* (n.b., the English "coral tree" is coincidental to the reference to coral in the *sūra*).

ous consequences. I will shackle that jacket-wearing *bāṅgālī* dog of a merchant and humiliate him. According to the custom in the Bhāṭi, he must make some token offering. Whenever and whatever thing gets produced here, half is yours, half is mine—it is a simple agreement. It is written that the act of hoarding and loaning money is an abominable practice, while the calculation of the debts of the poor will be forgiven."[49]

Unable to tolerate further Gāji's outrageous behavior, Dakṣiṇ Rāy interrupted and began to speak. "Who are you? Where are you from? And just what are these customary rules? You act as if you own the world, but you garner no respect in the villages. The more I forgave you out of our previous affection, the greater your arrogant swagger has grown, bigger and bigger. Just as the miscreant's heart and mind are submerged in sin, that haughtiness in the end meets with Yam, the lord of death. When a lowly person grows too big and waves his fist at the sky in defiance, every imaginable form of misery and anguish accrues, for the goddess of good fortune, Lachmi, will have fled. You should prepare yourself to meet a similar destruction: die or take flight and escape with your life to some place far, far away. No matter how many tigers have accompanied you, I will rip them to shreds, and devour them morsel by tiny morsel. Your tiger Khān Dāuḍā suffers you to mount his back. Hold that pose as this arrow is loosed."

As Rāy coolly addressed him as *beg*, the honorable one, the arrow called *siṁhaduḥkh*, the "scourge of lions," streaked forward.[50] The new razor-sharp arrow escaped with a scorching zip. It split the blaze on the tiger's forehead like a crack of lightning. The *pīr*'s tiger tumbled to the ground and writhed in the dirt. Baḍakhā̃ staggered up, his most noble mount gone. He called to his tigers, "Hey, come gather around me!" But they had scattered here and there. Who would stay and get mixed up in this kind of exchange? They blended in and disappeared into the throng of Rāy's congeries. Spewing with anger, Baḍakhān Gāji

49. The implication being that Dakṣiṇ Rāy engages in such un-Islamic activities as a zamindar, but that he also claims the offering of the merchant for himself alone.

50. In this construction—*balite balite bege siṃhaduḥkh bāṇ*—the author has skillfully captured the seamless action of Dakṣiṇ Rāy notching his arrow and letting it fly as he addresses Baḍa Khān ironically as *beg*, milord or your highness. The term */bege/* is a noun in the first foot, while serving as the verb for the second foot.

rigged his cannon-like weapon and let fly a venomous missile that resounded more loudly than a clap of thunder. While Dakṣiṇ Rāy's bow was split in two, the *pīr* quickly loaded another missile. With unspeakable anger the *pīr* fired a flaming missile that scattered the tigers, scorching their bodies. Rāy's mount, the tiger Hīrā was unsettled when his whiskers were singed, especially witnessing the terrible anger that gripped Dakṣiṇ Rāy Ṭhākur. The two—Rāy and Hīrā—escaped when Rāy invoked the arrow of Varuṇa, lord of waters.

Kṛṣṇarām says, fire is always extinguished by water.

SECTION 20

Brandishing his own incredibly terrifying missile,
and a sword blade that glinted total destruction
 so brilliant that it sent the sun scurrying,
the Lord of the Southern Lands
unleashed a deafening roar
 as he let fly his arrow at the *pīr*.
The release sounded harshly like ringing bells;
it was as if Yam waved his staff
 urging it on faster than the wind.
Rooted there fearlessly,
Gāji casually plucked that arrow out of the air with his left hand
 and broke it in half in a rage.
Calling on the beneficence of the gods,
Rāy in the meantime
 lit up the sky with fire.
The danger was inescapable,
doom and disaster fell all around.
 The *pīr* fervently meditated on the Prophet, *paygambar*.
A deadly missile-arrow split open his chest.
Gāji slumped to the ground dead, but
 in an instant he healed, shook it off, and rose again.
His new body was identical to the one
that lay resplendently on the ground—
 his prayer to the Lord worked its magic.
The trident of Śiv proved ineffective
as they remained rooted to the spot.
 The *pīr* called out to Rāy,
"Yam has cut off your progeny

as little life remains, and
    now I separate your head from your body.
"You son of a stinking *bāṅgāli* jackal,
you hide behind your women's skirts,
    but now you are found out, there is no going back.
You will find no protection there.
Where is your great palace now?
    You need to come to grips with your folly."
Under the guise of taunting in this way,
he feverishly pushed and pulled into place
    four hundred cannons, primed and ready.
His body trembling with rage.
He fired all the cannon balls
    as he brandished a razor-sharp sword.
The Prophet, the *paygambar*, had granted
him the power to strike a blow that never failed
    for Yam, Death, dwelled in its diamond-sharp edge.
Gāji rushed forward brazenly,
bristling with a limitless courage
    to kill Dakṣiṇ Rāy.
He securely corralled
and then massacred seven thousand tigers,
    their destruction aided by his magical incantations.
They all lay sprawled on their backs, staring blankly at the sky.
Then he came before Dakṣiṇ Rāy
    and with unmitigated anger cut through his throat.
He deliberately pulled out and raised his sword
with no need for show or flourish,
    such was his confident majestic dignity.
The head Dakṣiṇ Rāy had assumed in this earthly guise,
in a split second thudded to the ground and rolled in the dirt,
    as if it were himself.
An untimely doom had descended
when the two of them wielded their swords and shields,
    their armor clashing in anger.
The earth herself staggered and tilted, fearful as she
realized she would sink down to ruination—
    all the *devs*, the gods, were rattled.
Kavi Kṛṣṇarām personally notes
it was as if two lions had waged war
    neither one admitting a weakness to the other.

Listen to this extraordinary tale,
for the Lord, Īśvar, *personally came there*
to mediate and end the dispute.

SECTION 21

Half of his head was black,
a tuft of hair pulled to one side,
wildflower garland and rosary looping his forearms.
Half of the body was a dazzling white,
the other half the deep indigo of rain clouds,
the Korān in one hand and Purāṇ in the other.[51]
Both men beheld
the exact same vision at the same time,
and both fell and grasped his feet.
That lord of the universe lifted them up,
placed one's hand in the other, and made them to understand
they must establish a formal pact of friendship.
"Suzerainty over this Bhāṭi land
lies entirely with Dakṣiṇ Rāy,
so why have you kicked up a fuss, Pīr?
Is there anyone who does not show you honor and respect?
Is there anywhere you are not loved and honored?
Your name and standing are famous across the world.
You and Rāy are one and the same.
In this matter only knuckle-headed barbarians
see you as different and suffer all manner of misery for it.
There is one essential truth in all this:
whatever else you may see,
it is only the play of apparent, created forms.[52]

51. This image of divinity is unique in these tales. Kṛṣṇarām calls this lord *bhagavān*, the standard epithet in the Bangla-speaking world for Viṣṇu or Kṛṣṇa, but also generic for God. The image is one of the combined forms of the dark Kṛṣṇa and the light mendicant Prophet, *paygambar*. The rest of the image is straightforward enough: half of the figure has a wildflower garland, rain-cloud body color, and holds the *Bhāgavat purāṇ*; the other half has the traditional Sufi rosary, is white, and holds the Korān. This combination is, of course, the image of Satya Pīr that had been circulating widely for well over a century.

52. Forms (*ākār*) that are apparent, i.e., untrue or misleading (*mithya*). The suggestion here is that creation does not have any standing as permanently real.

Baḍakhā̃'s magically created body[53] will
from its grave emanate a charismatic power, *kerāmat*,
 that will allow people to gain their desires.
Wherever the name of the *pīr* is invoked,
that locale is designated an official court where
 any decree or settlement can be registered in his name.
May everyone worship in *pūjā*
the King of the Southern Regions in the form of a pot,
 which mimics his shaved head in this magical creation.[54]
Then his story and fame will proliferate
to every imaginable spot on earth, and
 images will come to reside in all those places."
Then with his auspicious glance
all the dead tigers sprang back to life
 and assembled together there on the battlefield.
He placed his hand on the head of
the tiger Khān Dāuḍā,
 and smiling said these words:
"When an arrow strikes your forehead
you will not lose your life—
 from this day forward I have granted this boon.
Arrows, gunshot, missiles, and pikes
will shatter and scatter harmlessly should
 any tiger receive a direct hit to the head.
The unpredictable, vile savages of the wild are like animals;
should you encounter them, they are likely to break your neck
 and for this reason you should avoid them.
When you try to catch them to eat,
you should be just as wary as when
 you encounter ordinary human beings.[55]
After twelve years or so
The cubs in your homes

53. Magically created (*māyā*) body or form (*ākār*); except in explicit Vedāntic passages, *māyā* in Bangla nearly always refers to the magic or wizardry of creation, and only in that sense is it illusory. The poet makes clear that the ontological reality of the two is in no way affected— i.e., it is simply the play of the created world—when Baḍa Khān Gāji is killed and Dakṣiṇ Rāy's head is lopped off.

54. I.e., the delusory (*māyā*) shaved head (*muṇḍa*), which takes the form of a water pot.

55. The vile savages (*duṣṭa jantu baḍa bāḍ*) are indigenous inhabitants of the deep forests.

may not always find the hunting successful.
When that happens, as soon as the sun rises,
fashion a lump of clay into a mound.
When you eat that, your hunger will go away.[56]
Now understand that Dakṣiṇ Rāy
is the overlord of all the Sundarban *bhāṭi*.
Kālu Rāy has Hijuli as his special place.
Sāheb Pīr has free rein in all areas.
Everyone must bow their heads to him, and
no one should show him any disrespect."
The lord god, Dev Bhagavān,
disappeared after delivering these words.
Who has the power to fathom the magic of his *māyā*?
His words are not to be forsworn
as every human in every home recognizes—
and when they admit that, they show proper honor and respect.
When the good and virtuous young merchant heard this tale,
he made his obeisance in an attitude of loving devotion
and took a flower as the leftover offering, *prasād*.
Kavi Kṛṣṇarām notes that
finding the winds favorable,
he boarded his ship and shoved off.

SECTION 22

With a heartfelt obeisance toward Dakṣiṇ Rāy, the Lord of the South, the young merchant caught the waves and sailed on. At the great pilgrimage site of Ambuliṅgā, the merchant prostrated himself to Śiv, Tripurāri, with a devotion immeasurable. At Chatrabhog, he performed a formal *pūjā* worship to Tripurā Bhavānī. The waves swept his ship past Kākadvīp Gajaghaḍi and soon Madhu's son left behind the abode of deadly snakes, Kālsāper Mahāl, and bypassed Magarā

56. As noted in the general Introduction above, this speech aimed at the tigers foretells the encroachment of humans into the Sundarbans and all the surrounding heavily forested areas to exploit their timber, salt, and honey, and for their agricultural domestication. This is a recurring theme in the *maṅgal kāvya*, and the taming of the frontier is bound up in the narrative of the spread of Islam in the region. Though not spelled out, the mounds of clay are homologous with Dakṣiṇ Rāy's "head," suggesting that he is the natural source of the tigers' nurture if all else fails.

altogether. The chop tossed them about as the boat slipped into the currents of the Gaṅgā, whose touch portended good luck. At this point the good merchant observed, "The mighty ascetic Kapila was a part of Viṣṇu and out of anger burned to ashes the entire lineage of Sagar. Scion of that lineage, Bhagirath, upon attaining the ultimate esoteric knowledge, utilized the fruits of his countless austerities to bring down Gaṅgā. When that *satī*, that pure and chaste woman, descended from the Himalayas, she took the name of Bhāgīrathī due to the gracious interventions of Bhagīrath. When she arrived here, she separated herself into a braided river of a hundred distributaries, each with its own mouth, and those untold numbers of Sagars who had suffered the *brahma*-curse of extinction were restored to life when they touched the liberating feet of her waters.[57] Now over there we see the Surdhunī as it flows into the ocean." A real delight rippled through the ship's pilot at this tale recounted by the good merchant.

They remained moored there that day, observing a fast. After they ceremonially bathed the next morning and made charitable donations, the seven ships pushed off. The son of the merchant called out the auspicious command of approval, "Everything is good, set sail!" and soon they caught sight of the main mouth of the Gaṅgā at Gaṅgāsāgar. There was a strong sense of belief that bathing there led to salvation of the fallen, so with a keen sense of devotion, he performed a *pūjā* worship directed toward Kṛṣṇa as Anantamādhav. The good merchant sailed toward the confluence with a calm confidence, then they swept past the curious kingdom of Bennatoraṇ. The wealthy merchant pressed on, again signaling his approval and barking the com-

57. The traditional tale, found in the Sanskrit *Mahābhārata* and other texts, indicates that Bhagīratha is a direct descendant of Viṣṇu, albeit more than thirty generations removed, and forefather of the Sagar Dynasty. Through his penance, he persuades Gaṅgā to come to earth to perform the funeral rites of the sixty thousand sons of Sagar, who enraged the sage Kapila when they interrupted his meditations (*tapas*), resulting in their incineration. Gaṅgā agrees, but fears the earth cannot withstand the force of her descent from the heavens, so Bhagīratha performs a thousand-year penance to propitiate Lord Śiva, who subsequently agrees to break Gaṅgā's torrents by allowing the cascades to flow through his hair, which slows the waters as they descend from the Himalayas and creates the Gaṅgā River, known as the Bhāgīrāthi River in Bengal. For a uniquely Bengali take on Bhagīrath's birth as found in the Bengali recension of the *Padmā purāṇa*, see the translation below of Kavi Vallabh's *Satyanārāyaṇer puthi*, n. 6.

mand to sail hard, as the ship swept steadily across the waves until well past the land ruled by Rājā Mārkaṇḍa. Afterwards they cruised by the settlement houses of Bāburmokām and quickly left the land of Karṇapūr in their wake. The merchant was unnerved when they were crossing the shoreless expanse of deep blue water, but soon they glimpsed Uḍiṣyā, the sight of whose stone temples, with their brilliant pennants waving on top, made the place as enchanting as the abode of the gods, Amarāvatī. The helmsman questioned the merchant, "What is this city that is so stunningly beautiful?"

The merchant replied, "Listen as I tell you its amazing story."

Kṛṣṇarām has written this captivating tale in pācāli *form.*

SECTION 23

"The overlord of Utkal,
a king named Indradyumna,
    was a veritable Rām for the Kali Age.
His posterity derived from focused meditation on the feet of Viṣṇu,
which made him supreme among rulers of men,
    his effulgent glory shone brighter than the moon.
A magnificent temple of stone
he labored hard to construct on the shores of the sea,
    giving shape to a long-held desire.
He had Lord Nārāyaṇ installed in that structure,
before he abandoned this life to
    become a permanent resident of Vaikuṇṭha heaven.
Descending from heaven in the Kali Age,
Nārāyaṇ assumed the form of Dārubrahma, the wooden god,
    accompanied by Subhadrā and Balarām.[58]
When he is viewed, no vestiges of sin remain,

58. Jagannāth is the Dārubrahma, the only icon in any major Indian temple fabricated entirely of wood; the images of Jagannāth, his sister Subhadrā, and his brother Balarām are replaced with new ones every twelve years. The images are said to self-manifest (*svayambhū*), each fashioned from a single piece of wood located in living trees by special priests and augurs. See Anncharlot Eschmann, Hermann Kulke, and Gaya Charan Tripathi, eds., *The Cult of Jagannāth and the Regional Tradition of Orissa*, South Asia Institute, Heidelberg University, South Asian Studies 8 (New Delhi: Manohar, 1978).

searing misery and pain are effaced,
    and one enters the eternal realm at Viṣṇu's feet."
The model son of the merchant continued,
"I have heard that with no more weapons to unleash,
    Indradyumna died on the Āṭhāronālā viaduct.
He assumed a divine body
and boarded an aerial vehicle
    which flew him to the city of the gods who never die.
What more can the god of death, Śaman, do?
for never will he be reborn again.
    Not even Indra is his equal.
More than any human being
within this Uḍiṣyā and even across the whole of earth,
    he had accumulated the greatest merit of all.[59]
Lord Jagannāth reigns over all three worlds, and
in his temple market, fine rice is prepared,
    along with wonderfully sweet yoghurt drinks.
To see this enraptures the mind, so that
one becomes greedy to possess all of it.
    The self-manifesting Svayambhū is equal to all the gods.
What more can I say?
Listen, brother helmsman,
    this Kali Age brings with it great danger.
People are given over to despicable actions;
they exercise no sense of discrimination,
    and their sins pile up higher and higher.
They conduct business dishonestly,

59. Tradition has it that Indradyumna—who is credited with building a host of stone temples to Jagannāth, Narasiṃha, and other forms of Viṣṇu, as well as constructing the Indradyumna Lake in Nilācal or Puri—is also credited with building the stone viaduct as the northern entryway to the city. His initial attempts were unsuccessful until he sacrificed eighteen (*āṭhāra*) of his sons and dropped their heads into the water, which enabled him to build the eighteen stone islands (*dvīp*) that served as the base for the arches (what today's engineers would call the foundation and pylons or piers), creating openings through which the water could freely flow (*nālā*), hence the name *āṭhāronālā* bridge. The merchant in Kṛṣṇarām's story appears to conflate parts of the tale of one Indradyumna cited in the *Mahābhārata* (*vana parva*) and the tale of another Indradyumna in the *Skaṇda purāṇa*, stories frequently retold in devotional tracts and pilgrimage guides in Bangla and Odia; see, e.g., the Bangla version by Viśvambhar Dās, *Jagannāth maṅgal* (Kalikātā: Śrīnaṭbar Cakravartī at Baṅgabāsī Ilekṭromesin Pres, 1313 BS [ca. 1906]), part 3, *kṣetra khaṇḍa*, 96–153.

they have no commitment to *dharma* or *karma*.
This is how people act in the age of Kali.
The many social ranks, starting with the *dvija*, twice-born,
will in the end become indistinguishable
from the foreign *jaban* and other groups.
Mired in times like these, I sincerely believe
that glorious Jagannāth, the great lord, Mahāprabhu,[60]
will rescue those sinful people, for
Brahmā and the hosts of other gods
aid him with extreme zeal and perseverance.
But what do I know of the full extent of their majesty?
Let us go and see for ourselves this wonder,
his stainless moon face!
Today will be our lucky day!"
May your transgressions be wiped away,
so there need not be any fear of death,
Kavi Kṛṣṇarām narrates the heart of what counts.

SECTION 24

With a sense of inquisitive adventure, the merchant
went along together with the pilot
to see the lord Jagannāth.
All the oarsmen and galley hands
were truly delighted, for today
the earnest strivings of their hearts would be fulfilled.
When they entered the marketplace
they were giddy with wonder
for there were hundreds of stalls in row after row.
The men were more handsome than Madan
and the women were the equal of Padminī,
all buying and selling with an easy enjoyment.

60. "Great lord" (*mahāprabhu*) was also the favored epithet of Kṛṣṇa Caitanya (1486–1533 CE), identified with Jagannāth, the image in Puri being *acala*, or immobile, and the human Caitanya *sacala*, or mobile. Given that Kṛṣṇarām was writing more than a century after Caitanya's death, it is likely both meanings are conveniently signified. "When I hear the name of one, I hear the name of the other," one devotee told me. For more on this identification, see Tony K. Stewart, *The Final Word: The Caitanya Caritāmṛta and the Grammar of Religious Tradition* (New York: Oxford University Press, 2010), pp. 57, 96, 115–16, 119–21, 123, 140, 168.

They entered the temple compound
to get a view of the divinity who ruled Puri,
the most revered, the highest lord.
Pure gold adorned his arms,
around his neck hung strings of pearls—
all woes disappeared just to gaze at his face.
Cinching a cloth around his neck,
then making a deep obeisance,
the merchant stood transfixed before him.
He made an offering of numerous gemstones,
requested and then accepted *prasād* food offerings,
which he ate, and then touched his head in humility.
To take away, they purchased local curds,
along with a sweet drink made with rice water,
and *sandeś* milk sweets in great quantities.
They were pleased and in the highest spirits,
when the merchant and his crew
reboarded their ships.
All seven vessels, handsomely outfitted,
set sail to the rhythmic chants of the crew,
moving at a sprightly pace, faster than the wind.
They soon reached Setubandha,
where they propitiated with pious devotion
Lord Rāmeśvar, a boundless fount of compassion.
As they looked at the remnants of an earthen dam,
the helmsman, who was forward,
questioned the merchant.
"Please tell me, won't you, my friend,
who could construct that earthen embankment crossing the ocean?
Clearly, humans do not have the lusty vigor to do this."
The good merchant replied, "Listen, brother,
I will relate the story in detail,
for it is the unprecedented saga of the *Rāmāyaṇ*."
When one hears that tale, merit without measure
accrues to cancel out completely all sins and suffering,
so Kṛṣṇarām has written.

SECTION 25

"There once ruled a king, Daśarath, in the citadel of Ayodhyā, and he watched over his subjects as if they were his own sons. Among his seven hundred marriage liaisons, three women were favored: Kauśalyā, Kaikeyī, and the beauty, Sumitrā. Lord Nārāyaṇ took birth in four separate parts as Daśarath's sons: Rāmcandra, Bharat, Lakṣmaṇ, and Śatrughna. The daughter of King Janaka was Sītā, a paragon of beauty. Rām broke Hara's bow and won her in marriage. Kaikeyī had begged a boon from the king, and she requested that Rām and Sītā be forced to live in exile deep in the forest for fourteen years, making way to anoint her son Bharat as king of the realm. When he heard this request, the king fainted dead away. Together with Lakṣmaṇ and Sītā, Rām went to live in the forest. Pining in his consternation over Rām, the king's body gave way, and he collapsed and died. In the forest, they wore crude clothes of bark, and their hair became matted. They drank only water and subsisted on fruits and roots. There was a night-faring demoness named Śūrpaṇakhā who came to propose to Rām, "Please marry me!" But the mighty hero Lakṣmaṇ sliced off her nose and ears. So she fled crying to Kharadūṣaṇ. Ignorant as he was, he moved to kill Rām, bringing with him a legion of fourteen thousand night-faring demons. The Lord Nārāyaṇ annihilated them all. Rāvaṇ, the supreme ruler of Laṅkā, came to hear of it. He hatched a fiendishly execrable plan to kidnap Rām's Sītā. Hence he dispatched the *rākṣas* demon Mārīc, who had shape-shifted into a beautiful deer. Śrī Raghunandan gave chase to slay him, and while the hut was vacated, the ten-headed Rāvaṇ, Daśānan, seized Jānakī. Utterly distracted by his longing for Sītā, Rām wept so profusely that his tears completely drenched his clothes. Rām was completely enervated by his grief at losing Sītā until a bird, who had befriended Janaka, was able to deliver a special message. Meanwhile, having established an alliance with King Sugrīv, Rām slew his enemy, the stalwart Bāli. With the might of his own two arms, the righteous one killed Rāvaṇ, recovered Sitā, and returned to his own lands."

Listen, pilot, it was Lakṣmaṇ who built the bridge.[61]
Kṛṣṇarām has composed the synopsis of the story in song.

61. Hanumān and his monkey army are most frequently credited with constructing the land bridge, as the author later indicates; see §31 and §38 below.

SECTION 26

When the helmsman heard the tale of the *Rāmāyaṇ* as told by the merchant, he smartly observed, "There is no work for us here." So the ships sailed on, outrunning the wind. They soon caught sight of the eddies off the island of Śrīhādyā, where the sailors hove to and dropped anchor. Then they cooked, and everyone exulted in their respite. The tide came in and began to submerge the beach, so they floated out and quickly caught the running current. They soon reached Kā̃kaḍādaha, where, as the fearless son of the merchant meditated on the lord, Rāy, they roasted a number of goats over a fire and offered a sacrifice. Next, all the ships ended up at Jokādaha, the land of leeches, where the bodies of the leeches are wider than fan palms. The galley slaves were unsettled as they tried to steady and secure the merchant's vessel. They emptied numerous gunny sacks of quicklime into the waters, which terrorized and scorched the leeches, who dove for the murky depths. As they settled, the crabs and lobsters raised their mandibles and snapped at them with their claws. Looking into the waters, the young merchant laughed and said, "It looks like forests of bamboo shoots vying with clumps of flute reeds.[62] When I return home, I shall relish telling everyone this marvelous episode."

The helmsman replied, "O merchant, those are not flute reeds, those are aged crustaceans, lobsters and giant shrimps, snapping their mandibles and claws."

The seven ships wasted no time in sailing on, but they soon encountered magnificent knots of serpents directly in their path. The serpent called Jāniyat had an enormous gaping maw; if you can imagine, he was so big that he attempted to swallow the entire vessel! The pilot was quick-thinking and shrewd, so he devised a solution and meditated on Garuḍa to slay it.[63]

62. The common Bangla name for the flute reed or tall reed *Phragmites karka* or *Arundo karka* is *nalakhāgaḍā*; it is a robust, strongly tufted perennial in the Poaceae family, with creeping rhizomes that can grow as tall as ten meters and thin leaves as much as eighty centimeters long. Its willowy leaves are used for thatching, basket-making, brooms, and fodder. It is often planted to stabilize soil along waterways. It is impossible to determine the precise plant designated by the generic *kõḍā* bamboo. The image suggests tree-sized leeches in battle with ancient crustaceans.

63. As the giant bird mount of Nārāyaṇ or Viṣṇu, Garuḍa is a natural enemy of serpents, over which he always prevails.

Offering obeisance at the lotus feet of Rāy,
Kṛṣṇarām has composed this eloquent dramatic recitation.

SECTION 27

Up ahead of them, a flock of birds soared this way and that—birds, yes, but more like behemoths, the girth of their bodies that of mountains. It seemed as if they could gulp down an entire ship in just a single bite. The merchant's son wept in terror. "I know that today I am certain to die." Suśīlā's son was undoubtedly in a terrible, frightful fix. But the helmsman devised yet another ploy: they labored hard to pack the cannons with gunpowder and then fired. The thundering report was deafening and intensely threatening. The sound and shockwave stunned the flock of giant aerial creatures. Afterwards, the merchant-chief celebrated, everyone clapping hands in unison, fast and slow, blowing auspicious sounds with conchs and cowries.

They sailed past Kālidaha, with Siṃhala off to port,
until they approached Rājadaha, narrates Kṛṣṇarām.

SECTION 28

As the merchant's ship made its way to Rājadaha, the lord Rāy created a palace in the middle of the ocean. First, a sandbank rose up in the middle of the ocean on which were untold numbers of elegant and beautifully shaped mansions constructed of gold. Nārāyaṇ was ensconced on his majestic throne, all of his servants assembled before him. On his left, an image of Nīlāvatī stood out.

You must understand that all of this was a magical, illusory display by God.

On his right was Sugrīv, kneeling with his legs reverently tucked under him, fanning the body of the Lord. The place was surrounded by trees of infinite varieties, and though they were but saplings, they bore beautiful fruits: cocoanut, jujube,[64] mango, and betel

64. The Indian jujube or Indian plum, *Ziziphus mauritiana* in the Rhamnaceae family, is called *kul* in Bangla. There are at least a half dozen varieties cultivated in the Bangla-speaking world. It can grow up to eight meters tall and has yellowish flowers. The berries, are approximately three and a half cm in length.

nut.[65] One could see huge numbers of mynah birds[66] at rest; from one moment to the next, they flew up and flitted about, then just as quickly alighted. The *vakul*[67] trees' blossoms delighted throngs of bees. There were birds of every imaginable type, displaying every imaginable color. Together in a single place carnivores that hunted moved freely with their normal prey, all side by side: humans, tigers, deer, and buffalo. The peacock and serpent played together, maned lions mixed freely with tuskers, bull elephants. Then the earth herself emitted a terrible groaning sound.

Witnessing all this, the good merchant's heart was truly confounded, narrates Kṛṣṇarām using the lively pācāli *meter.*

SECTION 29

The good merchant said to the pilot,
"Look at this stunning marvel of marvels:
  an enchanting citadel right in the middle of the ocean!
Bejeweled buildings without rival,
a majestic throne whose beauty enthralls,
  and a dozen celestial nymphs, *vidyādharīs*, dancing and singing.
Just look at this wonder manifest before us!
I shall report this to the king,
  and attest to it to any and everyone.
Such a miraculous event exceeds the already unprecedented.
What a blessed privilege it is to witness such a magnificent sight,
  one had never previously imagined in the three tiers of the universe."
As they listened to the rapture of the good merchant,
one by one, starting with the helmsman,
  a disturbing uneasiness crept into the crews' hearts.

65. The betel or areca nut, colloquially called *guyā*, which is valued for its mild narcotic properties and variously used as a breath freshener, a digestive, and an aphrodisiac, is the seed of a feather palm, *Areca catechu*.

66. See nn. 21 and 23 above.

67. The botanical name of the *vakul*, a small tree in the Sapotaceae (Mahua) family, is *Mimusops elengi*. It provides dense shade and is valued for its aromatic flowers, commonly used as offerings in worship, which produce a perfume that lasts long after they drop. In ancient lore, the plant is said to put forth its blossoms when sprinkled with the saliva of a beautiful woman.

They cast their gaze in all four directions,
but apart from the young merchant, no other actually saw
the magical illusion conjured up by God.
The pilot gently ruminated to himself with an uneasy laugh:
"Though in his heart he is fully convinced by it,
our merchant must have witnessed all this in some dream.
His story is so exceedingly absurd,
how can he say anything was out there when the ship
was cruising in deep blue waters out of sight of the shore?"
Savvy to the ways of the world, the helmsman
offered no reply, voiced no opinion, but
just sputtered noncommittally, "Wah, everything is good, sail on!"
A number of days passed and
the merchant, with his fleet of ships, had crossed over
the expanse of deep water and reached shore.
When the ship put in to the landing ghat,
trumpets blared loudly
and numerous open palms pounded kettledrums.
When the local king heard the resounding report
of the cannons and other weapons being fired,
he grew nervous and uneasy, indeed, worried.
Meanwhile, the merchant was in high spirits,
first bathing, then performing worship with great fanfare,
before consuming a well-cooked meal.
Meditating on Dakṣiṇrāy,
Kavi Kṛṣṇarām sings,
"May you grant a boon to your hero!"

SECTION 30

When they landed up at the ghat and dropped anchor, the deep rumble of the war weapons resounded like booming thunder in a rain cloud. In the midst of the ear-splitting uproar, the king, Surath, called his chief of his police force and said, "All manner of instruments are blaring and the commotion is generating a racket. What great king, what *mahārāj*, has landed up in my kingdom? Am I to understand that he has come to overrun us by force? Go and find out, and be quick!" yelled the king, himself a mountain of virtues. The chief of police went, taking a large number of foot soldiers and accompanied by large bull elephants carrying howdahs. The soldiers' faces were more burnished than fired copper pots, their complexions black as black can be, their hearts ill-tempered. They discovered that seven large ships had anchored at their docks, with Puṣpadatta seated on a golden cot.

The chief of police questioned him, "Tell me, where are you from? If you desire good to come your way, then you need to honor the feet of my lord, my king. His majesty, Sāheb himself, has summoned you. So let us go to Gidhijāi. I want you to set aside any thought of treachery. But to my mind, daughter-fucker, you are most certainly a highwayman, a dacoit. If so, the Sāheb himself has already ordered your beheading."

When he heard this, the merchant Puṣpadatta replied, "I have not had even a sip of water after arriving in your city, and now you are threatening me just because I've landed up on your shores! It is your good fortune that it is not someone else. Come, let us go into the king's city."

The helmsman queried, "Why is the ruler so angry? You are the chief of the king's police, so you can protect us." Then the merchant calculated and gave him twelve rupees' worth of goods. The items he wanted were presented to him as gifts.

Then the merchant gathered all kinds of delicacies and precious goods to take to his meeting with the king. He carried large quantities of cocoanuts and betel quids, ghee, vegetable oil, rice, and an assortment of garments. He found the ruler seated, leaning on a bolster, while attending servants fanned him from both sides. As he looked around the city of this regal lord of the world, the merchant observed that it compared favorably to the city of the gods, Amarāvatī. At the center crossroads, the bazaar was teeming with shops, and the men and women looked like the deities of love, Kām and Rati. Fully accomplished *yogīs* were to be seen set in their various postures, clothed only in ash, serenely unperturbed. Graciously adorning the banks of the ponds were pillars, completely wrapped in gold. *Kadamba* trees[68] were in abundance, mixed in with champak magnolias,[69] both blanketed with aromatic flowers. A short while later they arrived at the king's

68. On *kadamba*, see n. 28 above.

69. Champak is now a recognized English spelling for the *cā̃pā* or *cāmpā*, *Magnolia champaca* in the Magnoliaceae family. It is famous for its fragrant yellow-orange flowers and sturdy timber, suitable for woodworking. It can grow to a height of fifty meters and be as much as two meters in diameter.

quarters. A traditional teacher[70] instructed young boys through the medium of Farsi. With gold pens tucked behind their ears and inkpots on the floor in front of them, *kāyastha* scribes elegantly wrote in their books. Beyond that, the king, the lord of men, could be found in a spacious private chamber, to whose entrance the doorman restricted access. The chief of police reported to the king what the good merchant had said, so the lord of men ordered, "Bring him in." The chief of police left, greatly relieved, indeed very pleased, and escorted the merchant to the presence of the king. The son of the merchant produced and ceremonially placed in front of the king goods suitable for a formal meeting, then bowed to the king's feet, with the palms of his hands pressed together in respect. The king affectionately seated him at his side and inquired of the merchant the reason for his visit. The merchant replied, "Listen carefully, O king, to the reason for my coming to Pāṭan. My home lies in the kingdom of Baradānagar, where the ruler, Madan, is widely respected. My father, by the name of Devdatta, lived there and a very long time ago voyaged here to Pāṭan."

"To find out news of my father did I come here, O king, treasury of virtue.

Puṣpadatta is my name," so writes Kṛṣṇarām.

SECTION 31

Listening to the elegant speech of the good merchant, that king, great ornament of the world, spoke to him with compassion. "How can your mother bring herself to send her son such a great distance?"

Acknowledging this with respectful humility, the young merchant replied, "My mother is a pure and devoted wife, equal to Sāvitrī. In the absence of her husband, she feels that life is meaningless. She grieves constantly, all day and all night, until dawn finally comes. I am unable to bear the searing agony she constantly suffers. How could I remain at home when my father is lost in a distant land? Bear with me, O jewel among men, such is the duty of a son, to rescue mother or father when they are in danger."

70. The teacher is *ākhon* < *ākhūn*, the instructor of a traditional *maktab* or *kuttāb*, a public elementary school, the curriculum of which included Qur'ān recitation, reading, writing, and grammar, mingled with religious instruction.

The king replied, "Your life is truly a blessing, for only the most fortunate person has a son of your stature. Your father is undoubtedly fortunate to have sired you. Blessed, too, your mother that she carried you in her womb. Tell me more of your story, merchant, I wish to hear what you saw as you sailed, your ship passed so many different lands."

The good merchant spoke, "Great-souled one, please be mindful as I place my humble offering at your lustrous feet." And so he began to narrate the many details of things that occurred on his trip. "You shall see that fate proved fickle and we were beset with many vexations. At Gaṅgāsagar, the lord is called Ananta Mādhav, and his epithet of Patitapāban, 'Savior of the Fallen,' was appropriately reassuring. Listen, O king, the virtues and merit of a place such as that give salvation, whether reverently honored from the waters, on dry land, or from the skies above. I saw Lord Jagannāth on the shores of the ocean, and we purchased that god's leftover food, his *prasād*, and dutifully consumed it. During the descent of Rām, a massive land-bridge across the ocean was constructed by the great monkey for the sake of slaying Rāvaṇ. Now listen carefully to my description, O king, for it is in fact the truth: at Rājdaha I saw the most wonderful of all wonders. A spit of land jutted up in the middle of the ocean, an enchanted island where predator and prey sat side by side. A divine being was ensconced on a majestic throne covered with gems, and attending servants all around constantly fanned him with fly whisks." When that son of a good merchant made this claim, the king, ornament of the earth itself, laughed as he listened.

May you direct your grace and protect, O lord, the servitors of Nīlakaṇṭha, Śiv of the blue throat.

Kṛṣṇarām has written this at the direct command of Rāy.

SECTION 32

The protector of the world, King Surath, chuckled at the good merchant's words. "It was in your dreams that you saw a citadel floating in the middle of the ocean. Do not utter such nonsense again, lest your conduct start to resemble that of a swindling bastard."

The good merchant replied, "Please explain, lord among men, the reason for casting such aspersions? I will show you just how incredibly wondrous that city in the ocean really is! If I fail to demonstrate that what I said is true, then chop off my head and confiscate all seven of my ships. But if I am able to reveal it to you, then your loss will be my gain: Give me your entire kingdom and your daughter in marriage."

The king responded, "If I see for myself this city in the middle of the ocean, then I will have indeed lost and will make over my kingdom and my daughter to you." And in this fashion the two respected men confirmed their wager. Then each of them duly wrote down the terms, and each gave the other his promissory note.

Then the king wasted no time summoning the chief of police. He ordered, "Make the ships ready quickly, for we sail to Rājdaha." Divining the wishes of that lord of men, the chief of police made haste. He mustered large numbers of foot soldiers, their ranks forming an army. The king boarded a flat-bottomed barge, a *koyār*[71] sporting one hundred oars and took a seat amidships on a majestic golden throne, above which loomed a gem-studded parasol. Around the king were seated his ministers and advisors and an assembly of learned men, while the chief of his police boarded with a great many infantry soldiers. The merchant with his pilot led the way, their ship plowing ahead faster than the wind. On board the ship were large numbers of wicker baskets filled with gemstones, sparkling like the moon reflected in a mirror. White and yellow banners were affixed and raised in a glorious salute to the wind. Soon the soldiers and the king landed up at Rājdaha. The lord of men scanned the four directions and saw nothing save endless waters. The king said, "So speak, Merchant Puṣpadatta, tell me where exactly did you see this enchanting citadel?"

The merchant replied, "Can you not see it while staring straight at it? I will continue to insist over and over until I die: I declare it is right there! Look at it! See for yourself! There is your proof. And, as you yourself promised in writing in the presence of the goddess, the slayer of demons, I will now raise the umbrella of power and take over the reins of the kingdom of Pāṭan."

The king patiently replied, "I see nothing. Not one thing falls within my field of vision, not even a blade of grass. I see only the swells of the

71. The hundred-oared ship is better known as a *koś* or *koṣ*, because today the *koyār* is a flat-bottomed boat with a sharply pointed prow used for river navigation in shallow waters. It is capable of carrying only two or three tons of goods, with a standard crew of two, which suggests that either its classification has changed or the term is used generically here, since they were headed out into blue water.

deep blue sea. Because some of my own people may not always be counted on to speak truthfully to me, I will honor any eyewitness among your own crew. Speak up, tell me in no uncertain terms, helmsman, what do you see in this shoreless expanse of ocean?"

The good merchant blurted out, "My pilot is not blind. Now he will certainly confirm the presence of that city in the middle of the ocean."

The pilot replied, "O king, I speak the truth. I do not see anything but water. When we were on our way here, the good merchant said to me, 'All of you will be my witness when I report this to the king.' But I did not see anything then, nor do I see anything now."

When he heard this, King Surath was genuinely taken aback. The great king wasted no time in issuing the command to his police chief, "Tie up the merchant and throw him into prison. Tomorrow he will be executed in the southern cremation grounds. Now seize his ships and confiscate everything they hold." When the king imparted this instruction, the soldiers seized the ships as soon as they anchored, while the king disembarked and headed back home. The chief of police observed the king's order with a special vengeance, and he bound that son of a merchant from all sides. He lashed together both of his hands with an especially strong rope, and trussed him up like a common thief. They roped his waist, looping the rope round and round. Then they seized his gems and jewelry.

Meditating on the alluring lotus feet of Rāy,
Kṛṣṇarām Kavi has composed this in the pācāli *meter.*

SECTION 33

The merchant embraced the pilot, then said in all earnest, his trussed hands pressed together in supplication, "I implore you, listen, give me your undivided attention. There is no more work to be done here, so go, return to our homeland. There is no escape from what fate has written. I have come to Pāṭan to meet my death. I have never had a better friend and advisor than you. Please return home and share the news of my death. There is no suffering in this death, nor does it make me anxious, for all my life I have never known my father. And as a result, my mother Suśīlā has suffered a miserable existence. Day and night, she grieves with no respite. I will never be able to return to Baradānagar, nor will I be able to meet King Madan, that noble man.

Please go back to our homeland and perform this one act of compassion and kindness: inform my mother and give her solace and good counsel."

The helmsman replied, "I will not return to our homeland, for at your death, I have no good reason left to live and will not cling to this life. At the time of our leaving, good merchant, your mother put your hand in mine and entrusted you to me to bring you home. How can I return and show my face back home? How could I have the courage, much less the temerity, to tell of your death? At that time I warned you, but you would not listen, so you ended up telling a wild and nonsensical story to the king. Your troubles, brother, are solely of your own making, and now, whatever good or bad transpires lies in the hands of fate. How ironic that our ship, which did not sink as it navigated the ocean depths, by the simple fruit of your story has now foundered on dry land!" The chief of king's police then broke up their conversation, leading the good merchant off to a jail ghastly by any standard. When he saw the wretched place, the merchant was filled with fear. He felt that he had arrived in the realm of Yam, the god of death, but in the flesh. Thousands upon thousands of people had been impaled on tridents, many more hideously dismembered and tossed into the shallow creek. Packs of dogs and jackals tore at their flesh in a feeding frenzy, while crowds of vultures feverishly pecked and picked at the carcasses. It was here that the merchant was incarcerated, a huge stone lowered onto his chest. Feeling desperate, the son of the merchant cried out, meditating on Lord Rāy and singing his praises.

Using the cautriś *poetic form*[72] *to continue the story,*
Kṛṣṇarām has composed this heartening pācāli *tale.*

72. The *cautriś* poetic form, literally meaning "thirty-four," refers to the ordered consonants of the alphabet, in which the initial consonant of each couplet is the next letter of the alphabet, somewhat reminiscent of an acrostic. The form is deployed to allow the author to explore a topic in depth, here a highly-charged emotional outburst. In a further display of virtuosity, the second line of the couplet might also use the same letter, which is done in most of the couplets in this passage. There is some small deviation here where phonology, that is, identical pronunciation, is deemed equivalent to orthography (e.g., জ /j/ and য /y/ are pronounced as "j"; and / স /s/ and শ /ś/ are pronounced as "sh"). While the order is usually limited to consonants, we also find several couplets here that use vowels as well (e.g., আ /ā/, ই /i/, and উ /u/).

SECTION 34

"I petition you with palms pressed together in respect, Dakṣiṇ Rāy, please grant your grace, you who are the wish-fulfilling tree." The distress caused Puṣpadatta's thighs to twitch involuntarily and made his whole body spasm. "Seated on the king of all birds, Khagendra, you, who are a trove of virtues and who manifest a soothing luster, be pleased to mitigate my inborn tendency to baseness and protect me. You are proclaimed throughout every universe as an ocean of great qualities, yet you led us to this faraway land and sowed disorder and confusion. My mother remains at home all alone, because her husband and son are stranded in this alien land. The chief of police will soon behead me, so please quickly arrange my escape! As we made our way here, you delivered us safely across the rough chop of the ocean's waters, so why did you not again conjure up land in the middle of the sea? This king is confident and grounded in his action and word, in his character, in his vigorous strength, so the chief of his police, brandishing his brilliantly sharp sword, will certainly come to execute me. I have witnessed for myself the full power of your chicanery through the magic of this creation. By a simple deception, life and wealth easily evaporate, such is the nature of the inauspicious. I have suffered great misery in my birth in this world, so much so that not even Brahmā, the four-faced one, could grasp enough to narrate it."

In anticipation of carrion, flocks of vultures jockeyed for position, circling overhead, mimicking the whirling sword of the chief of police, who arrived to perform his duties. "With a face that puts the moon to shame, a beauty that exceeds that of Madan, the god of love, O Lord of the Southern Regions, please give me a sign that you will save me! You lured me here through the tether of memory, so please protect me from having my neck chopped, cleaving me in two. Please put a stop to that heartless chief of police, for he is a rogue and a scoundrel and with an unspeakable malice, he will slay me in a heartbeat. I cry out over and over, pleading in a voice choked with emotion, give me firm ground, for I have been overwhelmed, submerged in the waves of this ocean of existence. I am struck with fear as I look at the physical size and demeanor of that rogue chief of the king's police. Gripping a sword and shield, he rushes toward me seething with anger. Why did you bring your servant to this alien land only to kill him? Fear is written across my face and my voice gives way. In anticipation, the face of the chief of police has turned the color of a fired and burnished copper pot. My heart pounds wildly, my chest heaves, and I am breathless with fear. O Lord of the South, Dakṣiṇ Rāy, as you reside in this your territory, please pay heed: you can easily grant me a secure place at your feet, great-souled one. It is inappropriate to be angry over a lapse by a wayward servant. It is more suitable to show mercy when you see such abject misery. All of my wealth and my men have been lost; only my life remains. I meditate on your lotus feet so that you may grant me salvation. I bow over and over to you, the great-spirited husband of Līlāvatī. Please assuage the overwhelming fear I have. I know clearly that you are the supreme divinity, the *param puruṣ*, and you protect the life of your servant's son from error and ruin. You are Lord, *ṭhākur*, the girth of whose arms puts serpents to shame. I am confused, perplexed. Please relieve my spiraling fears! For all my years I have never met my father, who has always been lodged in some foreign land. As the Master who destroys the impediments of misfortune, please bestow your mercy. I arrived laden with goods brought from home, and I have meditated continuously on your feet as the source of sustenance. O Lord of the Southern Regions, Dakṣiṇ Ray, if you do not extend your affectionate regard and I were to die, what would happen to your reputation for sublime glory? O radiant one, in this birth I have never known my father. Please save me, you who are famed for dispensing the nectar of immortality. Save your personal servant, so that your glory may spread over the earth. Listen to these words of praise, and may you grant good sense to the king. If you do not intercede with dispatch and save my life, will anyone ever again turn to you for protection? O dear father, though I was never able to see you, or to serve you, and though you have turned away from me, please forgive my offenses. You promised me in a dream that everything would be made right, so please remove the misery of one who has turned to you as a refuge from suffering. O exalted one, you have powers equal to the six-faced Skanda. If you bestow your grace, then I will offer the formal worship composed of the six special offerings made to ancestors. As the son of Suśīlā, I was made your servant, so I desire nothing but the constant shade of your pleasing feet. I am in a horrible fix, with no escape. O Lord of the Southern Lands, PLEASE SHOW ME YOUR MERCY!"

In an earthen abode in Kalikātā, which lies along the banks of the Jāhnavī,

an exhausted and emaciated Kṛṣṇarām narrates at the feet of the Lord.

SECTION 35

Rāy divined through his meditation that
the son of the merchant was about to be dismembered,
    so he consulted his five chief advisors.
"He has fallen into danger and is about to die, so
he has directed his thoughts toward me.
    Please advise me what is the appropriate course of action?"
His wife, Līlāvatī, spoke,
"Listen, lord of my life, please listen.
    Your action can reverse the situation.
Suśīlā was an adolescent beauty,
blessed with an abundance of virtues,
    and apart from you, she has never turned to another.
For many long days has she been your servant.
Somehow she has managed to maintain her love
    for the twelve years her husband has been incarcerated.
Even though she bore an extraordinary son,
handsome, and endowed with the finest qualities,
    it was you who lured him to this faraway land.
Please fulfil my wish:
Rescue your servant from his imminent peril,
    for he is soon to be rent, cut to pieces.
Is there any reason not to eliminate his misery and suffering?
You are going to suffer such shame in the assembly of the gods,
    how will you even show your face?
From this I infer that your heart
is as hard and harsh as Indra's thunderbolt,
    with no room whatsoever for compassion.
Who will turn to you for protection?
If the son of the merchant dies,
    who will serve you ever again?"

When Rāy heard this, he got in a temper.
So that very day Kunil scampered off
    and assembled all the tigers.
Wherever they were, they dropped what they were doing,
and all came rushing to him,
    till the skies were ruptured by their dreadful roars.
Lohājaṅga and Rūp Rāy
came running, together with Belāki and others,
    converging en masse toward Rāy, guardian of the quarters.[73]
The Lord of the Southern Lands,
quickly gave the order,
    "All of you go to the city of Turaṅga Pāṭan.
The merchant and his pilot—
ensure those two are kept safe,
    but take the lives of all the rest."
As soon as they heard, they were off,
flying faster than the wind, and
    soon they arrived in the city of Turaṅga Pāṭan.
As was their custom, they fanned out as needed,
Like swarms of hornets buzzing,
    their growls generating a relentless thrum.
To execute their task of protecting the merchant,
the tigers surrounded the king's domain,
    the sight of which terrified the chief of police.
He had a hundred sharpshooters,
who in tight formation moved as one,
    quickly discharging shot in volley after volley.
Dhānukī advanced in a rage,
the men of his army were equipped with pikes and shields,
    the ranks swelling to hundreds of thousands.
As many artillerymen they could muster
all let off their weapons, while
    a myriad of war instruments swelled the cacophony.
When they encountered these armed men, the tigers
were maddened like ferocious demons and
    their roars swelled to a deafening pitch.
Kṛṣṇarām has written that

73. This *tripadi* is incomplete; missing the first three feet of the standard six, it is truncated.

it would be good if the chief of police
were to have his comeuppance delivered quickly.

SECTION 36

Incensed, the tiger named Lākeśvarī
dashed forward, and with a rippling, sinewy power,
plunged into the ranks of the soldiers.
He sank his fangs into the necks
of those who were mounted atop elephants, and
engaged in the thick of battle like one possessed.
Cued by the anger in Rāy's order, and[74]
with energetic dispatch, the tiger Vajradanta
in a rage pounced on the chief of police, and
ripped out his beard and mustache by the roots.
Lohājaṅga advancing in ill temper,
targeted the top of the chief of police's head,
and smacked him, using his paws for clubs.
Some tried to escape by climbing a tree,
but the testy tiger Lākeśvarī
pounced on the napes of their necks.
How can I describe the awesome ardor
with which he broke their necks and slurped their blood,
slaughtering them all, one by one.
Except for the merchant and his helmsman,
there was no one left living in that pit of death.
Doom had fallen about Turaṅga Pāṭan.
The part of town for foreigners, *jaban*, stood before them,
and the tigers swarmed in, their claws out.
*Sekh*s, *saiyad*s, *kāji*s, *mollā*s—
their bald heads, scalps neatly shorn of hair,[75]
were viciously attacked by swarms of hornets,

74. The first two feet of the six feet of this *tripadi* are missing. Some authors adopted this truncated form to signal the beginning of a section, but Kṛṣṇarām does not follow this convention anywhere in the text. This occurs several more times in the remaining tripadi sections, but not at the beginning of sections as would be expected.

75. It was a not uncommon practice in this period to have a king's retainers and personal staff and servants shave their heads so as to eliminate the possibility of their impersonating the king.

buzzed by countless droves of bees.
The result was mass confusion,
as they rubbed and slapped the tops of their heads,
and in anguish cried out *bismilla,* in the name of God!
The tigers ripped open their necks
and so much mayhem reigned that soon
bhūts, hungry ghosts, gathered to feast on the flesh.
Tigers even trapped cats and dogs,
ripping out their stomachs and intestines,
then scampered away dragging goats in their jaws.
As an ox desperately charged to get away
a tiger broke its neck.
Effortlessly did they slaughter.
The shopkeepers populating the market,
who had been busy buying and selling their various wares,
not one among their assorted ranks was spared.
Everyone took a great beating that day—
from cooking-oil vendors to prostitutes and weavers—
until all thirty-six social ranks were utterly routed.
Some escaped by fleeing on foot, running as fast as they could.
Crying and weeping, they breathlessly relayed the news
to their king, Rājā Surath.
"First came countless tigers devouring people,
soon followed by vampires, demons, and hungry ghosts, and then
swarms of hornets and bees surrounded us on all four sides!
They slew the chief of police,
but did not eat the merchant!
No one is left alive in Turaṅga Pāṭan!
The citadel was gutted, left completely deserted.
You must flee and escape to some faraway place!
That is what we feel best."
When he heard this breathless report, the king flew into a rage,
He shouted the order, "Prepare! Make yourselves ready!"
as he sped on his chariot to muster the cannons.
Small drums were beaten and tambours tapped,
kettledrums thundered, doubled-ended drums rumbled,
and trumpets blared the call to war.
Horses were saddled and caparisoned
in a show of great strength,
as the war trumpets blared and battle drums pounded.
With well-crafted words, Kṛṣṇarām describes

how the king prepared for war, and
all around him the forces were assembled.

SECTION 37

Great numbers of soldiers made up the *caturaṅga*, that traditional battle array of fighters on elephants, horses, chariots, and foot.[76] The cavalry wore special helmets and traditional loose-fitting uniforms. Surath, that ruler of men, arrived at the field of death, where he saw ravening tigers in numbers beyond counting. Displaying his own courage and power, the king screamed, "Attack! Kill them!" and his soldiers, their fury aroused, rushed forward as if one. Suddenly, the sky was blanketed with hornets and bees, which routed the ranks of soldiers with their stings. Those wounds burned unbearably, and their only recourse was to jump into the waters to soothe the pain and escape the onslaught. Mounted on their horses and elephants, the cavalry beat a hasty retreat. But artillerymen quickly set about their drills, packed the gunpowder, loaded the cannons, and lit the fuses. Great rings of fire incinerated the hornets and bees and wasps. In agonizing death they fell to earth by the hundreds of thousands. Then the king's soldiers to a man fell on the tigers with zeal, pummeling them with cudgels and maces. That further stoked the anger of those vicious tigers, who wrested away the cudgels and moved further onto the killing fields, generating unimaginable terror. Easily raising his massive paws like double-handed clubs, the tiger Lākeśvarī rained down vicious blows, breaking the hips and loins of horses and riders, pulverizing them both. The tigers went on to slaughter many more cavalry using nothing but their paws. Witnessing the broken ranks of his army anguished the king. So he let fly a special weapon, a missile with the name Siṃhamukh, the "Mouth of the Lion." With unimaginable speed that missile spewed fire and slew thousands upon thousands of *dānav*s, demon hordes. Shouldering their clubs, the remaining demons turned and fled, for they could not maintain their courage against the horrifying scream of that weapon. Seeing the *dānav*

76. Also called an *akṣauhiṇī*, a *caturaṅga* is an army composed of 109,350 foot soldiers; 65,610 cavalry on horseback; 21,870 elephants, and 21,870 chariots. The numbers are the products of primes and suggest an ideal and formulaic apportionment of infantry (50%), cavalry (30%), elephants (10%), and chariots (10%).

demons routed further incited the tigers. With a guttural chuff and deep-throated growl of "*ālum ālum*," they called for a retreat.[77]

When he saw tigers breaking ranks, Dhānukī rallied his forces and mounted an all-out counterattack. There was one tiger named Gajaskandha, "Shoulders like an Elephant," who was laying waste to the troops. No missile ever pierced his body; he was impervious to weapons. The cavalry mounted on horseback were unable to reach the merchant to cut him down with their sharp *talwār* swords, for an Iraqi horse is no match for a tiger. But there were rutting elephants all around, and one could wrap his trunk around a tiger and pound it mercilessly. Because the Iraqi horse is no match for the tiger, no matter how fast they ran, the riders could never land a blow. Watching the two tigers Rūp and Cā̃d crouching down and setting the trap of their ambush, the king simmered with anger. When soldiers on horseback made to ride off, the tigers leapt up, lacerating and biting them, eventually slaying them all. The foot soldiers wielding shield and pike were systematically butchered to a man and their corpses left floating in the Sunati River.

With mind fixed on the lotus feet of Rāy,
Kṛṣṇarām Kavi has composed this in the pācāli *meter.*

SECTION 38

That best of men, King Surath, was incensed at what he saw. At one go, he let fly three hundred arrows. Once released, the missiles split the air with breakneck speed. When the tiger Kadamba saw them coming, he fled in all-out fear. Agitated and unsettled, the tigers bolted in unruly streaks, while the king pursued, bellowing in the stentorian voice of authority, "Kill them, slay them!" Rāy seethed to watch the scattering of his tigers. He berated them mercilessly and ordered them to return to battle. The indefatigable duo of tigers, Rūp and Cā̃d, possessed a power unmatched. With a single well-timed leap, they landed atop the

77. The expression "*ālum ālum*" is an onomatopoeic attempt to mimic the deep-throated chuff and rumbling growl of the tiger. This seems to be the only documented instance of its use in early modern Bangla; see Mohammad Ābdul Kāium and Rājiyā Sultanā, *Prācin o madhyayuger bāṃlā bhāṣār abhidhān*, 2 vols. (Ḍhākā: Bāṃlā Ekāḍemī, 1414 BS [ca. 2006]).

king's chariot. At a stroke they slaughtered the charioteer and all eight horses. The king was beside himself with rage at having lost his chariot and driver. He let fly the arrow-missile called Mahākāl, the "Great Death," and immediately both Rūp and Cā̃d were felled. When those foremost tigers were cut down, Lākeśvarī was aggrieved and galled, and in a show of extraordinary courage, mounted the chariot without hesitation. He snatched the bow from the king's hands and lacerated and bruised the king's body till the blood freely flowed. But the king, who was possessed of tremendous fortitude, raised up his club and proceeded to bludgeon Lākeśvarī till he fractured his hip. Māmudā, Kumudā, Sudhā, and a host of other tigers bolted, making good their escape to a safe distance. Sensing defeat, Dakṣiṇ Rāy again erupted with anger, but this time he himself mounted a chariot to engage in battle. He took his bow in hand, accompanied by five ministers and, with the royal umbrella held above his head, made his way to the killing fields.

The king said, "Just who are you? Make yourself known. Why have you waged war on me?"

Rāy began to apprise him of his particulars, "The land here, the extended Āṭhārobhāṭī, the Land of the Eighteen Tides, is my sovereign domain. You do not offer me devotion or respectful worship, and you have abused my servant devotee. Out of affection for my devotee, I shall completely destroy all that is yours."

The king replied, "I understand that you are claiming lordship over this region, so let us fight it out, and may the triple world bear witness."

As the insults and calumny continued unabated until they engaged in combat,

Kṛṣṇarām has composed the auspicious epic of Rāy.

SECTION 39

The virtue-filled Lord of the Southern Regions vented his rage, matching his war of words by releasing hundreds of hundreds of thousands of arrows. The attack split the king's helmet in two, and he was battered and bruised. King Surath was forcibly unseated, leaving him completely bereft of his chariot and its protection. But he let fly the special arrow named Haritāni, "Tipped with Arsenic," which vomited a wide spray of venom like a cobra. The missile completely shattered the bow

Rāy held in his hand. Then the king let fly another magical weapon that targeted the five ministers, which left them prostrate and stunned. Blazing with an all-consuming fury, the Lord Dakṣiṇ picked up a club of enormous weight, called the "Legacy of Yam," the god of death, and swung at the king with all his might. When the king saw it coming, he knew no fear, but scrambled so briskly that the flapping of the hem of his billowing robes sounded like tiny cymbals clapping. As he fled, he raised his bow to his ear and shot an arrow over his shoulder, which split the heavy cudgel right in two. Once again what he witnessed enraged Lord Dakṣiṇ, and he countered by meditating on Maheś, Lord Śiv, and then let fly a celestial missile. Śiv's unfailing, irrepressible weapon accelerated meteorically, the sight of which instantly filled King Surath's heart with dread. The missile struck him square in the chest and split it open. The king slumped, sprawling as if to embrace the earth. The tigers one and all let loose jubilant roars of victory. Then all of those tigers who had been sent into battle only to die, were magically revived by administering *mantras*.

Kisanrām's story of how the powerful ruler fell in battle
is suffused with marvels and uncanny events.

SECTION 40

When the king's consort heard the news—
that the king had died in battle—
  she fled her home with her close attendants.
She ran so hard her hair fell loose, disheveled.
With tears streaming from her eyes,
  she cried out, "What happened! Tell me what happened!"
  Weeping uncontrollably, the queen flew
to the spot where the king had been killed.
There she gazed on a river of blood and
  pounded her head with her fists.
As she grasped the feet of her husband, she wailed,
"With which god have you fought?
  How could such madness ensue?
Without you I am helpless, lordless."
She wailed on, "I am all alone!
  Is this what fate has written on my forehead?"
Ensconced in his celestial chariot,

the great and majestic lord, Dakṣiṇ Īśvar,
    called out to the queen.
"I am the Lord of the Southern Regions.
You have failed to honor me with *pūjā* worship.
    You have abused the merchant son of one of my female devotees.
There really is no reason for you to cry.
First, you must honestly pledge that
    you will give your daughter to that merchant.
Were the king to construct an image of me,
and honor me with formal *pūjā* worship,
    then I would restore him to life again."
When she heard this, the queen made this promise,
pressing her palms together in respect,
    "My daughter will be gifted in marriage to the merchant.
The king will propitiate you
with a proper *pūjā* to the best of his power.
    Please restore life to my husband!"
As a result of the conciliatory words of the queen,
waters from the pitcher of the nectar of life
    spilled down onto the land of Turaṅga.
All those living beings who had died
were accommodated to Śiv, who
    with parental affection restored their lives.
After all of his soldiers were brought back to life,
the king, lord of men, previously filled with anger,
    suddenly sat bolt upright and wondered:
"Who could have restored life
to one who was previously killed in battle?"
    He was utterly mystified.
His consort, the queen, replied to the great king,
"You were felled in the midst of war,
    in quarrel with Lord Dakṣiṇ Rāy.
And it was he who gave you back your life.
Listen carefully to my words:
    If you proffer worship, you will receive his grace.
That young merchant is his devotee.
Usher him into our home and
    give him your daughter, Ratnāvatī, in marriage."
As she spoke, the queen made him to understand,
"This is the promise I have made.
    Do not even think to countermand it or do otherwise."

Meanwhile, Rāy spoke to the young merchant.
"Your fear and suffering are now mitigated, and
your mother Suśīlā's hardships will likewise dissipate.
Your father is held in this very same prison.
Go and liberate him, and
return without delay to your own lands."
Then the king, that ruler of men,
took the merchant by the hand and,
with great affection, addressed him as son-in-law.
He promptly gifted to the merchant
a necklace of incalculable value,
which he slipped from his own neck.
There was one Bhagavati Dās,
whose home was in the village of Nimita,
born into a class of scribes, kāyestha.
His descendant, Kṛṣṇarām,
has composed this song
with a single-minded effort.

SECTION 41

A formal gathering was convened of such learned and illustrious advisors that everyone commented that their collective brilliance outshone Vidhudev, the moon god. The king opened the proceedings, "Presiding priest, *purohit*, it is with some urgency that you fix an appropriate day for me to give my daughter in marriage without delay." That considerate and thoughtful best of twice-born sensed the anxiety behind the king's gravity and wasted no time in calculating the most auspicious day, but not without some curiosity.

As this was happening, the merchant spoke directly to the king's person, "Grant me one thing, and then I will go through with the marriage: All those prisoners who are incarcerated in the prison, please gift all of them to me, O great *mahārāj*."

The king replied, "From this very moment, I grant them all to you. Release them or do whatever you wish." The king had the chief of police fetched right away and instructed him, "Escort my son-in-law to the prisoners' dungeon."

The chief of the king's police was nonplussed, but made a formal polite salute, and with hands pressed together in respect, said, "Revered son-in-law of the king, please come with me." The merchant forged ahead wearing the brightly colored wooden sandals signifying privilege. In no time at all, they arrived at the prison house.

The merchant gave the order, "Bring out the prisoners one at a time, but make sure that none makes a formal bow to me.[78] Thieves and pickpockets, lecherous offenders, and all the other kinds of prisoners were brought at the command of the good merchant. One by one they were paraded before him and their particulars identified: their *jāti* or social rank, the location of their homes, and the names of their fathers. The young man, son of Devdatta, presented each and every one with new clothes and ornaments, then freed each one, bidding him a formal farewell. He slumped down to the ground, weeping, thoroughly dispirited. "After suffering such misery, I have failed to find my father, that treasure of virtues. I shall not return to our home country, nor shall I go through with the marriage. What incentive, what need is there for wealth, for other people, for a wife or a child?"

Just at that moment, a disembodied voice boomed from the skies, "Listen, young merchant-trader, your revered father is detained in a secret chamber deep in the bowels of the prison."

He was shocked and curious to hear the revelation of that divine oracle, so he slipped out of the assembly and went further inside the prison. The innermost chambers of the prison house were inky black, even during the bright of day. Though apprehensive, the young merchant searched methodically. Suddenly, the chief of police lifted up something bundled in a gunny sack, grabbing a man by the hair, and exclaimed, "I've got him, I've got him!" He pulled the prisoner out, a shaggy, unkempt, filthy mess. The well-bred merchant retched with revulsion and loathing. The man's body was emaciated, no meat, just skin and bones. His beard had grown shaggy, like a bear's, his nails were claws. He was instructed not to bow, so the prisoner stood motionless near the merchant, hands pressed together in servile respect. The son of the merchant inquired, "What is your name? Why are you imprisoned? Where is your home, in what country? Who is your first wife, your first son? What is your social rank, your *jāti*? Have no fear, speak bluntly. Who is the king in the principality from which you hail? If you speak honestly, then I shall grant your freedom."

78. This smartly avoids the possibility that his father would bow to his son.

Hearing such sweetly reassuring words, Devdatta spoke.
Kṛṣṇarām Kavi tells of the glory of the divine.

SECTION 42

"I reside in the kingdom of Baradānagar, throughout which its king, Rājā Madan, is honored and adored. My lineage is of the perfumers and spice-trading community, the *gandhabāṇik kul*. Listen, honorable sir, my name is Devdatta. My wife was five months pregnant when I received the directive of the king to undertake this venture. At Rājdaha, I witnessed an astounding marvel, but when I brought the king there, he saw nothing. As a result, he immediately appropriated my seven ships, the chief of his police incarcerated me in this, the vilest southern part of the prison, the cremation grounds and killing fields. There was no one who could come to my rescue. Bidhātā, the god of fate, had turned his back on me, so who could I blame?"

When he heard his personal details, the young merchant, Puṣpadatta, understood that the man standing before him was his father, that ocean of virtues. It was as if the child in him had finally managed to pluck the moon right out of the sky,[79] or a shriveled and desiccated tree suddenly burst into bloom from mere words. The young merchant had a barber brought to cut his father's nails and beard, and then he presented him with a brightly colored garment. They cleansed his body of caked dirt, anointed his head with oil, cleansed and trimmed his hair, then had myrobalan brought and applied.[80] They smeared his body all over with a bowl of *nārāyaṇ* oil,[81] after which he was bathed in water scented with camphor. They fed him thickened sweetened milk pudding and *sandeś* milk sweets, at which point he realized that it could only have been Bhagavān, God Himself, who had been gracious to him. Devdatta feared that with this preparation, he was about to be executed, so he waited nervously beside the young merchant, his hands pressed

79. See n. 13 above.

80. Myrobalan here is an oil or unguent from *Phyllanthus emblica*, a tree in the Phyllanthaceae family there are three species (*emblic*, *chebulic*, and *beleric*) whose fruits are often combined in Ayurvedic medicine to treat infections, diarrhea, and inflammations, no doubt here in response to the prisoner's pathetic condition.

81. Fragrant *nārāyaṇ* oil, compounded from sesame oil, clove oil, eucalyptus oil, and peppermint oil, is an ancient yogic rub for stiff and sore muscle relief.

together. "You have released all the other prisoners to their freedom. So why have you so deliberately kept back this one unfortunate?"

When he heard his father's query, the good merchant Puṣpadatta's eyes welled with tears and he spoke, his hands pressed together in respect. "Suśīlā is my mother and you are my father. My name is Puṣpadatta. Listen to my real story."

The elder merchant replied, "How can you say such things, honored sir? You are the son of a great man and the son-in-law of the king. Why do you mock me and treat me like an ignorant plebian?"

Kṛṣṇarām has composed his song with elegant, emotion-filled language.

SECTION 43

The honorable elder merchant spoke,
though he found it exceedingly hard.
    Please give me a hearing, your lordship.
This turn of events makes me terribly afraid
Listen, please listen, my good sir.
    Why do you call me your father?"
The young merchant spoke, his hands pressed together,
as tears streamed from his eyes, drenching his clothes.
    "In truth, I am your son.
I had been in my mother's womb for five months
when you departed for Pāṭan.
    Please listen, my good sir.
Out of concern for the attitudes of self-righteous people
toward Suśilā, who is a gem of a woman,
    you made sure that her pregnancy was well known.
You informed the twice-born,
who duly recorded it on cotton paper,
    and attested in your own hand."
His heart was bubbling with agitation
as he submitted this in so many words,
    then he handed his father the paper.
Seeing his own handwriting
thrilled him beyond measure,
    and now it was his clothes that were drenched by tears.[82]

82. The versification is once again truncated.

He knew with certainty that this was his son.
He clasped his son tightly to him,
and in a voice choked with emotion said,
"Today my fortune has finally turned for the better.
I am indeed exceedingly blessed,
for there can be nothing better than this:
to have a son like you.
Tell me, I'm listening to the wondrous news,
how did you manage to come here,
manage to cross the shoreless ocean?"
The young merchant Puṣpadatta beamed,
a moon outshining even the god of love, Madan.
"Please listen, my great-souled one.
With the express permission of the king,
I undertook the journey to Pāṭan, and
many days have passed since I left.
Without you, I have been tormented.
I have had no joy by day or night, and
within our residence, everything was a shambles.
Truly, the eyes of my mother
were ever filled with tears
by the absence of your feet.
My mother would sit and talk
endlessly, telling all tales of you,
every scrap of information there was to be had."
The meeting of father and son produced
unbounded joy, which displaced all prior misery,
as Kṛṣṇarām sweetly describes.

SECTION 44

While the father and son were reunited, the chief of police went to inform the king. Right after that, Devdatta the merchant, still basking in joy, also followed to see the king. When the king spotted his son-in-law with his father, he stood up, and, with an excited flourish, had them sit beside him. The king then spoke, "You have suffered immeasurably for an exceedingly long time, do understand that no fault accrues to me, for it was clearly the dictates of destiny, it was what fate had written. Whatever miseries you endured, please give me to understand. Listen, that is what I beg of you, you who are the possessor of all virtues."

The elder merchant listened, then responded, "Do listen, great one, can the master ever be discourteous? Or be guilty of uttering incivilities to his servitor?"

When the king recognized the good humor in the words of the merchant, he began to joke pointedly with his new son-in-law. "There were untold thousands of prisoners in that prison house. How were you able to know which one of them was your father? Perhaps you never really found your lost father and have brought someone else. How could you know for sure, since you had never once in your life seen your father?"

Puṣpadatta laughed and said, "Listen, great one, there are indeed many stalks surrounding any single blooming lotus flower. But I submit this before you, O king, how does one distinguish the moon from all the stars that cluster around it? Is not shiny fired glass easily detectable when compared with gold?" The *rājā* then laughed and embraced his son-in-law. He then directed his son-in-law and his father to their private quarters and afterwards sent them a supply of proper foodstuffs and other provisions,[83] which included fresh fish and an assortment of meats from wethers and deer. He had pots of ghee and pitchers of cooking oils sent along, and he dispatched his personal servants to see to their needs. The merchant Devdatta then prepped and cooked the food. The king had requisitioned golden bedsteads for their sleep, then he himself went to pay them a courtesy call. That king, the best of men, wore ceremonial golden slippers studded with gems, and he was accompanied by his primary advisors and friends. "The king has arrived," it was announced, and the merchant roused his tired body. The king, accompanied by his queen, then left with much merriment and fanfare.

The night passed and sun revealed itself, so Kavi Kṛṣṇarām observes, this new day marks the preparatory adhibās *rituals for the wedding.*

83. The initial word of this phrase, *sidhā*, indicates the supply of foodstuffs for simple cooking from people of lower social rank to those of higher rank, so that the recipients can prepare their own food and maintain ritual purity, here an act of humility on the part of the king.

SECTION 45

There was great jubilation when an auspicious day was determined so that they could initiate the preparatory purification and protective rituals for a successful wedding, those prescriptions called the *adhibās*. They retired to the private quarters of the virgin bride, where all the beautiful women of the king's court gathered with great pageantry and merriment, to perform the *adhibās*. Propitiating the sixteen mother goddesses, or *mātrikās*,[84] they painted auspicious marks on the wall with a mixture of ghee, honey, and turmeric in a rite called the *vasudhārā*. Meanwhile, the king and his companions performed the traditional rituals to honor departed ancestors, the *vṛddhiśrāddha*. Līlā, the wife of the king, whose face shone with the beauty of a blooming lotus, called for all the married women to come. The bride Ratnāvatī then seated the groom on a golden seat and proceeded ritually to wipe his limbs with her hair. The womenfolk had the bride and groom bathe and then smothered them in ornaments—*it was all much too lavish for me to describe!* When it was time for the wedding proper, the groom was immaculately outfitted, and when they finally set eyes on him, everyone expressed their admiration at his stunning appearance. Following ritual custom, the king formally confirmed the betrothal to the groom, while all the women executed the prescribed women's ritual conventions. The king then made a formal gift of his daughter in marriage, and at the stipulated time, the bride and groom were escorted inside. Everyone celebrated as the wedding night passed, then on the second day of the wedding, everyone gave gifts that made up the dowry. The bride and groom did not meet at all for the whole of the

84. In the context of discussing the goddess Ṣaṣṭhī, who protects children, and Manasā, the goddess who rules over serpents, the Sanskrit *Devī bhāgavata purāṇa* (9.1.71–95; 9.47.4–8) mentions sixteen *mātrikās*, but does not identify them by name, though this widely circulated and popular reference is most likely the one to which Kṛṣṇarām refers. Lists dating back several thousand years record a range of from seven to eight, sixteen, sixty-four, and one hundred eight *mātrikās*, each with tremendous regional variation. Ṣaṣṭhī, who is often referred to as the most important *mātrikā*, seems to serve as a metonym for the set of sixteen. It should be noted that, like Ṣaṣṭhī herself, the *mātrikās* are capricious and not always benign, hence the need to propitiate them ritually, especially in the contexts of weddings and childbirth. In some forms of *tāntrik* and *śakta* worship, they are aligned with the fourteen vowels plus *anusvāra* and *visarga* in the traditional Sanskrit alphabet and invoked for meditative purposes.

second night, which is called the *kālarātri*, the "the dark night of death"—*reserved for the divine, I believe the name is well taken!*[85] The next day the couple took to the nuptial bed of flowers where the passion each held for the other intensified as their love play blossomed. And so it came to pass that the young merchant was duly married, watched over in his meditations by the Lord of the South, Dakśiṇ Īśvar.

This is how the first half of the all-night vigil passed.
Kṛṣṇarām narrates, keeping his mind focused on the feet of Rāy.

SECTION 46

There in his in-laws' home, the handsome young merchant was so consumed by his liaison with the young woman that he completely forgot his mother and father. But one day, Rāymaṇi spoke to him through a dream, "Hey, merchant, listen carefully to what I have to say. You have been loitering here in this foreign land in the company of this woman and have completely forgotten your mother, your father, and everyone else. Even though you are learned, you have not acted sensibly. First thing in the morning, you should head back to your homeland, lest you be shamed for these careless actions." After delivering this message, Rāy returned to his own abode. The next morning, the son of the merchant started to regain his senses. The recollection of that dream jolted the him wide awake. He sat up on the bedstead and quietly wept in his anxiety. He castigated himself and pounded his forehead with his fists. "I have been lost in the infatuation of my new wife, and so failed to remember my mother and father. While I have been preoccupied with the pleasures of my bride, who knows whether or not my mother is even alive?"

The king's daughter, Ratnāvatī, lay snuggled up against him and soon her body was soaked with the tears streaming from his eyes. When she woke, the beautiful young woman sat bolt upright. She was

85. The *kālarātri*, or "dark night of death," originated from the story of the legendary ideal bride Behulā, whose husband Lakhindār was killed by snakebite on the second night of their wedding, death coming as the result of a conflict between Lakhindār's father, Cāṇḍo, and Manasā, goddess of serpents. Behulā's devotion resulted in the restoration of her husband's life. Note the association of Manasā with Ṣaṣṭhī in the previously mentioned ritual dedicated to the *mātrikās*.

shaken to see how emotionally disturbed her husband had become. With her hands pressed together respectfully, the young beauty carefully questioned him, "Please tell me, you who are the lord of my life, what anguish causes you to weep so? You are now the son-in-law of the king and precious to everyone. Has someone said something untoward or upsetting? Please make it known. Anyone who fully understands insolence and still speaks ill of you will have to face Śani, the evil eye of Saturn, when Bidhātā, the god of fate, turns his face away. Then Saturn will move into his eighth zodiacal house, with Mars entering the fifth, a destruction-causing combination—and that will generate a bizarre spectacle as the individual wends his way to the citadel of Yam, the god of death."

The good merchant gently demurred, "No malcontent has spoken maliciously to me. I witnessed in my dream this morning, just at the tail end of the night, that I have not met any of my friends or companions, and that oversight has me agitated and has caused me to weep without break. At this rate, I fear that it is I who shall certainly be destined for the nether regions. Tell me, virtuous woman, will you accompany me home or not? As the daughter of the king, you are the very life of your mother. If you leave your father's palace, who knows what kind of inconveniences you may suffer when you accompany me to my humble home."

The king's daughter understood fully well what was behind the merchant's words, so with a tearful countenance, she replied, "Listen, when Rām entered the forest in order to uphold righteousness, Sītā, the beautiful daughter of Janak, did not linger behind at home. Damayantī underwent severe trials as she suffered in some godforsaken wilderness. Draupadī, too, never hesitated or looked back with sorrow as she departed the assembly."[86]

The words of the king's daughter were like the nectar that staves off death, yet when the virtuous merchant listened, they burned like poison.

86. Ideals of wifely conduct: in the *Rāmāyaṇ*, Sītā accompanies Rām to the forest in exile; the *Mahābhārat* tells how Damayantī was estranged from Nala when he was possessed but never abandoned him, and the *Mahābhārat* likewise tells how Draupadī accompanied her five husbands, the Pāṇḍav brothers, into exile.

Who can fathom why the woman's words were poison.
Kṛṣṇarām sings how she was warned not to go.

SECTION 47

The merchant heard the woman's words but did not really pay heed. He then made his way to present himself to the king to bid a formal farewell. He bowed in obeisance and then spoke in a voice choked with emotion, "Please grant me leave, O king, to return to my home." When he heard this request, the king grew visibly agitated. That best of men pulled his son-in-law close to his side and then spoke, "In our land, you are now the one designated to hold firm the royal umbrella of succession. So, instead, I shall arrange to have your mother brought here."

The young merchant weighed those words, then replied, "Listen, honored sir, you need not make any arrangements, for I am returning to my own land, that much is certain." The lord of the earth made every effort to dissuade him, but that scion of the elder merchant would hear nothing of it. So the king promptly summoned the chief of his police and commanded, "Prepare seven ships to sail and load them full of treasures of all types, and be quick about it!" Somewhat nonplussed, the chief of police complied and executed the direct command of that lordly king. From the treasury he had stores of gemstones loaded onto the ships. He brought out vast quantities of aloe wood, sandalwood, conchs, rubies, coral, and black and white fly whisks. He mustered copious quantities of gold, silver, copper, and brass, and flawless rubies and diamonds, elephant pearls, and various trifles and trinkets. He requisitioned a number of elephants, and even larger number of horses, both Iraqi and Turkish. Seeing all this, the young merchant was more than a little astounded. Finally, the laborers conveyed vast stocks of camphor, pepper, cumin seed, and nutmeg to the ships, among a huge variety of other difficult-to-procure items. The virtuous young merchant then paid his sincere respects to Dakṣiṇ Rāy in formal worship, bowed in obeisance, and made generous sacrificial offerings. The king returned to his palace, sobbing without respite. He then sent the order to the queen to send out their daughter.

Listening to the king and queen weep in their terrible grief,
Kṛṣṇarām has composed the auspicious tale of Rāy.

SECTION 48

Everyone was overwrought with the prospect that Ratnāvatī would be moving far away, and her own brother was especially moved with a tender compassion for her.[87] The tears that gushed from the eyes of the king broke like waves in the ocean. All of the relatives were deeply distressed and grieved openly. The king's wife pulled her daughter onto her lap and bawled, her chest heaving uncontrollably from the unbearable torment. "O you who truly understand, this is your home, your palace, how I can I bear to look at it when you are absent from it? When you were a child, you used to play with dolls here, but to look at that place now doubles my misery and makes my heart burn with grief. Now, I am reminded of those days I scolded you, and it rends my heart with regret. How can I hang on to life?"

The queen's close companion and confidante was a woman named Candrāvatī. She commiserated with the queen and tried to console her. "There is no reason whatsoever to weep, O queen, just consider carefully my counsel. Stop and think, examine the passing nature of everything in this world. Who is really one's son or daughter? Who is really one's mother or father? One who possesses the knowledge of insight harbors no such attachment, no sense of ownership. Where did you happen to be born? Where did you happen to live? Realize that the nature of the world's coming and going is conjured as an illusory magic."

The queen in turn endeavored to help her daughter understand. And the two women ended up soaked in one another's tears. "Even though you are intelligent, how can I explain it, how can I make you truly comprehend? You must go and do your utmost to serve your mother-in-law faithfully. You must always treat your servants, both male and female, fairly and be protective of them. Address all of them as 'Mother' and 'Father.' Never allow yourself to be angry, never speak with haughtiness or indignation. Only then will you earn a favorable reputation among them. If someone's heart is dead set against you, turn them little by little. If you are good and proper in your conduct, you have nothing to fear from anyone. You must always concentrate

87. Ordinarily the son would have been the prince who would inherit the throne, not the husband of the king's daughter; for the merchant to inherit the kingdom or even half the kingdom by marrying the princess was not stipulated in Dakṣiṇ Rāy's conditions to King Surath's wife for restoring her husband's life.

on serving your husband, for without him, you have no place whatsoever in either life or death." The virtuous woman sought to relieve her daughter's anxieties and then showered her with gifts. With various shows of affection, her daughter's apprehensive heart was eventually soothed.

The bearers arrived with the palanquin resting on their shoulders, and the king signaled, "This particular time is the most auspicious moment for departure." When she heard that, the young wife's face grew wet with tears. One by one she sought the blessings of all of her seniors.

Touching her father's feet, this virtuous woman begged leave as
Kavi Kṛṣṇarām sings the auspicious tale of Rāy, the Rāymaṅgal.

SECTION 49

The young woman, full of virtue, bowed and touched her mother's feet. The queen, agitated, pulled her to her lap. The young woman said, "Stay calm, dear mother, please control your emotions. By crying uncontrollably you make everything more difficult. You gave me in marriage to someone who hails from a place that lies on the opposite shores of the ocean, so what is the point of crying now? You know what the traditional instruction in moral values, the *Nītiśāstras*, teach, so what more can I say? No matter how painful it feels, the man takes away the bride so that they live together. Recognizing that reality, carry on as if you never had a daughter. You will not be able to fetch me back just any time, because the place is not at all close, but far, far away."

As the bearers carried the palanquin forward on their shoulders, the young daughter of the king pulled back the cloth curtain and peered out. Framed in the opening, she looked like a white-browed wagtail,[88] though more beautiful, with eyes wide and nervously dancing as they took in every part of her father's vast kingdom. For all her friends with whom she had played from childhood she openly grieved. She would not see them again.

88. The reference is to the *khañjan*, or white-browed wagtail (*Motacilla maderaspatensis* in the Motacillidae family), a slender bird, which has distinctive white bands setting off its darting eyes. To be *khañjan*-eyed is a mark of alluring beauty. Wagtails are often caged as pets, like Ratnāvatī framed in the opening of her palanquin.

Understanding that the time was right, the elder merchant bowed in respectful obeisance in the direction of his son's mother-in-law and sent her word of their departure. Deferentially taking the dust of the king's feet on his head, this man, who was a treasure trove of virtue, then pressed his hands together in humble salutation and made the king to understand, "You are a great and trustworthy person, knowledgeable as a scholarly *paṇḍit*, and one on whom I will always be indubitably loyal and dependent." Then the father and the son bade farewell to the king, boarded their ships, and shoved off, back to their own lands.

As the merchants wended their way home, everyone cried, "Hari, Hari bol!"[89]

Kavi Kṛṣṇarām narrates at the direct command of Rāy.

SECTION 50

With Puṣpadatta comfortably seated in the commanding spot under
 the bimini,
he gave the command, "Wah, everything is auspicious, set sail!"
 and the ships flew even faster than the wind.
Musical instruments reverberated through the town,
mixed together with the din of hundreds upon hundreds of voices
 as untold numbers lined the shore.
As they sailed away from Turaṅga Pāṭan,
they eased past the magical waters of Rājdaha,
 where Rāy as lord once exercised his magical powers.
At Kālidaha in the mouth of the Padmā,
they laid up with great pleasure,
 filling their boats further with conchs and cowries.
The ships sped along, carried by the wind.
Sailing through the area of Setubandha,
 they paid their heartfelt respects to the feet of Hara.
Leaving untold numbers of distinctive regions in their wake,
they clanged their cymbals loudly,
 and pounded their barrel and kettledrums.

89. Though often exclaimed, regardless of religious orientation, as a signal of triumph or good fortune or on the completion of a task, "Hari *bol!*" literally means "Say the name of Hari, Kṛṣṇa!"

Lord Jagannāth resides in Orissa,
his leftover rice offerings are fashioned as ingestible grace, *prasād*,
which people purchase and consume for immortality.
There is no discrimination of social rank, or *varṇa*,
for upon death, devotees attain the supreme feet of the lord,
for the place is equivalent to Vaikuṇṭha heaven.
What is the point of expanding the narrative?
They passed the kingdom of Bennatoraṇ,
and following that, the Bāburmokām.
The citadel of Mārkaṇḍa Rājā
and the land of Karṇapur were soon left in their wake,
as that virtuous merchant sped on.
The sailors on all the ships, snapping their oars,
pulled hard past the *saṅgam* confluence,
pushing their ships to speed.
The oarsmen and galley slaves
redoubled their efforts, so they soon
left behind the turbulent land of Magarā.
The route they sailed was not a rhumb line,
but veered according to the whim of the pilot,
tacking to circumvent Dhāmāibetāi.
As they chanted together in a chorus,
this king of traders sped them past
Kākadvīp, or Crow Island, and Gajamuḍi, or Elephant's Head.
Meditating on Dakṣiṇ Rāy,
energized the boatmen
to pull harder on their oars.
Passing by Ṭīyākhol,
they then bathed at Gaṅgadvārā,
and soon landed up at Chatrabhog.
At the great pilgrimage center of Ambuliṅga
a place that has no equal, no peer,
they paid their respects to Lord Viśvanāth.
As they tacked past Hājāviṣṇupur,
mellifluous instrumental melodies wafted out.
Jaynagar, too, was soon left behind.
Their minds focused on Lord Rāy, treasure of virtues,
the steady beat of the kettledrum
propelled them joyfully past Baḍukṣetra.
They put in at Bārāsat, where
the merchant was pleased to take everyone

to perform *pūjā* worship of Ṭhākur Sadānanda.
They sailed to Hāsuḍi, where they brought
all seven ships together in tight formation
and soon passed by Maluṭi.
To the beat of two large kettledrums,
the ships skimmed the waves without difficulty
past two abandoned forts.
Passing by Sādhughāṭā, the landing of holy men,
the ships beat past Sūryapur to put up at
Bāruipur, where they moored abreast.
Acknowledging her divine splendor,
they worshipped the goddess Biśālakṣmī, then
that virtuous merchant immediately set sail.
Mālañca now lay far in the distance,
as they sailed to Kalyāṇapur, where
they paid their respects to Kalyāṇamādhav.
There is no utility in naming
the myriad villages they passed to port.
They eventually landed up at their home docks of Baḍadaha.
They loaded the cannons with gunpowder,
fixing them in neatly arranged order,
and synchronized the lighting of the fuses.
The thunderous retort was deafening,
stopping everyone on shore in their tracks.
The blare of the instruments redoubled the cacophony.
There was one Bhagavati Dās,
whose home was in the village of Nimita,
born into a class of scribes, kāyestha.
His descendant, Kṛṣṇarām,
has composed this song
with a single-minded effort.

SECTION 51

After many long days, the elder merchant sailed back to his homeland and arrived, overly laden with rich cargo. When the great ruler and local king, Mahārāj Madan, heard the commotion, he was in a state of anxiety out of fear that some invading forces were landing troops. He dispatched an emissary to act as spy to ascertain what caused the commotion, when he learned that it was the elder merchant who had finally returned home. The younger merchant Puṣpadatta had been especially anxious, worrying, so he immediately sent a message ahead to his mother. The merchant's wife had been sitting with her closest friend when the messenger pressed his hands together in respectful salutation and delivered the blessed good news. "The father and son have made it home. They have just landed, their boats packed with a bounty of gems and precious cargo, and they are accompanied by a beautiful young woman." The moment she heard it, this dispatch infused her with new life; she was instantly revitalized, as if the nectar of immortality suddenly surged through the bodies of both her and her companion. It was as if a poverty-stricken unfortunate had suddenly recovered previously lost riches, as if a poor soul drowning in the ocean suddenly washed up on dry land. She made the messenger happy, rewarding him with gemstones of no small value. And with pleasurable anticipation, she flew to meet her son.

Kavi Kṛṣṇarām narrates at the feet of Rāy, for
the lord will shower beneficence on this husband, his devotee.

SECTION 52

As soon as she heard the words from the messenger,
her heartache was instantly cured,
  and she rewarded the messenger with a mix of gemstones.
Destiny had steered them across
their ocean of affliction;
  the couple had successfully navigated the sea of suffering.
She gathered her married friends,
which caused a minor delay as she walked to the landing,
  then she saw the face of her son's bride.
She hugged the young bride, her new daughter,
which made her heart overflow with joy, and
  which banished all misery to some distant place.
Bidhātā, the god of fate, had engineered everything.
The clothes of both of the women were soon damp
  as the tears of joy freely flowed.
Puṣpadatta, noble and thoughtful,
sang his mother's praises with great affection,
  and reverently took the dust of her feet.
Ratnāvatī, though the daughter of a ruler,

made obeisance with palms pressed together in respect.
His mother blessed them as a couple.
As everyone shouted in jubilation,
she escorted her son's wife with satisfying pleasure,
as they made their way back to their abode.
Chewing her betel quid with great gusto,
the merchant's wife very deliberately
first put it in the mouth of her husband.
She wanted to do the same for the fortunate young girl,
but it was Puṣpadatta who refused to chew it,
much to the grand merriment of the older women.
In welcoming rituals, handfuls of unhusked rice
were poured over Ratnāvatī's head,
as she cradled a golden water pot in the crook of her waist.
Red *kusum* leaves[90] were likewise poured over her head,
like a cascading spray of rubies.
Then the couple entered their own private quarters.
Newly cut straw was laid down evenly
and a cloth neatly spread on top,
on which the bride and groom sat close to one another.
They played the game of dice over and over
and the young woman repeatedly bested her groom.
Sitting on the victor's throne, she teased him mercilessly.
"When you stake your ego and play for yourself,
and you lose the game to the woman,
then she gets to keep you as her slave.
Everything then, rests in her hands.
Only when she allows you to, may you eat your rice, and
you must always address her as *ṭhākurāṇī*, your ruling goddess.
Should you dare to marry again,
then you shall have to pay substantial compensation—
may all the women present bear witness."
As for any other playfully amorous activities they may have enjoyed—
what can I possibly say about that?
But the bride and her groom were left together in a private room.
Then the beautiful young wife of the merchant went with great fanfare
to make the sacrificial offering of a black-and-white goat,
performing *pūjā* worship to the ships and singing their praises.
The goods and riches were offloaded from the vessels,

90. See n. 11 above.

their allotted shares pleasing the many members of the crew,
after which wealth was distributed to the poor and destitute.
Kavi Kṛṣṇarām now tells
how the young merchant, laden with gemstones,
took great pleasure in meeting the king.

SECTION 53

The merchant made his way to greet the king, and he carried an assortment of goods as gifts, the quantity of which defies enumeration. In order to carry the large volume of this largesse, a substantial retinue of servants was pressed into service, flanked on each side by a platoon of armed sentries. The king, that best of men, had been seated in royal audience, as if he were some glorious deity holding forth in Indra's heavenly court. When the merchant arrived there, the ruler of men immediately called out, "Please come, do come in!" The king, whom the Earth, Medinī herself, wears as her personal ornament, gestured for him to take a seat, and so the merchant sat at the side of the king and offered appropriate encomia to his feet. The *rājā* addressed him, "Your voyage lasted such a long time, young merchant Puṣpadatta, tell us about your adventures."

When he heard this request, he proceeded to describe everything in detail, especially noting how Dakṣiṇ Rāy had intervened to save him. Everyone in the court was duly astounded to hear it. Afterwards, the good merchant received the blessings of the king, his *prasād*, then he begged his leave.

In response, that most noble ruler of men sincerely—in mind, body, and speech—performed a *pūjā* honoring Rāy's holy feet, all in strict accord with scriptural injunction. Soon people in every household performed the *pūjā*, which gratified Dakṣiṇ Rāy enormously. Both merchants, the father and the son, were in high spirits as they, too, performed an appropriately elaborate ritual *pūjā* in honor of Rāy. Lord Rāy, that pearl of virtue, dispatched Viśvakarmā, the architect of the gods, who assumed a human form and descended to the world of men. With single-minded focus, Viśvakarmā received the commission and proceeded to construct a palace of exceeding splendor. Its floors were fashioned of gold, its walls studded with rubies, carnelian, and other precious stones. It was topped with beautifully curved, sloping roof, carpeted with woven gold. He installed doors behind a lion gate. When they beheld this edifice, a blissful joy rippled through the hearts and minds of the merchants, a joy that knew no bounds. An image of Dakṣiṇ Rāy seated on a lion was fashioned, his golden body radiating a beauty enchanting. The young son of the merchant employed a *purohit* priest and initiated a regular *pūjā* of Rāy, much to the latter's delight. The sanctified leftovers of the food offerings were always presented on a golden plate—the offerings only of the highest quality, ghee, curd, milk, and honey. A gilded box was copiously filled with camphor and betel leaves, and a multitude of animal sacrifices were offered.

Kṛṣṇarām sings of how the Lord himself, Dakṣiṇ Rāy,
appeared before their very eyes to accept the worship of his devotees.

SECTION 54

The merchant earnestly sang his praises, "You are a sea of mercy, a parent to your devotees. My hands are pressed together in humble obeisance and I plead: Please forgive my transgressions! You are an ocean of compassion, my Lord, Rāy, pearl of all virtues. Your face puts to shame the moon, your beauty is superior to Madan, the god of love. O king of the southern regions, who else is there apart from you? May the worship offered by this lowly one satisfy you. . . ."[91]

91. The last few couplets of the manuscript, which normally personalize the author's closing, are missing. It is not uncommon for these loose-leaf manuscripts to lose both the top and bottom folios, but in this case only the last is missing.

Scouring the World for Cāmpāvatī

Scouring the World for Cāmpāvatī

Introduction to Gāji Kālu o Cāmpāvatī Kanyār Puthi of Ābdul Ohāb

The saga of the Sufi figures of Gāji Pīr and his brother Kālu in search of the princess Cāmpāvatī that I have translated for this volume was composed by Sāyeb Munsī Ābdul Ohāb and finished in 1893.[1] It is a tale whose origins stretch back at least to the early eighteenth century, when Śekh Khodā Bakhś recorded the earliest attested version we have of the story, today titled simply by the names of the three protagonists: *Gāji kālu o cāmpāvatī*. The oldest extant dated manuscript indicates that that particular copy was completed in 1750 CE, but considering its length, it is safe to assume that composition was begun some time earlier. With its more than eighteen thousand lines, divided into fifty-eight sections (*pālās*), the text rivals in length and style the *maṅgal kāvya*s that were circulating at the time. Not long after Khodā Bakhś's earliest known manuscript, another poet named Kavi Hālumīr completed his *Baḍo khān gājīr kerāmati*, or "The Wonder-working Power of Baḍo Khān Gāji," which covered more than eleven thousand lines and followed the same plot line.[2] These two tales provided the master

1. Sāyeb Munsī Ābdul Ohāb, *Gāji kālu o cāmpāvatī kanyār puthi* (Kalikātā: Munsī Ābdul Hāmād Khān; Reprint: Kalikātā: Śrīmahāmmad Rabiullā at Hāmidīyā Pres, Es Rahmān aṇḍ San Printer, 1315 BS [ca. 1908]).

2. Ābul Kālām Mohāmmad Jākāriyā, ed., *Bāṅglā sāhitye gājīkālu o cāmpāvatī upākhyān* (Ḍhākā: Bāṃlā Ekāḍemī, 1396 BS [1989], introduction, 77–80; the text *Gāji kālu o cāmpāvatī* of Śekh Khodā Bakhś can be found separately paginated, 1–307, and Hālumīr, 309–510. According to Jākāriyā, Khodā Bakhś was born in either 1698 or 1699.

narratives from which all others derived. Ohāb's version translated here closely follows those two earlier eighteenth-century compositions, but is considerably truncated, about a quarter of the size of Bakhś's original composition.

The narrative began with King Śekh Śekandar of Bairāṭ town and his wife Ājupā, whose only son Julhās has disappeared chasing a deer—a classic opening for a romantic quest narrative. That adventure occupies a significant portion of the original story told by Śekh Khodā Bakhś, but was reduced in the nineteenth century versions to a precious few lines. We don't see Julhās again until the end of the story. Sickened by the loss of her son, Ājupā's spirits are raised when she retrieves a mysterious trunk floating in the sea, a trunk which contains a foundling, a young boy whom she adopts and names Kālu. Shortly thereafter, Ājupā conceives and is delivered of a boy child named Gāji. The two young boys are raised together as brothers and became truly inseparable. King Śekandar plans for Gāji to succeed him, but Gāji has already realized that his mission is not in statecraft, but in the religious work of a Sufi. Curiously, he appears to have been an autodidact, practicing the mystical disciplines on his own, so by the time he is slated to take his father's throne, he has achieved the exalted status of a *jindā pīr*, the most accomplished Sufi master. His father torments him for refusing the crown, subjecting him to ordeals, all of which he survives by calling on God, Khodā, who intervenes: they attempt to decapitate him, he is trampled by elephants, burned in a fire pit, and tied to rock and cast into the ocean, but the rock floats and he is saved. His final ordeal comes when he is forced to retrieve a needle from the bottom of the sea, a feat accomplished with the help of Khoyāj Khijir, the nearly immortal teacher of prophets and saints, an enigmatic figure whose path Gāji periodically crosses.[3] Shortly thereafter, he and Kālu leave home on their mission.

At this juncture their adventures begins in earnest. Gāji and his half brother make their way through Bengal to the Sundarbans, where they reclaim land, build cities, and aid God-fearing, generous people—ordinary people from all walks of life, from woodcutters to *brāhmaṇs*. Invoking a titillating scene from Qamar al-Zamān in the *Arabian*

3. For more on Khoyāj Khijir, see "Curbing the Hubris of Moses" below.

Nights,[4] curious færies spot Gāji sleeping on his cot and on a whim wish to compare him to the *brāhmaṇ* princess Cāmpāvatī, whose beauty matches Gāji's good looks. They swoop down and fly him to her father's palace, a vast distance away. One can but guess at what really transpires behind the closed doors of her heavily guarded bedroom, but before dawn they are separated and the færies fly him back to his mosque. Both Cāmpāvatī and Gāji are afire with their serendipitous newfound love, but smolder in *viraha*, the exquisite agony of love in separation that has occupied poets and mystics in Bengal for centuries. This *viraha* is, of course, the basis for an allegorical reading of the text. Much of the rest of the tale traces Gāji's quest to find Cāmpāvatī again. Kālu, being of a more ascetic temperament, is his sometimes reluctant companion, but out of love for his younger half-brother, he faithfully perseveres.

There is a significant tension between profane and divine love that builds as Gāji attempts to remain true to his calling as a mendicant *phakir*, while nurturing his love for Cāmpāvatī. For those wishing to emphasize the Sufi nature of the text, it is worth noting that Kālu, a foundling, is fully detached from the householder's life as a celibate, ascetic mendicant; Julhās, the first-born, assumes his expected social place by marrying into royalty, though he remains with his wife's family to inherit the kingdom since she has no brother; while Gāji is both an ascetic and married, a seemingly antithetical position which is what generates so much of the tension. With ascetic at one end of the spectrum and householder at the other, their positions conveniently suspend Gāji in the middle, and he seems to lean first one direction, then the other. Notably, the text does not mention any offspring for either of the married brothers.

In the course of events leading up to Gāji's marriage to Cāmpāvatī, we see a dramatic reprisal of the conflict between Gāji and Dakṣiṇ Rāy, the warlord and champion of Cāmpāvatī's father, Makuṭ Rājā. While the reasons for the conflict are different from those described in

4. See Ulrich Marzolph and Richard van Leeuwen, with Hassan Wassouf, "Qamar al-Zamân and Budûr," in *The Arabian Nights Encyclopedia*, 2 vols. (Santa Barbara, CA: ABC Clio, 2004), 1: 341–45; and Richard F. Burton, trans., *A Plain and Literal Translation of the Arabian Nights Entertainments, Now Entitled the Book of the Thousand Nights and a Night*, 4 vols. (London: Kama Shastra Society, 1885–86), 3: 212–348, 4: 1–29.

Kṛṣṇarām's *Rāy maṅgal,* translated above, they do share the common thread of social injury or displacement and insult, but unlike the earlier version, the real issue is eligibility for marriage. Here it becomes a pitched battle between Gāji's tigers and Rāy's crocodiles and demons—notably supplied by the mother goddesses Gaṅgā and Caṇḍī respectively—and in the end, Cāmpāvatī's father's army outfitted with modern European weapons and a secret magic well of life-giving water that allows the king to revivify his dead soldiers each night. While there is a rapprochement of sorts, it is Gāji who is the clear victor, whom the disfigured Dakṣiṇā Rāy must subsequently serve. It should be noted that while the conflict between Gāji and Dakṣiṇā Rāy emerges as the central tale of the *Rāy maṅgal,* at the end of Ohāb's telling—when he is recapitulating all that transpired, producing an impromptu table of contents for the story and recounting everything of significance—the conflict is not even mentioned; rather what is noted is the triumph of Gāji over Makuṭ Rājā, which legitimizes his claim to Cāmpāvatī in marriage.

Within only a few days of marrying his darling Cāmpāvatī, Gāji and Kālu set out once again, only reluctantly allowing Cāmpāvatī to tag along, but with much hand-wringing over the propriety of it. Eventually Gāji resolves his uneasiness by turning her into a flower, which he keeps in his turban by day, allowing her to resume her normal human form to cook and lie with him in the evenings. Even this arrangement eventually discomfits him, so he magically transforms her into a tree and does not return to collect her until months later, when he is en route home. After Mother Earth, Baśumati, reveals the subterranean passageway to Pāṭālnagar, where his brother Julhās has been living all those years with his wife, the brothers begin the long jaunt home. With Julhās and his wife in tow, Gāji and Kālu retrieve Cāmpāvatī, then retrace their steps, revisiting all the sites of their adventures along the way. The author leaves to your imagination what happens when the three brothers, two of whom now have wives, return to their natal family.

Versions of the Text. In the late nineteenth century, this tale enjoyed a renewed popularity, primarily through the retelling by Ābdur Rahim, which today circulates under the title of *Gāji kālu o cāmpāvatī kanyār puthi,* the "story of Gāji, Kālu, and the fair maiden Cāmpāvatī." For those who know the story, it is almost irrevocably connected with Rahim's name. The earliest edition of his text that I have located, printed by the author in Mayamansiṃha (Mymensingh) and dated 09 Māgh 1282 BS (23 January 1876), is in the British Library.[5] Over the past century and a half, reprints of Ābdur Rahim's text included several editions from Cak Bājār, from Ḍhākā, and from Kalikātā, with titles and paratextual apparatuses adjusted sometimes only slightly, at others significantly. Gaosiyā Lāibrerī in Kalikātā has circulated facsimile reprint editions of the old hand-set version from 1961 printed by Hāmidiyā Lāibrerī in Ḍhākā (only changing the publisher and date of publication each time).[6] Even though these reprint editions have had the widest circulation, I have chosen to translate Ābdul Ohāb's nineteenth-century rendition for several reasons that I feel compelled to make clear.

Rahim's text has undergone more than a few emendations over the past one hundred forty years. Whether by editors, *munśis*, *murśids*, or others is never indicated, but each of these interventions gives the appearance of a different hand in both style and substance. They include changes in the paratextual apparatus, such as titles given to sections, and the expansion of poetic introductions to sections and musical information that punctuate several of the more emotion-laden passages. Nearly all of these significant changes are to be found in the first half of the narrative. Rahim tends to dwell on and expansively describe the emotional states of Gāji and Cāmpāvatī, which is not surprising given the subject, but he does so with more than a passing interest in similarly effusive descriptions of the beauty of their physiques. The modified text that circulates today includes several homiletic additions that interrupt the flow of the narrative, including one lengthy aside on the nature of pure love (*prem*) that seems

5. Ābdur Rahim, *Gājikālu o cāmpāvatī kanyār puthi* (Mayamansiṃha: Śrī Ābdur Rahim at Rahimni Jantra in Mahakumā Kiśor Gañj, 09 Māgh 1282 BS [23 January 1876 CE]). There was quickly another printing from the same press dated 21 Phālgun 1284 BS [06 March 1878 CE]. There is another considerably later version of the text composed in heavily Persian-inflected *musalmāni* Bangla, which does not seem to have circulated widely; see Munśī Ābdul Karim Sāheb, *Dudumeher churat jāmāl o kālu gāji cāmpāvatir kecchā* (Kalikātā: Āphājaddin Āhāmmad, Chiddikayā Lāibrerī, 1336 BS [ca. 1929]).

6. Ābdur Rahim, *Gājikālu o cāmpāvatī kanyār puthi* (Ḍhākā: Hāmidiyā Lāibrerī, 1961).

somewhat out of context, though it may be an attempt to establish an allegorical reading to help audiences navigate the steamy sexual bits. That possibility is not out of the question because the tale does bear certain shadowy structural resemblances to the well-known Sufi allegories from Hindavī and early modern Bangla—most notably in this case to the tale titled *Mirigāvati* or *Mṛgāvatī*—but without the consistency and rigor one would expect. In other words, the narrative trajectory does not quite fill in the stepwise spiritual progression of the more sophisticated tales that are recognized as allegories.[7]

While a comparison of these seemingly small additions to and interventions in the integrity of the original story are in themselves potentially instructive of shifts in the use of the text and its consumption—an intriguing investigation for scholars of religion and literature or the history of printing—the emendations disrupt the rhythm of the narrative in sometimes puzzling ways. The more succinct diction and clearer narrative thread of Ābdul Ohāb's text, however, suggests a more coherently conceived and executed piece, which ironically makes for a more rigorous allegorical interpretation, and, in the eyes of this translator, for a more satisfying aesthetic. From the standpoint of lexical choice, Ohāb's text conforms to a more standard *dobhāṣī* or *musalmāni* idiom than Rahim's. Ohāb's text does bear the marks of one patently religious paratextual intervention: the frame of the opening pages, which were clearly composed by a different author, utilizing technical language familiar to Sufis, an exposition in a more Persianate idiom that attempts to establish an overtly religious tone. But as its author rightly points out, "Those who are learned and perceptive can infer meaning through hints, insinuation, and implication. Consequently,

7. For more on the allegorical traditions in Hindavī and Avadhī—specifically the texts of *Candāyan, Mirigāvatī, Padmāvat,* and *Madhumālatī*—see Aditya Behl, *Love's Subtle Magic: An Indian Islamic Literary Tradition, 1379–1545*, edited by Wendy Doniger (New York: Oxford University Press, 2012); Behl also translated the tale of Mirigāvatī; see Behl, trans., *The Magic Doe: Quṭban Suhravardī's 'Mirigāvatī'*, with an introduction by Wendy Doniger (New York: Oxford University Press, 2012). For a study of the early modern Bangla renditions of those stories, see Mamtājur Rahmān Taraphdār, *Bāṃlā romāṇṭik kāvyer āoyādhī-hindī paṭbhūmi* (Ḍhākā: Ḍhākā Viśvavidyālay, 1971). For more on the Bangla *Padmāvatī*, see Thibaut d'Hubert, *In the Shade of the Golden Palace: Ālāol and Middle Bengali Poetics in Arakan*, South Asia Research (New York: Oxford University Press, 2018).

this preface will appear to many as opaque and cryptically dense" (p. 3). And cryptic it certainly is—but that is the last we hear of any homiletic or overtly didactic voice in the text.

My good friend and colleague the late Anisuzzaman of Dhaka suggested that I should translate Rahim's text because it is better known. After long consideration, I concluded that the two stories are so close that the aesthetics of the language should prevail. A direct comparison of the last half of the two texts shows few variations, not only in the story itself, but in the details, for it would appear that Ohāb's and Rahim's texts were composed using the same source, or that Ohāb's text was copied from Rahim's, though the directness of Ohāb's narrative would suggest the opposite. To illustrate how close they are, let us look at a literal translation of the passage where the king having asked him to do battle to avert the marriage proposal, Dakṣiṇā Rāy pleads with the goddess Gaṅgā for crocodiles to fight Gāji's tigers.

> A *phakir* has come who wants to marry his daughter. I did not realize the *phakir* brought with him so many tigers. He has completely surrounded and held hostage Brāhmaṇā Nagar city. If you are compassionate, supply me with crocodiles, then I will be able to find out just how much of a *phakir* he really is!
>
> Ābdur Rahim, *Gāji kālu o cāmpāvatī kanyār puthi*, p. 58

> A *phakir* has come and wants to take away his daughter! I had no idea that he had brought so many hundreds of tigers with him. They have completely surrounded and laid siege to Brāhmaṇ Nagar. O Mother, please show your mercy and bestow upon me a float of crocodiles. Then I will find out just what kind of a *phakīr* he really is!
>
> Ābdul Ohāb, *Gāji kālu o cāmpāvatī kanyār puthi*, p. 59

A close reading does suggest a slight difference in tone—in the first Dakṣiṇā Rāy is somewhat belligerent, exhibiting a slightly more brusque contractual relationship of devotion to the goddess—but the closeness of these two passages characterizes the entire second half of the text, page after page, line after line. What this seems to suggest is the we are witnessing the old storyteller's craft, each author telling the same story in his own words—and the vocabulary used in these two passages is quite different—yet it must be the same story. With the fetishization of print and the extension of intellectual property rights all over the world, we today are likely to judge the similarity in a different, perhaps harsher, light, because Ohāb's text, which is dated later, seems to be something between a paraphrase and a translation: no two verses or even phrases are ever the same as Rahim's, though the content is nearly identical; but as already noted, Ohāb uses a more *musalmāni* lexicon. As shown below in the Satya Pīr text, such copying or sharing was not unusual. Confirmation comes at the end of Rahim's version of the text where he insists that his telling is *his* story and that no one try to copy it, which seems to crystallize an important historical moment in the shifting attitudes toward credit for originality and composition.[8] For those interested, I have from time to time noted potentially significant passages where the two versions differ. The paratextual apparatus of musical *rāgs* and rhythms, as well as the section titles, are all to be found in Ohāb's print edition, from which I worked.

8. See Rahim, *Gājikālu o cāmpāvatī* (Mayamansiṃha, 1876), 162, and to compare my translation here to the 1961 Rahim version, see the translated passages and summaries of Gāji and Cāmpāvatī's story in *Witness to Marvels*, ch. 5.

PRIMARY ACTORS, HUMAN AND DIVINE

Ajupā, Ajupā Sundari – wife and queen of Śāh Śekandar, natural mother of Gāji

Āllā, Khodā, Elāhi, Nirañjan the Stainless – God

Balirājā – king who lost in battle to Śāh Śekandar, father of Ajupā

Becu and Mechu, Michu Dvija – *brāhmaṇ* priests, parodies of the twice-borne greed

Bidhātā – god who inscribes fate on one's forehead

Cāmpā, Cāmpāvatī – princess daughter of Maṭuk Rājā of Brāhmaṇ Nagar; marries Gāji

Caṇḍī – see Gaurī, q.v.

Chekāndar – Śāh Śekandar, q.v

Chirā and Ḍorā –brothers, ferrymen at Brāhmaṇ Nagar

Dakṣiṇā, Dakṣiṇā Rāy – the Gosāi of King Maṭuk Rājā, his champion and guarantor of safety

Elāhi – God

Gāji, Gājī, Gājī Śā, Gāji Sā, Gāji Śāh, Gāji Śāhā, Gāji Jendā Pīr – the story's protagonist; the natural son of Śāh Śekandar, a Sufi *phakir* who gained the exalted status of *jendā pīr* at an early age

Gaṅgā, Gaṅgādevī, Mā Gaṅgā – the goddess Gaṅgā, the river Ganges, who fell to earth through Śiv's hair; as Gaṅgā Māsī she is the aunt of Gāji

Gaurī, Bhavāni, Caṇḍī – goddess, aunt of Gāji

Gosāi, Gõsāi – Dakṣiṇ Rāy, the champion and guarantor of the safety of Maṭuk Rājā

Hara – Lord Śiv

Jāmāl – man suffering from elephantiasis

Jaṅga Bāhādur, Jaṅgarāj Mālek – ruler of underground kingdom of Pātāla or Pātālanagar

Julhās, Julhās Śāhā, Jul, Jul Sāhā – first-born son of Ajupā and Śāh Śekandar

Kālu, Kālu Śā, Kālu Sāhā, Kālu Śāhā, Kālu Śāhā Deoān – foundling and older half brother to Gāji, a Sufi *pīr* from an early age

Kartā – God as creator

Khodā – God, Āllā

Khoyāj Khejer, Khoyāj Khijir – teacher of all the greatest Sufi saints, who drank from the fountain of life and so never dies

Maṭuk, Maṭuk Rājā – king of Brāhmaṇ Nagar, father of Cāmpāvatī

Mechu, Michu Dvija –see Becu, q.v.

Monāi – son of man with elephantiasis

Nilāvatī – queen of Maṭuk Rājā, mother of Cāmpāvatī

Nirañjan – God, the "Stainless"

Padyāvati, Paddā – Padmāvatī or Manasā, goddess of serpents; also a maternal aunt of Gāji

Pāñc Tolā, Pāctulā – daughter of Jaṅga Bāhādur whose name means "Five Measures of Gold"; married to Julhās

Param Īśvar – the supreme lord, God

Pārvvatī – wife of the god Śiv, q.v.

Poroyār – God as protector

Prabhu – lord, God

Śāhā Śekandar, Śāh Śekandar, Śāhā, Sekāndar, Chekāndar Sāhā—ruler of kingdom of Bairāṭ, father of Gāji

Śiv – supreme lord, husband of Gaurī or Bhavāni

Śrīrām Rājā – king of Cāmpāi Nagar

Yam, Yom – god of death

OTHER CELESTIAL AND EPIC FIGURES

Baśu, Baśumati – the goddess as Mother Earth

Bhagavati – a generic moniker of any goddess, here Gaurī, q.v.

Durgā – wife of the god Śiv, q.v.

Gaṇeś – the elephant headed god, son of Pārvatī

Ichā – Jesus

Indra – king of the gods, whose net of illusion blankets the world

Iuchuph – the biblical Joseph

Jelekhā – Potiphar's wife Zulaikha, whose longing for Iuchuph or Yusuf is a Sufi allegory of the soul yearning for God

Kālī – the goddess in one of her threatening forms and who prefers blood sacrifices

Kārttik – the goddess Bhavāni's son

Mariyam – mother of Ichā, Jesus

Rāhu – the cause of the moon's eclipse; an *asura* who sips the nectar of immortality only to have his neck severed by Viṣṇu before it can trickle into his body, so his head remains immortal, periodically swallowing the moon, which momentarily obscures it, until it emerges from his throat

Rām – the form of Viṣṇu who is hero of the *Rāmāyaṇ*

Rāvaṇ – ten-headed enemy of Rām who captures Rām's wife Sītā; his citadel is the epitome of style and beauty

Śāhā Pari – king of færies, or *paris*

Śura and Āśuri – demigods, or *dānavas* who aid Khoyāj Khejer

Vāsuki – king of serpents and the world underneath the surface of the earth

GĀJI'S TIGERS (ONLY THOSE NAMED, OUT OF MORE THAN 520,000,700)

Beḍābhāṅgā – Kenduyā's closest sidekick, transmogrified into a ram

Kenduyā, Kendurā, Kenda, Kendā, Kendo – always the lead tiger; transmogrified into a ram

The remaining named few: Aoan, Bāoan, Biṅgarāj, Cilācākṣu, Dāneoārā, Kālkuṭī, Kheḍi, Lohājuḍi, Menī, Nāgeśvarī, Pecāmukhā, Vāsuki

Scouring the World for Cāmpāvatī

Gāji Kālu o Cāmpāvatī Kanyār Puthi of Ābdul Ohāb

Is there anyone who can compose
praise sufficient to Āllā's majesty?
    So how much less likely when it dribbles from my own pen?
With but a gesture He conjured heaven and earth.
In his magnificence He is exalted as the Lord God
    by all the inhabitants of this expansive world.
His beloved Prophet—how can I describe
such beatific splendor that, in the twinkling of an eye,
    vanquishes all fear and distress?
The Prophet associated exclusively with
those of his followers who were
    counted as exemplary leaders among the pious.
His innumerable descendants
enjoy his inimitable divine love and
    through his favor rank above all others.
Those favored by God's benevolence
are worthy of honor, the dearest of whom
    have exceptional fortitude and are of Arabian stock.
The descendants of those companions
who are in the direct line of the Prophet
    make their homes throughout the Arab world.
Born in the house of Ābdullā,
Ābdul Mataleb was his grandfather,
    and his father was named Hāsem.
His father in turn was Mānnāph,
dear to the hearts of all in the community,

and foremost leader among the Prophet's lineage.[1]
There were many prophets born in that lineage
each of whom looked after the good of the community,
and who constituted Āllā's learned leaders.
The path they prescribed
was founded on the authority of their free will,
which Āllā had granted them for righteous rule.
With the certainty of firm belief ruling their hearts,
they followed the best practices
so that the devil Saytān could never strike.
If anyone in this world
looks to the Lord God, Āllā,
then he will embrace the Prophet's path.
There are four stages along this path,
which you may choose as you will,
and through that you will become Āllā's ally.
When you first start along this path
the four stages together form a ladder, and
you must climb deliberately, one rung at a time.
When you land on the first rung of *śāriat*,
that step appears difficult; and perched there,
you are but one among hundreds of thousands.
But then the path shifts to overt spiritual exercises, *tarikat*,
the encounter with truth, *hakikat*, and finally gnosis, *mārphat*—
these in succession, brother, constitute the four steps.
You must persevere, and forge ahead,
moving methodically, step by step, no matter what befalls you.
You must advance with vigilance, but not without proper guidance.
When you ascend the zenith, you will taste the liquid emotion of love
or *ras*.
By savoring that, eminence will accrue, and
you will become the lover of your beloved.
Only through arduous effort
can you gradually distance yourself

1. These are the well-known immediate forebears of Muhāmmad as described in the first hagiography of Muhāmmad; see A[lfred] Guillaume, trans., *The Life of Muhammad: A Translation of Isḥāq's Sīrat Rasūl Allāh* (1955, reprint: Karachi: Oxford University Press, 1967), p. 3: "Muhammad was the son of 'Abdullah, b. 'Abdu'l-Muṭṭalib (whose name was Shayba), b. Hashim (whose name was 'Amr), b. 'Abdu Manaf (whose name was al-Mughira). . . ."

from the world and all its ordinary people.
One's feet begin mired in the filth of this worldly latrine.
When that nasty bile finally rises to the throat, only
the fire of asceticism can overcome it, transforming it into cool water.
Only when it advances to the point where you are neck-deep—
a real force to be reckoned with—
does it generate the necessary anxiety to move one to action.
Take, for instance, the henna[2] leaves in the forest—
just listen to their story:
To make contact with the one they love, those leaves
diligently, indeed remarkably, manage to maneuver themselves
to be crushed underfoot,
simply to kiss the feet of the beloved.
Consider the form and function of a candle,
which will ignite itself and burn, even when wet,
to ensure the rendezvous with the beloved.
When a potter throws an earthenware jug,
it must be long baked in the high heat of fire
before it can grace the mouth of the beloved.
The metal comb must first endure red-hot tempering blows;
only then can it be used, raised to the head, and
run through the hair of the beloved.
When you desire to cut a lock of that hair,
the comb works well for it can easily lift the hair
above the head for clipping.
The barleycorn dissolves itself, its former shape disintegrated,
when it is sown in the ground of the earth;
but the result, its achievement, is the production of its fruit.
And so it is that any number of people in this world—
beings of every imaginable stripe—
endeavor to come close to the beloved.
But first you must suffer to efface yourself, to destroy your ego,

2. Henna is *medi*, also known as *mehndi*; its botanical name is *Lawsonia inermis* and is from the Crape Myrtle family (Lythraceae) and is one of the most fragrant flowers in South Asia. It is well known as the dye used for decorating the hands, feet, and other parts of the bodies of women at weddings and festivals; it is also used to dye the beards of men, especially those who have made the Hajj to Mecca. Stepped on, the blossoms emit a strong fragrance, alerting the beloved to their presence, and the crushed leaves leave their dye on the soles of the beloved's feet, another lingering reminder.

after which you will achieve many joys and pleasures,
and your stature and prestige, your *ejjat,* will grow accordingly.
All those who desire to draw close to Him
who is the truly divine, *hakīkī*, beloved
must first cleanse the veils of their hearts.
Along the banks of the river
you must toil to construct a landing ghat,
piling up, bit by bit, small stones and scree.
Build a fire pit of annihilation, *phānā*, into God.
Then climb onto it!
Taking the sparkle of love,
concentrate on the basic elements, *ākṣārā*, of human frailty and desire, *naphs*,
to set the tinder on fire and burn that dried wood,
immolating that part of you that doubts, your *kāphar* self.
Continue to stoke that fire with more wood
and burn all the way through to the innermost part, your heart.
Afterwards purify yourself the rest of the way down.
Then wash with soap and
with clean water
and when you are done, return to the ghat.
A dignified modesty should mark your deportment;
you should show restraint with money and in all other matters;
and your stomach should always be wanting food.
Purified by the *nur*, the light of Āllā, the High,
you must dry out the cloak of the heart with a searing heat,
then fold the cloak, and put it away for safekeeping.
Employing the protective aid of the testimony: *ellāllā*,
don that carefully folded cloth
every time you engage and struggle with the beloved.[3]
We could describe these actions in a myriad of ways;
were we to write all of them down in detail,

3. This complex and somewhat unusual image suggests that God's light (*nur*) shines on the covering or cloak of the heart, drying and thereby purifying it from the outside, while the heat of the heart's ardor for God dries it from the inside. Normally *ellāllā* is a shorthand signifier of the first syllables of the *śāhādat* and as an indexical form can be rendered any number of different ways so long as it approximates the sounds. But here, if taken more literally in its restricted form of "except Āllā," then it would seem to suggest that the strong affirmation of denial of any other God is the protective cover to engage and struggle with the beloved.

the book would grow unmanageably large.
Those who are learned and perceptive
can infer meaning through hints, insinuation, and implication.
Consequently, this preface will appear to some as opaque and cryptically dense.

THE STORY BEGINS

Listen carefully, you literary connoisseurs to this dramatic romance of Kālu, Gāji, and Cāmpāvatī delivered in a pleasing style of speech. Śāhā Śekandar ruled in the citadel of Bairāṭ. The beautiful Ajupā dwelled in his palace as his wife. Her beauty was such that færies and celestial nymphs were put to shame. It was as if the moon had come down from the sky to earth, making the citadel of the Śāhā comparable to heaven itself. Exceedingly charitable, the Śāhā made lavish gifts to all; there was no *bādsā* equal to Śekandar. Pacifying the lands from the east to the west under his dominion, kings everywhere paid tribute to Śāhā Sekandar. In his arrogance and pride, one king, Balirājā, declared publicly: "I will never make over anything to a *jaban*, a foreigner." Hearing this filled Sekandar Śāhā with rage. Mustering his laskars, Śāhā headed for Balirājā's territory. Brimming with rage, Śāhā launched a savage attack, and Balirājā quickly broke off the engagement in woeful defeat. By way of tribute, he tendered his daughter named Ajupā. As soon as he made over his beautiful daughter, the *mahārājā* escaped to Pātāla, one of the seven regions of the underworld, while Śāhā escorted Ajupā back to Bairāṭ. It was not long before Ajupā gave their house a son. His beauty glowed, more radiant than the sun and the moon. He was given the name of Julhās. How can I possibly describe the full waxing effulgence of this young moon; day by day did this boy steadily grow there in the inner quarters of the palace. Then he reached his twelfth year.

One day he went out hunting in the company of a large retinue of soldiers. He soon arrived at the edge of a forest and entered. He complained that though they had long hunted, they had found nothing. Then a deer was flushed out and bounded past. No sooner had Julhās seen it than he dismounted and shot off toward it.

The deer was actually an illusion; but when it was spotted, what did it do? It darted off down a narrow track.

When Julhās managed to regain sight of the deer, he bolted down that same path in wild pursuit, hell-bent on killing it. The soldiers fanned out through the thickets of the forest to locate Julhās, but they could not ferret him out. Though they searched far and wide, they found no trace; eventually—and with no small regret, tinged with fear—they resigned themselves to returning. Śāhā Julhās pressed harder and harder down the faint trail, until the dark drape of night made it impossible to see further. About that time, he happened upon a wondrous settlement—the buildings were palaces of exceeding beauty and they were made of gold. Everything was of golden hue—trees, flowers, animals, and even the birds. The lustrous dwellings were truly a wonder to behold. When he gazed upon them, Julhās Śāhā was mesmerized. With all due deliberation, he slowly entered the citadel.

Jaṅga Bāhādur was the name of the king of that place. He looked after all his subjects as if they were his own sons. When the king caught sight of Julhās he questioned him vigorously: "How did you manage to arrive at this place? What is your name? Where do you call home?"

Julhās replied: "My home is the citadel of Bairāṭ. He who reigns in Bairāṭ is named Sekandar. My mother is called Ajupā. I am an only son, and I have no sisters. Grief at my disappearance will surely kill my parents."

When Jaṅgarājā listened to all this, he was satisfied and pleased. Then, with all due respect and humility, he proposed to Julhās: "I have but one daughter in my household, an extraordinary beauty. I propose to give her to you in marriage, along with my kingdom. Because of her enchanting beauty the girl has been named Pāñc Tolā—'Five Measures of Gold.' In learning she is no less than a *paṇḍit*, and her beauty exceeds even that of houris and færies." Weighing carefully this unexpected offer, Julhās finally consented. And so it was that Julhās accepted this girl of exceptional beauty and in lavish ceremony they were formally joined in marriage. He gave up all thoughts of returning to his own land, so Śāhā lived on in the citadel of Pātāla in quiet contentment.

While this was going on, all those who heard of his disappearance were beside themselves. The soldiers had been unable to secure any intelligence regarding young Śāhā's whereabouts. They returned as a group and reported to Sekandar Śāhā: "The prince, your son, has been lost in the wilds. We searched everywhere but could not find him.

Young Śāhā spurred his horse forward hell-bent on slaying a deer, but afterwards the prince failed to return."

As soon as he heard this fateful story, Sekandar Śāhā fell to the ground, completely insensate. The king openly wept, making public his lamentation in loud sobs. Cries of anguish and heartbreak soon reverberated through the citadel of Bairāṭ. Ajupā, who was normally ever-so-gracefully calm and in full control, dropped to the ground and writhed in the dirt. She wept uncontrollably, bitterly. Servants, female and male alike, gave similar vent to their anguish. Wailing could be heard in all quarters.

Eventually, Sekandar Śāhā regained his composure and sent for the geomancer and several astrologers. The king commanded the group of soothsayers: "Calculate the whereabouts of my son, the prince, and tell me!" The astrologers listened and pondered the matter and carefully calculated: "You need not worry; rest assured the prince is safe. The prince is living comfortably in the city of Pātāla. He has married the daughter of Jaṅgarājā, Lord of the Battle. It may be a long while, but eventually the prince will return."

And so the king's fears were eased and he contemplated the glory of God, Khodā. So it was that the days gradually passed.

Then one day the queen spoke to Śāhā Sekandar: "I have a hankering to visit the ocean. Please arrange to take me to the seaside." Sekandar Śāhā immediately heeded her request and arranged for a palanquin to escort her to the ocean shores. As she gazed out over the sea, waves of contentment washed over the queen. About that time she espied a chest floating there. Its casing was wood and it floated straight toward her. In no time the box washed right up to the shore. Ajupā Sundari ordered her maidservants: "Fetch the chest to me and be quick!" But each time the maidservants tried to secure the bobbing box, it would recede, floating just out of their reach. One by one, all her maidservants failed, returning empty-handed. Finally, Ajupā Sundari herself waded out and stretched her hand toward the wooden crate, and no sooner had she done so than it floated straight into her arms. She lifted the box from the waters, and without hesitation she lifted the lid and gazed inside only to discover a baby boy about six months old. High in the sky, the moon paled in comparison to his beaming countenance. The queen immediately lifted up the child and gave him her breast, mounted the palanquin, and sped home. She brought the child home and busied herself with his care. Knowing nothing about his mother and father, Ajupā Sundari decided to call him Kālu. So Ajupā declared him to be her adopted son—her son born from the eighth mansion of the zodiac—the boy who fell from the heavens.

Now let me proceed to narrate the birth of Gāji, as I, Ābdul Ohāb, compose this captivating tale.

This song is in the *rāginī* called *jogiyā*—the rhythm or *tāla* is *āḍāṭhekā*.[4]

Give over your mind to constant worship of the Lord God,
for how else will your heart be rescued
from the shoreless ocean of existence?
After your ledger is reckoned, no loophole omitted,
will he come for you.
Alas, who else is there to rescue you,
to purify you of the fruits of your *karma*?
Keep your mind focused on the Lord
throughout every day and night,
and with the intervention of the Stainless One,
in the end, everything will be rectified and
you will be delivered from this ocean of life.

THE NARRATIVE OF GĀJĪ ŚĀHĀ'S BIRTH

After she had performed the ritual bath at the end of her menstruation and her mind settled, the charming and glamorous woman Ajupā gave herself over to delightful love play with her husband. Later that very evening Ajupā saw in a dream how the moon, high in the sky, descended and seemed to enter her womb. She awakened when she witnessed this event in her dream and she cried out in fright. Śāhā Sekandar heard

4. *Jogiyā rāginī* (f) is from *thāt bhairāva*, sung in the second watch or *prahar* of the morning between 6 AM and 9 AM; *Āḍāṭhekā* has three beats (*tāla*) with one off-beat (*phānk*) in a fast-speed sixteen beat cycle. In modern usage it is thought to express sadness or contemplation and is often used for devotional or light genres (*bhajan, ṭhumrī*). It uses the flat 2nd and 6th intervals. Known today as *tintāl*, this is the most common *tāl* of Hindustani music. For more detailed information regarding the *rāgas* and *rāginīs*, see Faqīrullāh (Nawab Saif Khan), *Tarjuma-i-Mānakutūlhala; & Risāla-i-Rāgadarpaṇa*, edited and annotated by Shahab Sarmadee (New Delhi: Indira Gandhi National Centre for the Arts and Motilal Banarsidass Publishers, 1996); see also nn. 24, 35, 36, and 37 below.

her and gently questioned her, "What has made you cry, my dear, tell me please." The queen replied, "Listen my lord . . ." and so she told him. "What I saw in my dream makes my heart quake. The moon from above has entered me and now rises in my womb." Sekandar instructed her, "My beloved, please say no more. A wondrous son will surely be born from your womb." As soon as the prospect of this fully registered, a thrill of pure joy rippled through the queen. From that point on, she fervently recalled the names of the Lord day and night, and in this fashion nine months quickly passed.[5] At a perfectly auspicious moment was born a boy who outshone the moon itself. The birthing room filled with the glow emanating from his beautiful form. It was as if the moon had dropped from the sky down to earth.

To describe his extraordinary beauty presents me with an impossible task—there was no figure anywhere in the triple world to compare with his glory.

When Ajupā Sundari beheld the exquisite form of her son, she could attend only to him and she soon forgot Julhās altogether. The Mahārāṇī bestowed on him the name Gāji. He began to form words early on and so he grew day by day. Twelve years gradually and quite predictably passed.[6]

Śāhā Sekandar sent for Gājī and spoke to him, "I want you to rule, my child, to sit on the throne in court. To see you deliberate and judge affairs would fill my eyes with tears of joy." Gāji replied, "Listen carefully to what I have to say, dear father. I have no desire whatsoever to rule."

When he heard this, Sekandar Śāhā rebuked him in anger, "Why else were you born on this earth, you unworthy, disobedient son?" to which Gājī replied, "Listen father, please pay attention to what I am trying to tell you. Do not lecture me about assuming your kingship. I

5. In his rendition of this scene, Abdul Rahim includes month-by-month description of the pregnancy covering fourteen couplets; its style resembles the popular *bilāp* or *bāramās* lament that carries through each of the twelve months. See Abdul Rahim, *Gāji kālu o cāmpāvatī kanyār puthi* (Ḍhākā: Hāmidiyā Lāibrerī in Cakbājār, 1961), 4.

6. Abdul Rahim (p. 5) describes how Gāji and Kālu grew up as two brothers never separated, day and night reciting the names of the Lord, never for a second one forgetting the other, immersed in love for one another. They were two bodies, but one heart, each always aware of the other. Gāji considered Kālu to be his *guru*, while Kālu recognized Gāji to be his *guru*. Then as the two reached the end of their childhood, they both attained a vision of the Lord God, Khodā. In Rahim's version, Gāji is ten years old.

have turned away from that and put behind me this endless intoxication with power and wealth. What pleasure would come my way from the managing of riches and handling the affairs of people? When I die to the world not even the tiniest shred of cloth will accompany me. I will become a *phakir* and pay my respects only to him who imagined and fabricated this universe we call creation. I will become a *phakir* and bow only to him who, with but a simple word, brought this world into existence." Sekandar Śāhā desperately tried to reason, "Listen my dear child, abandon this notion of becoming a *phakīr* and dedicate yourself to ruling." But Gāji had already achieved the exalted rank of a *jindā pīr* and would not listen to his father's argument. When Sekandar Śāhā heard him announce publicly "I will become a *phakir*," he seethed with anger. He issued the order for the executioner to put Gāji to death.

As soon as his courtiers received the order, an executioner was brought. He had decided in advance the way Gāji was to die. The executioner swung the curved blade of his *talwār* sword across Gāji's neck to decapitate him, but Gāji fixed his heart and mind on the Lord Khodā, and He, Āllā, showered his beneficence upon him. Not even a single hair on his head was grazed as Gāji remained serene. Ten times and more did the *talwār* rain down its blows, but Gāji's body never suffered a wound.

When he watched this, Sekandar Śāhā screamed his anger: "Fit out ten of the biggest, most dangerous bull elephants!" The mahouts heard and quickly brought ten such elephants. The Śāhā described precisely what he wanted the mahouts to do, "Stir up the elephants quickly to make them trample Gāji." The mahouts heeded his order and drove the elephants hard. The elephants first wrapped their trunks around Gāji and repeatedly hurled him against the river bank, each time ramming their tusks into his body. The elephants mangled and gored him, over and over and over, but Gāji remained unperturbed, his mind serenely fixed on Āllā. They pulverized and impaled Gāji's body absolutely to no avail; rather, it was they who suffered broken tusks, and when the distal pads of their feet were split, they were left crippled. The elephants made obeisance to Gāji's person and threw off their mahouts who, in a mad dash, barely managed to escape. Though Sekandar Śāhā witnessed this marvel, he once again boiled in a rage.

He then gave the order, "Build a fire pit and stoke it to an inferno, be quick!" The second they heard, his attendants hastened to dig that fire pit. Sekandar ordered them to hurl Gāji into the pit, and the moment they received that directive, they wasted no time in mobbing Gāji. When the flames were roaring high, into the pit they launched him. As he flew deep into the fire, Gāji's heart remained pure and calm as he remembered his Lord, Prabhu. With his hands pressed together in respect, Gāji called out to the Lord God, Master Creator, Prabhu Kartā, "Please send water to me, for I am your obedient servant." Suddenly cascades of water deluged him as the fire raged all around. Gāji sat calmly in the midst of that fire until after three days it burned itself out. When Sekandar saw this, he thought his eyes were playing tricks on him; he thought to himself, "My son possesses some kind of magic or sorcery."

Still not pacified, he issued the order to fetch ten massive boulders and to bind Gāji to those massive rocks, "Ah, cast him into the depths of the ocean so that he surely sinks." When they received the official decree, they bound Gāji and heaved him into the sea. As he sank into the ocean depths, Gāji meditated on Nirañjan, the Stainless One, "O Lord, Prabhu, come quickly to the aid of your lowly servant." The Lord God, Master Creator, felt compassion for Gāji. The shackles on his limbs sloughed off, and by the grace of God, Prabhu, the boulders floated. Gāji perched himself quickly on top of the rocks, and not too much time later, he made his way back to the town of Bairāṭ. When they saw Gāji, everyone was flummoxed and filled with awe.

Sekandar Śāhā met Gāji and said, 'You have one more chance to convince me that you are a *phakir*." The Śāhā then picked up one tiny needle and cast it far out into the ocean, after which he beckoned to Gāji and commanded, "Go and fetch that needle!" When he heard this Gāji shivered at the prospect. He eventually made his way to the shores of the ocean. Gāji appealed to God, "Listen, O Lord Prabhu, you are an ocean of mercy. The Supreme Lord, Param Īśvar, you can rescue any and every one. O Lord Prabhu, filled with grace, please hear my petition which I offer at the tomb of a saint. How will I be able to retrieve the needle from the ocean depths?" And in this fashion did Gāji Śāhā meditate.

At the express command of the Lord Prabhu, Khoyāj arrived there. Khoyāj Khejer said to Gāji, "Tell me what is troubling you." Gāji replied: "Please tell me who you are, then I will tell you tell you my tale of woe." Khoyāj Khejer then revealed his identity and as soon as he heard the name, Gāji made obeisance, offering salaams. He knelt down and clasped Khoyāj Khejer's feet and then detailed all of the troubles that made him suffer so. Khoyāj consoled him, "My son, be at peace."

The *pīr* then called on Śura and Āśvari.[7] They arrived, their bodies the size of mountains. They bowed in obeisance, making salaam, and inquired of their calling. Khoyāj Khejer spoke, "Listen to our predicament. Śāhā Sekāndar threw a needle into the ocean, and I need you to retrieve it. It is to execute this difficult task that I have summoned you." No sooner than they had heard than Śura and Āśuri descended into the waters. They drew the waters up and stored them up in the mountains.[8] The ocean was drained dry and only sand was left, so Śura and Āśvari dug, but could not locate the needle. They returned to Khoyāj and spoke to him, "Although we dug and mined and sifted the sand, we could not locate the needle anywhere on the ocean floor." So the Pīr took himself into meditation and then understood: Right at the time Śāhā Sekāndar threw the needle into the ocean, along came a man of the sea, a merman, who picked it up and then headed onward to the underworld city of Pātālanagar. He gave the needle to his young daughter, a færie, so she could pin up her hair, and so into her hair she wove it. Khejer then instructed them: "Śura and Āśvari, go back again. The needle is pinned in the hair of the young færie who lives in Pātāla; bring it back here straight away." When the two celestials, *dānav*s, received the command they headed for Pātāla at once and just as quickly returned with the needle. After Khoyāj vouchsafed the needle into the hands of Gāji, he took his leave.

After accepting it, Gāji eventually made his way to his own quarters, whereupon he immediately placed the needle in the hand of his father. Sekāndar looked hard at the needle and contemplated its significance. Feeling quite gratified, indeed overwhelmed, he embraced Gāji and kissed his lotus face hundreds of thousands of times. Sekāndar spoke, "My dear son, treasure of my heart, I have caused you much grief and suffering. Please do not hold a grudge against me for all the suffering, for you cannot possibly fathom what I truly intended. Look, my beloved son, I have on my tongue a poison pill. Had you died, I would

7. The names of these two appear to be versions of the Sanskrit *sura* and *āsura*, the feminine of the latter being *āsuri;* so demigods and antigods. The /v/ *bɔphalā* is not pronounced, but rather doubles the consonant to which it is joined, so *āśvari* and *āśuri* (as it spelled a few lines later) are pronounced in much the same way. Subsequently they are referred to as *dānavas*, often glossed as demons, who are foes of the gods but obviously here under the control of Khoyāj Khejer.

8. The line can also be read as "They stacked the waters up like a mountain."

have swallowed the poison. That poison would have eaten up my life right then and there. I take an oath before God, Khodā, to confirm the truthfulness of what I say. Listen, son, to what I now tell you. You are the one and only son I have in these three worlds. You must rule the kingdom with the aid of your ministers and confidants. When I look at you my heart and life are refreshed. My treasured son, you are the lamp that lights my lineage. Please honor my request and rule the kingdom with pleasure and ease. After I have died, only then should you become a *phakir*. I beg you to honor my wishes and calm my heart." And so in this way did Sekāndar make his various arguments and pleas.

Gāji gave no reply and remained with his head bowed. Gāji then properly made salaam to his father as the king, after which he sought out his mother, Ajupā, in the women's apartments. He grasped the feet of his mother in deep obeisance and then with tears streaming from his eyes, he buried himself in his mother's bosom. Seeing her Gāji like this, she broke down in loud lament, "In spite of the wretched misery that has been written on your forehead, my child, you are the defender of the ignorant and the wealth of those bereft. You are the life of my life, the jewel of this wretched woman. Your father has tortured you unmercifully, what more can I say? Please do not leave this house for the world—stay here with me in my quarters day and night! Just to look at you soothes my eyes." The winsome Ajupā then hugged Gājī close and tenderly fed him specially prepared dishes. When the day came to a close and darkness fell, Ajupā pulled him close and they lay down together.

When she lay on the couch, the queen eventually drifted off to sleep, and as soon as her guard was down, Gājī Śāhā quickly got up. Crying softly to himself, Gājī began to reflect privately on his sad plight: "In this king's world my father has inflicted great misery on me. I cannot describe the horrors my father has committed. To stay under his dominion is impossible, so this is my vow: I shall abandon this land and wander across the world, and, in the name of Āllā, I will become a *phakir*." Gājī then dressed himself in a traditional mendicant's robe woven with gold thread, and cinched a chain of gold around his waist. Gājī picked up a golden staff in his hand and slipped his feet into golden-hued sandals. He pulled a woven bag onto his shoulder and wrapped prayer beads around his ankle as protection against all troubles and fears. After hastily dressing in his *phakir*'s garb, he reverently honored his mother's feet.

Ābdul Ohāb tells of his remorse: Dear mother, your son is now a phakir.[9]

"Listen, dear woman, as I speak at your feet, though you be completely oblivious in the house of sleep. O mother, your son has become a *phakir*. Because of my commitment, beloved mother, never again will you see me, nor ply me with your specially prepared foods. Never again will you hear the word 'mother' pour from my mouth, nor will you be able to call me 'son, my son'. Nor will you will be able to nourish me with the endless flow of your milk . . ." His eyes brimmed with tears, his silent weeping inconsolable. He gripped his mother's feet and kissed them; then exhaling deeply, he checked his affection. Uttering *bechmellā*—In the name of God—Gājī departed.

At the moment of his departure, Gājī heard something like this: The injunction "Come!" was repeated three times in an especially soothing voice. Remembering Khodā, he made his way. All the sentries were fast sleep and so he was able to slip past the nine doors. Through the tenth doorway he saw Kālu.[10] When he looked up and saw Gājī, Kālu began to question him, "Where are you off to, brother? Are you abandoning me?" Kālu pressed him further, "Brother Gāji, what is going on? Did you plan to go and leave me behind?" Gāji replied, "Kālu brother, listen to what I share with you. You are most free to join me if you wish." Then Gāji took his brother and left. They soon left the city of Bairāṭ behind and embarked on their journey. Their minds content and calm, the two brothers made their way.

Gāji's mother eventually awoke from her deep sleep. When she could not locate Gāji, she began to weep inconsolably. Crying out in agony, "Oh my son!" the Queen slumped to the ground insensate. After a short while, her limp body revived and consciousness returned. Invigorated, she ran here and there searching frantically for Gāji, screaming in anguish. When Sekandar Śāhā heard the commotion, he

9. The translation of this passage including the attempts to punish Gāji and his determination to renounce can be found in Stewart, *Witness to Marvels*, 75–78.

10. While it may signal slipping unnoticed by the myriad of servitors in the palace, it more is likely a veiled reference to the mastery of the yogic body. That his elder half brother Kālu appears through the tenth door, awake and aware, would seem to signal an extraordinary level of spiritual accomplishment for the latter, evidence of which will be presented later in the narrative.

exclaimed in a loud voice, "Has that treasure of my life abandoned his mother and father? Where has he gone?" In this fashion they wept, their hearts broken.[11]

It was from that emotional place that the two brothers, Kālu and Gāji—still just very young men—had slipped away. The siblings serenely plunged into their adventure. They soon landed up on the shore of a vast expanse of water, but there was neither dinghy nor boat moored there.[12] The two boys sat on the water's edge pondering the situation. They prayed together to resolve their problem: "Please show your mercy to us, O Lord, the Stainless Nirañjan!" In response to Gāji's call, a disembodied voice called out, "Throw into the ocean that staff you hold in your hand. It will be magically transformed into a small boat and by my grace you will cross." Heeding those words from the sky, without hesitation Gāji hurled his staff into those waters as he continued to meditate on the Stainless Nirañjan. The staff that was cast instantly transformed into a dinghy. With immense relief the two brothers climbed on board. They pushed off the dinghy and floated into the broad currents.

The duo traversed one region after another where they finally landed up on the edges of the Sundarban forests. As soon as they landed, Gāji Śāhā then called all of the tigers—as many as were to be found in the Sundarban forests. They crept forward all and made obeisance to the person of Gāji as soon as he had established himself in the section of the forest called Sondal. After a short while Kālu Śā and Gāji assessed the matter and concluded that this really was not a very good place to establish a *phakir*'s residence, so before night could fall, the brothers broke camp and abandoned the place. Gāji admitted, "Truth be known, I have no desire whatsoever to stay in this area." And continuing their conversation in this frank manner, the two brothers resumed their peregrinations. At this auspicious moment, they came

11. Abdur Rahim expands the narrative of Gāji's leave taking and the royal couple's subsequent discovery of his departure by exploring it for more than fifty couplets (pp. 8–10), giving vent to the full range of emotions such an act would engender.

12. *Sāgar* is often translated as ocean, but can apply to the vast expanses of water formed by the rivers of the region, in some places stretching a dozen or more miles across, blurring the distinction between river and sea. As the next verses make clear, they are still quite far inland but headed to the Sundarban mangrove swamps of southern Bengal.

upon another particularly large body of water. When Gāji threw his staff into the waters, a dinghy was again instantly conjured. Remembering God, they steered across the waters to the other shore. After some two and one-half hours, the duo made landfall and were considerably more sanguine climbing ashore. Gāji questioned the first person he met, "What is the name of this land? And what is the name of its *rājā*?" That person listened politely and then replied, "Listen, here is the story. Know the name of this land to be Cāmpāi Nagar and the king, who is a veritable trove of good qualities, is named Śrīrām Rājā." Hearing this and more, the two brothers resolved to stay on in that place.

One day as they wandered, exploring the area, Kālu Sāhā said, "Brother, listen to what I propose. Today is for maintaining the discipline of silence: do not speak or greet anyone you may meet along the way!" Gāji Śāhā listened, but remained only warily quiet. The two brothers made their way ever so slowly down the road, when Gāji caught sight of Khoyāj Khijir sitting at the foot of a tree with two others. Gāji immediately approached and made obeisance to the feet of the three young men. As Gāji was prostrating himself in salaam, Kālu Śāhā grew increasingly annoyed. "Why on earth are you making salaams to these boys? They are just children." Much embarrassed, Gāji then broke his silence, "Do you not recognize Khoyāj Khijir in this form? Seldom, if ever, does one encounter *pīr*s as accomplished as these even through rigorous meditation."[13]

By this time the day had progressed into the second watch and a hunger gnawed at them. Śrī Rām was the name of the *rājā* who ruled this land. The two brothers, Kālu and Gāji, made their way and soon the two men found the king's palace. First reciting "*Ellellāha*" the two men began their *jikir* recitations. The king bellowed angrily, "Listen up, Constable, some foreign mendicants, some *jaban phakir*s have arrived. Get rid of them now!" The Constable jumped to the task. He manhandled the two and hustled them away. Gāji spoke, "Listen, brother Kālu

13. Ābdur Rahim (p. 12, ll. 6–17) adds to the narrative explaining Kālu's annoyance which stems from the injunction that one should only bow down to and worship Khodā and none other. Individuals bearing the title of *khijir* are everywhere, he continues, and he has no time for them. Khoyāj Khijir then angrily asks Gāji why he is traveling with such an imbecile village bumpkin and, without waiting for a reply, recommends getting rid of him.

Śāhā Deoān,[14] what blind arrogance to collar us and kick us out." But they persevered and continued their *jikir*.

Everywhere they traveled in that region, they encountered only native inhabitants of Hindustān; there was not a *muchalmān* to be found among them. The moment they were heard to beg a tiny morsel, the locals would without fail emerge from their houses to beat them. Still suffering from what had now become an acute hunger, they escaped to the wilds of a forest close by the village. They took refuge there, but found no means to assuage their hunger pangs. Eventually, their petitions for mercy found their way to Āllā's court, and as soon as their needs were realized, the Stainless Lord Nirañjan sent down food. Reciting *bechmellā*, "In the name of God," the two men consumed the welcome provisions. Once their bellies were filled, they were refreshed. By then content, the two settled themselves quietly in the forest.

Kālu Śāhā brooded and then his thoughts gradually took the shape of a plan: "Were the palace of the *rājā* to burn down, and then *jinn* come and carry off his wife, all of the townspeople would look to become *muchalmān*—then my heart's desire would be fulfilled." And so he continued silently to mull over this plan. God in his heavenly *dargā* acknowledged the plea to execute this plan and granted his blessings. A mysterious fire magically swept through the city. Houses and huts in all directions began to burn. The king and queen were both inside the palace, and just like that, the queen was lifted up and carried to the opposite bank of the river.

On that far side of the river stood a mosque, a *machjed*, and in this *machjed* the queen was held captive. Kālu and Gāji found Khoyāj Khijir there, and they went inside the *machjed* when the call to prayer was made. Kālu Śāhā again made a request for Āllā's intervention from heaven and right then the doors to the *machjed* were closed and blocked. In a flash, the *rājā*, Śrī Rām, realized the seriousness of the situation. Witness to the ravages of the fire, the stunned king was

14. I read *deoān* is an alternate spelling of *dāoān*, which indicates a pious individual who calls out the *da'wa* (Arabic) or *dāoyā*/*dāoā* (Bangla), summoning people to join the *ummā*, the issuing of the invitation, which is a form of proselytizing, but with implicit intention to establish Islamic conventions of governance and law (Arabic *sharī'a*), not just to invite individuals to participate. As a title it can be translated as "the Summoner"; see the tale of Badar Pīr in Stewart, *Witness to Marvels*, ch. 2; note esp. p. 47, n. 29.

beside himself when he could not find his queen anywhere inside her quarters. In his agony, the king gave a cry of distress. Someone reported to him, "Listen, here is the situation—remember those two *phakir*s who came to your court? They were from the land of Bairāṭ, from the house of Śāhā Sekāndar. It was his sons who showed up in your realm. You had them collared, choked, and then thrown out. For this reason you have been struck by this horrible calamity. If you wish to see to your personal welfare, O *rājā*, I advise you to reconcile with those two brothers. We have now traced the brothers to a known area of the jungle. If you wish to be saved from this calamity, then you must submit to them now."

The king took heed and gathered a number of attendants to help locate Gāji, then he went to meet him. The king made proper obeisance at Gāji's feet. But when Kālu spotted the king, he began to rant, "This is the one, O brother, who grabbed us by the scruff of the neck and beat us! My body has not stopped aching since that time he tormented us in his palace." Hearing the tirade, the king was contrite and wept openly. He then clasped Kālu's feet with both his hands in supplication. Kālu spoke out, "Here is your situation, my good king." And as he spoke, the *rājā* got the picture and all of its implications. Kālu continued, "Your land has been ravaged by fire. If you want to make it right, here is your solution." Kālu then gave his orders: "First, you must become *muchalmān*. Afterwards I will lay out the nature of this obligation." Hearing the command, Śrī Rām, the king, took his attendants and together they recited the *kalemā* and became *muchalmān*. The king's counsellor and his friends all grasped the feet of Gāji. After adopting the ways of the *muchalmān*, all of them, now observant of the faith, brought Gāji and Kālu back with them. Kālu Śāhā wiped some of the dust from Gāji's feet and threw it toward the city, which instantly cooled down. The raging fires subsided and were soon extinguished. The power of that master, *prabhu*, was witnessed by everyone. Then they all made for Cāmpāi Nagar, reconciled to the situation.

When the king and his courtiers beheld the city intact, they were greatly relieved. The king immediately entered the palace's personal quarters. When he failed to find the queen, he began to lament. Again the king approached Gāji to discover her whereabouts. Weeping with a heartfelt remorse, the king fell at the feet of Gāji. But it was Kālu who spoke, "Listen, O King, I will explain the situation. Three cunning reprobates kidnapped your queen. She is comfortably ensconced inside the *machjid* that sits on the opposite bank of the river. If you go straight away you just might get back your queen." As soon as he heard these words from the mouth of Kālu, the *rājā* summoned and dispatched a select group of his personal attendants. When they reached the *machjed*, they found the door was locked; the *mahārānī* was safely sequestered in complete isolation. They devised a proper way to retrieve her and as soon as the king saw his queen, a thrill ran through his body.[15] Meanwhile Kālu and Gāji stayed back in the forest.

The *rājā* took his *rānī* back to the women's quarters of the palace. Then the *mahārājā* brought the brothers Kālu and Gāji and seated them on his elaborately decorated throne. Perched above this golden lion-throne were royal standards. It pleased the two brother to be seated there. Attar of roses was brought and sprinkled over their bodies, while incense and scented sandalwood candles burned all around. And in this manner Kālu and Gāji took up residence in that land, where they remained for quite some time. Eventually, Kālu Śāhā said to Gāji, "As I speak to our situation, as a *phakir*, I do not desire to, nor think it meet to, live in such luxury, so I am going to abandon this place and travel to some other place far, far away." Gāji replied, "Brother Kālu, you have spoken well. Let us leave this place now, for we should not reside here, nor anywhere, permanently." Continuing to speak in this vein, Gāji departed without hesitation. When the *rājā* and his courtiers saw them about to depart, they remonstrated with them. The two brothers did not return anyone's gaze, looked no one in the eye, for a *phakir* cannot be bound by attachment to this world. Giving up the attractions of this world, they headed into the forests.

15. Ābdur Rahim (p. 14) narrates that Kālu had implicated Khoyāj Khijir and his companions (only two companions in this text, but three in Ābdur Rahim's) without Gāji knowing. When the king and his men arrived at the *machjed*, Khoyāj Khijir and his companions were deep in meditation, performing their *jikir*, while the queen was completely separated from them. The four *pīrs* were bound hand and foot and taken back to the city of Cāmpāi Nagar, where an amazed Gāji immediately recognized them and released them with apologies. Ābdur Rahim notes that only then did Gāji begin to realize the full extent of Kālu's power. Khoyāj Khijir and company left, the king and queen returned to the palace, and Kālu and Gāji remained in the forest.

This humble poet sings a refrain suitable to the moment:

refrain In fear does the mind hopelessly wander in this world,
though the Stainless Lord be a constant presence.
The aspirations of this worldly life
come to little more than dreams in the night.

THE NARRATIVE OF GĀJI AND KĀLU TRAVERSING THE LAND OF THE WOODCUTTERS

The two brothers, Gāji and Kālu, moved on with equanimity, wandering through various regions. In this way they rambled until they reached a particularly beautiful part of the forest, where they encountered seven men cutting timber. Gāji said, "Kālu brother, I do not have the strength to press on so hard. Come, let us stop here at the woodcutters' home." Gāji politely addressed the woodcutters, "We are *phakirs* and would like to rest in your place for the day." When they heard this pair's plea, all seven men bowed their heads and wasted no time in making obeisances of salaam. Acknowledging Gāji's request, they escorted the two mendicants and settled them into their home. They washed their hands and feet while someone scurried off to the kitchen to have food prepared. The women ordered them, "Go to the market and fetch back fish and mutton. Be quick!"

There was no money to be had anywhere in the house, so the seven brothers pondered how they were going to feed their guests. Whatever tools they had—mainly billhooks and axes—they pawned, then they purchased and hauled home a variety foodstuffs. When the women had finished cooking, they fed the pair, then Gāji insisted the seven men themselves eat. When all seven had eaten, everyone was happily sated, settled, and satisfied. Gāji addressed the seven men, "Come along with me. I want to give you compensation." Gāji took the whole group to the banks of the river while he meditated on Āllā. He called out, "Gaṅgā Māsī! Auntie!" After repeating the call three times, Gaṅgā Devī appeared floating on the waters. Gaṅgā said, "My precious child, why have you called me? Tell me, has some calamity struck?" Gāji replied, "O Gaṅgā, please supply me with an abundance of riches." And when she heard the reason behind his request, she headed straight for the underworld kingdom of Pātāla. Down and down she journeyed to

Pātāla, where she presented herself to Padyāvati,[16] and little by little explained her story. "From his home in Bairāṭ, your sister's daughter's son, your grand nephew, has come to me requesting riches for some men." Paddā replied, "I wish to lay my own eyes on the boy, so I will go to him personally and provide the wealth he asks." Paddā departed right then, toting all manner of treasures and carrying four golden standards. As she made her way, Paddā anticipated the pleasure of meeting, and when she finally saw Gāji, she said, "You give great joy to my heart of hearts." In the meanwhile, Gāji had boarded a dinghy and was right there as Paddā reached the river's edge. She greeted Gāji with a salaam. She handed over to Gāji a generous allotment of varied treasures and then chatted with him. When they had finished talking, she bade farewell and headed back to the underworld citadel of Pātāla. He filled baskets for the woodcutters with whatever valuables and jewels she had furnished, then he made his way back where he proffered those treasures with profound obeisance.

The two *pirs*, Gāji and Kālu, recalled the name of the Śāhā Pari, the king of færies, and Gāji called out in a thunderous voice. Hearing his summons, the færie appeared in a flurry, for everyone responded immediately to the command of Gāji. This king of færies humbly grasped Gāji's feet and inquired: "For what reason have you summoned me?" Gāji replied: "Listen, færie, I called you because there is enormous work to be done for the benefit of those living in these environs. Please log this entire jungle and level the ground, then construct a commons, a meeting hall, on the site. Next construct a golden *machjed* of beautiful dimensions, splendid to behold." Receiving his command, the færie reluctantly demurred, still grasping Gāji's feet, "That is too much of a task just for me alone." So that færie sent for hundreds and hundreds of færies to come, a veritable army of them advancing on the forest. The færies cleared the jungle, and, after constructing the *machjed*, they took their leave and departed. The two men, Kālu and Gāji, entered the *machjed* and seated themselves on two gem-studded lion thrones. Four golden standards, their flags flying high, were erected on the four corners marking the four directions,

16. Padyāvati is pronounced *poddābati*, which is the pronunciation of Padmāvati, or Manasā, Goddess of Serpents. In the next verse, he shortens her name to Paddā, which is Padmā.

and a golden canopy was hoisted above. When they beheld the new city, the people exclaimed: "Alas, this is so incredible we surely have died and gone to heaven, for we have never before seen such a beautiful city in all the world!" Truly, it was a city of gold. There Gāji established a marketplace and decreed there would be justice against misdeeds and protection against any calamity. Though the place enjoyed an abundance of inhabitants, not one was made to pay taxes, so everyone lived quite comfortably in their homes.

When Kālu Śāhā witnessed Gāji's immense power and authority, he was deeply troubled, so he closed his eyes tight. Kālu muttered, "O Lord the Calculator, I do not fathom your play, but your name is a noose around my neck. Please show your mercy to me and let it rain gold in the city for three days!" No sooner had Kālu Sā completed the thought than it was acknowledged, and untold amounts of gold rained down in that place. The hundreds of residents of the city watched in amazement as the gold fell, and they quickly scooped it up and hauled it home. When Gāji Śā witnessed this with his own eyes, he was deeply gratified, and he emotionally offered up his thanks there in the *darbār* court. When Gāji Śāhā was satisfied, he took Kālu, and together they wandered in and around the place. Only after some days of roaming here and there did they finally reach the ends of the city, which shone everywhere with an incredible opulence. Seeing the magnificent luster of the settlement, Gāji and Kālu were both deeply gratified, and they aptly named it Sonāpur, the City of Gold. Because they had been responsible for its construction, the *phakir* observed, "It would be inappropriate that we should leave after only a few days." So Gāji and Kālu remained taking up residence there in the city. They remained deeply contented and countless days passed. The two brothers whiled away their time in that magnificent place, keeping their minds focused on the Stainless Lord, Nirañjan.[17]

17. Ābdur Rahim ruptures the narrative at this point and inserts extradiagetically thirty-two lines of printed text (one *payār* couplet and ten *tripadi* stanzas) describing the nature of pure love (*prem*)—both human and divine—which introduces a didactic element that anticipates coming events. The text reads as follows (pp. 17–18):

> Pure, divine love, *prem*, flooded my heart—its experience indescribable. He who has experienced that immersion knows; is it possible for anyone else to fathom? The knowledge mediated by the physical body, the eyes, the ears, cannot perceive

Contented and settled in Sonāpur, Gāji lived comfortably. As long as Gāji and Kālu were present in the *machjed*, there was no end to the bliss of the markets of the city. The pair occupied their lion thrones with gravitas, quietly commanding respect. With their effulgent golden

---

or localize its miraculous power anywhere. How does this formless love operate on what is embodied? Pure love permeates it through and through. In the same way that particles of light from the sun distribute their luminescence uniformly, at once and all around, the formless permeates the bodily form. Its play appears like so many strands wound together to form a magical garland of illusion, its playful breeze tickles the heart, the mind. When one is smitten by pure divine love and sits with the gaze turned inward, he becomes oblivious to mind and body. For one whose eyes are opened in this way, the longer he looks in this meditation, the less he sees until there is nothing else but love. As the sun to the pink lotus, and the moon to the blue, so too is the world blessed by the blossoming of pure love. As the moth is held to be sublime for incinerating itself, offering its life to the beloved, so too one lost in the extremes of pure love will try to fuse his heart, his life-breath, with his lover's. The ways of love are like this: Only when one has become dead while alive, is it possible to become truly ennobled. The earth, the sky, the moon, the sun, the stars, and day and night—all of them are impelled by the love that is pure. In that flash when total annihilation occurs, the individual who has become dispassionate, detached, will perish, leaving no trace. Alas, from him who does not cultivate that priceless gem, that treasure will slip away through neglect. You should consult one who has lost his mind and body to the natural quality that is love.† In the beginning the Lord was formless, but he created the treasure that is love, and immersed Himself completely in it. By means of his effulgence, his light, did He will the form of Mohāmmad into existence, to descend. Maddened by His love, exercising His power of light, He created the three worlds. Were I to labor for a thousand years I would not be able to explore fully the limits of this matter. Enveloped in that orb of its effulgence, Ābdur Rahim advises: Exercise that pure love while you are still alive.

†Because of the reference several lines earlier to the catch phrase *jiyante marā*, "dead while living," there could well be an allusion to more esoteric bodily practices where *bastu* (here translated as "natural quality") could also mean substance, and is often enough used as shorthand for the very substance of life, that is, semen. Given the context, however, it would be the kind of inference left to the teacher to draw for the student—though this text would hardly seem to be one studied in this way. The physically generative nature of *bastu* has a centuries' old history among Bengali religious practitioners, from *nāth*s and *sahajiyā*s to *bāul*s, and when incorporated by Sufi practitioners of *yoga*, it was often connected with light, which is intimated here in several places. For more, see Shashibhusan Dasgupta, *Obscure Religious Cults*, 3rd ed. (Calcutta: Firma KLM, 1969), and Āhmad Śarīph, ed., *Bāṃlār sūphī sāhitya: Ālocanā o naykhāni sambalita* (Ḍhākā: Bāṃlā Ekādemī, 1373 BS [1969]).

hue, it was impossible to imagine the two brothers as anything other than close kin. At night they would stretch out to sleep on their cots. Who could have imagined that one night seven færies from Āllā's Makka happened by the place of the pair's residence, each of whom was mesmerized beholding the astonishing beauty of the city. They got down from their chariots to get a better look. The citadel reflected gold like the shimmer of a metropolis, as if it were Rāvaṇ's legendary citadel perched in the middle of Laṅkā. The seven took in the city's splendor and so approached the *machjed* to pray. Together as one they slowly tiptoed in and leaned over to see the magnificent forms of the *jauban*s: the two brothers were fast asleep on their beds, and a great bewitching light emanated from their bodies. Gazing at Gāji, one by one, each of the færies was utterly discombobulated and slumped down insensate in turn. Only after some time did they eventually come around and regain their wits. They all competed to praise his stunning good looks: "Alas such gloriously irresistible beauty outshines even the sun and the moon together." The færies quivered with nervous embarrassment at being in such close proximity to such a splendid body. Staring at Gāji's magnificent form, doubting, the færies wondered aloud, "Is there a woman anywhere who can match Gāji's beauty?" But there was one among them who spoke up, "There is a young maiden of singular beauty, the likes of whose sensuous charms are nowhere else to be seen. Her voice is sweet like the *kokil* bird[18]—there is none more beautiful in the triple world." Another færie interrupted her, "Tell us details. What is the name of the king? What is his daughter's name?" Answering these and similar queries, the færie replied, "In the south there is one Brāhmaṇ Nagar whose king is known as Maṭuk. It is hemmed in on all four sides by rivers, which sets off its idyllic splendor. Only *brāhmaṇ*s live there; it is populated by no other social groups. The king's Gõsāi, his guarantor and second, is named Dakṣinā, while the king's daughter goes by the name of Cāmpāvatī. With seven brothers, this prodigious beauty is the youngest of the siblings. One hundred thousand armed men surround her. This maiden is never seen except in the company of that entourage." The færie continued, "We should fly

18. The *kokil,* or Asian koel (*Eudynamys scolopaceus*), is a large member of the cuckoo order of birds, the Cuculiformes; the male's pleasing, distinctive "coo-hoo" call, often perceived as erotically charged, has given it a notable role in Indian belles-lettres.

Gājī Śāh there, for the two joined together as a single couple would present an image of beauty perfected." And forthwith they picked up Gāji's cot and off they flew.

The author says, "Listen all you friends, What fate has written can never be undone."

THE FÆRIES FLY GĀJĪ ŚĀH TO BRĀHMAṆ NAGAR

Gājī lay dead asleep, so the group bent down and picked up the bedstead with Gāji on it. Up and away they flew the bed and soon they arrived in Brāhmaṇ Nagar. As they drew near the palace pavilion they looked all around and saw that all of guards had fallen asleep; they all lay oblivious in their respective quarters. So the group of færies easily entered Cāmpā's private pavilion. They gathered round, beholding Cāmpā's beauty. Then they settled Gāji's bed beside hers, on the right-hand side. They scooted the beds together as if they were one, and then they systematically compared the unparalleled beauty of each, attempting to discriminate any difference. Gāji's beautiful form was matched precisely by hers. It was as if the sun and moon had come together as one. The beauty of one fully matched and emulated the beauty of the other; they were identical. It was as if they had maneuvered into an astral syzygy—that traditional conjunction of the sun and moon yoked together—two heavenly bodies perfectly aligned and matched. One of the færies then proposed, "Think about this: what if this couple were to get married some day? There would be no end to their joy." And talking like this, they all went into the king's gardens, and there in Maṭuk Rājā's estates, they beheld the various flora in perfectly neat rows, in the midst of which stood a golden pavilion surrounded by a riot of flowering plants. Imagining what might transpire, they perched and swung playfully on the branches of a profusion of fruiting trees, the bounty of which the færies soon greedily ate. And in this manner those færies romped through the king's gardens. Now listen, everyone as I write about the end of Gāji's death-like sleep.

Lying on his bed, Gājī Pīr was in a deep, deep sleep, his body totally inert like a corpse—but that sleep was a spell cast by divine intervention. Then Gājī Śāh's hand fell on Cāmpā's breast. The moment his hand touched her body, the virgin girl's heart palpitated wildly, and she sat bolt upright. The young woman imagined that it must be the servant girl, but what servant girl had ever dared to touch her breast? What met the young woman's eyes was this: she found herself holding Gāji's hand. Looking upon Gāji's prepossessing form, the young woman involuntarily shuddered with spontaneous delight. Beguiled, she stared in disbelief at his exquisite body and silently gasped in alarm, "Oh, what has my all-compassionate Lord seen fit to arrange for me?" Staring over and again at Gāji's arresting beauty, the young woman fidgeted, agitated in the extreme. The blessed one slipped ever so slowly back onto her bedstead. Carefully scrutinizing every part of Gāji's physique had unsettled her completely, but instinct took over and the young woman quickly assumed her place in Gāji's bed. In her heart of hearts, Cāmpāvatī worried to herself, "I do not know him or anything about his rank and birth." But his irresistible good looks overwhelmed her, and the young virgin was positively overwrought, completely intoxicated. She began to run her hands over Gāji's body. And the time passed just like that. Anxious, flustered, the young virgin muttered, "Wake up, you master thief, how much longer are you going to sleep?" The unfortunate Cāmpā cried out, "I want to look into your eyes!"

That exclamation finally interrupted Gājī's sleep, and their eyes locked. He beheld Cāmpāvatī seated at his feet. The moment he saw Cāmpāvatī, Gāji was smitten, instantly passed out, and fell back onto the bed. The young woman fetched some rosewater and gently dabbed it on Gāji Śāh's face; he slowly awoke and sat up on the bed. Gazing at Cāmpā's exquisite body, he trembled violently. "Where is the *machjed*? Where is my brother Kālu? In what strange place have I landed up? I do not know this maiden whose body would slay even the demon Murā.[19] I cannot understand to whom this golden palace belongs." Staring at Cāmpā, Gājī mulled over these puzzles and, feeling embarrassed, indeed humiliated and thoroughly confused, Śāhā could only pound his head in wonderment.

19. Murā was an *asura* who had won the boon of being able to slay anyone he touched, but after challenging successfully every god in the universe to battle—and they all refused to engage—he went after Yam, the god of death, who refused to accept Murā's order to stop killing. Yam argued that he answered only to Nārāyaṇ, so Murā headed to the ocean of milk where Viṣṇu lay on the serpent Śeṣa. As Murā was on his way, Kṛṣṇa descended on Murā's citadel, broke down the barriers, slew his sons, and eventually killed Murā, hence Kṛṣṇa's epithet of Murāmathana.

Cāmpāvatī spoke, "You burglar, listen to this piece of intelligence: Surely you have heard the name Maṭuk Rājā and you know who he is! Know you are in Brāhmaṇ Nagar, where everyone is a *brāhmaṇ*. Listen carefully to what I say: there are no other social groups. The king's *gosāi*, his champion, goes by the name of Dakṣiṇā. He can lay waste the earth in the batting of an eye. My mother, Nilāvatī, has seven sons, all my elder brothers. Maṭuk Rājā is my father, and this palace belongs to him. Where did you come from, you housebreaker, where is your place of residence? What is your name and what is your birth? Tell me everything about you! I am impressed by your incredible boldness—how did you manage to sneak inside my private quarters? How could you evade the guards all around? How did you not fall into their hands and avoid capture? Father's strongman, his *gõsāi*, is known as Dakṣiṇā Rāy, and in the morning he is sure to come. He will lay hold of you, and just as surely he will eat you!"

Gāji Śāhā replied, "Listen, you who have stolen my heart. Let me now tell you my story. My father is well known in this world as Śāhā Sekāndar, and my natal home is in Bairāṭ Nagar. There are untold numbers of kings in this world, and all of them pay tribute to my father. You should know that when he went to the home of the insurgent Bali Rājā, the latter was terrified and feared for his life from the moment he spotted my father. He fled. Bali Rājā's virgin daughter was the beautiful Ajupā Sundari—to save his life, Bali Rājā bartered that princess to my father in marriage. It was from her womb that I was born. Eleven years passed as expected, then one day the Bādsā sent for me: 'You must assume the lion throne and rule.' But kingship was not for me; I could not, would not rule. I became a *phakir* and threw this coarse patchwork cloak over my shoulders. In his anger, my father threw me under the feet of elephants. When the elephants saw me, they all fled, and seeing this made my father even more angry. He bound a boulder to my throat and threw me into the sea. I took the name of the Lord, repeating it mentally, and the Stainless Lord, Prabhu Nirañjan, buoyed me. My father then took a needle and cast it into the ocean and ordered me to go and fetch it; I did. So I took leave of my mother and father, paid my earnest respects, and set out for any land that would take me away from there. I made good my escape when my mother was sleeping, and under the cover of night I abandoned that place. The crown and kingship—everything I had till then—I disowned. With the patchwork cloak around my neck I left. I have an adopted older brother named Kālu, and he, too, left with me. We came to a vast expanse of water, and my staff carried us over the waves to the other shore. By nightfall we arrived in the environs belonging to one Śrīrām. The only people we met in the entire area were *hinduyān*, so we tried to get them to recite the *kalemā* and become *machalmān*. We soon bade goodbye to the place and not long after arrived in the forest where we took up residence. For three days we failed to encounter a single human being until finally we stumbled across seven woodcutters deep in the woods. We accosted them as they were working, and they graciously took us back to their house. There they fed us until we were sated. We in turn provided them with an abundance of riches. Together we cleared the jungle and founded a city there. Once we had dreamed it into existence, we named it Sonāpur, the City of Gold. Large numbers of people swarmed there, and we erected a *machjed*. There the two of us were lying comfortably on our golden bedsteads—so how on earth did I land up in your private quarters? You call me a thief, but it is you who have stolen me."

The composer of this poem says, "Both of them were overwhelmed by love. Go ahead and marry to your mutual hearts' delight."

Paying close attention to Gāji's explanation,
the blessed Cāmpāvatī replied,
    "That story is a deceitful sham.
Listen up, you hardened criminal,
your head will soon be severed,
    so why have you come here only to die?
Your only great accomplishment
is that you, a *machalman*,
    managed to get into my private quarters!
When my father lays hold of you,
he will dispatch you to Dakṣiṇā Rāy's quarters
    to be cut to pieces.
Why have you slipped in here?
How can you speak so fearlessly
    when I am going to make a sacrifice of you?
Were the multitudes of guards to hear you,
they would apprehend you in an instant and
    you would end up with neck severed."
Gāji countered, "Listen my lovely maiden,

your beauty is all I treasure,
so why do you keep repeating these threats?
You show your fear of Dakṣiṇā Rāy,
but I feel no trepidation,
no dread on his account."

Gāji continued, "Pay heed you beautiful maiden to what I submit. I had lain down to sleep in the *machjed*. I had not even imagined Brāhmaṇ Nagar in my dreams. Just who are you? Whose residence is this? Yes, you are a *brāhmaṇ* beauty and I a *jaban*—but I certainly do not wish to die. Your beauty alone rattles me, makes my body shake and shudder. I harbor fear of neither the king nor Dakṣiṇā Rāy. Were I to be separated from you, my heart would never survive—better that a sword cut me in two. Looking at you, my chest mysteriously swells beyond constraint." Declaring himself in this way, Gāji struggled with a profound emotional trauma and could only weep.

This daughter of the king was an accomplished scholar of the sacred texts, and so she examined the astrological treatises and ran her calculations. She realized through her computations that whether in heaven or on earth, whether above ground or below, wherever they appeared, Gāji would be her husband, her lord, her *svāmī*. Campā breathlessly spoke, "Get up, my lord, do not cry, for you are indeed my husband, my *svāmī*, the life of my life. You are the one who is my husband, and I am always your wife, just as Śiv and Pārvvatī could never be separated."

To recover, Gāji drank some water and washed his face. He sat up, feeling strangely calm and refreshed.

Cāmpā continued, "Listen to my words, my lord: Fate has written that we are to be married to one another. Mother, father, relatives say that in this worldly existence, no one can counter what Fate has written on one's forehead. I am a virgin *brāhmaṇ* girl, you are a *machalmān*. I will take you to my father straight away. I will explain to him what the sacred texts say—and that I know deep within my heart that we are to be married. Since you are already a *phakir*, I will become a mendicant *phakirāni*. Going door to door the two of us will beg food and eat; wherever we land up is where the two of us shall stay, just as Śiv and Durgā were ever together. The beauty that you, Gāji, possess will manifest greater and enhance further my womanly form, as if the sun and the moon have risen together in the sky."

Gāji slipped one of his rings onto her finger and Cāmpā's ring he placed on his own. Then they sat on the bed together and exchanged chewed betel quids.[20] Cāmpāvatī then divided her hair into two parts and bound each of Gāji Śāh's feet. "I am ritually binding your feet so that they never abandon me. You will know me to be your supreme servant to the judgement day at the end of time." Gāji replied, "You—whom I now call the beloved of my heart—may God's mercy be with you should you ever have to abandon me."[21] Then Gāji lay down on Cāmpa's bed and drifted off to sleep, while she nodded off on Gāji's bed. Together as one did they fall into a deep sleep and in that slumber, the two had entered heaven.

What happens at this juncture is going to drive both the lovers mad—listen, everyone, as I write about the actions of the færies.

There in the king's gardens, the færies were busy absentmindedly over-indulging in the remarkable selection of fruits when suddenly one of them remembered Gāji's situation. One of the færies said, "Elder sister, listen up, remember we brought Gāji to Cāmpā's personal apartments. His brother, Kālu, was left alone in the *machjed*. Come, let us return Gāji to his place. The night is coming to a close, we must do something to rectify this, to set it straight, before night settles." So right away they flew off to Cāmpā's private quarters. When the færies reached, they gathered around the bedsteads. Staring at the couple they began to talk excitedly. "My goodness, I know that Gāji and this beautiful maiden must have coupled. They have exchanged beds and rings with one another." And so they feverishly prepared to whisk Gāji back to Sonārpur, the Golden City. "There is no avoiding it—the affliction wrought from missing Cāmpā is sure to kill him. And it will be the same for Cāmpā when she fails to see Gāji. Each will wail and weep and, in their distress, seek to abandon their lives. I see no way out of the mess we have made. We are certain to be reckoned sinners in Āllā's *dargā*. I cannot imagine what can be done to rectify what has hap-

20. The exchange of chewed betel is an act of love that generally symbolizes consummation or its intent, but, appropriately enough in this tale, the author does not make that explicit.

21. Binding the feet of the groom with the bride's hair is a traditional ritual act of marriage, indicating both submission, but more importantly, future fidelity.

pened." Another færie then suggested, "Listen, this is the real story: If that particular fate was written on both of their foreheads, then it is certain that the two will be reunited." With that sensible observation four of the færies grabbed hold of the Gāji's bedstead. They lifted it up and let the wind help carry them along. So it was that the færies ferried Gāji in his bed and it was not long before they caught sight of the Golden City of Sonārpur. Still lost in his heavenly sleep, Gāji was aware of nothing as they safely deposited his bed there beside Kālu Śā.

Listen attentively to what transpired after the færies took their leave.

The night passed and the day finally broke. Kālu woke up and sat up. He prodded Gāji to sit up, chiding him, "You have slept long enough! Open your eyes, the call for prayer has already sounded." Gāji awoke and quickly jumped up. When he looked around he was speechless. He was back in the *machjed* beside brother Kālu. He caught no glimpse of the beautiful maiden of the previous night, yet he was on Cāmpā's bedstead with her ring on his finger. Slapping himself to try to make sense of it all, Gāji looked, but simply could not see; he was agitated, mad, and speech utterly failed him. It was as if a bolt of lightning had suddenly struck his head. Gāji sat on the bed, immobile, forsaken and forlorn; his breathing grew shallow. He collapsed as if he were dead. Gāji wept uncontrollably and cried out in sheer agony. Seeing Gāji's flustered state, Kālu slipped into another room and fetched cold water, returned and doused his face. Kālu Śā then interrogated him, "Why are you crying out, brother? The two of us, we brothers, slept together here in the *machjed*, so tell me, what did you see in your dream?" At first Gāji was unable to respond and could only sob, ever more deliriously, for it would be impossible for Kālu to fathom the truth of his mad adventure. Gāji was speechless and could give Kālu no clue as to the cause. Now himself fretting in panic, Kālu fell at Gāji's feet. And all of the farmers and other people in the land grieved when they saw Gāji's abject condition. Gājī could manage to speak to no one at all; he simply sprawled listlessly on the bed, weeping.

Gāji Śāhā persisted in this helpless condition back in Sonāpur. Now listen, everyone, to Cāmpāvatī's indisposition.

When the night had passed and dawn broke, the rays of the sun prompted Cāmpāvatī to sit up. Perched on her bed, Cāmpāvatī looked all around, but nowhere did she espy her beloved, yet she had his bed and his ring. Out of control, wailing from grief, Cāmpāvatī erupted in flood of tears. Her eyes saw nothing as a darkness seemed to fall across the room, and she stretched out on the bed in a fit. The young woman tore off and smashed her traditional eight ornaments. She mussed her hair and ripped off her necklace. Her clothes refused to stay on her body and down came her hair, disheveled, completely undone. She went mad, writhing in the dirt and grime as she wailed.

Cāmpāvatī had fifty female servants in the house, and they were frantic when they saw her in this state. They went flying to the queen, who was in her quarters, and between sobs they excitedly apprised her of the situation. "Listen, dear madam, you must go quickly to the princess! The young maiden Cāmpāvatī weeps uncontrollably and thrashes around in the dirt and dust." To hear this certainly unsettled the queen, so she quickly took herself to Cāmpāvatī's side. "My child, my dear child," she tried to soothe her as she pulled Cāmpāvatī onto her lap and hugged her close. "What has happened, my child, to make you cry so?" Her mother sat her down in front of her and pulled her hair back up, tightly bound, as she questioned her, herself now quietly weeping. "What did you see in your dreams, my child, tell me now. More than my seven sons, I love you, little one. You are most dear to me. You are my precious darling, the apple of my eye; you are my life breath."

As soon as the local *brāhmaṇ* women heard of the commotion, they came to console her, but she offered no response, her eyes only brimmed with tears. When Maṭuk Rājā finally heard, he himself came to her rooms, and along with him came Cāmpāvatī's seven brothers. All nine of her maternal uncles arrived to inquire of her, and all of her aunts came bearing flower garlands. Each of her uncles in turn asked her about her crying, but the young woman offered no explanation, and the cascade of tears simply would not stop. The chief physician checked her pulse and then gave his diagnosis: "I have determined beyond doubt, it is the madness of love."[22] The various doctors then prescribed medicines and talismans, but no matter what they tried, Cāmpāvatī remained unsettled.

22. As far back as the *ayurvedic* medical text of the *Caraka saṃhitā* (ca. 2nd century BCE), madness is reckoned to be from three things: from physical maladjustments, from possession by hungry ghosts and spirits, and from *bhāva*, love, which can also manifest as religious love.

Cāmpāvatī passed the next three nights sobbing. For three days straight she ate absolutely nothing. The king and everyone else had been grieving over Cāmpā. So finally Cāmpā said to them, "Please everyone leave and go back to your places. I will explain everything to my mother now." So Cāmpā finally spoke, "Listen, my dear mother, let me tell you the real story." Cāmpā continued, "O mother, listen carefully to my words, but please promise to protect me, for what I have to say is extremely difficult. What I must tell you is tearing my heart apart."

"Your story is safe with me, my child, so speak honestly. May I eat your head if I share it with anyone."[23]

Cāmpā replied, "Listen carefully to what I'm telling you, mother. In the same manner that you protected and nurtured me in your womb for ten months and ten days,[24] please, you must keep my predicament confidential, to yourself."

"I promise, my child, I give you my word. Whatever you tell me will go no further."

The poet says—Listen, everyone, to what Cāmpāvatī shared with her mother.

Amidst bouts of weeping, she spoke to her mother, "What I have to tell you, mother, is rending my heart. What I encountered, my dear one, I am at a loss to describe. It is driving my heart and mind to distraction, alas, I feel I am dying. Dying! How can I tell anyone what exactly has afflicted me deep down? It tears at my heart to relate the tale of that thief of love. There is no man like him anywhere in the world. His face shone brighter than hundreds of thousands of tens of millions of moons. Such physical beauty exists nowhere else in the triple world. Compared to him the gods, *devatās*, and celestial musicians, *gandharvas*, are just so much rubbish; compared to him the færies are like so much burnt ash—that is the kind of stunning beauty that Bidhātā, the God of Fate, granted him. I am not mistaken, not deceived in any of this, even to the tiniest degree; I cannot forget any detail. His physical

23. To take an oath on the head of one's child places the child in danger if broken, a marker of seriousness of the most extreme promise, hence the expression "May I eat your head . . ."

24. Ten months and ten days, the traditional calculation of gestation based on the lunar calendar.

stature bespoke an extraordinary strength of character. Alas, I feel I am dying, dying, simply dying from the shame! What blemish, what stain has he left on my own spotless character?" Interrupted with bouts of weeping, the young maiden managed slowly to eke out her story. "What can I say when the words coming from my own mouth are not even in my own voice? Just to speak of this makes my heart stand still."

"Please listen, please, my dear mother, give my your full and affectionate attention. I was dead asleep on my bed. How could that cunning thief have entered without me being in the least aware? His bedstead was pushed right up beside my own. We were sleeping soundly when the beds were somehow joined together as one. I was lost in a profoundly deep sleep when I was suddenly awakened by a hand fondling my breast. I was agitated, I trembled, and then, filled with indignation, I thought to fetch a sword to hack the miscreant to pieces. It was only then that I actually looked at him. My eyes were riveted. It was as if the full moon had suddenly risen before me. The splendor of his moonlike face exceeded that of tens upon tens of millions of ordinary moons. I fainted from the sight and fell back on the bed. Sometime later, my dear mother, I came to and regained my senses. I clasped his feet and woke him. I made him to understand how much his actions had frightened me. Then he wept, expressing a profound grief—and to see him cry like that, mother, simply broke my heart. Taking the end of my sari, I wiped his face, and he stole my heart. I questioned him. 'How did you manage to make your way into my private chambers? What is your name? Tell me, what is your social rank, your *jāti*? Who are your father and mother, and where do you reside?'"

"Hearing this interrogation he then settled himself and in a sweet voice spoke. 'The town of Bairāṭ Nagar is my home, my name is Gājī Śāhā. My father is Chekāndar Sāhā, a veritable treasure of virtue. My mother is Ajupā and my *jāti* is *mochalmān*. That was the place of my birth, but now I reside in Sonāpur, the City of Gold. I have one older brother by the name of Kālu, who remains with me. We two brothers lay down on our beds and slept. How I got here and for what reason I do not know. What is the name of this place, where is it? Is it a place I have not previously heard of? How am I supposed to tell you how I managed to land up here? I have no recollection of coming—and for that my death is surely found in this bed. With no protection, my life will be finished. When I realize that I will never see my brother Kālu again, I can only weep in grief.'"

"With a feeling of intense sorrow, I fell at his feet. Grasping both of his feet I began to cry. 'Whatever the *māyā* of this created world has brought about, so be it,' and with that I pulled him to my lap and hugged him. Only then did a calming peace enter both our hearts and minds. In order to do things properly, to uphold *dharma*, I swear this oath: I am his wife. He alone is my husband. I will remain with him for all my days. And so it has come to pass that though my heart leaps with joy, I am truly dead. I exchanged my ring and bed with him, so this ring on my finger belongs to him. See now, this is the cot on which he has slept. Alas, alas, I feel I am dying, I am dying, for I see no way out. What am I to do since the lord of my heart has abandoned me?"

Between her whimpering and crying, Cāmpā repeated this over and over: "The treasure I had found I have lost. What am I to do? How can I go in search of him? I see no alternative but to slit my own throat. Aiee, aiee, O lord of my life, you have such a hard heart! You tossed aside your weak, submissive servant, but where have you gone? In the deadly tow of this undercurrent I am helpless, foundering in the waters of a shoreless sea—what can I do? I am surely drowned, for I do not know how to swim. When are you, the lord of my life, going to rescue me, this wretched woman, from this vast ocean of life? Hey, life of my life, my soulmate, where are you? This miserable woman is pleading with you, pitiful and in great distress. Please find me and save me, lord of my heart, for I am certain to die out of grief for you. O my lord, come back and grant me just one more look, then surely my life will be salvaged. If by chance fate had made me a bird, I would flap my wings and off I would fly to find you. Wherever you have gone, my lord, I will track you down. Do tell me please where I can search you out. I cannot forget you for even a minute. This obsessing and fretting will, in the end, kill me. When you disappeared, you rendered my body and life worthless. I will die, incinerated by the flames of separation from you. What can I do, O my lord, where can I flee? When I look at your ring and your bed, my insides are ablaze—but those two priceless objects signal my sure death. There is nothing more but to greet the day of my demise. In this way my body will burn up everything, for the flames cannot be checked even for a moment."[25]

Ceaselessly did our heroine prattle and weep. But the Holy Protector will ensure that you meet your lord again.

refrain Through the fires of my separation from you, life
slips away.
O lord of my life, reveal to me where you are!

Over and over again Cāmpāvatī cried and vented her anguish. "Where have you gone, turning me into a most unfortunate wretch? The fate now revealed to me is surely monstrous. Alas, I die consumed in the fires of separation from him. Oh, Gāji, what was going on in your heart? Why on earth did you swear an oath of love? You had sworn, you promised, 'I will not abandon you,' but you did! What blunder, what horrible imperfection, what flaw do I have to make you abandon me, this miserable creature? I will find no husband in the world equal to Gāji. Without him, my life is useless rubbish. Cut off from my lord, how can I survive? I want only this: may my life desert this wretched body."

And in this distraught way Cāmpāvatī wailed and wept. The sweet woman slumped to the ground, crying in endless anguish. Watching this display, her mother, Nilāvatī, could not check her own weeping herself, so she picked up her young daughter and gently pulled her to her lap and hugged her. Profoundly the two sobbed together, their eyes overflowed. Eventually, her mother did manage to calm her down and get her to sit still. The queen consoled her and commiserated with a motherly affection, "Do not cry anymore, my beloved child, what comes of weeping? Your mother and father only are responsible for your birth in this world, but the sacred texts say that what you yourself do is guided by the hand of Bidhātā, the god of fate. If it is truly written on your forehead that he and he alone is your husband, rest assured

25. There is more to this conceit than simply the searing agony of pain when separated from the beloved (*viraha*), for in traditional Indic culture, the perfect wife who mounts her husband's funeral pyre to immolate herself and become *satī* is believed to spontaneously ignite the pyre from her immeasurable purity and fidelity.

that it is meant to be so. You were born as the direct result of my worship of Hara and Gaurī. You are special, my only daughter among seven sons. Listen carefully to what I am telling you and take it to heart. If people hear of this, your social standing and elevated ranking will surely be ruined. Take care, my child, never to appear in public. By the grace of God may you remain safe here at home."

The young woman heeded her mother's counsel, and she remained isolated and alone, pointedly meditating on her husband. This beautiful maiden applied herself, striving ever so hard to follow her mother's lead. Whenever she looked in someone's direction, she turned her gaze inward, and within that piercing gaze she conjured up Gāji's glittering form. Her eyes would brim with tears as she contemplated his brilliant moon face. Whether up or down, this way or that, she saw nothing but Gāji's beautiful body. Gāji's figure was mesmerizing, an enchanting ocean of beauty. This lovely young maiden constantly reached out for the farther shore of this ocean that was his alluring charm, and in this way this singular beauty immersed herself in Gāji's splendor. Apart from his image, she recognized nothing. Even when someone else was present, the maiden could only imagine Gāji in her mind's eye. Bereft of her senses, she no longer knew what had transpired or what was going on around her. Cāmpā was drowning in an ocean of *prem*, a pure and unadulterated love. As she bobbed up and down, a sapphire, the pure blue jewel of *prem*, rose from the depths, and this virgin girl accepted this treasure with joyful praise, and wore it around her neck as a protective talisman.[26]

O brother, is there anyone on earth as blessed in their faith as the one whose heart has journeyed into the depths of the pure love, esk, *that is true? Remain calm and still, my dear Cāmpā, and have no fear. I will go quickly and report to Gāji.*

Now, as the pen decrees, you must move quickly back to that place where Kālu and Gāji remain in Sonāpur, the City of Gold. Listen atten-

26. The allusion here is to the characterization of Rādhā's love for Kṛṣṇa, which was elegantly and poignantly characterized by the *vaiṣṇav* Rūpa Gosvāmī in his treatise titled *Ujjvala nilāmaṇi*, "the blazing sapphire of love," the standard text by which to measure the greatest possible form of love. The narrator in the following signature line equates this *prema* with *esk* (Persian *'ishq*), passionate love characterizing the burning love a Sufi has for God.

tively, all of you discriminating connoisseurs of love, to a vivid description of Gāji Sāhā's condition.

After Gāji was safely deposited with his brother Kālu, the færies flew back to their own country. The two brothers slept away there in the *machjid*. As Āllā commanded, the night finally came to a close. The birds perched on the branches of trees sang mellifluously and the chickens scattered throughout the compound began to cluck. The muezzin arrived and delivered the morning call to prayer, and Kālu got up to begin his required prostrations. Preparing his tobacco, the diligent man tried to awaken Gāji. "Up, up, get up, brother! Sleep-time is over." Hearing his call, Gāji Sāhā arose to a shock: looking around, Sāhā took in his surroundings. "Where is the beautiful princess? And where is her private chamber?" Upon seeing her bed and her ring, he was completely undone. It was as if a lightning bolt had struck his head. He cried out, "Cāmpā, Cāmpā!" and slapped his chest with his hands. With a loud cry, Sāhā fell to the ground. When Kālu Sāhā witnessed this, he was astonished. Gāji gasped for air so violently that he hyperventilated, his breath escaped into the sky—he passed out.

GĀJI SĀHĀ'S VEXATION OVER CĀMPĀVATĪ

Sāhā awoke
just as the dawn broke.
    He opened his eyes and
called out to his brother Kālu.
When he failed to see Cāmpā.
    he immediately slumped down.
Crazed, totally insensate,
he fell to the ground;
    nothing remained of his mental faculties.
A short time later, with his fists
he battered his head and
    called out in agonizing sobs,
"Oh, aiee, Cāmpāvatī!
You make the sparkle in my eye!
    But where are you?
It is beyond me! I cannot say
just how I managed to slip

into your bedroom.
Just who are you, my love?
I have no idea,
but the minions of Āllā must.
I broke my solemn promise when
I left you and was returned here.
Just exactly who are you, my beloved?
If I am separated from you,
if I cannot be with you,
how will I survive?
The breath of my life is slipping away,
for I see no solution;
how can my heart be calmed?
I am going mad
because of you!
I must find a way to Brāhmaṇ Nagar.
I will surely slit my throat
to sacrifice my life,
if I cannot find you.
Alas, that woman, queen of my heart,
is making me so delirious that
my heart bursts day and night.
How can I go on?
A fire rages inside when I look
at that ring you gave me.
Alas, my life is slipping away,
please tell me
how this can be resolved?
Here I feel am dying, so
I cry out in distress, while you
remain hidden in your private quarters.
Focus your attention on me,
aiee, please rescue me,
lest I suffer a sure death!
Oh, my sweetheart,
I am totally flummoxed;
however will I find you?"
Gaji carried on with senseless blather,
whining and keening,
until he slumped to the ground, spent.
Kālu, distressed, cried out in empathy,

and grabbed hold of him,
    pulling him in close embrace.
He drew him up in his arms,
as his own eyes brimmed with tears
    questioning Gājī's besottedness.
"Tell me, dear brother,
what is behind all this madness?
    Who has stolen your heart?"
Completely overwrought
choked and unable to answer,
    Gāji began again to weep.
Kālu grasped his feet,
which rendered Gāji immobile.
    Then he began the interrogation.
But no words emerged from Gāji's mouth;
he remained deflated, head down,
    weeping, his sorrow flowing.
Soon many people
came crowding in and reverently
    fell at his feet to inquire,
but he could offer no response.
He could only shed tears,
    which further alarmed them all.
Soon, different people offered
various homespun remedies and medicines,
    but Gājī Sāhā refused to swallow any of them.
When the patient is infected with love,
can any medicine be effective
    in healing that sickness?
All the town's inhabitants
came together and
    offered up their earnest prayers.
Seeing Gājī in this abject condition
unnerved everyone present,
    causing them to grieve and wail.
In his pathetic state
Gāji finally addressed Kālu Sāhā, but
    he spoke slowly and deliberately.
"I am too distracted to stay;
I must leave and
    quit this country.

I can remain here no longer.
I must get away from this place—
listen brother to what I propose:
Why not come with me? Come!
Together let us search for Brāhmaṇ Nagar,
for love is running amok in my heart."

When all those gathered heard what Gājī had declared, they were so upset that they could only beat their heads and weep. Without exception the denizens of the city were unhinged, emotionally overwrought. Kālu Sāhā found himself growing increasingly exasperated as he witnessed it all. He grilled Gājī: "Brother, tell me what is the reason for this sulk, this incessant sobbing? By the grace of Āllā, Sāhā, tell me what is going on!" As soon as Gājī Sāhā heard the invocation of Āllā, he again began to weep, but sat up, then he looked straight at Kālu, drew near him, and finally opened up. "Listen, brother, my blessed and dearest kin. I no longer have the heart to remain in this place, so I will fly from here to parts unknown. Everything that is in my heart, what I feel, I promise I will eventually explain and leave out nothing."

When the people of the city heard his plan, their mourning swelled to a fever pitch, and they vented their distress. "Ah, Gājī Sāhā, what are you saying? When you abandon us, where will you go? How can we manage when you have forsaken us? Gloom will engulf the entire region when you go. The whole of Sonāpur, that glimmering City of Gold, will be doomed." Lamenting in this vein, the townspeople expressed their heartfelt anguish. Each and everyone paid their respects to Gājī, sobbing in despair. In their homes, women grew similarly agitated, disconsolate; they could but weep.

When he saw how wretched everyone felt, he promised them: "I will never abandon you. Wherever I am, you need only meditate on me, and then you will behold me present in your hearts and minds." Pronouncing the blessing of *bechmellā*, Gājī then made ready to leave, and Kālu joined him as traveling companion. Departing, they espied a snake passing by on the right, and when Gāji said, "Let's go!" they heard a gecko chirp over their heads. A woman was seen breastfeeding a child on her lap. Some distance further on, they witnessed a mahout sitting atop his elephant. The flowers in the baskets of all the garland weavers scattered to the winds as a result of their passing. Women walked by carrying large clay pots filled with water, and a cattle farmer could be heard loudly hawking his surplus milk, for a cow had given teat to her calf till its mouth overflowed. Delighted, Gājī's spirits were buoyed witnessing all of these positive omens—he knew down deep in his heart that all of his desires would be fulfilled.

"Let us be on our way, brother!" Gāji said to Kālu, so off they went, walking until the day came to a close, then the two spread their pallets at the base of a tree. Kālu gave over his heart and mind to recitation, to the formal remembrance of Āllā, then he lay down on his makeshift bed. Gājī Sāhā silently repeated the name Cāmpā[27] and privately wondered, "O dearly beloved, where exactly do you live, where will I find you?" Suffering quietly, Gāji Sāhā sang a special song, deeply soulful in a way that told of his misery.

Beloved of my life, cooling moon, destroyer of misery,
how can you make me pass this night alone?
To be separated from you, my beloved,
is for my heart to abandon my body.
I have no recollection of where you reside.
Had I any inkling earlier that
I would be torn from you, my beloved,
I would have foregone sleep.
My eyes I must scold:
Why did you slip into such fathomless sleep?
It was your fault that I lost my dearly beloved.

With this song he sought to express his wretchedness. The tears that streamed from his eyes bathed his face. Finally Kālu turned to Gāji coaxed him, "My dear brother, what is making you so wretched?"

Gāji finally replied, "Listen, brother, I will explain how it is." But he choked up, and only with difficulty did he the words slip from his mouth. "That misery which has landed on my forehead, brother, when you hear of it, you are certain to revile and censure me."

27. The Sufi practice of *jikir* (Persian *zikr*, Arabic *dhikr*) that Kālu is performing is the recitation of the names and qualities of God. Gāji is performing *jikir* as well, but has substituted the name of his beloved Cāmpā in lieu of the names of God, which he justifies in his conversation with Kālu below. The first line of the song he sings next gives three of her epithets. The following exchange captures the tension of the Sufi's desire to approach God as the beloved to the point of losing or annihilating oneself in His presence.

Kālu responded, "That which remains hidden in your heart, brother, this involvement with a woman, is unprecedented; you never see anything written in the scriptures about it. For all those on this earth counted among the saints—the *pīr*s and *oli*s depicted in the scriptures—there is nothing like it. The inkpot must have run dry, since nothing has been written about this situation, nothing about this grieving, about this kind of entanglement with a woman: it is simply unprecedented."

Gāji countered, "Pay attention to what has been recorded in the Book wherein God Himself has written about Iuchuph and Jelekhā.[28] Has one not heard the stories of the lineage of Ādhām and Ebrāhim who became the chief pillars of Āllā's saints, his *kutub*? Do not preach to me, brother, think it over, and I'll say no more."

Kālu replied, "Gāji, brother, there is one intractable complication with this woman which you have not yet mentioned: she is *hindu* and you are *mochalmān*. How is it possible for her to be considered your equal? How is it possible for a *hindu* to be joined together with a *mochalmān*? You know in your heart that this business with the woman will never work out."

Gāji quickly answered, "Āllā makes all things possible—it is within his power to channel and adjudicate this kind of passion."

Kālu observed, "What kind of passion comes from a woman? It will only wrap your body tight in the chains of this illusory world."

Gāji came back, "My eyes, my soul are no longer my own. Cāmpā has snatched them away. How can I retrieve them?"

Kālu said, "What you will get is this: you will remain stupefied, spellbound, totally bereft of your good sense."

Gāji said, "I am unable to forget this woman."

Kālu argued, "You will forget Khodā on account of this woman."

Gāji responded, "By meditating on this woman will I gain Khodā."

Kālu countered, "Khodā has no bodily form."

Gāji replied, "Everything you see is Khodā's form."

"Where and how will you find Cāmpāvatī?" Kālu Sāhā finally asked.

28. This is perhaps one of the two most celebrated romances in the Islamic world, the story circulating in a multitude of languages; for the most popular early modern Bangla version, see Śāh Muhammad Sagīr, *Iusuph-Jolekhā*, edited by Muhammad Enāmul Hak (Ḍhākā: Ḍhākā Viśvavidyālay, 1984).

"I will do whatever it takes to find her." Gāji continued, "I will go and immerse myself in the ocean of her beauty. I will even become *hindu* in order to land on the ghat of that ocean. And I will join together with her, merge together so that the two of us become one."

Kālu persisted, "Where is Cāmpā right now?"

"Wherever she has gone, I trust my eyes will lead me in that direction."

Kālu again asked, "How much longer are you going to be like this?"

Gāji promised, "I will never knowingly give it up."

Kālu then pushed, "But what if this passion, this love, kills you?"

Gāji just as quickly responded, "Then I will gain her in heaven."

Kālu queried, "What if you got married here in this world?"

Gāji replied, "Then my *karma* will have reached fruition."

Kālu exasperatedly said, "What nonsense are you blathering? I cannot understand any of it."

Gāji patiently replied, "There is no easy path from here to there."

Kālu then asked, "When you get married, who then will be worshiping whom?"

Gāji answered, "We will be strung together in our hearts."

Kālu complained, "You are always saying 'Cāmpā, Cāmpā.' But she certainly is not going mad over you."

"She eats nothing, she drinks no water. Day and night is she overwrought on account of me."

Kālu finally said, "Enough, let's stop this kind of talk. I advise you to constantly take the name of Āllā and your illness will be healed."

To hear such dismissive talk grieved Gāji, who again said, "Talk like that again and I will slit my throat! Were I severed into many parts, I would never renounce her. How can I even begin to describe to you the incredible beauty of her body, which I beheld with my own eyes? Her gorgeous splendor outshines tens of millions of suns and moons together. The magnificence of her winsome beauty is a sight to behold. Her speech is sweeter than honey—it would create a false analogy to compare her voice even to the mellifluous cuckoo. Her eyes would dart and dance, and when she looked at me my chest fairly burst open; she draws out the very breath of my life. Her hair is darker than the pitch black of the bumblebee. There is no sage whose heart and mind could remain unperturbed were he but to catch the tiniest glimpse of her hair. What features, what arms, what feet, what nose and ears—but for all that, it was the simple movement of her eyes that stole my heart away. The Creator fashioned her body in such ideal proportions that its perfection simply slays me. I cannot imagine another woman her equal anywhere in the universe. When my sweetheart ornaments herself with precious jewels, they pale in comparison to her beauty; they seem suddenly dim like so many glass baubles. Whatever pearls and other precious stones drape her form, they too appear dull as old ivory, for her body radiates light brighter than the burning midday sun. Whose heart can fail to be smitten when beholding her beauty?" And going on and on like this, Gāji finally talked himself into a faint, and slumped down in the dirt.

Kālu consoled him, "Listen, brother, calm your mind. We'll leave tomorrow to trace her. Are you able to say where, in what part of the country she is located? It is north or south, west or east?"

Gāji replied, "How can I say for sure? But I believe that it must be in the southern regions."

Then Kālu said, "Tomorrow we'll set out." And with this decided, the two settled down for the evening at the foot of a large tree. Punctually, at the precise time for early morning prayers, Kālu awakened and then bowed down to pray. Afterwards, he took Gāji in tow and they headed for the southerly regions. They traversed many lands, slowly meandering through what must have been a myriad of places. Along the way, they crossed countless braided rivers, with their many channels and canals. Seven long years passed like this, but no matter where they landed up, they could not track her whereabouts. Still they pushed on for another three months, through swamps and marshes and bogs, crossing untold numbers of rivers and streams.

Finally, in the distance, the city of Brāhmaṇ Nagar materialized before their weary eyes. Defined and protected by rivers on all four sides, those waters flowed the color of milk. Four landing ghats made of gold had been constructed along the perimeter. The royal palace was a blaze of brilliance as if made of fire—mansions and monastic buildings, indeed every structure, was golden-hued. Everything sparkled in brilliant display. Splendid flags and pennants adorned all parts of the city. All manner of birds sang their serenades, while the bees flitted, wildly abuzz. Dazzling structures had been erected adjacent to the landing ghats along the banks of the river, and *kadamba* trees[29] towered over the ghats all around. This particular place where they had first landed was a village outpost called Kāntapuri, and the two brothers make their way toward it. The giant *kadamba* tree they saw loomed with inviting resplendence, its fully matured, fragrant blossoms dropping into the cooling waters. Exhausted, the two brothers took their seats at the foot of that tree just as some women from the city approached. Their bodies shimmered with the grace and elegance of heavenly nymphs; they carried golden water pots on their hips, and smaller pots with spouts glimmered in their hands. Each and every one was draped with breathtaking ornaments inlaid with rubies. Their diamonds and pearls refracted the red glow of the sunlight, which played on them in a most delightful way. Kālu finally said, "Goodness, how these women take one's breath away. They glow with the same luster of the city that sits on the opposite bank of the river."

Kālu was just as astonished when he beheld the citadel of this king's capital, and when he looked at the women, even he, too, was struck speechless. He was astounded to see that king's city, for he had never laid eyes on any comparable metropolis anywhere in the world. Rāvaṇ's magnificent citadel was a mere hovel by comparison. "This city's artistry exceeds *behest*, heaven itself, in its beauty. How could a man, a mere mortal, construct such a place? You really have gone mad, my brother, for who could possibly enter that fortified citadel? Who has the kind of power and presence to gain entrance to it? And besides, we have heard that its champion, the king's enforcer, is the valiant Dakṣiṇā Rāy. The denizens all worship him in fear and devotion, for every time he has caught a *jaban* he has slain him without fail." Kālu continued, "Gāji, you are extremely intelligent, but do even I have the power to make you understand? Cāmpā is there enjoying the good life without worrying over you, without giving you a second thought. Yet

29. The *kadamba* (previously classified as *Nauclea kadamba*, but now *Neolamarckia cadamba*), is a fast-growing fir tree with distinctive highly aromatic orange globular flowers, long associated with Kṛṣṇa, who plays his flute beneath it; it is sometimes called *haripriyā*, or 'beloved of Hari, Kṛṣṇa." There are four other flowering trees that go by the name *kadamba*, but this is the variety most often described in older texts. It can reach a height of 45 meters. See also p. 56, n. 28, above.

you are driven by a false hope for her. You do not even know precisely where Cāmpā is, in which compound she lives. A *mochalmān* cannot even enter that place across the river. Tell me, truthfully, how are you going to find her? Give up this fantasy and come along with me. We have no work here, nothing to do, no business at all."

Gāji interrupted, "Kālu brother, what are you blathering about? I have no fear and do not hesitate to enter, whether it be the king's citadel or the fire pit. If I have to jump into a pit of fire, I am not afraid. Listen carefully to what I propose, brother Kālu: The two of us should stay put for two or three days. Whatever is written in my fate will become clear, for surely she will be spotted on the landing ghat. No more than two more days will we remain here, after which I will abandon all hope of gaining the young woman."

Kālu replied, "You have spoken well. If Cāmpāvatī shows on the banks of this river, then we will know truly that Khodā has decreed it, and I will ease your marriage. But you must promise honestly: if the young damsel fails to come, then you will give up your hopes and dreams for her."

Gāji promised, "I can agree to that truthfully, and what is more, never again will I utter the name Cāmpā."

Kālu said, "Finally, I have been freed from this fix. We'll wander and witness with our own eyes the full expanse of God's creation afterwards." And so they continued to discuss the matter as they hunkered down to keep watch over the ghat. As they sat, they fixed their minds on Āllā.

Who can fathom the full majesty of the Creator, brother? That night Cāmpāvatī dreamed. To convey properly what the princess dreamt as she slept requires the more elaborate three-footed tripadī *meter to describe.*

CĀMPĀVATĪ DREAMS OF GĀJI AND GOES TO THE GHAT TO SEE HIM

Sheltering at the foot of the giant tree
Gāji and Kālu in nervous anticipation
    wait and watch for the young woman's arrival.
On the opposite side of the river, Cāmpāvatī
weeps the whole night for her beloved,
    incessantly repeating the name of Gāji.
No food passes her lips,

her eyes show that she has had no sleep,
 the young maiden just sits quietly and sobs.
The separation from Gāji burns,
its searing passion ravages her body,
 flames that rise without respite.
That night the ever-chaste Cāmpāvatī
is so agitated that she writhes on the ground,
 haunted by the memory of the lord of her life.
Her consciousness fades as she grieves,
focused on the one who has stolen her heart;
 after a while she nods and drifts off to sleep.
At the direct command of the Lord
an angel flies there
 and speaks to her in her dreams.
Sitting on the edge of her bed,
the angel promises her,
 "Your miseries will soon be relieved.
Pay heed to what I am telling you, Cāmpāvatī,
your husband and brother-in-law
 have arrived at the riverbank opposite.
By the ghat on the north side of the river
they have camped right on the bank,
 and they have taken somber vows.
If they spot you there tomorrow
in the company of your friends,
 they will come around.
If not, the two will depart
and Gāji has declared, indeed, vowed, that
 he will never take up your name again.
Listen, my dear girl, to what I am telling you:
Tomorrow you must go to that precise spot,
 uttering Gāji's name over and over.
If you make your way to the northern ghat
you are certain to meet him,
 for Gāji will be sitting there, waiting."
Realizing her dream had the ring of truth,
this unblemished beauty is delighted, but stunned,
 and she rises up wide awake.
The longer the night drags out,
the more fully aroused she is, her heart rippling
 with joy unabated as she mulls over the prospects.

No more sleep is in the offing
but after some indeterminate time
    the night finally manages to crawl to an end.
Following the cue of the birds breaking into song,
the sun awakes and rises higher and higher,
    till it floods the eastern sky with its light.
Listen everyone with rapt attention,
for the next phase of the story
    will be conveyed in the meter of the payār *couplet.*

refrain Ah, off the maiden goes, laughing and joking.
Alas, she is heading to the riverbank with her friends.

As night gave way to day, the sun rose and Cāmpā called for her mother. They talked. "Listen, mother dear, to what I propose. I am utterly wrung out, my poor body has been consumed by the fire of a separation that smolders without respite. I simply cannot stay here in my quarters any longer, so I wish to go to the river and bathe. I have not visited the river for many days. So please do give your permission that I might go and soothe my soul in its clear running waters." Her mother responded, "My child, why would I keep you from going? I would never forbid you, so be off with a light heart and have fun." Soon Cāmpāvatī departed, accompanied by a gaggle of five maidservants, and a chaperone troupe composed of nine aunts and seven sisters-in-law, all laughing and joking. The smaller girls danced the whole way. A number of women from the neighborhood dressed up and accompanied Cāmpā as well. Some of them carried spouted water pots, while others carried smaller pitchers filled with oils variously scented with musk and other fragrances. Some of them toted large golden pots in the crooks of their arms, and that rested on the curve of their hips. The train of women moved along, carefree, breasts swaying. In their ranks, some walked, swinging their hips with the grace and gait of elephants, others more animated moved their limbs with youthful zest, while a few strutted like wagtails. Slim-waisted women, their eyebrows raised in laughter—all moved forward, bubbly and vivacious. They marched on as if to war, their hips moving in time. To see their slender waists made one's heart race. A few darted forward like slithering snakes while others plodded along ever more deliberately. A few of them were veiled, while others left their heads uncovered; some did their hair up with artistic flair and others let it hang loose, completely unbound. A few draped garlands of flowers around their necks, deep black mascara circling their eyes, vermillion dotting their foreheads, and golden anklets of small bells dressing their feet. They adorned their limbs in every imaginable color, sporting saris of the sheerest of silks. The troupe moved along, each member chewing a betel quid with liquid pleasure. How their bodies shimmered, a moving constellation in the midst of which the moon itself had risen—but alas, in the continued agony of her separation from Gāji, the demon Rāhu had momentarily eclipsed that moon, Cāmpā.[30] On the surface, her appearance was unkempt, her limbs appeared dingy and soiled, her body smeared with dust and dirt, like a sun covered by clouds. Her hair was matted, neither oiled nor combed. Still, in spite of that, her natural beauty was electrifying, more effulgent than a flash of lightning. Were a sage to see her luscious form, he would lose his soul and pine for her, run after her. A special light radiated from the body of this king's daughter for she was going with her girlfriends to see her husband. Cāmpāvatī led the way, her maidservants on her left, her sisters-in-law flanking her on the right, and her numerous aunts and aunties trailing.

She finally arrived at the bank of the river, her beautiful form beginning to sparkle as if a full moon. Gāji Sāhā was on the opposite bank under the stately *kadamba* tree. Gāji pointed her out to Kālu. "Look, brother Kālu, see her there on the opposite bank. Cāmpāvatī has come as I just knew she would." When he heard this, Kālu Sāhā got up, turned, and stared across the river and there the moon-faced Cāmpā stood on the riverbank. Kālu Sāhā looked and saw she was a real person, standing right before his very eyes, brilliantly illuminated by the sun. Then Kālu turned to Gāji and said, "Your eminence, you have truly passed the test as you already knew in your heart you would."

30. Rahu is an *asura* who in a battle with the gods manages to sip a drop of the nectar of immortality churned up from the ocean of milk, but Viṣṇu hurled his discus, severing Rahu's head from his body. Becoming immortal, the head periodically reenacts this by swallowing the moon, producing an eclipse. Exiting from the severed neck, however, the moon invariably resumes its course. In some versions, attested to in the epics and several of the Sanskrit *purāṇas*, the sun is swallowed as well.

And just then, the king's daughter said to her companions, "All of you stay here, keep your distance."

refrain Look, look, all you companions, look, for I know
the one who sits on the opposite shore is the thief of
my heart.

So saying, the young woman stood lingering on the ghat. Then that maiden fixed her gaze on the opposite shore and there she made out the two brothers seated at the foot of the *kadamba* tree. As soon as she caught sight of them, Cāmpāvatī's heart flared. She began to weep uncontrollably and lost consciousness. When she fainted she slipped down into the mud. Seven of the women ran up and splashed water on her face to bring her around. Then the womenfolk crowded around and hugged her. Wiping her face with the ends of their saris, they consoled and cajoled, "We were all laughing and having such a good time. What has rent your heart to make you tear up?"

The young woman replied, "Listen, I promise not to cry anymore, but I must go alone and pay my humble respects to the river goddess Gaṅgā. Do not come with me, just stay back. I fear that if you accompany me, the goddess Gaṅgā will not show herself." Hearing this reasonable request, they all hung back at a distance. Cāmpāvatī then went down and immersed herself in the river. When she submerged herself in the river's waters she fixed her garment up around her neck. She made obeisance to her husband, pressing her hands together in respect. Then she bowed down in the direction of the northern bank. "May you live long, beloved of my heart, and may you prosper." Seeing Gāji in the distance, the tender-faced Cāmpā's eyes brimmed with silent tears that soon joined the river's currents. Crying harder, she slapped herself on the head, "Had the Creator but given me wings, I would fly over and land at your feet. I have revealed to you the misery that is in my heart." The young woman then stood up and gazed, staring in the direction of Gāji, still as a picture. Her tears formed rivulets down and around her breasts, but her face remained fixed in that direction and no other.

"Cāmpāvatī, hurry up and finish washing," her aunt called out. "And why, my child, do you keep staring at the opposite river bank? Be quick with your bath before someone tears my head off. You were laughing and cheerful when you came to the ghat, why have you grown sullen all of a sudden?"

Cāmpā replied, "I can tell you at last, but later you must promise not to share this with anyone, even if asked." The women present listened and then said, "O daughter of our king, please go ahead and speak. With Śiv as our witness, we won't tell a soul. If we do tell anyone, then may we go blind in both eyes!" Cāmpā then unloaded her heartache to her aunts. "If any of this gets out, my dear aunties, then may your uncle turn out to be your father." Then the princess wept as she spoke. She told the whole group everything that was troubling her: how she and Gāji had got together, where his home was, whose son he was, and so forth. Little by little, she spun out the entire story. Raising her arm, she pointed to him on the opposite shore. "Look there, the thief of my heart is sitting. And beside him sits my brother-in-law. It is on account of him that I have been weeping, dying day and night. That thief has stolen my heart. Alas, I feel I am just about to die, my chest is about to burst, and my heart aches. Would that I could fly up and land at his feet."

When they took in all she said, those *brāhmaṇ* ladies immediately stood up and stared at Gāji and whispered excitedly. They saw him standing there beneath the *kadamba* tree, and his imposing presence made him glow more brilliantly than tens of tens of millions of moons. When they got sight of Gāji's elegant form, they gasped, felt faint, and in their distraction slipped down in the mud. One after another exclaimed, "What a sculpted physique, I would die for that! The extraordinary handsomeness of this man complements the beauty of his wife perfectly. The god of fate, Bidhātā, has fashioned a single figure from two equal parts. It is extraordinarily fortunate that this woman has found this perfect match, and equally so for the brothers. Such a man is almost never found in this universe." All of the married women present grew agitated with envy and the entire circle of sisters-in-law, when they saw him, went absolutely mad. Recovering their wits, they all began to joke about Gāji, expressing feigned contempt. Some exaggerated surprise. Others berated him and called it the end of the world, saying that nothing good would ever come from this: "If this has come to pass, we shudder to think what will happen next!" Then they turned toward Gāji and stared. One of them waved at him, while another flirted, winking and making faces, and finally another waded into the water up to her waist and splashed water in his direction. Even though he was quite a distance away, one hearty companion managed to spray him, at which point the aunts and aunties began to bite their tongues, pretending embarrassment. They pulled the veils over their heads in sham modesty and turned away, but still stood there.

"Just look at them standing there pointing their backsides at us," Kālu Sāhā said to Gāji then. "I don't particularly want to know any of those ladies any better. None of the bottoms of these women strike me as particularly enticing. Can you figure out which one of these fine relations is to be your mother-in-law? But seriously, listen to me, brother, I have no more worries, the doubts that plagued my mind have been banished. It is clearly written that this young woman is destined to be your life mate. I saw for myself that this maiden is smitten, thinking of you and only you. No need to worry further, you can rest easy." Exchanging these kinds of words, the two brothers stood where they were.

At that moment, the princess came forward with her companions and dipped into the waters to bathe. Submerging themselves in the water, they all gazed at Gāji. Ever so deliberately, they washed their arms, their legs, and every conceivable part of their bodies. When Cāmpā washed her torso she made sure Gāji got a good look at both her breasts. She washed her nose, washed her face, washed her ears, then again made sure Gāji saw clearly as she massaged her nipples and breasts. She let down her hair, shaking it out. It was as if a black storm cloud had moved across and covered over the moon. Her hair was blacker than black and hung a full three arm lengths long. When she pulled her hair up into a bun, she was so fair that it seemed a lightning bolt had erupted from a blue-black cloud. After that Cāmpāvatī settled down in the water up to her neck. Her wet limbs flashed, coruscating more brilliantly than tens of tens of millions of suns. Just out of the water, her face glowed with beauty marks that exceeded tens of millions of autumnal moons. Eventually, some of the women emerged from the river, climbed onto the ghat, and put on their clothes. But Cāmpāvatī remained alone, submerged in the water. That was when Gāji signaled with his hand to say, "Go, go now, love of my life, go back to your home. We will soon be together again as quickly as I can make it so." Then Cāmpāvatī, that pure devoted wife, that *satī*, pulled her garment around her neck, made obeisance to her husband, and left. As she made her way to the shore, she kept looking back, like a frantic bird desperate to escape its cage. At every step she took, she looked back twice. Tears streamed down her cheeks. Her female companions surrounded Cāmpāvatī and, with her safely in their midst, whisked her away.

They walked briskly back to their respective homes, but Cāmpāvatī detoured to the Śiv temple. She shook out her hair and gave her clothes a good shaking, while her serving girls fetched the items necessary for performing *pūjā* worship. Lamps, parched rice, aromatic incense, ripe bananas, sugar, sandalwood paste, vermillion, flowers—all were gathered. After that the princess shed her regular wet clothes and wrapped herself in a Bānāraśi silk sari of elaborate design. After she wrapped herself in that exceptional ritual sari, one with precious gold threads woven into it, she then sat down to perform the worship. She began the *pūjā* in the established manner. First, and in proper order, the young woman performed *pūjā* to Nirañjan, the Stainless One, that God responsible for the creation of the triple universe. After that, while contemplating the feet of Gāji, she supplicated Gaurī with devotion and heartfelt focus. Gaurī felt compassion and tenderness for her, so the goddess herself appeared on her chariot to grant Cāmpā a boon. When the wife of Hara arrived, she advised Cāmpā in a divinely mellifluous voice, "Listen carefully, you who are the daughter of the king, why have you summoned me?" The young woman replied, "The reason is my husband. I am very much in distress, Mother, please grant me a boon. Please fulfil my heart's desire."

The goddess Bhavāni responded, "My child, may your heart and mind be calmed. What has been inscribed by fate cannot be undone. You will be joined to your handsome husband, a *mochalmān* by social standing; and from that know too that your beloved is my cousin-sister's son. You will learn that his name is Gāji Jendā Pīr. He gave up his seat on the lion throne of kingship and now, after becoming a *phakir*, he wanders as a mendicant. You should know that his father is Chekāndar Sāhā. He constructed the city of Bairāṭ Nagar from his stores of gold. The daughter of Bali Rājā is Ajupā Sundarī: she is my cousin-sister and your mother-in-law. Gāji is my dear nephew and I am his aunt. I love him more than either my own Kārttik or Gaṇeś. Listen, Cāmpāvatī, I grant you the boon you ask: May my sister's son become your husband."

And having spoken like this, Gaurī departed, riding her chariot back to *vaikuṇṭha* heaven. En route, her meditative eye espied Gāji and Kālu stretched out asleep at the foot of a *kadamba* tree.

About that same time, Śiv mounted his own chariot and merrily made his way to Gāji. As soon as he saw Śiv, Gāji made obeisance. Śiv in return granted his blessings and began to speak. "I was visiting your in-laws' house today." Kidding him a little, he said, "Listen my child Gāji. When your uncle's wives and all the other women get hold of you, they will cling to you like leeches. The more I think about it, I figure you will be stranded, alone as Kṛṣṇa among all the *gupī* maidens. They will push and pull and finally tear you apart, my son. When you get in the clutches of these lubricious women, you will surely lose your heart, if not your life. The king's queen is to be your mother-in-law. She has had seven sons, but she is a young woman yet. Knowing how weak your father-in-law is, I know he does not discharge his duties properly, for if he were not so lazy, then he would certainly have had many more sons." Śiv continued his joking in this vein which caused no small embarrassment to Gāji, who kept his head down. Śiv kept up the banter. "Why are you brooding so, my child, why are you afraid? Whatever Bidhātā, the god of fate, has written is irrevocable. Know for certain that you will gain Cāmpā. And I too will help you, so be fearful of no one and no thing. You will best Maṭuk and be triumphant. So tomorrow dispatch Kālu to Brāhmaṇ Nagar." Lord Śiv departed as soon as he had delivered this advice.

The two brothers remained transfixed at the foot of the tree. But the next morning Gāji made clear his intentions. Assuming the stance of someone asking a favor, he said to his brother Kālu, "Listen, brother, listen carefully: you must act as the emissary of my heart. I cannot live any longer without Cāmpā, I feel my life-breath slipping away from my body. Please go this morning to the king's palace. Take pity on me, on my skittish heart, which I can no longer hold to this earth as it flutters like a frightened bird trying to take flight. What else can I do to get her? Understand how rattled I am without her. So please this morning take yourself straight to the king's quarters, and when you gain entry, tell him the whole story. What else can I say? You know the tale from the beginning to end."

"I will visit his eminence the king" Kālu replied. "But I want to say something to you first. If I fall into danger, is there any way to send word to you to come and rescue me?"

Gāji said to him, "Brother Kālu, listen carefully. Recite the names of Āllā and meditate on me, calling me three times. That will cause my turban to fall from my head. I will know in my heart when you have fallen into difficulty and I will immediately come to your aid." With this reassurance, Deoān Kālu recited *bichimillā* blessing "In the Name of God" and got up, made ready, and headed off to Brāhmaṇ Nagar. He recited "Āllā, Āllā" as he walked. Kālu reached the ferry's landing dock in no time. Chirā and Dorā were the two brothers in charge there. Kālu accosted them and spoke, "I need to cross the river, can you take me across?"

Chirā replied, "Let me put it to you this way: Have you come with a death wish? If you are keen to suffer a sure death, then fill a large water pot to the brim, tie it to your neck, jump in, and drown yourself in those dark waters. Under no circumstance should you go to Brāhmaṇ Nagar. What could a *jaban* possibly want on that side of the river? If a low-caste *śūdra* happens to go there for some strange reason, they beat him unmercifully and drive him away. There is a monstrous strongman there, a *deo* by the name of Dakṣinā. Whenever he catches a *jaban*, he simply eats him. Give up this crazy wish and just move along. Go somewhere else to beg for your food."

Kālu calmly replied, "I must go to the other side, so ferry me across. Whatever my destiny happens to be, so be it."

Chirā said, "If you really are determined to go across, then you must pay me the fare in advance. You must give me cash, cowries, worth twenty-one measures of gold. Only then will I take you, and it will be within the hour."

Kālu heard him out and boarded the boat. Meditating on Āllā, his shoulder bag was suddenly full of gold and by that miraculous power, the *kerāmati* of God, Kālu tendered a handful of gold. Just like that the ferryman took him across to the other shore. When he reached the bank, Kālu cinched a sash around his waist and headed quickly in the direction of the king's palace. He arrived at the king's dwellings in no time and sought entry, expressing his desire to have a personal audience with the king. The *mahārājā* was sitting on a bejeweled lion throne holding court. He was in good spirits as he consorted with his courtiers and friends. His seven sons and nine sons-in-law and a host of other people were present. His seven sons sat around him on splendid chairs. Any number of *brāhmaṇ paṇḍit*s were seated in neat rows, animatedly reciting the *Mahābhārat* and *Purāṇ* in sonorous tones. Male and female dancers performed more gracefully than celestial nymphs, *vidhyādharis*. They were singing the six classical musical forms, *rāgs*, and thirty-six secondary forms, *rāginīs*, accompanied by different instruments, diligently marking the rhythm with their claps.[31] They were acknowledged to be better than the great musicians Tānsen and Bṛkabālā, his *guru*,[32] as they played to the hordes crowding the court, and to all the sepoys standing by and the mahouts atop their elephants.

Repeating "*Elellā* . . .", Kālu Sāhā presented himself and stood before the king. As soon he laid eyes on him, Maṭuk Rājā Gosvāy erupted. He screamed for the constables and with that telltale roar the knowing constables jumped nervously. They inquired of the *mahārāj* what he commanded. The king shouted, "Look, see that *jaban phakir*! Grab him by the scruff of the neck and kick him out of here! I am never to look upon the face of a *jaban*, but now that I have, I will have to do penance for three days. Go quickly and forcibly remove this *jaban* and, if you cannot manage it, then inform Dakṣiṇā Rāy!"

No sooner had they heard the king's command than they apprehended Kālu. But Kālu insistently spoke out, "O *mahārāj*, please listen to my request."

The king ordered them, "Hold on, let us hear what this bugger has to say." Receiving their revised direction, the constables released him.

"Mahārāj, please listen to what I have to say," Kālu said. "In the city of Bairāṭ Nagar there dwells a king who is a treasure trove of virtue. The Sāhā's name is Chekāndar and his name and fame are widely known. There is no other king on earth his equal. The triple world quakes when it hears his name. No one on Āllā's earth is his peer. Bali

31. A few years immediately prior to the composition of this version of the story, Nandalāl Śarma's *Saṅgītasūtra* (Calcutta, 1870) listed the thirty-six *rāginīs*, while Kṣetra Mohan Gosvāmī's *Saṅgītasāra* (Calcutta, 1879) contained descriptions of eighty-eight *rāgas*. See also Suvarnalata Rao, Joep Bor, Wim van der Meer, and Jane Harvey, *The Rāga Guide: A Survey of Seventy-four Hindustani Ragas* (Wyastone Leys, Monmouth, UK, and Charlottesville, VA: Nimbus Records with Rotterdam Conservatory of Music, 1999).

32. Originally from Gwalior, Tansen was the ranking musician of Akbar's court; he is famous for his *rāgas* and the development of the *dhrupād* style of music. His *guru* was Haridās Svāmī, referred here by the reference to his home of Bṛndāvan in Braj, so Bṛkabālā < Bṛjvālā < Brajvālā, one who dwells in Braj.

Rājā engaged him in combat and lost, so he gave him his daughter in marriage. Know that Sāhā Chekāndar is extremely pious and given to truth. He erected Bairāṭ Nagar completely of gold. Understand, too, that his son, Sāhā Gāji, is an exalted *jendā pīr*, that he abandoned kingship in favor of becoming a *phakir*. Upon seeing his eminence and recognizing his saintliness, any number of *brāhmaṇs* have taken off their sacred threads and become practicing *jabans*. In the city of Chāphāi, the king went by the name of Śrīrām. He came to Gāji and in his presence recited the *kalemā*. By virtue of his miraculous power, *keramāt*, Gāji then built Śonāpur, the City of Gold, and in it a *machjid*, where we two brothers had settled down. Your daughter is named Cāmpāvatī. By some fantastic magic, Gāji was transported to her room. Their beds were switched and rings exchanged; she had given Gāji her own bed and ring. Cāmpāvatī used the excuse of having to bathe when Gāji had come to the opposite river bank to gain sight of her. After consuming the offering of food from your very own *pūjā* worship, Bhagavati granted Sāheb Gāji an extraordinary boon. Yesterday, the goddess Caṇḍī herself went to visit Gāji and told him, 'I am granting you Cāmpāvatī as your boon.' Lovesick, Gāji Sāha will not even consume a single chickpea or drink a sip of water. He is constantly calling out 'Cāmpā, Cāmpā' in his distress. Will you grant them this marriage or not? Please do say."

As he listened, the king put his head down in utter humiliation. Those present who had heard the story nodded in total agreement with everything Kālu had explained. "Everything is true, that *phakir* has not exaggerated in the least. Cāmpāvatī has gone truly mad over him."

But as he listened to Kālu, the king seethed, his fury welling up. He screamed at his constables, "Take this *phakir* and slam him into a jail cell. Shackle his hands and feet and find a boulder of at least several hundred pounds and place it on his chest. My limbs, my entire body blaze in anger listening to his blather." When they heard their command, they arrested Kālu, took him to jail, bound him, and pressed the stone hard on his chest.

"Why are you manhandling me, brothers," Kālu cried out. "I am not the king's son-in-law. I am the go-between, the matchmaker, where am I at fault? Go and capture the one who wants to get married." But the constables would hear nothing of it and restrained Kālu further. They executed the direct order of the king with gusto and roughly spirited him off to jail. The cell was constructed of iron, with not even the tiniest crack anywhere inside it. It was oppressively desolate, and the only door was one hand high and opened to the south, but even so the cell remained totally dark even in the middle of the day, so it was no different even on a full-moon night. They bound him hand and foot as they incarcerated him in that suffocating dungeon. Somehow they maneuvered a stone of several hundred weight onto his chest. Kālu Sāhā recited the name of Āllā and repeating "Gāji" over and over wept.

Elsewhere, Maṭuk Rājā continued to vent his anger as he strode through the citadel in search of Cāmpāvatī. When he saw Gāji's bed in her private quarters, he smashed that bedstead and chopped it into so many pieces. After destroying the bed, the king flew into an even wilder rage. Sword in hand, he looked to thoroughly dismember his daughter. Terrified, Cāmpāvatī jumped and fled to her seven sisters-in-laws' quarters. Cāmpā hid behind them, covering herself by grabbing the loose ends of their saris and wrapping herself in their folds. Eventually, the *mahārāj's* rage subsided. He slumped back down on his lion throne and uttered not a word.

This humble servant speaks, deploying the three-footed tripadī *meter. Listen with all your heart to something of Kālu's plight.*

refrain: Be merciful to me, you who are ever filled with boundless grace!
I have fallen into dire straits, so I am calling out for you.

KĀLU ŚĀHĀ IS IMPRISONED AND GĀJI SUMMONS ALL THE TIGERS

Imprisoned in a dank cell
Kālu Sāhā wept and sobbed;
Over and over he called for Gāji.
He wallowed in misery,
"When I do not see your face
my life slips away.
Brother Gāji, you promised me that
any time I would suffer
you would come to my rescue.
Your face, younger brother, is nowhere to be seen.
Though my chest splits and my heart is rent,

you have yet to appear."
Kālu wailed in the burning fire of his misery,
his limbs awash in a flood of tears—
all this Gāji discerned through meditation.
The turban atop his head
slipped and fell in confirmation.
Gāji spoke, choking his tears in distress:
"You, my brother, are my life breath!
I did not think through this ill-conceived plan.
Why did I send you?
I should have known in advance that
in that city of *brāhmaṇ*s, Brāhmaṇ Nagar,
you would fall into danger.
But selfishly and only on my behalf, my brother,
I felt compelled to send you anyway,
knowing full well you could lose your life.
O brother, I do not know now
whether you are alive or dead."
So Gāji wept, bemoaning his brother's fate.
When his lament was spent,
up into the skies he flew, born by the wind.
He came down in the Sundarbans.
Moving deep through those enchanted forests
he finally paused at the base of a large tree
and began to summon all the tigers.
Hearing Gāji's clarion call
tigers by the hundreds of thousands came running.
He properly greeted each of them when they arrived.
They returned his salaams, and when
they were settled on the ground around him,
the leading tiger spoke, "Where is Kālu Pīr?
We did not catch sight of him in the swamps.
Tell us, what has transpired? What has happened, Pīr?"
Gāji then wept as he spoke.
He narrated in great detail
everything that had transpired,
the entire story from beginning to end.
The tigers all reassured him, "O Pīr,
may your heart and mind rest easy.
Do not worry, for we will remain with you.
We will depart right away,

not even stopping to eat or drink,"
They all concurred, "Let's go, let's go now."

refrain The massive ambush of tigers made ready to depart,
and their roar shook the ground of the earth.

As he bounded about, one tiger said, "May your heart and mind remain calm. Why else do we serve as your servants? Within a half hour we will all head toward Brāhmaṇ Nagar. We will see just how much power this Maṭuk Rājā really has. After we destroy Maṭuk Rājā's family and lineage, we will rescue Cāmpāvatī and bring her to you." Saying these and similar comforting things, the tigers prepared themselves. Kenduyā always performed as the lead tiger, the chief of all the tigers: he routinely captured *rakṣas* demons for his meals. The tiger Beḍābhāṅgā manifested an unbelievably ferocious power. He would easily slay demons and lions, utterly destroying them and sending them to the lowest of the seven hells. Dāneoārā tiger would jump and attack savagely, so angry that he wanted to rip the sun right out of the sky. The tiger Biṅgarāj's mass loomed as large as a mountain, and when he roared Vāsuki, king of serpents, trembled in his underworld kingdom of Pātāla. The tiger named Kālkuṭī had an unparalleled strength that allowed him to carry off whole elephants, mahouts and all. Cilācākṣu tiger could always be spotted lazily rolling his eyes, but in a trice he would pounce on a man and devour him head-first. Kenda tiger, whose tail stuck straight up in the air, would eviscerate and consume cattle and goats within seconds of their being slain. The tiger called Menī would roam back and forth constantly, then, when he spotted a dog or a jackal, he would pounce on their necks before you knew it. The tiger Lohājuḍi would stalk with a deliberate, studied stealth, but as soon as he picked up the smell of an ewe, with blinding speed he would dart into the shed for the kill. Pecāmukhā of the deformed back came with Kheḍi, while Aoan and Bāoan appeared with Nāgeśvari.

I have provided some of the names of the tigers who assembled, but were I to record all of their names this book would never end. Seemingly untold numbers of tigers rallied, and I could name more, but altogether there were fifty-two crores and another seven hundred. There may have been others, but it is impossible to enumerate, but even to imagine those numbers is terrifying.

Once they were prepared, they headed for Brāhmaṇ Nagar and Gāji went along with them carrying his staff in his hand. The tigers passed through a number of towns and villages and all those poor folk who laid eyes on the tigers understandably trembled in terror. Some said in wonder, "Look at that *phakir* character. He clearly commands a powerful magic—that is the only way he could possibly bring these tigers along with him." And everyone speculated in this fashion, but when he overheard them, Gāji was actually embarrassed by the spectacle. As a *jendā pīr*, Gāji was discomfited and grew increasingly self-conscious, so he recited *bichmillā* and blew it over the tigers. When Gāji blew his breath over the tigers, they were all transmogrified, taking the shape of sheep, allowing the tigers to amble forward as innocuous rams and ewes, while Gāji, holding his staff in his hand, accompanied them as the sheepherder.

In village after village, the locals ventured forward and proposed to Gāji, "Since you have all these sheep, you should sell some. Do take whatever price you think is appropriate. If you do not wish to sell the whole flock, give us one and take what you need to cover your travel expenses."

"Impossible, for they are not mine to sell," Gāji replied. "All of the sheep you see belong to Maṭuk Rājā." Enduring many similar exchanges, Gājī pressed onward with the sheep in tow.

After some days, they reached the town of Kāntapur. On the opposite bank Gājī could see Brāhmaṇ Nagar, so he wasted no time going to the ferry's landing ghat. The two brothers named Chirā and Ḍorā were the ferrymen. Seeing the sheep, the pair began to scheme. Chirā commented to Ḍorā, "Take a look at that. Here comes another halfwit bastard *phakir* herding a large drove of sheep. Those sheep are certain to destroy our ferry, their hooves will tear up the planking, then our boat will founder and be lost and we will have no way to make money. Quick, let's move our ferry across the river and then the imbecile of a *phakir* will have to turn around and leave." Talking themselves into that decisive action, they slipped their moorings to push off.

"Wait, wait!" Gāji cried out loudly. When they heard Gāji's yell, somehow they were compelled to reverse course and return. Gāji came up to board the boat with his ewes and rams trailing. They sized up Gāji and began to interrogate him. "Tell us, where have you come from and where are you headed?"

Gāji replied, "Listen, Chirā, brother, listen and I will tell you. Brāhmaṇ Nagar—that is where I am going."

Chirā replied, "I'm thinking that you must have a hankering for death! Are you somehow connected with that other *phakir* we met who is now languishing in prison? Now I think I understand your death wish. Go ahead, indulge your whim and you will end up in Yam's abode, the house of death. Yearning for that will lead you to walk right through Yam's gateway, for the moment you do, Dakṣiṇā Rāy will lay hold of you and eat you!"

"Listen to what I'm proposing, ferryman," Gājī calmly replied. "That *phakir* lying in manacles is my brother. The king entrusted the two of us with a large sum of money. He commissioned us to procure the sheep, but we were late in delivery. That's why my brother was incarcerated. Both of you brothers, hear me out and take my request seriously. You really must take me across the river quickly."

Chirā replied, "Okay, but first you must hand over full payment in cash. I will accept no less than one hundred cowries."

Gāji countered, "Today I have no money, no cowries, in hand. But as soon as I sell all my sheep, I will pay you, brother."

Chirā responded, "You idiot, you really believe you can outsmart us. If you are going to get across the river, you need to cough up the cowries now."

"If you do not believe that I will settle up, then take my golden staff in exchange."

As soon as he heard this, Chirā exploded in anger, "All you thieves come to me in the same way all the time. You are a thug, a master swindler, and the way you work is well known. You dye your staff yellow with turmeric and call it gold."

"Listen, Chirā, take the patchwork cloak off my back to ferry me across," Gāji said.

Listening to him, Chirā's face grew dark, "So many of these cloaks are nothing more than a mishmash of rags and strips of torn bark."

"Why, brother, do you pull such a long face?" Gāji countered. "Keep my gold chain and take me across."

"Scamming like that won't cut it," Chirā retorted. "That chain has the counterfeit ring of polished brass."

"Why are you stalling?" Gāji asked. "Accept this spun gold thread and take me across."

"I'm not that crazy," Chirā replied, "the discolored yellow-green cast of copper shines through. Why do you keep trying to swindle me? I have stitched my own torn garments with thread just like that."

Now failing to control his laughter, Gāji impishly suggested, "What else can I give you? Take the shorts I'm wearing and ferry me across."

"Brother Ḍorā," Chirā called out, "what did this bastard just say? This rogue wants to kill me by stopping me from pissing. If that's not enough, were I to wear shorts, I couldn't fart, my stomach would swell up, and I would die. And finally, if I wore those shorts, I would not be able to shit, nor would I be able to get it off with a woman!"

Gāji then suggested, "Chirā brother, take me across the river. Take the diamond, the pearl, and the ruby wrapped in my turban."

"I'm sick of hearing you say 'take me across.'" retorted Chirā, "I have never encountered such relentless skullduggery as yours. You are a *phakir* with your hand out, you bastard, what do you say now? Your father never saw a ruby, so how would you? Someone was probably performing *pūjā* to Durgā and submerged the image, from which you stole that shiny cloth and that's why you pretend there is a ruby embedded in it. You have never seen a ruby even in your wildest dreams!"

"Chirā, brother, consider this offer." Gāji countered, "Please accept two of these sheep, a pair, to take me across."

This time Ḍorā chimed in, "Chirā, at the end of this year we will need to perform our father's funerary obsequies, and with the sheep we will have no problem serving our relatives and friends."

"Go quickly to the bank, bring back two sheep, brother." Gāji quickly replied, "Tie a lead around their necks to secure them, then you can ferry across the remaining sheep."

As soon as they heard this, the two brothers moored the ferry, picked up oars, took rope in hand, and went off to choose their sheep. They looked over all the rams and ewes in the herd and their mouths watered at the prospect of eating that rich mutton. Kenduyā and Beḍābhāṅgā were the two largest, dominant rams—so the two brothers naturally slipped ropes around their necks. There was a banyan,[33] an imposing fig tree, spreading its canopy next to the landing ghat. They tethered the rams underneath that banyan, then proceeded to haul Sāheb Gāji and all the remaining sheep to the bank across the river. Rippling with delight, Gāji rounded up those sheep and they entered Brāhmaṇ Nagar later that night. He led the tigers, still disguised as sheep, and settled them at the northern ghat, then Sāhā Gājī began to meditate on the Stainless One, Nirañjan.

Listen everyone as I tell something of the story of who else had landed up there. Subject to your trust and dependence on Āllā, I will continue narrating, for Āllā manages to rescue those who have fallen into distress.

THE ARRIVAL OF THE FÆRIES UPON HEARING OF KĀLU'S PLIGHT AND THE EPISODE WITH THE FERRYMEN

Now give over your heart and mind and listen to a little more of the tale, how the færies managed to be present.

The very day that the king incarcerated Kālu, a single færie had flown to that city of Brāhmaṇ Nagar. She witnessed Kālu's distress and horrible condition firsthand. She flew back at speed to report to the Queen Færie. When the Færie Queen was fully informed, she was deeply disturbed and wept in sympathy. Recovering her composure, she mustered three hundred thousand færies and flew to Brāhmaṇ Nagar in her chariot, while others in separate chariots were dispatched to Sonāpur, the City of Gold. From Sonāpur they secured Gāji's bed, replete with banners, and, like the wind, spirited it away, lifting it as if it weighed nothing. In the wink of an eye they reached Brāhmaṇ Nagar. The færies soon landed at the bivouac where Gājī Sāhā had assembled the tigers. They made their salaams with hands pressed together in respect. In return Gājī extended his blessings. They then handed over Gāji's cot—which was, of course, Cāmpāvatī's—and Gājī Sāhā was both relieved and deeply gratified. He promptly seated himself on it. Right after Gājī Sāhā had taken his seat on the bedstead, its four golden

33. *Ficus benghalensis*, the banyan fig or Indian banyan; its aerial roots, which easily serve as a tethering post, hold up a thick canopy that can serve as a natural shed or tent.

banners were hoisted on their standards. When Gājī then gazed at his party of sheep, he meditated on the Stainless One, Nirañjan, and blew three times in their direction: in an instant all the sheep that had been herded there were magically transformed back into tigers.

Let us hear now about the ferrymen and how their situation soon deteriorated into a fiasco.

They took the two tigers-as-rams and tethered them in the cowshed, gathered up two sheaves of grass, and dropped them within easy reach of the rams' mouths. After they had fed and watered them, they went into the house. Satisfied with their bargain, indeed feeling quite smug, the two men sat down to eat. Meanwhile the two tigers looked askance at the grass and began to whisper to one another. The more they talked the more annoyed they became. The tiger Beḍābhāṅgā said to Kenduyā, "Go ahead, chow down on the fodder and water because we are in the guise of sheep." Gājī knew their natures and nearly died laughing at the joke: he had magically transmogrified those vicious carnivores into docile sheep and then made them go vegetarian, to eat forage and drink water!

The next morning the two men boarded their ferry while the two tiger brothers remained tethered in the cowshed. About that time Ḍorā's mother, an old crone if there ever was one, wasted no time in going to look over the rams. Bent over and brittle she could only get around by leaning heavily on a broom as her walking stick. When she reached the door of the cowshed she raised her head to look around. When she saw the rams, she was all aflutter, thrilled at the prospect of getting to eat mutton, the saliva involuntarily welling up in her mouth. As he watched, Beḍābhāṅgā decided to prank her, so he butted her in the loins one time. Somehow the butting accentuated her hunger, so when the ram butted her again, her anger erupted and she struck him with her broom, two, then three times on the top of his head. Enduring the first whack of the broom, but not one to suffer any rain of blows, Beḍābhāṅgā's temper flared. He grabbed the old woman by the hair and slapped her, jabbed her with his hoof, then butted her again. She fell to the ground and rolled over in the fodder. He did not beat her to death, for he wanted to keep her alive to even the score. The old hag managed to scramble out of the cowshed, went back to the house, where she dropped to the ground and curled up in a corner niche of the wall and pulled her rags tight about her. About that time, Chirā and Ḍorā returned and entered the hut. The old hag, who was shivering, called out to them, "The rams knocked me about and now I am suffering a fever. I have no strength and cannot get up. I fear that at some point that ram is going to knock someone dead, so let's not wait, let's make the preparations for father's funeral obsequies today."

So they quickly issued invitations to ten or twenty neighbors. When the other ferrymen received the invitation, they wasted no time arriving at Ḍorā's home. Two *brāhmaṇ* priests, both *purohit*s, Becu and Mechu, naturally showed up then they got wind of it. As soon as the two twice-born, *dvija*s, looked over the rams, they were ready to eat them raw right on the spot. One of the priests called out to Ḍorā, "Make sure you give me the bulging testicles of these outsized rams. If you hand them over to anyone else, I will lay a monstrous curse on you."

The other priest, Mechu, heard this and quickly commanded the ferryman, "No, I will take the gonads of those rams; do not grant them to Becu. My wife has told me that she is pregnant and is especially craving ram's testicles."

Becu promptly interjected, "Michu Dvija, the testicles are mine!"

"Listen, Becu," Michu retorted, "what you are about to eat is a slap in the face!"

And so the argument escalated. They punched one another, they wrestled, they grappled, they grabbed each other around the waist, all the while heaping scurrilous abuse on one another. At this point the ferrymen together intervened, and with hands pressed together in respect, they gently suggested, "Please, you most eminent of those who are twice-born, entertain our modest proposal. There are two rams and therefore four testicles. If each of you takes a portion, then there is no disgrace in that. Becu Dvija, you take two of the testicles, and Mechu, you take the other two for yourself. Then be content that each of you has a pair of nuts." And this way these best of twice-born finally resolved their disagreement.

The ferrymen wasted no time in fetching a long knife for butchering. They went to make ready the Gaṅgā water, wood-apple leaves,[34]

34. Wood apple is *Aegle marmelos*, also known as *bhel* in Bangla; other common English names include Bengal quince or stone apple; the use of the wood apple in sacrifices dates back to the Ṛg Veda and is found in early Ayurvedic texts.

ghee, bananas, sugar, incense, resin, mustard oil, and vermillion. When they returned, they bathed the rams and with rope nooses tied them to a stake in the sacrificial pit. Then the two twice-born recited *mantras* as they placed wood-apple leaves on the heads of the tigers. Kendā said, "Beḍābhāṅgā, did anyone say that we were supposed to remain quiet as our bodies are butchered and we are killed?" Anxious and worried, as they called on Āllā they let out an ear-splitting roar. They instantly resumed their own forms as tigers and roared as they leapt away. "Listen, Beḍābhāṅgā brother, *chāheb* did not give us permission to kill the men," Kendu reasoned, "so let's just give those two best of twice-born a real taste of our balls and then go scout the area for cattle." As their anger welled up, they sprang forward in attack mode with tails straight up in the air. They pounced on the two twice-born and proceeded to smack them around until their cheeks were swollen. They twisted their noses and boxed their ears until they were scarlet. They thrashed them to the point of death, but they pulled up short and did not kill them.

Then what did the two tigers do there? They slaughtered as many sheep and cattle as were in the vicinity, whole herds of them. They slew one hundred thousand oxen and two hundred thousand cows, and so many calves and sheep they cannot be calculated in this writing.

The ferrymen were stunned, overwhelmed with fear. Everyone scrambled helter-skelter and fled as fast they could. As the two brothers Chirā and Ḍorā looked back, it finally dawned on them that the *phakir* was behind this and the tigers were his accomplices. They cut holes through the mud walls of the house so that everyone in the extended family could escape. Constantly looking over their shoulders in fear, they ran for cover. "For as long as I stay alive, I will never take another cowrie from a *mochalmān phakir*!" Chirā swore, "Before today I had absolutely no idea what wondrous powers they possessed. Had I known, why would I have asked that *phakir* for money? When a *phakir* shows up at my ghat, I will carry him across the river on my head if I have to. If those two tigers leave my house, I will offer *śinnī* to the goddess Kālī in the name of Āllā.[35] I will learn how to practice the *din*, the

35. The favorite of Satya Pīr, who is the combined form of God as Nārāyaṇ and Khodā, *śinni* is the traditional offering to powerful *pīrs*, consisting of rice flour, banana, sugar, some mix of spices.

religion of Mahāmmad, and then I will construct two more public landing ghats as penance."

While both Chirā and Ḍorā were making many such promises of this sort, listen everyone to what the tigers got up to next.

When they paused and stood still, assessing the situation, they reasoned, "We do not have the *pīr*'s express command to slay the two ferrymen, and since there is nothing more to detain us further, let's go now to be with *chāheb* Gājī." After they had taken the decision, the two tigers let out a mighty roar and sped off. Leaving a telltale commotion in their wake, they exuberantly bounded across the river, landing on the opposite shore. They shortly arrived in the presence *chāheb* Gājī.

The tigers stood before him and made their salaams of greeting. He gave them his blessings and then began to question them. "Tell me, how were things at the home of the ferrymen?" The two pressed their hands together in respectful obeisance and began to describe how they were tethered inside the cowshed. Little by little, they revealed all the details. As he heard them out, *sāheb* Gājī was delighted. Then he summoned all the tigers and færies and addressed them as a group: "My brother is struggling simply to stay alive in his prison cell. I place this before all of you—what else can I say? We must do whatever it takes to rescue him." The tigers and færies responded, "We want your blessings. Stay here and sit tight while we generate a spectacle."

refrain With ear-splitting roars the tigers bounded about,
leaping as if they were the monkey hordes laying siege
to Laṅkā.

THE TIGERS AND FÆRIES BESIEGE THE CITY OF MAṬUK RĀJĀ AND ENGAGE DAKṢIṆĀ RĀY IN BATTLE

The tigers roared, sprang up and bounded about, then took off. Their flight was unruly, the sounds of their gnashing fangs piercing. The tigers had soon surrounded each and every house there in the city. They blocked every lane and landing ghat, back and forth they patrolled growling and roaring. The tigers managed quietly to encircle the whole of the city, while the residents of that enclave remained completely ignorant of their presence. As soon as the residents got up, they headed outdoors with their pots used for ablutions, as was their morning habit. But once outside, they encountered rows and ranks of tigers at every turn, and, astonished and indeed ravaged by fear, they beat a hasty retreat back indoors. When the *brāhmaṇ* women toted their large gold pots to fetch water from the river, they encountered the tigers and, startled, involuntarily cried out, "O Lord, O Lord!" They dropped their precious pots and fled in every direction. They shook with fear, their terror driving them to the point of unadulterated hysteria. No one in any house dared to set foot outside. The cowherds could not drive the cattle out of the cowsheds, and everyone had to stay indoors to shit and piss. They used cooking pots and even ladling cups to hold their urine and excrement until those vessels were overflowing, then flung the contents outside. The sound of the tigers' roars reverberated, shaking the ghats, indeed the very ground of the earth. *Brāhmaṇ* men and women were terrified equally. Some loudly pleaded, "Stay away! Please stay away!" while others could be heard screaming "It got me!" Any number of people cried out, taking an oath, "O Mother, O Mother! I'm going to die!"

Then someone sent word to the king. "Brāhmaṇ Nagar is on the verge of destruction. You imprisoned that *phakir* and now his brother, Gāji Jendā Pīr, has arrived. I do not know just how many tigers he has dispatched, but they are eating the people and plundering and laying waste to every thing everywhere. Sāhā Gājī has ensconced himself on a palanquin with four golden pennants raised on standards on each of its corners. Atop his head sits a ruby-encrusted hat, while færies hover above and fan him with their whisks. Please take yourself quickly to meet with Gājī, lest his tigers eat up all of us."

"Say nothing more of the kind!" was how the king responded, "What possible fear could I have when Dakṣiṇā Rāy is present? When news of this reaches Dakṣiṇā Rāy's ears, he will slay all of the tigers and Gājī along with them." After this pronouncement, the king went to see the tigers for himself. He climbed up on the roof of one of his sturdy brick-built fortifications. Settled there on the roof, he gazed out and saw rows of tigers in neat ranks patrolling the entire area. For every tiger he singled out, he saw a hundred more. To see so many tigers left him dazed, as if a flame had suddenly ignited inside his head. As he looked out at the tigers, the fever made the *mahārājā* quake with fear, the pain more violent than that of a woman in labor.

Now terrified, what did the mahārājā *do? He took himself forthwith to meet Dakṣiṇā Rāy.*

The king took an array of comestibles with him, and when Dakṣiṇā Rāy saw all that the king had brought, he was very much pleased. There was milk, sugar, *sandeś* sweets, and a cornucopia of fruits, raisins and almonds, bananas and coconuts. For meat there was antelope, buffalo, and goat, and for fowl, duck and goose and any number of pigeons. Of course, the king also brought along fish—hundreds of different varieties.

The variety of foodstuffs was so incredible I cannot even begin to record it all. This much and more did the king have sent along, and when Dakṣiṇā Rāy saw it, he was pleased beyond measure. He cooked and savored each delicacy one at a time, until all had been consumed. After he had eaten and drunk his fill, the virile hero sat back sated and satisfied. Only when the *mahārājā* could control his anguish no longer did he kneel down and grasp Dakṣiṇā Rāy's feet in the most profound obeisance. Taking it in, Dakṣiṇā Rāy was compelled to ask, "What is the reason for this distress, my king, tell me please." The *rājā* replied, "Listen great-souled one, what can I say? Aiee, my social standing and lineage, my *jāt kul*, are totally lost. A *phakir* by the name of Kālu recently landed up. That little son of a bitch had the audacity to tell me that I needed to prepare the traditional *bāṭā* foods offered to my new son-in-law, his brother, who goes by the name of Gājī. He wants my daughter in marriage! Kālu came to arrange it all as the official matchmaker. I wasted no time in having him apprehended and remanded to jail, but listen to this report of what has now transpired: His brother has arrived with his tigers in tow, and they have completely surrounded the city. I cannot even begin to calculate how many tigers he has brought together, but they are certain to lay waste to my city, destroy it all. No one can leave their homes, for they are rattled to the core by the roaring of the tigers. The tigers are attacking and eating up cows and humans alike."

Hearing him out, Rāy chuckled to himself, "Is this the only reason you are so upset, my honorable king?" Then he smiled and said, "Be at your ease, for I will certainly go and slay the whole lot of the tigers and the *phakir* along with them." And having declared that course, the heroic protector left and went to don his armaments for war. On his head, the valiant warrior placed an eighty-maund[36] helmet. Around

36. A maund is variously calculated as 25 to 28 pounds, or ten pounds troy.

his waist, he wrapped a thousand-maund chain, cinching it over his *dhuti*. Over that he placed a breastplate and back plate and then slung beneath his armpit an eighty-maund sword. He picked up his twelve-hundred-maund club and, exulting in his weapons, headed out to wage war.

At the precise moment he headed out, someone sneezed on his left, then a fly buzzed him and landed on his left eyelid. As he continued moving forward an insect bit him on the hand, then a woodcutter with a load of wood crossed his path from the right. Behind him he heard someone mutter, "Stop, stop!" Then a corpse materialized right in front of him. A crow called out, its cackle amplified by the large empty pot on which it sat. A full crew of sailors had taken seats in an empty boat, while a bird squawked, perched on the branch of a dead tree. These worrying omens struck the valiant warrior as serious cause for alarm, but out of pride and embarrassment, he could not turn back. The warrior fretted as he continued forward amidst the sounds of jubilant ululation made by the women in every house he passed. Conchs blew and small bells rang out from all directions, and sounds of horns and other musical instruments could be heard everywhere around. Maṭuk Rājā sat underneath a royal parasol to watch as the valiant warrior Dakṣiṇā headed out to fight. All of his sons and sons-in-law had assembled with him and all of them eagerly watched, with their hands pressed against their cheeks in anticipation. Now fully equipped, Dakṣiṇā Rāy entered the field of battle.

Though he was quite some distance away, Gāji immediately espied him. As soon as Gājī saw Dakṣiṇā approach, he called out to his tigers and gave instruction: "Assume orderly ranks and surround him from all four directions." The tigers heard the command and tore out in great leaps and bounds. When the tigers approached, it was as if they swarmed through his field of vision—hundreds upon hundreds of thousands of tigers advanced, each primed to kill. Where he encountered one tiger he saw ten. The bravado he wore on his face was erased, and his voice failed him. A fear gripped Rāy so completely that he could only shake violently. In his heart of hearts, he realized that it was his life that would be taken: he was about to be killed. "I am but a solitary figure, but the tigers number in the hundreds"—these kinds of thoughts cycled through his mind and spawned an unremitting panic. "If I pick up my club and kill one tiger, hundreds of thousands of other tigers will come to take its place." With these thoughts racing through his head, the valiant warrior quit the battlefield in retreat and made his solitary way to the river.

He took a seat on the bank of the river and called out for the goddess Gaṅgā in an anguished, loud voice. Hearing his plaintive call, Gaṅgādevī floated up to the surface. Fixing his eyes on Gaṅgā, the warrior made deep obeisance. Then the goddess asked him what was his wish: "Speak, tell me, virile one, for what reason did you summon me?" And so the valiant warrior began to speak between his anguished sobs. "O Mother, please listen as I explain everything to you. I have been in the service of Maṭuk Rājā for a long, long time. And I have served ceaselessly all of his people. But today, dear Mother, the social standing and lineage of this king's family is threatened. A *phakir* came and wants to take away his daughter! I had no idea that he had brought so many hundreds of tigers with him. They have completely surrounded and laid siege to Brāhmaṇ Nagar. O Mother, please show your mercy and bestow upon me a bask of crocodiles. Then I will find out just what kind of a *phakīr* he really is."

Gaṅgādevī replied, "O valiant one, tell me precisely, what is the name of this particular *phakir* and where does he hail from, where does he call home?"

Then Rāy explained, "Listen my dear Mother, I have heard people say that Gājī Sāhā is his name. He hails from Bairāṭ Nagar somewhere west of here. Chekāndar Sāhā is his father and master of that place. His mother is the beautiful woman called Ajupā. I have heard this from the mouths of others, but cannot vouch for it myself."

When she heard the details, Gaṅgā spoke, "There is nothing for it, your *brāhmaṇ* has already lost his status and will become *mochalmān*. Listen my dear Dakṣīṇā Rāy, you do not realize that that boy Gājī is my sister's son and I know him very well. He is as dear to me as my own flesh and blood. I have lavished my grace and affection on him since he was a child. Gaurī and I both have ensured his well-being. Who has the power to thwart his marriage to Cāmpā? Were the entire world to unite as one and engage Gājī, they would surely lose. You need to go to the king and explain to him that he must hand over his daughter in marriage to Gājī."

When he registered this, the warrior put forward this proposition: "Why did I even bother to call out to you, Mother? If I turn tail and flee, people are bound to laugh, and the tigers are sure to trap and eat me! Whether I am slain or I am victorious, I want only to engage with him on equal terms. Please grant me the crocodiles and I will be off."

Gaṅgādevi replied, "I most certainly will *not* supply you with crocodiles. Gājī Sāhā would be furious and rebuke me soundly."

Then the warrior ratcheted up his whining and pleaded, "Know well that my life will be lost at the hands of the *turuk*.[37] But do you imagine that any *turuk* will ever perform your *pūjā*? It is my misfortune that you are so heartless. If you do not equip me with the crocodiles, Mother, then I have little choice but to commit suicide right now, right before your eyes, making you responsible."[38] And with this declaration the warrior picked up his club and began to hammer himself on the head. Witnessing this fatal spectacle, Gaṅgā called out, "Stop, stop, valiant one! I will fetch and hand over the crocodiles. But you must say nothing of this to anyone; keep it as our secret! Under no circumstance must Gājī hear of this conversation!" Gaṅgādevī then started to call the crocodiles, each by name, and they began to float up, rising to the surface of the river. Fifty-two thousand crocodiles surfaced and the warrior was pleased and herded them away. As they lumbered forward, they leveled the jungle, the dragging of their stomachs digging ruts that became new river channels.

The warrior then entered the fight with his crocodiles, while the *mahārāj* eagerly watched from his rooftop outpost. "Rāy has mobilized the crocodiles!" he observed to everyone gathered around, "Now that will force the *phakīr* and his tigers to flee."

When Gāji spotted the crocodiles, he addressed the færies: "Look, look at that! Has my aunt, Gaṅgā Māsī, provisioned him with crocodiles? You do understand that her expression of love is self-serving. She cuts the root of the tree while pouring water on its leaves."

Meanwhile, Dakṣiṇā Rāy had arrived, bristling to fight. The great warrior instructed his crocodiles to attack the tigers. When he heard this, Gājī Sāhā commanded in a loud voice, "All of you tigers present, go and punish them! Pounce on the crocodiles and kill all of them!"

37. Turk, a foreigner, or *jaban*, but implying a *musalmān*.

38. To commit suicide in front of someone or on the stoop of their house confers responsibility on that individual, which generates an inescapable blame and social opprobrium that is impossible to counter.

Receiving Gāji's command, the assembled tigers descended on the crocodiles and engaged them in open-field battle. The city of Brāhmaṇ Nagar quaked with fear from the roar of the tigers. *Brāhmaṇ* men and women alike were paralyzed with terror. Even the valiant warrior himself was unsettled and began to tremble, while a flood of tears streamed uncontrollably from Maṭuk Rājā's eyes. As they roared, the tigers raised their tails for the hunt, then they pounced, bounding on and around the crocodiles. With blood-curdling roars they fell on the crocodiles, biting hard. But they quickly cried out with their own frustration as their nails and fangs failed to penetrate the tough leathery hides of the crocs. When they bit down, they found their fangs breaking off, so too their claws. Suddenly neutralized, even rendered powerless, the tigers were utterly confused and perplexed. Then the crocodiles grunted and bellowed, turned and trapped the tigers, snagging their legs between their jaws. Some tigers had their paws and legs utterly crushed, others their heads cracked open. Rattled and uncharacteristically unnerved, the tigers turned tail and fled. With that advantage, Dakṣiṇā Rāy cried out, "Kill them, kill them! Slaughter the whole lot of those tigers!" But the tigers were speedy and quickly escaped to a safe distance. They reassembled in Gāji's presence and whined, giving vent to their complaints. "The bodies of those crocodiles are like iron. Look at how our fangs and claws are jagged and broken off. We are utterly exhausted and cannot continue to attack. That is what forced us to break off and retreat here before you."

When Gāji heard them out he became extremely distressed, so he earnestly supplicated the Lord through his *dargā*, his heavenly court: "O my Lord, filled with compassion, please grant me your mercy. I have fallen into grave danger and need to escape. To extricate me from this particular disaster, in your compassion, you could make it happen something like this: provoke the sun to shine hotter than the fire of conflagration, and this dire situation is certain to be salvaged." The prayer offered through Āllā's court was granted, and the sun slowly began to heat up till it turned into a sizzling fireball. The crocodiles began to overheat, some even giving off smoke, smoldering like burning incense. They were enervated and without the watery mud, they began to thrash and wallow desperately as their life forces withered and dried up. One after another their life-giving energies eked away, weakened in their desiccation; the crocodiles were in desperate straits.

Snipping at their lumbering backsides, the tigers herded them, driving them away. Witnessing this shift, Gāji Sāhā screamed, "Slay them! Kill!" The tigers erupted this way and that, nipping the crocs' tails, climbing onto their backs in furious attacks. Some they killed by pouncing and splitting open their heads, others they simply battered senseless with their paws. Any other survivors they found, the tigers head-butted into oblivion. Having suffered a humiliating defeat, the crocodiles fled, roiling the waters as they plunged back into the river. The crocodiles made for the underground realm, Pātāl Nagar. Witnessing the spectacle, a dispirited Dakṣiṇā Rāy could only lament. Then the tigers returned and completely surrounded him. Finding himself in this desperate fix, the warrior began to grieve. Moaning and weeping plaintively, he cried out, "What is the way out? Who can possibly deliver me from this impending doom? It is only now that I fully comprehend exactly what Fate has written on my forehead. I am to be slain, slaughtered by the tigers. Were I to retreat, indeed, turn tail and run, I'd be the laughingstock of all and sundry, and Maṭuk Rājā would have to eat the ashes of humiliation."

Pondering his predicament from every angle, what did the warrior do? He screamed in anguish to summon another goddess, this time, Gaurī.

With a profound devotion, the valiant warrior called and petitioned Mā Bhavāni. "O Mother, please grant your mercy to this obedient servant. Where else might I turn, dear Mother, for you are the destroyer of all obstacles. Grant me your grace and deliver me from this vile predicament." In this manner Rāy loudly belabored the issue with the goddess. His fervent cries finally reached the goddess's throne, and, understanding instinctively, the goddess mounted her chariot. The goddess, Devī, arrived and presented herself before Rāy. The moment her chariot descended from the sky and landed in that place, Rāy acknowledged her and bowed deeply in profound obeisance. Perched atop her chariot, Gaurī then questioned him: "Speak valiant one, why have you summoned me?" Grief-stricken, the warrior aired his plight to the goddess, "Please look favorably on what I will share with you. The tigers of that *turuk* have me completely compromised—outnumbered and surrounded. They have already killed untold numbers of the city's inhabitants. It is on account of them, my dear Mother, that I called out to you. Please provide me with hordes of hungry ghosts, *bhūts*, and blood-thirsty demons, goblins, and *piśāc*s, so that I can destroy the tigers and that son-of-a-bitch *phakir*! Please grant me this boon right here and now, my dear Mother."

Gaurī replied, "Listen, my child, stop this war and sue for peace. Fate has written that Gāji is destined to marry Cāmpā. You must go back and make Maṭuk Rājā understand in no uncertain terms: 'You must hand over your daughter to Gāji!' He is my sister's son, so I am his aunt. If your king fails to make this marriage, then I promise to flood the whole of Brāhmaṇ Nagar with the ocean's waters and there will be no kin left alive to light the lamps for the transmigration of his lineage. Kārttik and Gaṇeś both love Gāji dearly—I know this to be true. I will place my own necklace on Cāmpā's neck, then I will take some of the food offerings to the gods, *prasād*, and head back to heaven. Go and explain to Maṭuk Rājā: 'It will redound to your benefit to make over your daughter to him.' Your king is burdened with hubris and a self-serving nature. But Gāji's father is no one's servant. Gāji's mother is the daughter of King Bali in Pātāl, while his father is the crest jewel, the epitome of all great kings. There is no fault or shame in Maṭuk Rājā giving his daughter to Gāji. Even with unlimited wealth, one could never purchase a better a son-in-law."

As he listened to her lecture, the warrior's face was pinched, expressing his aggravation and grief. He spoke bluntly to Gaurī. "Listen, dear Mother, why did I bother to call you? If you do not grant me the hungry ghosts, demons, and goblins, then I will smash my head with my own club and kill myself!" It was no idle threat, for he picked up his battle club and began to batter his own skull. "Stop!" Devī yelled quickly to cut short the valiant warrior. She promised, "I will hand over the hungry ghosts right away. But Gāji must never hear of this. If he does get wind of it, I am sure that that sweet boy will be furious with me." And with these words Devī let fly a resounding roar and wild blood-thirsty witches, female spirits, and savage hungry ghosts began to gather. Antigods and disgruntled demigods joined the ranks of the witches, making for tens and tens of millions in all. Bhavāni was at the battlefield, and there they gathered. They ground their teeth impatiently and questioned: "For what task did you summon us, dear Mother. Tell us! Speak! Explain!" She then gave the group the order to fight, at which point the goddess Devī flew off to *vaikuṇṭha* heaven, where she normally dwelled. Right after that, the hungry ghosts and others prepped themselves and set off to do battle with the tigers.

From the mountains they gathered rocks and boulders and then, flying up in the skies, soon rained them down on the tigers. They scanned the horizons in all directions, but the tigers could see nothing. A hailstorm, not of ice but of stones, showered down, hundreds and hundreds of thousands, and the tigers could not escape by any route. They were felled by the hundreds, their bodies pummeled—many paws and legs mangled, countless heads smashed. Those that could came running to Gāji Sāhā. They wept and complained bitterly to Gāji: "What are you doing? How can you just sit there? There is no saving us! All the tigers are going to be massacred! Not one of us has the power even to sit or stand up. We cannot tell where the boulders are coming from nor who is behind their deadly rain. We are in a fix, and all the tigers will soon be eating their doom. Most of us are too weak to fall back and regroup here."

When he received this urgent report, Gāji began to meditate. Through his mind's eye, he soon found the source. It was the goddess who had mustered the witches and goblins and hungry ghosts. So *chāheb* Gāji quickly recited *bichmillā*, "In the Name of God." Three times he blew the incantation as he looked in each of the four directions. When Gāji finished reciting and blew the *bichmillā* to the winds, the heads of the ghosts and goblins were set alight. Shocked and disoriented, the ghosts could find no escape, for the inferno raged catastrophically in all directions. What appeared to be stars twinkling in the sky were actually the heads of the ghosts igniting brightly and bursting into flames. Cries of agony resounded through the blazes that fanned through the four directions. The demonic hordes dispersed helter-skelter, frantically searching for an escape here, there, and everywhere. Eventually, they found a route through the northern quadrant of the skies. As soon as they found this exit through the north, they wasted no time making good their escape.

Witnessing the rout, panic swallowed the warrior Dakṣiṇā, for everywhere he looked, the tigers had him trapped. In orderly ranks and on all sides the tigers fenced him in. Reckoning his position intractable, a litany of anxieties bored through the great warrior's mind, leaving him to draw but one conclusion: "My end is here—the tigers are certain to eat me before the day is out." Agonizing over the futility of the situation, the warrior cinched tight his waistband. Then that warrior, the protector of the king, valiant as ever, let fly a blood-curdling roar in a reckless rage. It reverberated through the sky and caused the earth to quake, so much so that Vāsuki, king of serpents, shook in fear all the way down in the underworld of Pātāl Nagar. The gods and celestial beings alike began to quail, and pregnant women instantly aborted. The concussion knocked the tigers flat out, and they fell, unconscious, in piles that littered the ground. The færies beat a hasty retreat from the bedlam and chaos before them. All alone and still, *chāheb* Gāji sat unperturbed, engrossed in meditation, peering deeply into his mind, while the warrior Dakṣiṇā girded himself and advanced. The club in Dakṣiṇā's hand generated a steady whirlwind, a thrumming, deafening whirr as he swung it. With menacing bulk, the *gosvāi* pressed forward to slay Gāji. Alert to this advance, Gāji picked up his staff and gave it marching orders: "Listen, my good staff, go forth and do battle with the only other person whose face you see, Dakṣiṇā Rāy!" Reciting *bichmillā*, he launched his ascetic's staff. The rod gyrated away, moving in dizzying circles, and, with dance-like precision, pounded Dakṣiṇā's chest. The beating soon made blood ooze from his mouth. Then with evasive pirouettes, the stick flew back and thrashed the crown of his head, before tattooing his face. Then it began to weave back and forth, coiling around and around like a serpent till he was immobilized, unable to shake it off. He tumbled to the ground. Fretting and desperate, the valiant one reached for his club, raised it, and smashed the staff, which broke in two, its splinters flying to the ground. After he shattered the staff, he picked up the two large pieces and hurled them into the waters of the sea. Those waters instantly evaporated, drying up completely. Gaṅgā knew in her heart what had transpired, so in an act of affection, she dispatched the staff to Cāmpā's private quarters. As soon as the staff reached Cāmpā's rooms, the waters were restored as before.

Standing there the warrior Dakṣiṇā took his club in hand. When that valiant one had gathered himself, he advanced to slay Gāji. Watching him approach prompted Gāji to stand up, but looking in all four directions, Sāhā could see no one else. He calculated his options, "Is there anyone for me to call on, to command to help?" Then he happened to look down at the ground and there sat his sandals. Gāji addressed his sandals: "Go forth and engage Dakṣiṇā Rāy in battle!" In a loud and raging whirlwind, the sandals flew up, then began to rain a torrent of blows on Rāy's head. They thumped out a violent *dhum*

dhum rhythm on his skull, then with a quick "thwack thwack" they battered his mouth and nose. They assailed him, flying up in the air and then diving down to pound the full length of his body. The valiant warrior absorbed the blows, but eventually he fell, prostrate, writhing on the ground in agony. Those sandals flailed him relentlessly, flying here and there, up and down, the way the rice flies when women beat flat the paddy. Eventually, blossoms of blood rose all over his body from the relentless barrage of beatings. So thoroughly was he thrashed that he seemed little more than a shapeless pulp. Numb and insensate, the warrior sprawled on the earth.

When he saw his immobilized condition, Gāji Sāhā picked up a dagger, sat on the warrior's chest, and cut off both his ears. At this most elemental of humiliations, the despairing warrior cried out: "Rām! Rām!" Then *chāheb* Gāji brought the knife up in a move to slit his throat. Watching this filled Dakṣiṇā's gut with fear. He blurted out, "By the mercy of Āllā, Gāji, please don't stab me, please don't eviscerate me! I am already dead from the humiliation of having my ears cut off. Listen, listen, Gāji Sāhā, please don't take my life! I will remain forever at your feet as your loyal servant. I will immediately make my way to the king and convince him that he must give his daughter, Cāmpā, in marriage!" When he heard this promise, Gāji actually believed him, so he did not slay him. He did, however, bind his wrists together firmly, after which he grabbed him by his topknot. The topknot that sprouted from Dakṣiṇā's head was a good thirteen hands long, and the girth of his enormous body was equivalent to a mountain. His ears had been the size of an elephant's. Gāji Sāhā grabbed his topknot with one hand and tied it tight to the leg of his cot.

The færies watched this, and as soon as the news spread, they all came and gathered around Sāhā. Gāji Sāhā said, "O hey, listen up, færies, why did you fly off and abandon me?" The færies responded, "Sāhā, let us explain what happened. The power of that warrior's roar hurled us flying into the distance. The impact of that shout knocked us all silly, unconscious. We did flee and leave you, Sāhā. Oh, please forgive us this offense. May the beneficence of Āllā be upon you! We sincerely wish for your well-being. We take this oath so that all of your wishes will be fulfilled." Gāji Sāhā was gratified to hear this honest confession, and with great affection, he seated the færies all around him. The færies in turn expressed their heartfelt thanks to Gāji Sāh for how he had managed to subdue a warrior of such incredibly enormous stature.

After that all the tigers came to his venerable presence. Having formed into orderly ranks, they stood straight with their hands pressed together in supplication. With a scolding laugh Gāji spoke to the tigers, "Every one of you fled! All of you abandoned me!" Gāji gently scolded the tigers thus. "I saw only too well how you hung back in the distance." The tigers replied, "You clearly know everything. The roar made by Dakṣiṇā Rāy was inhuman, and the force of it knocked us all unconscious, absolutely silly. Well done, kudos to you, Sāhā, for subduing that virile warrior! Now, Sāhā, we will rip him to pieces. Give us leave to move quickly, Sāhā, so we can eat and fill our stomachs!" Bheḍābhāṅgā said, "I will feast on the offal—the lungs and the liver." Kenda said, "I will disembowel him and eat my fill of his guts." Overhearing this, that mighty warrior shook with fear. Pressing his hands together, he spoke to the eminent Gāji: "I beg you, please do not cut me up and feed me to the tigers. I will go right away and arrange your marriage to Cāmpāvatī!" When he heard this declaration, Gāji smiled knowingly, while the færies struggled to contain their laughter. Shouting out to all the tigers present, "I am not going to surrender Dakṣiṇā for you to eat, because he has just promised to arrange my marriage to Cāmpā! And given that, I simply cannot hand him over to you to devour." Then all the tigers and the færies burst out in gales of laughter. So, Dakṣiṇā was bound, but on account of Cāmpā, survived. Gāji, now quite happy, stayed right where he was.

The news soon reached Maṭuk Rājā that the mighty warrior Dakṣiṇā Rāy was captured. Seeing that it was true, Maṭuk Rājā cried out in a loud voice.

refrain Alas, aiee, is my life to come to an end this day?
How did Gājī manage to subdue such an intrepid warrior?

MAṬUK RĀJĀ HIMSELF THEN MOVED TO ENGAGE GĀJI ŚĀHĀ IN BATTLE.

Head in his hands, the king fretted over the incredible strength of Gāji manhandling Dakṣiṇā. "He demonstrates a power like no other—he put an elephant into a headlock and effortlessly threw him to the ground. Once Gāji Sā engages, who can possibly triumph over him. I am in an impossible situation, what shall I do? My social standing, *jāti* and *kul*, will be compromised, and after that the tigers will devour us! Aiee, aargh, I do not see any way out!" His ministers and close friends consoled him, "Do not give yourself over to worry and despair. What can a solitary *phakir* do by himself? You have a massive army of twelve crore nine hundred men, untold lakhs of rifle and archery units, with shot and arrows galore. There are twelve lakhs of elephants and horses. What power can the *jaban* muster to wage war against that? The cannon shot will kill him and reduce the tigers to ashes. This can be effected in the twinkling of an eye." Hearing this, the king was mollified and convinced. He issued the command to the army, "Waste no time, prepare every one. Arm yourselves, and go quickly to the battlefield today! Slay all of the tigers. Lay hold of the *phakir* and drag him to the Kālī temple and dispatch him as a blood offering." Acknowledging the command of the king, the elephant troops and cavalry in numerous divisions were mustered precisely as ordered. Elephants in massive numbers were caparisoned, mounted by musketeers and archers, which were then assembled in orderly ranks on the open field of the maidan. Some men brandished *talwār* swords, shields strapped to their backs, and behind them, men carrying cudgels were without number. As the foot-soldiers moved into position, kettledrums rumbled, their relentless beat hammering the rhythm into the ear. All the war trumpets sounded, a cacophony of intermingled sounds vying one against another, while conchs blared long and loud. Untold numbers of *jayḍhāk* drums resounded, and flutes by the hundreds trilled, as thousands upon thousands poured onto the battlefield. The thwacking of *bheul* drums split the air, kettledrums and bells rang out, sounding an endless din.

refrain. The *rājā* was giddy at the deafening tumult
of his army mobilizing and heading into battle.

The soldiers yelled, "Victory to the king! Victory to the king!" In house after house, the womenfolk trilled their auspicious ululations. The twelve lakhs of horse and elephant cavalry moved forward in smart, orderly ranks. The pounding of the infantry's footsteps made the earth quake. As they advanced, Maṭuk Rājā's heart rippled with pleasure. Still bound in his jail cell, Kālu Sāhā heard the commotion, and he began to call after the king. "Take me along with the soldiers, otherwise you will not survive. Gājī's tigers will catch you and devour you! In the presence of your armies, you are conceited, puffed up with pride, but rest assured that Gājī will be victorious in this battle. Were all the people in the world to band together as one, make no mistake that Gājī would slay them all. All of those soldiers will be killed for no good reason. Make over your daughter to Gājī, who is an appropriate match."

When he heard this, Maṭuk Rājā rejoined, "Do you not fear to make such grandiose speeches, you degenerate mendicant? When the day is done, all of the tigers will be killed. I will lead Gāji back, ropes binding hand and foot. At the fixed time for Kālī's worship, I will surely be offering her a blood sacrifice of both of you!" As he listened, Kālu remained with his head down. Keeping his anger in check, his thoughts to himself, he stifled his retort and remained silent. Making ready, Maṭuk Rājā headed to the battlefield.

Elsewhere, Sāheb Gāji focused his mind on Khodā. "O God, Āllā, the Protector of this Earth, the Pure, there is none other than You who can save me!" Gathering all the tigers and færies around him, Prabhu, firmly seated, called out in a loud voice to the stainless Nirāñjan. While this was transpiring, Maṭuk Rājā's army arrived. All in neat, disciplined ranks, they prepared their artillery. Gathering his tigers around him, Gāji sat right where he was, stationary, while the artillery troops and archers surrounded them on all sides. Finally, Maṭuk Rājā gave the order: "Everyone fire at once!" As soon as the order was issued, the artillery fired in unison. The ground shook at its terrible sound. All of the trees, the shrubs, the leafy ground cover burst into flame, the cannons incinerating everything there. When each and every artillery piece had discharged, the earth was dark, blanketed in a thick smoke. The pall of darkness was still lingering after more than four hours. Then Maṭuk Rājā announced, "That son of a bitch *phakir* has been killed and the crisis averted!" The jubilant cry of "Hari *bol*!" rang from every quarter.[39]

39. *Hari bol* is literally "Say the name of Hari, Kṛṣṇa!" an exclamation of praise, an interjection to punctuate good news, a greeting, an exclamation of victory, and so forth, originally among *vaiṣṇavs*, followers of Kṛṣṇa, but not limited to that group.

At the command of Āllā, the cloud of smoke began to clear, and through that haze the tigers materialized, standing in tight formation. Not a single hair or whisker of any tiger was ruffled or singed. With all of them gathered around, Gāji Sāhā sat blissfully unperturbed. When he saw Gāji, the king was astonished. Distressed, he pounded his head, wailing in agony. "Now I know for certain that that son of a bitch *phakir* commands a great magical power. Twelve lakhs of cannon shot were fired without effect. I brought fifty-two crores of foot soldiers with me and I was unable to slay even a single tiger. I am not able to engage this *phakir* in further battle. I had harbored false hope, only to be throwing away my life." Gripped in fear, the king turned tail and fled, while the tigers closed in from behind. Gāji Sāhā saw what was happening and called out to his tigers, "See there how Maṭuk Rājā is running away, and see how he is taking all his soldiers with him. Surround them and kill them now!" As soon as the command was issued, the tigers leapt to the task, sinking their claws and fangs into countless men, tossing them to their deaths. Ignited by their own brutish anger, they became like fire incarnate and slew thousands upon thousands of men. When the men scattered in fear, the tigers together leapt forward and surrounded and toyed with them. Anyone who heard the low-pitched growl expired of his own accord before he was even touched. The magnificent roars of the tigers Beḍābhāṅgā, Kendo, and Kālkuṭī made the *nāg* serpents in the underworld city of Pātāl shiver in fear. One by one the tigers, betraying a spiteful malice, slaughtered all of the horses, elephants, and camels gathered on the maidan, then with the same cold-blooded intent the tigers turned to track down and butcher all of the soldiers riding those mounts. All the finery and expensive clothes that marked the king as king, he shed, tossing them to the ground as he fled. He rushed into his palace and slammed shut the shutters. *Brāhmaṇs* all around scattered crying in despair. Some artisans broke their arms and legs as they fled, while some workers knocked out their teeth in their haste to escape. Some fled terrified into silence, with no sound at all leaking from their mouths. Regardless of how, everyone there made to get away. The tigers continued their search until there were no more humans to find. The tigers had routed all the soldiers, after which they returned to Gāji elated and satisfied.

Feeling lucky to have escaped, what did the king decide to do?

There was a magic well located in the king's compound whose waters could bring the dead to life. The king filled a large earthen jug with that well-water and that night hauled it to the battlefield and sprinkled it over all the soldiers lying there. On all the elephants and horses that had been slain he sprinkled those waters, so too on the bodies of all the men who had been killed. Everyone who had died magically came back to life and the elephants and horses likewise got up, revived. Everyone got the gift of life and arose. And off they went to engage Gāji in battle once again. All those men who had been killed on the field of battle were repeatedly resuscitated when they were sprinkled with the life-giving waters. In this way the battled dragged out day after day. And so twenty days passed in this routine. The tigers were utterly exhausted and no longer able to fight. Repeated battles left their faces mauled, their fangs and claws chipped, splintered, broken off. The tigers then turned to Gāji and spoke, "We cannot understand how the king musters all these soldiers. Whatever number we slay, their numbers remain the same. We are banged up, claws, fangs, faces mutilated. We are fatigued, overtaxed, our bodies enervated, drained of strength."

Listening carefully to their report, Gāji closed his eyes and in his meditation he had a vision of the well that contained that nectar of immortality. Gāji said, "Listen carefully, tigers, to what I have to report. In the king's compound there is a magic well whose waters bring the dead back to life. That well is located in a special place on the palace grounds. If you slaughter a cow and tip it into the well, then from that moment you will be guaranteed victory in battle, for its waters will no longer have the power to revive anyone." When they heard this, Bheḍābhāṅgā sprang up and away and soon brought back a cow he had slain. A færie picked up a meaty piece of its thigh and flew it to the well, dropped it in, and quickly returned. After that, all the tigers and færies girded themselves, and then, moving as one, sallied forth to engage the king's soldiers amassed before them. The tigers and færies pushed into the midst of the attacking soldiers where hundreds of hundreds of thousands died by claw and fang on the ground, and toting *talwār* swords, the færies slashed the soldiers from above. Men by the thousands were savagely hacked to death, and the tigers soon bathed in the pooled blood of those men. It was so deep that the tigers had to swim through that blood, which flowed in every direction, and anyone they happened to spot, they instantly pounced on his neck. Maṭuk Rājā had twelve crores of soldiers, along with numerous elephants, horses, and camels, who fought until none could engage further in battle. The tigers and færies together slaughtered the entire lot; war's full horror closed in, and no single man remained alive.

So later that day, Maṭuk Rājā brought those special waters and sprinkled them over the limbs of the corpses. He drizzled the waters throughout the night, but not a one sprang up revived. The king finally realized that someone must have polluted the magic well by dumping cow meat into it. "Aiee, aargh, where can I go? What else can I do? Now the tigers will surely track me down and eat me!" Worrying himself sick, one fear building on another, the king fled to one of the cooler, less exposed, parts of the inner palace where he slammed shut the doors figuring there was no way the tigers could break in.

The tigers were thrilled with their victory in battle and together immediately headed off to the prison house to look for Kālu. They pounced on the sentries and guards defending the jail and devoured them in a gulp. They banged on the doors with hard staffs and eventually broke them down. They fanned out searching for Kālu and they soon found him bound in his iron shackles. Kālu closed his eyes and recalled the name of the Lord, Prabhu. The tigers huddled in a group around his feet and one by one they wept and solemnly touched his feet. Kālu Sāhā managed to calm the tigers. Using their teeth, they broke the iron shackles. Then from behind, the tiger Kenda grasped Kālu's body and hoisted him onto his back. All the tigers pranced around, before, and behind Kendurā with Kālu riding on his back. It was not long before Kālu was reunited with Gāji. They began to weep, but they were tears of pure joy. Gāji said, "Hey, brother, where have you been? It is on account of me that you have suffered such awful misery!" Teary, Gāji hugged Kālu Sāhā around the neck, and the two commiserated, overcome with emotion. Their turbans soon unraveled and slipped down, but they let them lie and did not bother to retie them. Witnessing their weeping, the tigers and færies too began to shed tears as they crowded around them. After a while, calm was restored, and the pair sat, settled on the cot, which served as a palanquin, their hearts gently rippling with pleasure.

Looking over at Dakṣiṇā Rāy, Kālu Sāhā spoke, "How did you manage to subdue that demon, Gāji?" Laughing, Kālu continued, "It is our great fortune, brother Gājī, that you managed to tie up the king's *gosvāi*, his champion, at the foot of the palanquin." At that moment, Gājī Sāhā bubbled with glee. Then he called for Kendo and Beḍābhāṅgā. Gājī spoke to the two tigers with great affection, "The two of you are dear, like sons to me. Go and arrest Maṭuk Rājā and fetch him back here. The earth will resound with your glory."

As soon as they heard, the tigers roared and were off. They managed to force their way into the king's compound. The tigers were astonished, gazing in wonder at the splendor of the citadel. Looking around their eyes grew wider and wider in amazement. The temple, the monastic quarters, the palace itself were constructed of gold. The walls were studded all over with emeralds, pearls, and rubies set in gold, and delightful, even entrancing, were the various paintings covering their walls. Indrapuri, the citadel of the king of the gods, itself could not compare. There were untold hundreds of towering buildings and not one the same. They were constructed with carnelian-studded walkways, while doorways by the hundreds were set with diamonds. Gazing at this opulence the tigers began to chatter, "Aiyee aiyee, I am slain by such magnificence! How did mere humans manage to construct such a citadel?" The duo of tigers looked for the living quarters, rummaging through corridor after corridor in search of the king. But all the rooms had been securely locked down. They searched the entirety of the properties but failed to find him, nor anyone else for that matter. To the south there was a towering building, the women's quarters. They kicked with all their might until they broke open the door. Once they had shattered the door, the tigers entered and searched all around. The wives of Cāmpā's brothers—her sisters-in-law—were all huddled there, shaking with uncontrollable fear at the sight of the tigers. Suddenly feeling quite embarrassed over the intrusion, the tigers beat a hasty retreat. Then they broke open the door situated to the west. The tigers entered and surveyed the room where they found Cāmpā's aunts—the wives of her father's brothers—cowering anxiously. Taking stock of the scene, the tiger Kenda began to speak, "Listen, brother Beḍābhāṅgā, watch me while I have a little wicked fun. I'm going to tease Cāmpā's aunts. Raising his tail straight up as if to hunt, he let out an ear-splitting roar. "Oh, my, O mother!" they screamed as they fell to the floor, writhing in fear. In their terror, the clothes of a few slipped off, and they scrambled naked. Some pissed themselves, and at least one shat herself, and others flung off their garments as they were being chased. The tiger Beḍābhāṅgā said, "Listen, Kenda brother, enough of this joking around. Let's get on with the business at hand."

Next, the pair loped down the corridor to the north door, which they broke down. Inside, they spotted two women—Cāmpā and her mother sitting on a bedstead. Seeing the tigers, Cāmpā jumped onto her mother's lap. The two tigers, motionless, looked steadily at them and calmly said, "Have no fear in your heart or mind, O mother. Honorable woman, we are your servants because you are soon to be the mistress of *chāheb* Gāji's house." The two then bowed down and grasped the young maiden's feet, made formal obeisance, and then departed.

They broke down the door to the cool inner chamber, where they finally located Maṭuk Rāja crouching down inside. When he spotted the tigers, he recoiled in horror. His eyes filled with tears, but he was politely escorted outside. One of the tigers placed him on his back and leaped forward to take him to Gāji. When they were still a ways off, Kālu espied the king. He ran out, barefoot and sans shirt, to meet him. He retrieved the king from the tigers and, with a show of great respect, led him forward by the hand. Weeping and whimpering, the king addressed Kālu: "Please intervene with Gāji and make him understand my position. If he spares my life, then I promise to hand him my daughter in marriage. I will adopt the *mohāmmadi* faith and practices. After I cut off my topknot, I will be a *muchalmān,* and I will regularly utter the *kalemā* of the Prophet. And I promise to do whatever else he might tell me."

And so Kālu immediately escorted the king to meet Gāji and explained the situation: "Please reduce your judgement of Maṭuk Rājā's offenses, which for a king are really not so grave. He promises to give his daughter in marriage, and he promises that he will become a *mochalmān* as well." When he heard these pronouncements, Gāji grew genuinely happy and personally raised the king up and had him sit beside him. At that juncture, all the tigers and færies gathered around and began to joke affectionately with the king. One of the færies said, "O king, what do you think? Should we cut off your ears to match Dakṣiṇā Rāy's." Chuckling mischievously another one queried, "What kind of cook is your wife? Please explain how the queen makes her pickle? Does she remember to put the salt in the spinach? How does she prepare her goat-stuffed breads, her butter breads? Go on, tell your son-in-law what how she excels as an accomplished cook." In this way the færies prattled in light-hearted humor, while the *mahārāj* remained silent, too embarrassed to retort.

After that encounter, Gāji called out to Kālu, "Go ahead and release Dakṣiṇā. Let us not delay for there is nothing more to be done. Have the tigers and færies take a break and we shall head to our new home." The king then approached Gāji and in a conciliatory voice said, "Listen, listen, my dear son, to what I have to say: My daughter Cāmpāvatī is an ocean of virtue. She is my only daughter born amidst seven sons. Please maintain her always with compassion. If she ever makes a mistake or errs, please forgive and forget. With your eye constantly on God, the Merciful, may you always treat her with a gentle hand—may she never suffer any physical abuse or undergo other miseries." When he had heard him out, Gāji stood up and then turned his attention to Rāy and released him from his fetters. To the tigers and færies he said, "You have suffered much, gone to great pains on my account. Please do not harbor any resentment because of it. So now let us part. All of you should return home, back to your own lands." The tigers and færies listened attentively, made their obeisances, and took their leave, after which the *mahārāj*, too, headed back to his palace. The two brothers, Gāji and Kālu, accompanied him.

As the entourage trekked along, the warrior Dakṣiṇā took the lead. They arrived as a group in the king's quarters, where the two brothers were soon seated in a pleasantly cool room. They were inwardly thrilled to be sitting there, and they were fed an assortment of brilliantly cooked dishes and refined delicacies. The pair's appetites thus stimulated, they ate with gusto. Counsellors and ministers, select subjects, and any number of other people were formally received. All recited the *kalemā* and became *mochalmān*. All ranks of *brāhmaṇs* clipped off their sacred threads, cut off the tufts of hair on their heads, and one and all became *mochalmān*. Afterwards the *mahārāj* called his counsellors and instructed them to make the preparations for the wedding. As soon as the counsellors received the order, they busied themselves with those arrangements. All the relatives directly related to the king—his *jñāti* and *kuṭumba*[40]—were then assembled.

40. Generally, these terms designate relatives of one's own (*jñāti*) and relatives by marriage (*kuṭumba*). The two sets are overlapping. For an insightful and precise explanation, see Ronald B. Inden and Ralph W. Nicholas, *Kinship in Bengali Culture* (Chicago: University of Chicago Press, 1977); see esp. the first chapter for the distinction.

There simply was no limit to the joy wafting through the king's household.

The poet, though unskilled, writes in his sweetest voice.

refrain Ah, what bliss, what pleasure filled the king's palace.
Shouts of jubilation erupted from the homes of the city's denizens.

THE NARRATIVE OF THE MARRIAGE OF CĀMPĀVATĪ TO GĀJI SĀHĀ

Professional dancers performed and accomplished vocalists sang, and the soothing voices of all manner of instruments blended beautifully. *Mṛdaṅga* and smaller tom-tom drums punctuated the soaring melody of the flutes. Kettledrums and victory bells kept time to the tinkling of anklets. The sonorous double-ended *pākhoyāj* barrel drum beat different rhythms, to which the singers began to sway in dance. All around musicians played in small troupes composed of tabor, drum, and small kettledrums. Everyone was enchanted, entirely captivated with the bliss of the moment. For seven days the music and entertainment continued. Everyone—from the most illustrious citizens to the poorest of the poor—ate all together in the king's palace, with men and women freely mixing together. Eventually the *mahārāj* took his place in the assembly hall. After calculating precisely the auspicious moment of the most propitious day, he gave the order to make ready the groom and his daughter. Next the barber made his mandatory appearance. The youngish barber, a bit of a cheeky scoundrel, clipped a single nail and then ordered two or three maunds[41] of grain be bound up as his gift. And after another quick clip, the greedy shyster had the audacity to say, "I am still due a gift of lentils, *ḍāl*." He kept muttering "*ḍāl, ḍāl*," over and over, as if under a spell. When he received the *ḍāl*, he next demanded oil. The reason for the oil was that he also wanted quince or wood apple. When he got the oil and the quince, he then announced that he was due a measure of salt. This obnoxious man went on blathering "salt, salt," until he was nearly murdered. The barber then smartly took his honorarium and escaped. Afterwards, the bride and groom made their final preparations.

41. See n. 36 above.

This poet, though unskilled, speaks in his sweetest voice. Now, everyone, listen to the three-footed tripadi *meter.*

Gāji Sāh was very calm as
everyone gathered, jostling to get a
glimpse of him being dressed.
Sāhā Gāji was quite pleased when they
fitted a garment woven with gold thread,
enhancing his already striking presence.
Around his neck they draped a string of massive *gajamati* pearls,
which further complemented his radiant figure, and
topped this with a turban of gold-woven cloth.
His already prepossessing good looks
erupted like a flash of lightning,
mesmerizing all who held him in their gaze.
When the womenfolk cast their eyes on the groom,
they involuntarily exclaimed, "Aha, I could just die!
What heavenly charms has the stainless Nirāñjan, fashioned!
It seems a full moon has
fallen down to the earth, or
the sun's rays streak through a dark raincloud."
In this way did they make ready Gāji,
taking him in hand to be ensconced on a
brilliantly iridescent mobile throne.
When the groom's party was fully assembled,
they carried him on that seat of honor through
all the quarters of the city before returning.
Dancers and musicians led the way,
large *daṅka* drums punctuated the music, while
naobata kettledrums atop lumbering elephants marked time.
English horns blared, signaling that the
honorary sepoys were properly mustered.
The city resounded with the trill of auspicious ululation.
Hundreds upon hundreds of elephants
and horses were on parade, and ahead of them,
the roadway was ceremonially swept with peacock feathers.
Fireworks rained down their showers of sparks,
leaving billows of thick smoke lingering behind.
The groom's crowd surged up to the king's personal quarters.
Everyone was in high spirits as they led the groom
to the assembly hall and placed him in the seat of honor,

a high cushion interwoven with gold thread.
Afterwards, everyone else who followed
was seated in the assembly in strict accordance
to their status and station.
A troupe of female dancers then entered, followed by
traditional classical dancers, whose torsos undulated,
posed to convey the full range of the emotions of love.
Jugglers and other entertainers by the hundreds appeared,
all taking their turns to perform for the gathering.
Everyone present sang out their blessings and benedictions.
Meanwhile, in the women's quarters,
all the ladies huddled around to prepare Cāmpāvatī,
massaging oil in her hair, turmeric on her limbs and scalp.
The lowly poet says,
Listen, everyone, with a happy heart
to the preparations of Gāji's bride.

A bevy of intimates busied themselves with Cāmpāvatī's toilet. She rivaled a heavenly nymph, a *vidyādhari*, her beauty more blindingly radiant than the sun. They massaged her body from head to toe with a mixture of turmeric and oil. They bathed her and then scented her with fragrant rose water. They combed her hair, wove strands of gold through it to affix ornaments on her head. They draped her with elegant finery garnished with pearls and emeralds. Her beautiful form glistened as if her limbs were ablaze. They furnished her with ornamental drupes of pink pearls set in gold. So startling and brilliant was the effect, she seemed to sparkle like the rays of the sun. In this glamorous fashion did they adorn Cāmpāvatī.

About then, Kālu Sāhā calculated that the auspicious moment had arrived, so he sent for the lawyer. In the presence of this legal authority, Cāmpā gave her formal consent, and Gāji, in turn, agreed to the legal terms of the marriage. Through the conventional ceremony of matrimony the two were joined as one. When the marriage was completed, a thrill raced through Gāji's heart as he headed toward the screened women's quarters to experience that solemn first look at Cāmpā's face. He entered that mysterious sequestered realm of the women. Gāji's beauty filled their quarters with a soft light. The ocean of Gāji's charms complemented hers, like a lamp aglow with sunlight. The attending færies were utterly spellbound when they beheld his magnificent form.

The play of light off his body illuminated the special nuptial room. When they caught a glimpse of his stunning presence, the women there caught their breath, totally transfixed, as if frozen in their tracks by the sight of a swaying cobra. None was able to keep her calm. At least a few lost consciousness and fell to the ground in a dead faint, all reason and understanding disappearing in a flash. When they gathered their wits and got up, they blurted out things like, "Sister, I can only hope to become a serving girl and devote myself to this Gāji." When the wives of Cāmpā's brothers glimpsed Gāji they quite lost their minds, ensorcelled by his irresistible glamour. Then the young woman's mother announced to all the other women gathered there, "May I formally present to you my son-in-law, who is a peerless *pīr*." When she showed him to the princesses, they, too, fell dumb, stunned, but eventually, albeit slowly, regained their senses. The queen began to speak to those in the group, "I have never previously encountered such a wonderfully handsome prospect for a son-in-law, nor could I have ever foreseen that I would be giving my daughter in such a marriage. What can I say? It is my great good fortune that he is the one who is to become my son-in-law. Who else could take his place, for there is no one like him."

As they were listening to this, the servant girls began to joke and carry on as they escorted all of the princesses inside. Afterwards the womenfolk gathered as a single group and crowded into the special nuptial chamber. They all sat close to Cāmpā and ceremoniously lifted the young bride's veil to reveal her face. Gāji's and Cāmpā's gaze met, the couple's eyes locked. They were smitten, each lost in the mesmerizing, ever-increasing beauty of the other.

Cāmpā's sisters-in-law laughed and joked and conspired to play some pranks. Somehow, no doubt by mistake, they slipped chili peppers into the areca nut[42] for paan and then gave it to Gāji to chew. Somehow someone managed to mix in pungent leaves of leadwort[43]

42. The areca nut is the seed of the *Areca catechu*, a feather palm, valued for its mild narcotic properties and used as a breath freshener, a digestif, and an aphrodisiac. Its exchange by a couple, once chewed, is heavily symbolic of their erotic connection. The chili pepper is *Capsicum annum*

43. Leadwort is *Plumbago zeylanica*, also called doctorbush. Its bitter leaf is ground and used in Ayurvedic medicine for its carminative properties, as an aid to digestion, to expel nasal mucus, and in sufficient dose, as an abortifacient..

with the betel leaves used to wrap that catechu,[44] while somehow another mistakenly mixed pellets of rabbit droppings into the tobacco that laced the betel quid for additional flavor. Somehow one more innocently blended the flowers of the leadwort into the parched rice, which they all pressed Gāji to eat.

Gāji Sāhā looked at the concoctions and instantly understood all they had done. Smiling, he grabbed the women by the ends of their saris, pulled, and said, "Listen you beautiful ladies, I am embarrassed for you. But I feel constrained to speak since I am your new son-in-law. It is clear that you have never been touched by the hand of a real man. Not even in your dreams have you encountered a real man. All of you women present here should understand that joking and buffoonery with a man is not conducive to the art of love. I understand that your husbands must act like so many low-caste barbarians, blockheads. Take control of the domestic realm, be the women you are meant to be! It is clear you have not studied the *rati śāstra*s, the manuals of erotic love. Were you conversant with them, they would teach you how to present yourself in a more sophisticated manner." After Sāheb Gāji lectured them like this, the women, shamed, pulled their saris over their faces and fled.

A huge variety of foods and condiments were then brought so that the group could ceremonially feed Gāji. After he ate and drank, Gāji lay down on Cāmpā's bed. He and Cāmpā coupled in a wonderfully erotic play of love. Cāmpā cut and pinned a rose-scented paan. She lifted up the quid and romantically slipped it into her husband's mouth. She then spent the entire night making ardent love with her husband. The couple's heads came together as their lips locked in kisses. They began fervently to scuffle, to mate in every conceivable way. Eventually, the raging fires of their passion subsided and the pair floated on an ocean of pure bliss. They completely forgot all the miseries that had afflicted them. The couple bobbed in the vast river of pleasure as they experienced every imaginable act of lovemaking, not once, but all day and night. Soon more than a few days had passed in this fashion. But in the midst of this joyful recreation, a discontent wormed its way in.

44. Betel is the leaf of the *Piper betle* (*Piperaceae*) used to wrap the areca nut, to which is added slaked lime paste (calcium hydroxide) to make the betel quid.

While Gāji basked in ecstasy back in Cāmpā's quarters, Kālu remained all alone, isolated, outside of the compound. Kālu's worries grew alarmingly serious. "Erotic love of this woman has utterly bound my brother, and once a man is trapped by *māyā*—the magical allure of woman, that enchanting net of Indra—it is virtually impossible to cut through its bonds."

Listen, listen friends, you must understand fully: no one, no one at all should be immersed in the love of a woman.

"No amount of effort, brother, can sever the entanglement of this net. That he became a *phakir* in the name of Āllā was clearly a sham. If Gāji's mind and heart were so besotted with desire, why did he give up his kingship to become a *phakir*? By what power could he be made to show his face in Khodā's heavenly *dargā*?" Thinking like this, Kālu grieved.

Gāji fathomed what was in his heart, which prompted him to come outside. He saw that Kālu Sāhā was quietly weeping, and seeing him grieving thus, placed his arms around his neck and hugged him. Tenderly, he asked, "To what end are you lamenting, brother? Tell me what troubles you. If you cannot speak truthfully, brother, then take an oath on Āllā."

Kālu replied, "You are what has made me grieve, when you succumbed, hopelessly enthralled by the love of that woman. Know that any woman is born a ghoul, a *rākkasi*, of this magical world of *māyā*. O brother, he who keeps her in intimate company finds himself committed to two different families, this-clan and that-clan. Let me explain the analogy. When one becomes the lord, the husband, of a woman, he has in effect split himself into two different people. Explain to me, Sāhā, how does one determine the correct commitment? In this life your heart can only pledge to one love. If you give that to your wife, what will you give to Khodā? When you produce a child, this world of *māyā* will spirit you away, for when you look into the child's face, your love for Khodā will fade and evaporate. When your boat is securely berthed at the ghat, would you scuttle your goods, throwing everything overboard? Would you allow your stores of grain to slip through your hands at a loss? There is a story told in the Korān: Mariyam, the mother of Ichā,[45] was a faithful, devoted woman; her heart was totally immersed

45. Ichā is Issā or Jesus.

in a pure and unalloyed love for the Lord. So singular was her focus that she completely forgot herself. Showing compassion toward her, He dispatched angels from heaven to her house. They bore many different kinds of heavenly fruits and other edible provisions, which they gave to this favored *bibī*. When she ate those morsels, an heir, the Prophet Ichā, was conceived. Her affection and attachment grew every time she lifted the child onto her lap and gave him her breast. Then He declared, 'You used to sing my praises as the favored of Ālla. But you have not called out to me with that tone of singular love for quite some time. Now that you have a son, you have quite forgotten me altogether, for you are torn between two loves. You will be fed no longer in this comfortable setting. You must leave this place straight away and with your own hands will you have to forage for food in the forested areas. You will no longer receive sustenance through the service of the angels.'[46] When there are two loves, look at what a mess it makes. Listen, my dear brother, what more can I say? Who among intelligent people possesses the disciplined fortitude to make you understand?" And with that, Kālu concluded what he had to say.

Smiling, Chāheb Gāji spoke, "I have not become incapacitated by the love of a woman. What woman has the wherewithal to hold me captive? Listen, brother, I will leave this very night. You must not say anything to the king or queen. When that beautiful young princess heads off to bed, then, just after she falls asleep, we'll depart." And in this way Gājī and Kālu discussed their plan before the two of them headed inside to Cāmpā's apartments. Gāji Sāhā stretched out to sleep, but remained alert, while Kālu Sāhā lay down just outside their door. Cāmpāvatī snuggled up against Gāji. Soon all three were settled in to sleep. But Cāmpā sensed that something was troubling Gāji and, as she mulled over the possibilities, this blessed woman grew more and more uneasy. "It seems clear that the lord of my life is about to abandon me." This faithful woman lay there for a long time, silently weeping, sleep eluding her. When the sky indicated that two watches of the night had

46. This precise story of Mariyam is not found in the Qur'ān. In Qur'ān 3.37, there is reference to provisions for Mariyam made available directly through God's intervention. Later, in Qur'ān 19.25–26, when Mariyam is standing giving birth, she steadies herself by holding onto a palm tree and is instructed to shake it for fruit to eat in order to alleviate her pains.

passed, Sāhā Gāji woke and quickly got up. Moving ever so quietly, Gāji Sāhā aroused Kālu. As soon as he heard the word, Kālu was up and in no time at all the two men were ready to depart. Remembering the name and power of God, the two slipped out. When she saw them leave, Cāmpāvatī chased after them like a mad woman, dress disheveled, hair a flying mess. She clasped Gāji's feet, groveling on the ground, inconsolable. Tears streamed from her eyes, her breasts hung unbound. "Where are you going, my lord, are you leaving me? Wherever it is, you cannot go without me. You want to cast me aside! Where are you headed, lord of my life? If you disown me and leave, you eat my head, making me crazy!"

Gāji answered, "Listen my beloved, I am never coming back. You are dear to me, but I am a *phakir* of Āllā. Living in comfort and luxury is not appropriate for a *phakir*, so I cannot take a woman and set up house on a permanent basis."

Cāmpā replied, "I was not made aware of these constraints before. Previously you made love to me, only now to throw me away like so much rubbish. So all that nonsense you muttered was to deceive me. The so-called love you made was a deceitful pretense, and in the end I am left to weep. Now the truth outs and I fully understand, my lord, that you are an unprincipled scoundrel, truly a thief of love. And now you will flee, while all I have left to cling to are the words of a charlatan. Previously I was naïve, ignorant of how this would play out. You took an oath that I was your dearly beloved, only in the end to run away. Listen, listen carefully, lord of my life, to what I'm telling you: You are not going to abandon me! Go ahead and try to leave if you think you are strong enough."

refrain: Listen, listen carefully, Lord of my life, to what I am telling you:
By some instinct I secretly realized that your heart was hard.

As she finished speaking, Cāmpāvatī wept. Gāji Sāhā truly understood how she felt and consoled her in a voice filled with sweetness.

refrain: My darling, I love you more than life itself.
Be patient a while longer, my beloved, and stay here at home.

After Gāji Sāhā tried to comfort Cāmpā with those words, he made to leave, but Cāmpāvatī prostrated herself, clasping Gāji's ankles hard.

"Why, oh, why, are you abandoning me, my lord? I cannot live without you, my beloved. Bereft of a husband, a wife simply cannot carry on. The life of a woman who has lost her husband is less than useless." Cāmpāvatī wept and pleaded and whimpered in this manner, groveling in the dirt, still clinging to Gāji's feet.

refrain: Don't say, "I'm going, I'm leaving," while I am holding your feet.
When you abandon me, my lord, you slip a noose around my neck.

NOW HEAR THE STORY OF HOW GĀJI ŚĀHĀ TURNED CĀMPĀVATĪ INTO A TREE

"Aiee, alas, what more can I say, lord of my life?" Saying this and much more, she beat her chest in despair. "Do you not feel even the smallest touch of compassion in your heart, my beloved? How can you be so merciless as to leave me? Separated from you, I am bound to go mad! Out of fear and shame everyone in my family relinquished their social standing, their *kul*. It was for me that my father, my brothers, all gave up the heritage of their birth, their *jāti*. I, and I alone, now bear that dark stain of being responsible for those senseless acts. How can you go? How can you forget me, lord, and leave? Without you, my beloved, I will surely die! Rām took Sītā when he entered the forest in exile. Śiv saw fit to save Gaṅgā Devī in his hair. So how can you, my beloved, abandon me? Who is there to protect a woman bereft of her master? Come, let us go, lord of my life, I will accompany you. I, too, will become a mendicant, become a *phakirani*, and be your constant companion. If you give me up and leave, my beloved, I swear to Khodā that you will see me dead."

And just like that Cāmpāvatī was ready to swear in the name of God, Khodā.

Listening to her, the *chaheb* Gāji was worried, confounded. He asked Kālu, "Is there a solution? What can I do? The beautiful Cāmpā insists on coming with me." Kālu responded, "If you want to take Cāmpā with you, then do it. Let us go and quit worrying about it. You have already sedulously besmeared, indeed, bathed your body, with the filth of worldly illusion. Bring her along, and we'll worry about whatever transpires later. Those who have recourse to the shelter of the forest would never wish to eat arum root,[47] but how does anyone find enough food to put in one's mouth otherwise? Finding the tamarind tree might seem a game, but how else does one locate the arum?"[48] Gāji listened carefully, then began to meditate on God. Finally he decided to go ahead and take Cāmpāvatī along on his travels. That night, they made good their escape from the city of Brāhmaṇā Nagar, and they soon reached and entered a nearby forest.

Here is the story of those left behind.
Pay attention, everyone, to the tale of Maṭuk Rājā.

Early the next morning, Maṭuk Rājā arose as usual, but he soon received the news that the trio had bolted. Openly lamenting his lost Cāmpā, the *rājā* wept. "Aiee, alas, Cāmpāvatī has vanished—but where has she gone?" Queen Nilāvatī wept and writhed on the ground. "You have abandoned me, my dear child, where have you gone? Be strong and have patience first of all, everyone. Kālu, Gāji, and Cāmpāvatī can't have gotten far, you hear, they must be some place close by."

But actually Kālu and Gāji had already whisked Cāmpā far away from that place. Striking out, the three of them seemed to be settling in, getting adjusted to the circumstances. Making their way through the forest, they came to a town, where Gāji Sāhā spoke, "Listen, Kālu Sāhā, as my brother, you are as dear to me as life itself, but Cāmpāvatī has already become a burden, like a too-heavy necklace that chokes my throat. When we set out, there was no way I could leave her behind. But how can I continue to bring her along? When people meet us, they will laugh and say, 'What kind of *phakir* keeps a woman for company?' This is the fix I'm in."

47. The root of the arum lily, *Arum maculatum* in the family Araceae, commonly called jack in the pulpit or lords-and-ladies in English; its flowering parts resemble male and female genitalia, suggesting copulation, giving rise to its many gender-related names. The starchy root is edible when roasted well but the red-orange berries are extremely poisonous, and the reference here is no doubt a commentary on the trap of eroticism.

48. Tamarind is *Tamarindus indica* in the family Fabaceae, well known for the pungent pulp found in its pod-like fruits, which in addition to its culinary uses has a wide range of medicinal ones; the English name comes from the Arabic *tamar-hindi*, or Indian date. Kālu's somewhat opaque metaphor seems to suggest that one must "get one's hands dirty" to survive once mired in the created world.

Kālu replied, "I am sure you will think of something, so just do it." When he heard this, Gāji meditated on the Creator, Kartā. Then three times he blew his breath across Cāmpā's body. When Gāji blew on Cāmpā's limbs, that *bibī* magically transformed into a yellow turmeric flower,[49] which Gāji then took and secured inside his turban. At that point the two brothers were greatly relieved and ventured forth. The pair entered the city to beg food. Afterwards they retreated to the thickets of the forest, whereupon Gāji turned his mind toward God, The Protector, Poroyār. Once again he blew three times across the yellow turmeric flower and Cāmpāvatī magically resumed her previous human form. She gathered the lentils and rice and whatever else the pair had begged and cooked all of it, then dutifully served the two brothers. After they had finished, she took only a small portion for herself to eat. Then Gāji took Cāmpāvatī and they lay down to sleep for the night, while Kālu Sāhā moved some distance away for his rest. At daybreak, in time for morning prayers, Gāji again blew his breath on Cāmpā and turned her into a turmeric flower and tucked it into his turban. On other days, he would transmogrify her into a ring, which he wore on his finger. Then, later, she would be restored to her form as a woman and cook for them, after which, when it was dark, they lay down to sleep. When she was in her human form, she and Gāji lay together intimately and coupled.

And so they continued this routine as the days began to blur together, yet all that time Gāji never ceased to worry about finding a more satisfactory solution. For days Gāji bore his burden calmly, outwardly unruffled, but he was always mulling his predicament, "How can I continue to suffer this unfortunate turn of events? What is the solution? What might alleviate it?" Worrying himself sick, he finally came to a decision. Once again, he blew his breath three times toward Cāmpā, only this time she was transfigured into a sandpaper tree.[50]

49. The inflorescence, or flower cluster, of the turmeric plant, *Curcuma longa*, colloquially called *haridrā phul*, is topped by a display of waxy bracts, which are usually greenish or tinged with purple, while its small yellow-orange flowers are borne beneath it in the axils. The rhizome of the turmeric is ground for the spice.

50. The sandpaper tree, *Streblus asper*, which is in the Moraceae (mulberry) family, can grow as high as ten meters. The leaves are rough, hence the English name, and used for a variety of domestic chores, such as cleaning cooking utensils and sanding. It has a variety of uses in Ayurvedic medicine, especially for treating alimentary and urinary tract disorders, and can also be an abortifacient; its tender twigs are used as toothbrushes.

Seeing her thus transformed, Gāji Sāhā was relieved. And so the two brothers decamped from that spot and resumed their wanderings. As she watched them leave, Cāmpāvatī understandably wept in distress. "You have abandoned me, lord of my life, where are you going? I will be your lowly serving wench if you but take me with you! What horrible offense have I committed to warrant turning me into a tree? I am transfixed, rooted to this spot, all alone, while you flee. O lord of my life, do not jilt me, don't leave me stranded like this! If you are determined to cast me aside, I will appeal to Khodā for justice!"

This song is in the *rāginī* called *purabī* in *tāl āḍāṭhekā*.[51]

You are merciless in love, my friend, how can you abandon me?
I can atone for my failings if you will but take me as your servant.
I am so desperate for your love that I will become a mendicant
vairāginī.[52]
Like a serpent devoid of its crown jewel, I can no longer live at home.
But now, when I leave here, how can I carry on, for
you taught me the beauty of love? With whom can I share this misery?

Weeping uncontrollably, Cāmpāvatī gave her grievance to song, her voice was feeble, and wavered in abject humility. Tears streamed down her face. She continued to cry as she sang of fortune's cruel reversal.

This song is in the *rāginī* called *pīlū* in *tāl jat*.[53]

51. The *puravī* (*purabī*) is a relatively old sunset *rāga* associated with a young woman longing for her lover; it is alluded to in texts dating from at least the seventeenth century. A few decades after the current text was composed, the theoretician V.N. Bhaktikhande designated its scale as one of the ten foundational scales (*thāṭ*) of Indian music; it has a flat 2nd and 6th and a sharp 4th. As previously noted, *tāla ādāṭhekā* is a fast-speed, sixteen beat cycle.

52. A *vairāginī* is technically a *vaiṣṇav* female ascetic, but also generic for any woman who renounces the householder life; as Gāji has already intimated in his worries, it carries connotations of wanton behavior and at the time of this text's composition was commonly used despectively.

53. The *rāga* name *pīlū* appears in nineteenth-century texts and has been one of the most popularly familiar *rāgas* since then. It can use eleven of the twelve possible tones of the octave in distinctive characteristic phrasings. It is thought to be derived from regional melodies. *Jat tāl* has a fourteen-beat cycle.

I never dreamed the business of love was so painful.
I will never survive its flames as it sweeps through my body.
Love of that man slipped a noose around my neck.
To him I served up my maidenhood—how can he renounce me?
I was a princess, then I took the dress of a renunciant *sanyāsinī*,
and you took me with you; now you abandon your devoted servant!
You are the love of my life, so listen! Go anywhere, but take me along.
If you do not stop this masquerade, how will I endure?
Ābdul Ohāb says: This business of love is fraught with jeopardy.
When one cries so plaintively, what can be done?

Gāji listened to this lament voiced by Cāmpā. In dulcet tones he sang a song of his own in response.

This song is in the *rāginī* called *basanta* in *tāl madhyamān*.[54]

Why do you indulge in this kind of talk, my dear woman?
I am your servant and in my heart I meditate on no other.
In search of your love I gave up my own country.
Once conjoined, how could I possibly cast you aside?
Just manage for a few days, for I am not abandoning you.
I garland your neck with modesty every morning when I see
your face.
I am a tree, you its leaves; you are the flower, and I your creeper.
Where could I escape when you ever dwell in the temple of my heart?

Cāmpāvatī listened intently to Gāji's song. She remained with her head bowed and contemplated the portent of those troubling words. Gāji Sāhā asked, "Why do you cry so, my beloved? I took an oath before Khodā that I would never leave you. I promise I will return from my peregrinations in just a few days. Focus on Khodā and may you receive a vision from this vantage point." In this and other ways did Gāji Sāhā try to pacify Cāmpā. Then Gāji Sāhā took Kālu and they set out on their tour to visit all the various sites in the region, to fill their eyes with the wonders of Khodā's creation.

54. The *rāga* name *basanta* has been well known since the sixteenth century as a son (*putra*) in the family of *rāga hinḍol* and as a *rāginī*, *vasantī*, in the same family. It is associated with the god of love, Kāma, or with Kṛṣṇa, and so with the spring season. It uses the same basic scale as *puravī*, noted above. *Madhyamān tāl* is a slow, sixteen-beat cycle with additional strokes that fill in the slower-paced beats.

refrain The sweet song of the *kokil* incites love in my heart.[55]
And so Jendā Gāji with his brother Kālu began
their travels.

NOW HEAR THE STORY OF GĀJI SĀHĀ CURING A MAN WITH ELEPHANTIASIS

The two brothers began their odyssey, meandering this way and that until they finally reached some unnamed city. That day, as they were walking along, feeling light-hearted, they happened upon a man with elephantiasis who had fallen on the road. Ironically, his name was Jāmāl, the Beautiful, and he suffered elephantiasis in both legs. Seared by the excruciating pain of the elephantiasis, he could not walk. He also suffered a testicular tumor that weighed two maunds,[56] so that each of his gonads was as large as an egg basket. When he struggled out to the fields, the cowherds pelted him with clods of clay. When he headed to his house, his wife greeted him derisively, "Look, the diseased sister-fucker has arrived." The misery inflicted by the searing pain of the elephantiasis beat him down, until he finally made a firm decision: "I will give up my life." And he lay down in the road to do just that. It was just then that Kālu and Gāji arrived. They greeted the diseased man and began to question him. "Why are you lying in the middle of the road? Why have you given up on life?" The elephantiasis-wracked man begged them, "Please, just beat me with your thick staves until I am dead! I am sprawled on the road because of the unbearable pain. Clearly, there can be no one in all of creation who is a greater sinner than I. I cannot walk. I cannot suffer the intolerable agony of this elephantiasis any longer. It would seem that even the god of death, Yom, has completely forgotten me."

Gāji listened carefully to what the diseased man said and then responded, "Your misery can be relieved, you can be cured, so despair no longer." With this promise, the two men placed their hands on his diseased legs and began to squeeze firmly and with purpose. They drained and collected the oozing lymph onto a lotus leaf, most of which they hurled in the direction of Vikramnagar, but a small

55. For *kokil*, see n. 18 above.

56. See n. 36 above.

portion of which fell short at Nāṭarnagar. Some of it managed to reach as far as Sāntipur in Nade.[57] And from there it managed to pretty much spread everywhere across the world, but at least half of it landed in Ḍhākā and Vikrampur. A tiny bit fell onto the leaves of bananas and onto those tiny ordinary limes. It might take as long as three or four months, but anyone who eats those will develop elephantiasis or testicular hydrocele. There is, however, a curious story about Sāntipur and Nadiyā in connection with this. The women of that region have enormous, pendulous breasts; even young just-pubescent girls look as developed as fully grown women.

After completing their ministrations, Gāji and Kālu felt quite gratified with the result, so they invoked the general blessing of Khodā on Jāmāl. Then they directed more specific blessings on him and instructed him, "Now go to your home straightaway. If Āllā wills it, you will become a successful maritime merchant. Listen, dig at such and such a place and you will find great riches. You will have a son named Monāi and he, too, will become a merchant. You will soon become the wealthiest in this district, and so it will be for the next seven generations." After the intercession Gāji made on behalf of Jāmāl, the two brothers departed and continued on with their journey.

On another day, they landed up on the shore where the river meets the sea. There they found three hundred *jugi*s performing austerities and chanting the names of the goddess. The arrival of Gāji and Kālu disrupted their ascetic practices. Incensed, the *jugi*s rose up to beat them. Picking up staffs and batons, they threatened to flail Gāji. Watching this unfold, Kālu Sāhā interrupted, "Hey, wait now, tell me, to whom are you directing your austerities?" They replied, "Our mortifications are aimed at Mā Gaṅgā." Gāji Sāhā replied, "Listen, all you *jugi*s. I will make Gaṅgā appear for your personal audience if and only if you agree to become *mochalmān*." They replied in unison, "If you can grant us a vision of Gaṅgā, then we will become *mochalmān*s as you propose. Have Gaṅgā come up on the bank to grant us an audience, give us *darśan*." Then Gāji assembled them on the river's bank and addressed the waters, calling out three times, "Auntie, sister of my mother!" Floating up from the depths, a figure soon appeared riding a *makar*—the goddess' mythical mount. Gaṅgā spoke, "Why did you call

57. Nadiyā.

for me, my child? Tell me quickly, what does your heart desire?" Gāji replied, "Please listen to my request, auntie. For countless days these *jugis* here have been performing austerities and chanting your name in order to gain a vision of you. Please grant them their wish now. Please climb up and take a seat on your lotus throne. Grant them the vision, give them *darśan*, and fill their eyes with what they seek." No sooner had she heard this than Gaṅgā Devī mounted her lotus throne, and the *jugis* all were able to behold her body entire. Gāji then said, "Thank you, Auntie, you can take your leave now." Gaṅgā Devī acknowledged him and headed back to the underworld of Pātāl. The *jugis* excitedly declared, "Many thanks, how fortunate indeed, Sāhā Gāji! We have been worshipping this Gaṅgā for such a long time. Clearly, there is no community on earth the equivalent of the *mochalmān*, for a vision of that Gaṅgā Bhagirathī is incredibly difficult to attain." Then the *jugis* kissed Gāji's feet. All of them accepted the tenets of the faith and became *mochalmāns*, after which Gāji Sāhā took all of the *jugis* and built a *machjed*.[58]

The masjid was built, encrusted with diamonds and rubies,
observes Ābdul Ohāb, for the benefit of all.

Gāji Sāhā was very satisfied
as he directed the *jugis*
to build a *machjed*.
They constructed the *machjed* so that it was
dotted with carnelian and rubies and laced with
lines of decorative bricks studded with diamonds and pearls.
For some indeterminate number of days
the duo remained there, serene and tranquil.
Then Gāji respectfully confided in Kālu.
"I cannot remain here any longer.
I plan to go to Pātāl
where my elder brother lives."
Announcing his intention, Gāji Sāhā
took his brother and headed out,

58. Badar Pīr has a somewhat similar experience with meditating *jogis* seeking a vision of Gaṅgā but has first to compel her to grant their vision; she then floats stones up the river so that the *jogis* can build their mosque. For a translation of the story, see Stewart, *Witness to Marvels*, 48–51.

leaving the *jugis* to care for the *machjed.*
After the two brothers had traveled
for quite a few days,
they called out to Baśu, Mother Earth.
"Please hear us, Baśumati,
we wish to go to the underworld of Pātālnagar.
Please show us the quickest route."
The entire earth quaked and shook with a resounding crack
and suddenly a path appeared, clean and straight,
with horses and elephants at the ready for their conveyance.
The two brothers were more than pleased,
and so they resumed their journey along that roadway,
in constant contemplation of the glories of the Lord Creator.
After some indeterminate number of days,
they finally reached Pātālnagar,
which was ruled by one Jaṅgarāj Mālek.
Beholding the grandeur of the citadel of Pātāl,
Gāji blurted out, "I must have died and gone to heaven,
for I have never seen such a place anywhere."
Everything to the last detail shone with the luster of gold,
even the earth had turned green-gold in color, and
the foliage of the trees, too, produced a golden hue.
Even animals and insects—
everything had a fresh golden luster.
The two of them were dumbfounded.
The fabulous array of brilliant golden hues,
so transfixed their hearts that they could only proceed slowly,
but eventually they did reach that city.
The city itself had the
appearance of Indra's heavenly gardens, with
pearls and gemstones strung here and there.
Recovering from that overpowering vision,
the two methodically plodded on, and
finally took rest at the foot of a tree.
Look! Who can fathom the where, the why,
the wizardry of the Lord's grace?
That night, Julhās had a dream,
and in that dream he came to know that
his two brothers Gāji and Kālu,
had arrived there in Pātāl.
He saw that beneath a fruiting tree,

those two brothers, Gāji and Kālu,
had paused to rest.
As Julhās's dream unfolded,
it made him weep, made him feel miserable.
He felt a sudden longing for his mother and father.
When the day broke the next morning,
just as the sun was rising,
Jul Sāhā took himself to that very spot.
Kālu and Gāji were patiently waiting.
When Julhās reached them, he questioned them
seemingly innocently, but with friendly affection.
"What are your names? Where is your home?
Who are your father and mother?"
Gāji listened and then replied with these words:
"Our home is back in the land of Bairāṭ,
our father is Chekāndar, and
the beautiful Ajupā is our mother."
The lowly Ābdul Ohāb says,
When he fell at Gāji's feet,
the three brothers were united.
Take Julhās along, go!
Go to Bairāṭnagar where
your mother and father wait expectantly.

NOW HEAR THE TALE OF HOW GĀJI, KĀLU, TOGETHER WITH JULHĀS, RETURNED TO THEIR HOMELAND

Gāji Sāhā said, "Listen, here are our personal details. Our home is in Bairāṭnagar and our father is Chekāndar. We have heard that we have a brother living here in this land. It is for this reason that we have come in search of him." Jul wrapped a quilted scarf around Gāji's neck, hugged him, and began to weep. "I am taken aback for I am that very brother of yours. But tell me brother, how are our mother and father?" Gāji divulged, "On account of you they ache and yearn, for they have been unable to say whether you are still alive or dead. Come, brother, let all of us return to their place together." Julhās replied, "Would that we could up and fly away to Bairāṭnagar right this moment."

After this, the two brothers accompanied Julhās to his residence. When Jaṅgārāj Sāhā met them, he, too, questioned them. "From where have you come to land up here? You have the bodies of *devatās* or *ganddharvas* or at least færies: I have never encountered in person such incredible beauty before." Julhās listened and said to the king, "These two men are my dear brothers. They have come to Pātālnagar in search of me." As soon as he heard that explanation, the king jumped up and arranged to have Gāji and Kālu properly seated. From within the women's quarters, Pāctulā heard the news: my husband's younger brothers have come here from the land of Bairāṭ. When she heard the news, she was moved with a profound joy. The princess herself went to cook for them, and when the food was fully prepared the princess sent for them. Receiving that invitation, the two brothers dutifully made their way into the private quarters. The king's daughter led Gāji by the hand and then, in a sweet voice reminiscent of the *kokil* bird,[59] she proposed the following: "Listen, brother Gāji, you are the younger brother of my beloved husband. Now that you have come to Pātālnagar, please take me to visit Bairāṭ city. I do not know anyone as unfortunate as I, because my birth will always be counted deficient if I only live in the home of my mother and father and never have the chance to serve my father- and mother-in-law. There is no woman on earth more wretched, more miserable than I, for I have never been able to take the dust of their feet in reverent salutation. Listen seriously, my dear Gāji, my brother, there is nothing to be gained by waiting. Please eat quickly and then address my father. Let us make haste to take our leave and go." After pleading her case, she straight away offered them food. The three men ate until they were full and genuinely content. Soon afterwards, Gāji Sāhā spoke to the king. "We do not wish to tarry any longer, so please grant us leave to depart. We plan to take Julhās with us to go back to our own land. There is no need to procrastinate and we have nothing more left to do. My elder brother and his wife, we will all go together. As soon as you grant us permission, we will be on our way."

When the *mahārāj* heard the request, he blessed Gāji, "Go in happiness, I hereby grant you leave." The king supplied a number of sepoys to accompany them. He also gifted them more riches and gemstones than can be described. His darling daughter Pāctulā took along five hundred female servants, while the young woman herself was seated in a golden palanquin. Gāji, Kālu, Julhās, and Pāctulā all together made

59. See n. 18 above.

their obeisance to the king. Three hundred thousand people initially accompanied Gāji. They concentrated on Āllā as they set out along a scenic path. Eventually they veered off that scenic route and landed up at the *machjed* that had been erected previously by the *jugis* and left in their hands. The crowd of three hundred thousand and the three brothers reached the *machjed*, entered, and took a seat. They felt extremely contented, with no worries crowding their minds.

Gāji then called out to Kālu and said, "Cāmpāvatī is still rooted as a tree somewhere back there. Take Pāctulā and her servants and quickly fetch her back to me." As soon as heard, Kālu prepared to leave, so he gathered up Pāctulā and her serving women. All of the women mounted palanquins and they managed to make their way to the place where Cāmpāvatī had been rooted. They all took their seats at the foot of that special tree, then, standing in front of it, Kālu Sāhā gave three sharp cries and called Cāmpāvatī by name. Within the hour Cāmpāvatī had regained consciousness, then slowly she emerged from the trunk of the tree and resumed her winsome form. A soft light emanated from her body to illuminate the forest. When Pāctulā took in Cāmpā's ethereal beauty, the young woman was smitten and fell to the earth, unconscious. Then Cāmpāvatī queried Kālu, "Just who is that woman who is crumpled on the ground?" Kālu replied, "Dear one, that charming woman is Pāctulā. She is the child of Jaṅgarāj in Pātāla. This woman was given in marriage to the valiant Jul Sāhā, so she is Gāji's brother's wife; listen, Cāmpāvatī, that makes her your elder sister-in-law." When this registered, the good and pure woman instantly scurried off to fetch water to pour on the woman's face. Pāctulā immediately came to. Taking her in, Cāmpāvatī made obeisance. Pāctulā then queried Kālu about her, "In whose lucky house was this beautiful woman born?" Kālu replied, "This alluring beauty is the daughter of Maṭuk Rājā. She is married to Gāji, the younger brother of your husband." Then the comely Pāctulā heard all about her, hugged her neck, and addressed her as "sister." Then the two women huddled together in extended conversation. The bearers set the litter down before them, and they climbed into the palanquin as passengers. They soon returned to Gāji.

Gāji gathered everyone together and guided them along. As they made their journey, he constantly turned his thoughts to Elāhi, God. After a few days they were able to access the trunk road, and they soon reached Brāhmaṇā Nagar. Once in the realm of his father-in-law, Gāji respectfully addressed Kālu with this request: "Listen brother Kālu Sāhā, please you go ahead and inform the king that we are on our way." Kālu fully understood Gāji's request, and he went on ahead to alert the king: "Chāheb Gāji has returned." Then he shared with him in great detail everything that had transpired since they left. When he heard the news, Maṭuk Rājā was thrilled beyond measure. They made everything ready to escort them to the residence. Instrumental music played, waving lamps cast a reddish glow, and the subjects of the realm began to assemble. Lamps were lit in every house so that the entire city looked as if both the sun and moon were blazing forth. In each and every dwelling people began to sing: "The two brothers—Kālu and Gāji—have come home." The king lodged them in the Ruby Room of the palace, and he made arrangements to accommodate the hundreds of thousands of people who accompanied the brothers.

They prepared a veritable banquet and fed everyone with such a variety of dishes I cannot even begin to name.

When Cāmpāvatī and Pāctulā reached there, just imagine what the women in the private quarters did. They proffered flowers and the like, and offered them assorted betel quids, breath fresheners, and sugar. The seven sisters-in-law gathered around and they laughed and smiled giddily. They showered them with gifts, sacred *durbā* grass,[60] and flowers, then took them in tow and quickly disappeared into the palace complex. The two women, Pāctulā and Cāmpāvatī, then made humble obeisance to the latter's mother. The queen blessed them and embraced them. As she held them close, Queen Nilāvati was truly overjoyed. She then fed them a variety of prepared foods, and the two ate happily and with gusto. After they had finished eating, what was left was placed on banana leaves, which the seven sisters-in-law then came together to eat. The seven sisters-in-law and nine aunts all sat together and made the two young women feel comfortably right at home. And so in just this way any number of days went by.

Then one day Gāji Sāhā conferred with the king, they took their leave, and departed. It took a year for the entourage to reach Sonāpur, in which city they remained for three or four days, after which they

60. *Durbā* (Skt, *dūrvā*) grass is *Cynodon dactylon*, a plant in the Poaceae (or Gramineae) family, commonly known in America as Bermuda grass. It has a long sacred history, associated with the earliest Vedic rituals, in the Indian subcontinent.

decamped. They made their way to Chāphāi Nagar. All the townsfolk of Chāphāi Nagar came out to greet them. When King Śrīrām heard of their arrival, he was very pleased. He made his profound obeisances at Gāji's feet. Afterwards everyone pitched in to entertain them and a general feeling of good will was felt in every home. Gāji Sāhā rested there for five days, then, with his thoughts centered on Elāhi, God, he set out and resumed the journey. They continued on the roadway for a number of days, until they reached the banks of the large river where it all began. It took them several days to make their way across to the opposite shore. They were eager to return to Bairāṭnagar, but with only three or four *kroś* left to go,[61] Gāji halted the entourage at a group of houses, where they paused. He spoke to Kālu, "Brother, please go on ahead quickly to the palace and give them news of our arrival." Receiving his instruction, Kālu immediately set off and reached his destination to inform Chekāndar Sāhā, who was lounging on his royal divan.

When Kālu Sāhā arrived, he made his obeisance, then stood smartly before him. The king wept and then began to question Kālu. "Tell me, my son, how many days has it been? You took Gāji away, so where is he being kept, when will he return?" Kālu replied, "All of us have come back together. Gāji Sāhā stopped at a nearby village and sent me ahead to alert you." When he heard this, Chekāndar was overjoyed. The king took Kālu into the palace living area, where the queen, Ajupā, could be found in her private chambers. When she caught sight of Kālu, she broke into tears and said, "Now that you have come, tell me, where is Gāji?" Kālu responded, "My dear mother, there is no need to cry. I have come in advance to give you the news of Gāji. My two brothers—Jul Sāhā and Gāji Śāhā—have both returned. And they have brought two wives to meet you as well." Then he recounted everything to his mother: how they both had been wandering *phakir*s; how they crossed the broad waters at Sāgar; how they went to Chāphāi Nagar where they destroyed the caste standing of Śrīrām Rājā; how they constructed the golden city of Sonāpur and its bazaars; how they went to sleep on their beds and how the mysterious meeting with Cāmpā drove Gāji mad; how they made their way to Brāhmaṇā Nagar; how they waged war against Maṭuk Rājā; how Gāji was wedded to Cāmpā; how magnificent Gāji and Cāmpā looked at their wedding; how Gāji Sāhā went to Pātāl

61. A *kroś* is about two miles.

and found Jul Sāhā and brought him along. One by one, he related every single detail of their every adventure to the queen.

When she had taken in everything Kālu had said, the queen brimmed with motherly joy. It was if a poverty-stricken person had suddenly stumbled onto riches beyond measure, or a peasant happened upon a gold coin. It was as if one who had gone blind could once again see, or the body of one dead was reanimated and made to sit up. Chekāndar Sāhā went out first with an entourage and with great affection fetched his sons and their wives. As joyful music sounded through all four quarters of the estates, they arrived at the palace residence in a state of great joy. Julhās, Gāji, and Kālu, the three sons, all made formal obeisance at the feet of their father, after which their wives fell at the feet of their father-in-law, made their obeisances with heartfelt pleasure, and were formally introduced. After that, the sons and their wives went together to make their obeisances and pay their respects to the queen. One by one she affectionately pulled her sons and daughters-in-law to her lap. The overflowing love of the queen spilled onto everyone. After this, Gāji Sāhā told their story in the august presence of his mother and father until the whole saga was complete. All the miseries they suffered and the joys they had had, Gāji Sāhā described, until they knew every last detail.

Now this tale has come to an end. I make a thousand salaams to aesthetes who can savor it. On the twelfth day of the month of Aghrān *in the year 1300,*[62] *I have completed this manuscript. Ābdul Ohāb says: May mercy received as the auspicious gift of salvation be granted to the feet of all peoples.*

62. 27 November 1893.

Glorifying the Protective Matron of the Jungle

Glorifying the Protective Matron of the Jungle

Introduction to Bonbibī Jahurā Nāmā of Mohāmmad Khater

The *Bonbibī kecchā*, today better known as the *Bonbibī jahurā nāmā* of Mohāmmad Khater,[1] tells the story of the woman who became the "Mother" of all the inhabitants of the Sundarbans, the Āṭhārobhāṭī, or Land of the Eighteen Tides. She was given the epithets of *bibī,* or matron, and *pīrānī*, female Sufi saint. She had a fraternal twin in her brother Śājaṅgali, himself a *pīr* of no small stature, but she was always his senior and in command, while he acted as her second. Like many of the other sagas, this narrative is divided into three distinct tales. In the first part, the narrator describes how Khodā summoned the twins Bonbibī and Śājaṅgali in paradise, *behest*, and sent them down to the devout Berāhim and his second wife, Golbibī. Because of a rash promise by Berāhim to his first wife, Phulbibī, he abandoned his second wife, Golbibī, in the jungle just as she was nearing term. She gave birth alone, save for wild animals. Distraught in the recognition that she would be hard-pressed to care for one child there in the jungle, much less two, she chose to abandon the girl-child, Bonbibī, in order to save her son, a culturally conditioned choice that, given the circumstances, would surprise no one. At the command of Khodā, or God, Bonbibī was then miraculously raised by the deer and the other animals of the jungle, making good on her name as the lady (*bibī*) of the forests (*bon*).

1. Munsī Mohāmmad Khater Sāheb, *Bonbibī jahurānāmā* (Kalikātā: Śrī Rāmlāl Śīl at Niu-Bhikṭoriyā Pres, 1325 BS [?] [ca. 1918?]). The translation gives priority to the readings in this text.

After they had matured, the twins somehow managed to reunite and together left to fulfill the mission assigned to them by Khodā. They headed to Madinā where they received advanced training in the ways of the Sufis, after which they received official sanction. They returned to settle in the Sundarbans. The second part of the story describes Bonbibī's celebrated battle with Dakṣiṇā Rāy's mother, Nārāyaṇī, after which Bonbibī consolidated complete administrative control over the Āṭhārobhāṭī, assigning each portion to interested parties to ensure cooperation and reduce competition for the limited resources.

The final episode, which covers more than half of the text, tells a story essentially independent of the two first episodes, sufficiently so that Amitav Ghosh made this the subject of his dramatic verse retelling in *Junglenama.*[2] It relates the romance of the attempted sacrifice of the young boy Dukhe by his uncle, Dhonā, a corrupt honey-gathering merchant, concluding with a reconciliation of all the stakeholders in the Sundarbans. Bonbibī flies to his aid, materializing out of thin air any time he calls on her. She visits people in dreams to accomplish her goals, and even shape-shifts into a white fly to deliver succor and advice. At one poignant moment, Bonbibī has to explain to her twin brother the burden of responsibility she bears as "Mother" of all the inhabitants of the Sundarbans, the mantle of *baraka*, the charismatic power bestowed by Khodā on his most accomplished of Sufi saints. The story closes with Dukhe establishing an ideal estate that is tax-free for the *ryots*, or peasants, run by officials and officers free of corruption, with justice administered fairly in an environment beneficial to all concerned. Bonbibī's support, which sustains Dukhe's rise from a position of pathetic, poverty-ridden vulnerability as a child to that of a righteous ruler establishing an *ābādī*, the properly settled and functioning ideal Islamic community, is the closest approximation of a Bildingsroman to be found in the various *pīr kathās*, not only in this anthology but more generally.

The *Bonbibī jahurā nāmā* verges on, but does not succumb to, a didacticism unlike other stories in this anthology. Its message relates how people must suppress their personal desires to work together to survive, and be respectful of one another, which in turn results in a

2. *The Jungle Nama: A Story of the Sundarban*, retold by Amitav Ghosh, illustrated by Salman Toor (Noida: Harper Collins Publishers, India, 2021).

better quality of life for all, but in it we begin to see hints of the politicizing of religious identities that became the norm in Bengal by the early twentieth century. While the text suggests a clear hierarchy of religious belief and practice, with *musalmāni* forms proving superior to *hinduyāni*, people who revere Bonbibī in their daily lives in the Sundarbans do not seem to accept those neat divisions, preferring a more pragmatic inclusiveness as response to the vagaries of their existence. Following the lead of Bonbibī, high-minded personal conduct generates a prosperity that is ultimately guaranteed only by judicious governance. Bonbibī alone is responsible for showing the way and, regardless of other allegiances, her devotees abound throughout the southern reaches of the Bangla-speaking world.[3]

Versions of the Text. The Bengali scholar Sarat Chandra Mitra reports that the earliest attested text, composed by Bayanuddīn, was published in 1877. Copies of it remain elusive, but a revised edition appeared in 1920.[4] I have been unable to lay eyes, however, on either edition. The version translated here was composed by Mohāmmad Khater and is easily the most popular version of the story, which has circulated in print since its composition in the late 1870s.

The popular text of Mohāmmad Khater (also spelled Khāter) was first printed in 1880, only three years after Bayanuddīn's work. In the opening passage, he identifies his composition as the *Bonbibī kecchā*, or tale of Bonbibī. The title by which everyone knows the text today, the *Bonbibī jahurā nāmā*, or "The Book Spreading the Glory of Bonbibī," was apparently conferred on it later. That is the title of the earliest version I have seen, an edition dated 1918, on which this translation is based. For the second half of the twentieth century, a hand-set, poorly reproduced edition of the text has seen multiple reprints,

3. For more on the rôle of the *Bonbibī jahurā nāmā* in the Sundarbans, see Annu Jalais's essential *Forest of Tigers: People, Politics and Environment in the Sundarbans* (New York: Routledge, 2010), as noted in the introduction to this volume.

4. Munśī Bayanuddīn, *Bonbibiījahurānāmā* (Sisvādaha: by the author, 1284 BS [ca. 1877]), cited by Sarat Chandra Mitra, "On a Musalmāni Legend about the Sylvan Saint Bana-bibī and the Tiger-Deity Dakshiṇa Rāya," *Journal of the Department of Letters* 10 (1923): 156. For the revised edition of Bayanuddīn's text, see Munśī Bayanuddīn, *Bonbibījahurānāmā* (Kalikātā: Āfājuddin Āhāmmad, from 337-s Upper Chitput Road, 1327 BS [ca. 1920]).

attesting to its popularity.[5] That edition served as the basis for a digitally printed version with clean laser fonts, which I surmise was copied from its predecessor, based on the replication of identical typographical errors from the hand-set versions and the reproduction of the earlier title page with dates changed.[6] But that digitally generated edition has altered the earlier text, introduced lexical modifications, and generated a small number of grammatical mistakes not previously found. In every instance I could find, the hand-set version was heavily smudged, in some cases to the point of being illegible, so alterations seem to be as much from the mechanics of reproduction as deliberate meddling. Some of those mistakes in the laser-typeset edition have actually changed the tenor of the text in a few passages, whether intentionally or not. It also modernizes some spellings and occasionally replaces a word with what the compositors apparently considered to be a more current contemporary equivalent, though on occasion one with a more politically charged valence. In an effort to capture the tenor of the text closer to Khater's original, I have chosen the 1918 version as my source text, but I have triangulated some readings with the hand-set version of 1961 and sought clarifications from the laser printed copy dated 1987.[7]

5. Munśī Mohāmmad Khater Sāheb, *Bonbibī jahurā nāmā: Nārāyaṇīr jaṅga o dhonā dukher pālā* (Kalikātā: Nuruddīn Āhmmad at Gāochiyā Lāibrerī, 1394 BS [ca. 1987]. It should be noted that the title page spells the name of the printing house in two ways: Gaosiyā and Gāochiyā. The earliest version of this hand-set text I have examined (unfortunately severely damaged and containing only the first five pages) was dated 1368 BS (ca. 1961).

6. Munśī Mohāmmad Khater Sāheb, *Bonbibī jahurā nāmā: Nārāyaṇīr jaṅga o dhonā dukher pālā* (Kalikātā: Nuruddīn Āhmmad at Gāochiyā Lāibrerī, 1401 BS [ca. 1994]. The digitally printed version simply reproduces the earlier hand-set edition's cover, with both the spellings Gaosiyā and Gāochiyā. It should also be noted that recent editions have appended several pages describing some of the miracles of Śāh Jālāl of Sylhet, which have nothing to do with the story of Bonbibī and are obviously later emendations (they were not present in the 1918 edition I examined), the purpose of which is unclear. I have chosen not to translate those extraneous pages.

7. A number of other authors have told Bonbibī's story, which has remained especially popular in the *jātrā* theater circuit throughout the Sundarbans and has often shown the kind of situational creativity one expects from live performance. For more on the printing and performance history of this text, see Stewart, *Witness to Marvels*, 123–24, esp. n. 27, n. 28, and n. 31. And as is now well known, Amitav Ghosh wove the story of his novel *The Hungry Tide* (London: HarperCollins, 2004) around the Bonbibī

According to Jatindra Mohan Bhattacharjee's *Catalogus Catalogorum of Bengali Manuscripts*, there are no extant hand-written manuscripts of the *Bonbibī jahurā nāmā*,[8] which suggests that the author took the book straight to print. This would seem to be confirmed in the opening section of the text, where Mohāmmad Khater writes of the locals begging him to compose Bonbibī's tale.

> Without exception, they petitioned me like this:
> "Brother, write the story, the *kecchā*, of Bonbibī and
> please get it published in print.
> When you do this, your *puthi* text
> will easily find a place in every home
> throughout the land."
>
> Mohāmmad Khater, *Bonbibī jahurā nāmā*, p. 1

The author confirms the impulse to go straight to print again in the closing lines, where he begs the reader's indulgence in the event of an omission or mistake that may deviate from the story as it had been told to him. Toward the end of the text, he complains that he had not enjoyed particularly good health during the writing, but composed it in response to the demands of an eager public.

In another twist in changing attitudes to texts and their circulation, prior to the nineteenth century and the advent of print, newer, cleaner hand-written copies of manuscripts were often preferred to older, often worn texts. It was not unusual for an older manuscript to be ceremonially submerged in the river upon completion of a copy. But several colleagues in Kolkata and Dhaka have indicated in personal conversation that since the advent of print (and, presumably in this case, in the absence of any hand-written manuscript), the older printed editions of Khater's Bonbibī story are now especially treasured by her

---

narrative, which has had the additional salutary effect of bringing attention to the environmental threats to the Sundarbans and has served as a lens for larger environmental issues. The environmental issues are the subject of two of Ghosh's recent works, *The Great Derangement: Climate Change and the Unthinkable* (Chicago: University of Chicago Press, 2016) and *The Nutmeg's Curse: Parables for a Planet in Crisis* (Chicago: University of Chicago Press, 2021).

8. Jatindra Mohan Bhattacharjee, comp. and ed., Catalogus *Catalogorum of Bengali Manuscripts* [*Bāṃlā Puthir tālikā samanvay: Saṅkalak o sampādak yatīndramohan bhaṭṭācāryya*] (Calcutta: Asiatic Society, 1978).

devotees in the Sundarbans and are considered to have greater sanctity than the later reprints. In a tradition probably not much more than a century and a half old, the earlier print editions have become physical artifacts that carry a greater weight of authenticity, a near-iconic value (though the content remains the same), which transports their owners and readers closer to the source of inspiration, hence closer to Bonbibī. Older may be better to those devotees in this vibrant living tradition, but regardless of the source, each telling of Bonbibī's story helps to spread her message, so irrespective of a scholar's meticulous concern for best editions, textual emendations, and lexical irregularities, for those who earnestly believe in Bonbibī's motherly duty to the inhabitants of the Āṭhārobhāṭī, any version of her tale is still her sacred story.

PRIMARY ACTORS, HUMAN AND DIVINE

Barakhān, Barakhān Gāji, Baḍa Khān Gāji – a warrior Sufi *pīr* or *phakir* who shares leadership of the Sundarbans until Bonbibī's arrival

Berāhim Śāhā – father of Bonbibī and Śājaṅgali

Bhāṅgaḍ Śāhā – informant who meets Bonbibī and Śājaṅgali as they enter the Sundarbans

Biṣam Rāy – brother of Dakṣiṇā Rāy

Bonbibī, Bibī – matron of the Sundarbans, raised by the animals of the jungle, an accomplished *pīrānī*

Cāmpā – Dhonāi's daughter, married to Dukhe

Dakṣiṇ Rāy, Dakṣiṇā, Rāy, Rāymaṇi, Rāi – the controller of the Sundarbans prior to Bonbibī's arrival, a *rākṣas* who can shape-shift into a tiger

Dhonāi, Dhonā – greedy merchant, Dukhe's paternal uncle

Dukhe, Dukhe Śāhā – an only son, Dhonāi's paternal nephew, who signs on for voyage to the Sundarbans; a devotee of Bonbibī and eventual exemplary ruler of parts of Bengal

Elāhi, Āllā, Elāhi Āllā, Khodā, Echam, Nirañjan the Stainless – God

Hajrat Nabī – the Prophet Mohāmmad

Golāl, Golālbibī – daughter of Jalil of Makkā, second wife of Berāhim, and mother of Bonbibī and Śājaṅgali

Jadurāy – chief minister, estate manager, and construction overseer for Dukhe

Jalil, Phakir Jalil Śāhā – father of Golālbibi, prominent in Makkā

Khodā – God

Mohāmmad, Nabī, Hajrat, Mostaphā – Mohāmmad the Prophet

Monāi – brother of Dhonāi who does not agree with Dhonāi's need for further trade

Nārāyaṇī – mother of Dakṣiṇ Rāy who loses to Bonbibī in battle

Nirañjan the Stainless – God

Phātemā – Phātemā Bibī, the Prophet Mohāmmad's daughter

Phulbibī – Bibī, Berāhim's barren first wife

Rāy, Rāymaṇi, Dakṣiṇ Rāy, qv.

Śājaṅgali, Śā Jaṅgali, Jaṅgali – Bonbibī's younger twin brother, a *pīr* of superior standing

Sanātan – a minion of Dakṣiṇ Rāy's

Śāhā Sekandār – father of Barakhān Gāji

Seko – Bonbibī's magnificent magical crocodile, which can travel at unheard-of speed

Glorifying the Protective Matron of the Jungle

Bonbibī Jahurā Nāmā of Mohāmmad Khater

Āllā, the Pure, the Protector,
the Sustainer of Creation,
    is a boundless ocean of compassion.
Do I even know enough to voice
proper words in praise of Him,
    considering the paucity of my narrative skills?
In the beginning, through His *nur*, His light,
he created the Prophet of Light, the *nurnabī*,
    and from that light emerged the *nabī*, the Prophet himself.
Everything that can be found
within each of the fourteen worlds
    He created through His kindness.
After He had completed the world and,
at long last, fashioned the Apostle, *rachul*,
    He initiated his work in the city of Makkā.
The Apostle's renown served as an example to sinners;
He became the spiritual leader, the *emām*, and established
    legal tribunals in the community of the faithful, *omma*.
People will be saved after the resurrection
thanks to his compassion alone,
    as is written in the Korān.
How can I possibly write effectively of the splendor
and the full scope of majesty and glory
    He as Creator has fashioned?
With teeth clinched in humility and head bowed,
I make my obeisances to all those

who number among the companions of the Prophet.
I bow to Phātemā Bibi,
the pure and holy daughter of the Apostle,
whose religious faith is a beacon to the world.
I bow to Phātemā's two sons,
the pair, Hāsen and Hosen,
who function as guarantors of the faith.
To my mother, my father, my teacher,
my patron, and well-wishers—
to them all I sincerely bow in earnest.
Paying homage to all those respectfully acknowledged,
I make salaams at their feet.
Now listen everyone to the story I tell.
I trust that you will be patient with
the record that I have composed in the form of a *kecchā*,
for it was not something driven by personal desire.
I have taken the matter of this book
from people who reside in the
the eastern regions, the mangrove swamps.
I have composed this manuscript
with the sincere hope of preserving and reproducing
faithfully what they have told me.
Without exception, they petitioned me like this:
"Brother, write the *kecchā* of Bonbibī and
please get it published in print.
When you do this, your *puthi* text
will easily find a place in every home
throughout the land."
For those suffering agonies of the heart,
listen to the majestic subject of this tale,
then meditate on the virtues it generates,
for the *Bonbibī kecchā*
which I have labored so diligently to compose,
will in the final reckoning prove its worth.
This tale was composed alternating both
the elegant three-footed *tripadī* and the *payār* couplet,
so everyone please study it well.
I exist only to serve,
so if this tale affords you a sincere pleasure,
please proffer your blessings.
The prolegomena to the composition

runs up to this point
but now I will turn to the tale proper.
Pay close attention, everyone, to what I have written,
as I narrate the full and complete story
of the *Bonbibī kecchā*.

THE BIRTH OF BONBIBĪ AND ŚĀJAṄGALI IN THE FIRST WATCH OF THE NIGHT

By repeating the name of Āllā, everyone may focus their hearts and minds, so listen carefully, one and all, to a summary of the story of Bonbibī: How Bonbibī and Śājaṅgali were twins, sister and brother; how they were born deep within the forest; how they journeyed to Makkā and then returned to the mangrove swamps of the low-lying lands; how they waged war on Nārāyaṇī, after which they established their home base in the vicinity of Bhurkuṇḍa; how they eventually toured the whole of the low-lying regions and then deep within those forests established a market for the trade of honey; how the two traders Dhonāi and Monāi prepped seven ships for transporting honey; after handing over Dukhe to Dakṣiṇ Rāy, how Dhonāi left Kẽdokhāli and returned home hauling beeswax and honey; how Bonbibī was filled with compassion upon hearing of Dukhe's plight, and at the very moment, he was dangerously threatened, how she intervened; how she then affectionately took Dukhe to her lap and dispatched him out of the low-lying lands of the eighteen tides; after sending Dukhe home riding on the back of her crocodile, how she bestowed enormous wealth on Dukhe, rewarding his devotional merit; how she was merciful to his steadfast and loving mother and ensured that she receive a new home as a result of Dukhe's good acts; how, after bestowing great wealth on Dukhe, she made him the ruler, *rājā*, of the land, and how he properly managed the affairs of all those who were his subjects; how anyone falling into danger in the forests would receive her grace simply by calling out to her as Mother; how through her virtuous qualities they would be saved. These are the glories of the Mother of which I will now write—and I will describe all of them in complete detail. So pay close attention to the finer points of these episodes as I now tell the saga of Bonbibī and Śājaṅgali.

Brother and sister were born in the deep forest, and now for that episode I narrate the particulars. Just listen with pleasure, everyone, to the nature of fundamental faith. One of Āllā's *phakir*s was named Berāhim, and he made his home inside the city of Makkā. He possessed a youthful vigor and was an honorable, upstanding man who wished to be married. His bride went by the name of Phulbibī, and they appropriately enjoyed the life of a happily joined couple for quite some time. But there were no children to fill their home, and this misery was the source of a daily-visited grief. With arms raised in supplication, Berāhim appealed to Āllā at his *dargā*. "What fault, what sin have I committed that leads me here to your *dargā*? I have been diligently tilling my land, but the flowerless tree produces no fruit.[1] People gossip, referring to that tree as barren, good for nothing but firewood. As a result, one can imagine the predicament in which I find myself now: I will abandon this life by immolating my body in the flames of the fire produced by that wood."[2] And in this fashion the *phakir* grieved in the *dargā* of Elāhi, of God, raising his arms in supplication and giving sad voice to his lament.

Afterwards Phulbibī suggested to the *phakir*, "Please go, my beloved, and make formal petition at the tomb of the *rachul*, the Apostle. Through his compassion and by the grace of God, Khodā, may a boy and a girl be born within our home. Should that not come to pass, then we will know it was not ordained, that we were not fated to have a child."

Hearing this satisfied Berāhim as appropriate action, and so he went to the grave of the Holy Prophet in Medinā. At the tomb of the Prophet, he cinched a cloth around his neck, pressed his hands together in supplication, and wept as he pleaded his case. He presented his desire in a formal petition. The Prophet, being of exemplary nature, listened from his tomb. Then the noble one spoke in a disembodied voice, "The determination of offspring does not fall to me. To oversee these matters, it is God, Elāhi Āllā who has the vested authority. Submit your desires to Him, and He will decide. That being the case, give

1. In this transparent euphemism, there is a pun on "flower," or *phul*, the name of his wife.

2. The image invokes an inversion of the traditional *hinduyāni* ideal wife (*satī*) immolating herself on her husband's pyre to ensure transmigration and continuation of the lineage, where here Berāhim's lineage will come to an abrupt halt.

me leave to approach Phātemā, if she is agreeable, for Phātemā is responsible for organizing things in heaven. It is she we should ask whether or not children are in the offing." With these words Berāhim was consoled, and the Prophet, Hajrat himself took off for heaven.

When Phātemā saw him, she inquired of the Prophet, "Tell me, my beloved one, why have you come to see me in person?"

Hajrat replied, "O Mother, the reason I have come is this: Why is the house of Berāhim bereft of children?"

Phātemā replied, "Please be seated and wait. The Korān is right there on its throne, so I will look it up." And with these words Bibī went to consult the Korān. She soon returned and announced to Hajrat Nabī, the Holy Prophet. "It records that there will be two offspring in the house of Berāhim. But they will not be born of Phulbibī. He must couple with another woman in marriage, then he will have children. Go and give the news to Berāhim."

As soon as he heard, the Prophet returned to his dwelling in Madinā. Remaining invisible, he relayed this to Berāhim in a disembodied voice. "Long have you been beloved of me, an immaculate learned saint, a *sāi*. But there will be no children issuing from Phulbibī's womb. Understand that what is required is for you to join together with another in marriage. From her womb will be born a girl and a boy." When he heard this Berāhim was relieved and thrilled. He made a thousand salaams in obeisance before the Apostle, at his tomb. Then he took his leave and headed back to his home.

Phulbibī questioned Berāhim about all the intelligence that he had gleaned. "Tell me, what has the noble Prophet ordained?" Berāhim replied, "Bibī, how can I put this? Here is the story." The moment she heard, the news made her sick at heart. "He told me to take a second wife in marriage because you have no children in your belly, Bibī. You may choose not to believe this report, but He gave me the express command to marry again and then children would emerge from that union to fill my house."

When Berāhim explained what the Exalted One had conveyed, Phulbibī's head split as if struck by lightning. Weeping uncontrollably she beat her head in grief. "What did He decree for me in connection with you? Has He dictated that my fate is to be so deplorable? What am I to do when my lot is to be nothing but an empty vessel? Well, here is my decree: you must promise a settlement."

Berāhim replied, "What kind of agreement do you want? Whatever compensation you want, I will make happen."

Bibī said, "I am not going to say right now. What exactly you will grant me, you will give only when I make up my mind."

Berāhim replied, "Bibī, I promise to honor that request. Whatever you desire, I promise to fulfill it. Were I to ignore or disavow this promise, then I would be culpable, a sinner in Khodā's court, his *dargā*."

Bibī responded, "With only God, the Pure and Holy, as witness, if you do not fulfil my wish, meet my demand, your Great Protector will punish you unsparingly!" Having warned him, she said, "Go, my dearly beloved, go and make that marriage that you were instructed to do!"

When he heard her response, Berāhim Śāhā was satisfied, if not pleased. He systematically searched from house to house in the city of Makkā looking for a *phakir* by the name of Jalil who was resident there. His explorations finally led him to his home. Jalil had a daughter by the name of Golāl. This young woman was fourteen years of age, she was still there under his protection, she was not yet married, and this young *bibī* was a virgin. When he learned of his visitor, Jalil Śāhā was exceedingly pleased and he said to him, "Please take a seat, my honorable friend."

"I have come to make inquires about your daughter."

"If she is amenable to what is proposed, then I shall give her over to you in marriage." And with these righteous words Śāhā disappeared into the inner apartments, where he apprised Golāl Bibī of the overture.

Golāl heard him out and then said to her father, "If you find this agreeable, then I am amenable, dear father. Whatever terms you negotiate privately with him, I will be bound to honor. From my end, I will not renege or attempt to disavow any of it." Hearing her heartfelt confirmation, Śāhā Jalil came back out and apprised Berāhim of the good news. Listening carefully, Berāhim was made one very happy man. The demure agreement of his newly beloved made him overflow with joy as he stood up.

The humble Khāter says: Because both of you are in agreement, waste no time in arranging with the kāji, *the judge, to effect the marriage.*

THE MARRIAGE OF GOLĀL BIBĪ TO BERĀHIM

Phakir Jalil Śāhā was very satisfied. He arranged for Berāhim to bathe and made ready as the groom. He quickly issued invitations to each and every person found in the neighborhood. Everyone came and sat to constitute a formal assembly or *majlis*, where Golāl was properly wed to Berāhim. They brought the individuals required to act in accord with legislated custom: they summoned an *ukil*, a legal expert, and two other people to act as official witnesses. When she gave formal consent, the *ukil* brought Golāl Bibī before the assembly. When the judge received confirmation of the consent to marriage from the *ukil*, he duly married Golāl to Berāhim. Placing their hands together, the prayer of benediction was pronounced. Everyone showered the bride and groom with their blessings of good will and then dispersed, returning to their own homes. Berāhim stayed for a while in the home of his father-in-law, where he made delightful, fervent love to Golāl. Lost in that happy state, there they remained for three or four days. With a profound delight, he eventually took his *bibī* back to his own home, where Phulbibī was there waiting in her own quarters. He entrusted the care of Golāl Bibī to her, but of course when she saw her co-wife, it was as if that anger that had been smoldering in Phulbibī's heart suddenly burst into flames. Giving no reaction either good or bad, Berāhim remained unruffled and said nothing. Checking her sadness and grief, Phulbibī eventually quieted down. Berāhim had fully registered the anguish in Phulbibī's heart, so he installed the two *bibī*s in separate, private apartments, in which—when he visited each in turn—he passed his time most pleasantly.

In this fashion some number of days passed uneventfully, then God determined it was time for the great event of the birth. Āllā summoned Bonbibī and Śājaṅgali, both of whom were residing in heaven, and issued this command: "In the house of one Berāhim, there is a woman, his wife, named Golāl. Go and take birth from her womb. Rāi and Gāji are the resident powers in the Āṭhārobhāṭī, Land of the Eighteen Tides. It is there that you must establish your fame and glory." Listening intently, Bibī made full prostration at the appropriate moment and, in the presence of Khodā, in his *dargā*, she spoke with a keen mindfulness, "At Your express command, O God, Elāhi, we will go to Your created earth. Neither of us— brother or sister—will bring embarrassment or humiliation upon ourselves, for it is by your assistance that all obstacles are shifted and removed. Except through You, no one can be saved." Confirming this, Bibī and Śājaṅgali then went to be born from their mother's womb.

That very night Berāhim lay with Golāl and they coupled with great desire and joyful intent. When God breathed into their father's head,[3] the twins entered their mother's womb in the shape of a miniscule black dot. By the grace of Khodā, those twins, brother and sister, grew little by little every day, hidden there in that impenetrable darkness of the womb. One or two months passed like this, then it registered on Golāl Bibī. She approached Berāhim and spoke, "Śāhā, listen, take this to heart: by the grace of Khodā, I know that I have become pregnant." When Śāhā Berāhim heard, he was exultant. Before Khodā, in his *dargā*, he gave a thousand salutations of praise.

The humble Khāter explains: In this way did Bonbibī grow gradually in her mother's womb.

In the first month it was but a tiny dot floating in the waters
and no one knew that it was there;
    but in the second month came streaks of blood.
Little by little, day after day,
they became recognizable, taking the shape of tiny toy dolls;
    from these slips of a figure were the twins gradually fashioned.
Then they entered the third month,
and veins and sinews began to take form,
    knitting together the bones and flesh.
In the fourth month, hands and feet,
ribs and the organs of the thorax,
    were sheathed in covering muscle.
Wherever and however things were arranged, including
the order of the gut, the stomach, the intestines, and so forth—
    all developed in their proper anatomical place and sequence.
After the nose, mouth, eyes, and ears,
there was nothing left to be fashioned, so it was
    during the fifth month that the five senses were activated.
The life breath that was incipient in the body

3. This is likely the moment of ensoulment for new human life.

could remain still no longer, as the
    many conduits of energy started up in concert.
Impelled by the energizing sound of "*hu hu,*"
the fetus would not remain motionless in the womb,
    for the various openings of the body were becoming active.[4]
In the sixth month the sinews and veins and connective tissues
knitted together with ever-greater complexity
    making the body whole and without blemish.
In month seven, the boy and the girl
stretched their limbs out straight and grew longer, and
    they began to squirm and rock back and forth like lovers
        possessed.
During the eighth month, the wind whips
waves of breath through the eight organs, the ghats,
    but two of those organs remain dormant.
That organ which is the most powerful, the most important,
is astounding in its development,
    for there is where cognition takes place.[5]

4. *Bhāṭi* [many] *ujāner melā* [the interplay of the streams or flows, i.e., lines of energy and fluids, in] *āṭhār* [openings or wounds (in the last line of this *tripadi* stanza) in] *cij* [critical parts], punning on *bhāṭi* and *āṭhār*, inasmuch as the Sundarbans are called the Āṭhārobhāṭī, low-lying lands (*bhāṭi*) of the eighteen tides (*āṭhāro*) The wording hints either that as soon as the fetus is viable, the call of Bonbibī's mission to the Sundarbans will impel the final development of the fetus, or, perhaps more pointedly, sets up a homology between her body and the Sundarbans, the welfare of one being the welfare of the other.

5. This verse describing the developments of the eighth month is obscure. The image of the wind whipping up waves along the *ghāṭs* (Eng. ghat), as would happen on the river, suggests the full activation of the various organs, breathing activity into them, and most likely the two that remain enervated are for alimentation and excretion. At first blush the term *ghāṭ* might seem to signify an "opening" in the body (usually there are nine), in the way a *ghāṭ* along the river functions as a point of entry/exit, embarkation/disembarkation. For several millennia Indic medicine had been well aware of the hydraulic nature of bodily organs as they move various fluids in and out (suggestive of the waves), so the image is not as far-fetched as it might first seem, but the second half of the triplet clearly indicates the organ of cognition and intellection, corresponding to contemporary notions of the brain, so thinking of the *ghāṭ* as an opening does not follow. The preferred reading is *ghaṭ*, a small metal or earthenware pot, a container, which in image and function more closely approximates an organ; importantly, *ghaṭ* can in context explicitly signify the brain or head as it does in the aniconic image found in the *Rāy maṅgal* above, so the author seems to be playing with the *ghāṭ*/*ghaṭ* pairing. Reading *ghāṭ*/*ghaṭ*/ghat as "organ" is not without precedent; in the passage that opens Ābdul

By the ninth month, the babies were
clamoring to escape the darkness,
    desiring to open their closed eyes.
By the time the tenth month had rolled around
the babies were feeling pain, cramped in the womb
    and made it clear "We will stay here no longer!
Now is the time to come out,
and to look, to cast our eyes about, to see for ourselves
    how the people act in the ways of the world."

The lowly Khāter speaks
at the feet of Bonbibī,
    a friend of the Protector Who Knows No Limits.

And in this way Bonbibī grew bigger, day by day, in her mother's womb, joyfully and full-term without complications.

After the ninth month had passed and the tenth had finally arrived, Phulbibī spoke to Berāhim, "Listen, Sāheb, remember that at the time of the wedding you promised me a boon. Now you must honor that solemn oath."

Berāhim replied, "Bibī, tell me what you want. I'm listening."

Phulbibī then declared, "Now I want you to abandon your Golāl Bibī deep in the forest."

The moment he heard that request, it was as if a lightning bolt had struck his head. He cried out, "Oh, what awful thing has happened to me, for I am duty bound to honor this ghastly demand! From a terrible misery that plagued me—no children—I again got married, though I was at an older age. Through the blessings of Khodā that woman became pregnant. To have children was my driving desire. How can I now abandon them to that swampy forest?" These and more worrying thoughts flooded his heart and mind, so he said, "Bibī, how can you demand such a thing? She is pregnant and weak. How can I possibly desert her in the forest? This act will anger Elāhi Āllā and, at the end of time, standing in his *dargā*, in his presence, I will be judged a vile sinner. Forgive me, but please take back this request. Except for that, I will give you anything you want."

Ohāb's rendition of the *Gāji kālu o cāmpāvatī kanyār puthi* (p. 145 above), the diligent Sufi practitioner is instructed to purify the *ghāṭs/ghaṭs* within the body, but in a more explicit yogic physiology (that purification being an analogue to or variant of *tapas*, the generation of heat).

Phulbibī replied, "But that exception is it. I do not want anything else from you. You knew fully well that you were in the presence of Khodā when you made that commitment. So today you must fulfil that agreement."

As he listened, Berāhim was flummoxed and lost his bearings. Over and over he mulled the possibilities of how he might discharge this debt. Under what conditions could he bring a pregnant Golāl Bibī to the forest and then leave her all alone? He worried himself about what in the end must be counted a truly evil transgression. He wept profusely as he made his way to Golāl Bibī's quarters. Tearfully he hugged Golāl Bibī and then spoke solicitously, in her interest, "Considering your condition, there is no one here to offer proper care, neither your mother-in-law nor my sisters, your sisters-in-law. Come, let me take you to your father's home where you can deliver at ease. Your mother is there and she will attend you." As Golāl Bibī listened, her heart was much relieved and she prepared to leave with her husband.

As he walked ahead of her, Berāhim's heart grew heavy, while following along behind, Bibī found the going difficult. After walking some distance they detoured into a heavily forested jungle. Bibī noticed and began to question Berāhim. "Tell me, why have you chosen to veer off the main road, leading us into this forest?"

Berāhim answered, "Listen carefully and I will explain, my beloved. There is a saint's shrine, a tomb, close by here. I had made a formal vow prior to my wedding that were my wife, my Bibī, to get pregnant, I would certainly bring her to acknowledge our good fortune: I will come back to the grave, to the blessed tomb. That is why we have left the main road and entered the forest thicket."

As she had done many times before, Bibī heard him out. Afterwards they moved on, but got only a short distance. Sitting down under a tree to rest, Bibī said, "I simply cannot go any farther. The pain that grips my belly has grown unbearable." As she said that she spread out a small cloth and uttering the name of Āllā and the Apostle she lay down to rest. A gentle breeze wafted over her and she gradually succumbed to her torpor. As she closed her eyes, sleep soon overwhelmed Bibī.

As he watched her, Berāhim then began to calculate the possibilities: "There is no human traffic through this place." His love and kind regard for his wife conveniently deserted him right then and there. "I will leave her all alone and return to my home." Taking this decision, he called out to her three times. "Get up, Bibī, we cannot stay and must be on our way." Bibī was so deep in sleep she did not even twitch, totally incapable of hearing him call to her. Berāhim then proclaimed, "Āllā, no fault can accrue to me. I called out to my Bibī and she never responded." In an effort to exonerate himself with these words, the illusion of his compassion evaporated. Committed to this heinous act, he headed back home.

When his first wife Phulbibī spotted Berāhim, she was delighted and faithfully served him.

Back in the forest where Golāl Bibī had fallen asleep, she eventually emerged from her stupefaction, and was now fully awake. Berāhim was nowhere to be seen. Filled with anxiety, Bibī looked all around, but no matter which way she looked, she found no trace. Crying out in anguish, she wept and beat her head. She moaned, "Alas, what incredible disaster has befallen me! How will I manage? Where can I go, how can I survive in this jungly forest? The man dearer to me than life brought me here only to deceive me. He has abandoned me here in the underbrush of this swampy forest. Aiee, my beloved, what on earth was in your mind? You have sacrificed me to the fires of utter misery! A woman alone is helpless and loses her social standing, her *jāti*. And in this case, as Elāhi Himself desired, I am pregnant. How could you have exposed me to this horrible situation here in the forest? What I have only learned is that the hearts and minds of men are cruel, devoid of feeling. When it is convenient, they are solicitous; but when it is not, they are duplicitous and it becomes someone else's problem. I have now come to understand that in this world everyone tends to treachery: in good times one has lots of friends, but in bad times none, they disappear. With the exception of Elāhi, God, friends grow scarce in distressing situations. I have come to realize that no one else comes to your aid; He alone looks after you in every critical situation. No one else is filled with compassion as is He." With this lament, Bibī raised her arms to address Khodā and made her appeal, saturated with the ring of genuine agony. "Alas, Āllā, the Pure Ocean of compassion. Apart from you, I have no one in this jungly forest. I have fallen into extreme danger: please show your mercy! Please help me out of this trouble!" After crying out like this, the anxieties in her heart were miraculously alleviated and losing consciousness, she slumped in a heap on the ground. In response to Bibī's lament, Āllā did show pity on her, and on the spot he summoned four færies. At Khodā's command they assembled and they stationed themselves in vigil around her. When she came to, Bibī opened her eyes and beheld the four female figures standing guard around her. Bibī asked, "Who are you and where you have come from?" They replied, "We live here in the jungle. We were coming this way and spotted you here all alone. In the name of God, we have remained here for you." With these words all of them settled in right there. They fetched food from heaven, *behest*, and fed Bibī.

By now, the tenth month had passed, so she was full-term; soon the labor contractions began to surge through Bibī's womb. Bibī writhed in agony at the sharpness of the pains. The færies reassured her, "Do not be afraid. Khodā is looking after you. Within the hour you will deliver." In this way they contrived to elevate her spirits. Bonbibī was born shortly thereafter and by the command of Āllā her umbilical cord was knotted, and she was carefully laid on the ground. To look upon her caused a thrill to course through the hearts of all as they circled back over and again to catch a glimpse of her face. Then Śājaṅgali dropped from her belly to the ground. The brother and sister had shared the same womb, and it was by Khodā's directive that the twins were now born. When Golāl Bibī first looked on her two children, all of her previous heartache simply evaporated. She fixed her eyes on them, enrapt, and was instantly and thoroughly besotted. As this was happening, the four færies slipped away; they mounted a special conveyance and returned to the confines of heaven, *behest*. When Bibī raised her head and looked around she saw no one. It was then that Bibī fully realized that the aid they had furnished was by the grace of Khodā. This she verbally acknowledged as she pulled her two children onto her lap.

She continued out loud, "Where can I go? Or should I stay put here?" After weighing her options, she decided in the end to leave both of them in the jungle. Saying goodbye, she struck out in some uncertain direction. "Āllā the Pure and Holy will determine their fates," and with the words she laid them down.

Just at that moment a doe turned up and rebuked her, "After bearing in your womb two children who have emerged like golden twin moons—how can you possibly abandon them here in the forest? You are the most heartless, merciless person in the triple world! How can you embrace such an evil action? Has your heart completely forgotten God, the Protector? Listen, my child, for six months I dragged around the corpse of my dead fawn. I am a beast of the jungle and eat only grasses, but my eyes never tired of looking on her face. How could you leave your children here in the forest? Have you forgotten your principles, has God the Protector fled from your heart?" After lecturing her, the doe bolted back into the forest.

Mulling her words, Golāl Bibī reconsidered. She said to herself, "Now I have two to look after, but what will I do? How can I raise them, provide for them? So for the sake of the baby boy, I will leave the girl behind. Now I must get out of here; should I not leave now, how will we survive without food? I might manage to survive here for a few days, but for everyone, Nirāñjan—the Stainless, the Pure, the Protector—He alone decides who dies and who survives. Should He not kill her, but save her, then certainly He will send her protectors."

Having reasoned this through best she could, she picked up Bonbibī and took her deeper into the forest to abandon her. Bonbibī plaintively looked up at her mother's face and thought, "Oh, mother, what you have determined is this: your heart is filled with compassion for your infant son, but can you say why you do not harbor that same love and affection for your daughter? Both boy and girl shared a single womb, but one enjoys the good fortune of your compassion, the fortune of the other, not at all."

In the end Golāl abandoned Bonbibī to the forest, then weeping desperately, gathered up Jaṅgali and held him tight. She began to wander aimlessly through the overgrown forest, scavenging wild fruits and leafy greens to eat. And that was how she came to meander without purpose or direction through the jungle.

But wait, who was there to take care of Bonbibī?

Devoid of all decency and compassion, Bonbibī's mother abandoned her crying newborn in the forest and went on her way. Bonbibī prayed to Khodā, "O Āllā, please show me a tiny bit of your grace. You were responsible for dispatching me into this world, may you now bless me with your loving mercy." And after that, Āllā showed Himself to Bonbibī as the Compassionate. He issued a command to all the deer of that jungle: "Bonbibī is lying in the forest crying. All of you together go find her and raise her." With that express order from Elāhi, the deer dashed off and they nourished her with their milk as they did their own young. This is how it came to be that Bonbibī and Śājaṅgali separately grew to adulthood in the forest.

Mohammad Khāter says: Khodā showers mercy on all those who have become his companions, after which they will suffer no misery in any place or circumstance, for Khodā's bounty produces ease and joy in them all.

BONBIBĪ AND ŚĀJAṄGALI TAKE LEAVE OF THEIR MOTHER AND FATHER TO GO TO THE HOLY CITY OF MADINĀ TO TRAIN AS STUDENTS

Through the grace of Khodā, all the deer of the forest together were able to take care of Bonbibī and raise her without interruption. The færies descended from heaven and carried her on their hips in the way that women carry their young as they move about. They fed her whatever fruits and other edibles they managed to scavenge in the forest undergrowth. Meanwhile, Golāl Bibī carried Jaṅgali, the two of them managing to scrape along through different parts of the jungle. Those fruits and suitable foods they found they ate with gusto to satisfy their hunger. Though both Bonbibī and her brother Śājaṅgali grew up deep in the forest, they were hidden from one another. The twins remained separated, completely apart, neither one hearing or seeing a trace of the other. They managed this way for seven years, until they both started to mature as young adults. Then Khodā issued a command to the twins: "Take yourselves to the city that is deep within the mangrove swamps of the low-lying lands." And according to that directive they each did just that.

Now listen, everyone, to something of Berāhim's story.

Many, many days later, Berāhim Śāhā was thinking remorsefully about the twins, so he confronted Phul Bibī with tears in his eyes. "In order to meet your demands, I abandoned Golāl Bibī in the forest. Even though she was completely without fault, I deserted her in the mangrove swamps. Much time has passed, yet I failed to search for her, and for that I have accrued a great sin. What can I plead in my defense before the judgement of Khodā? You stay here at home in your personal quarters, Bibī, while just this once I go into the jungle to search."

Announcing his intentions, Berāhim remained deeply troubled as he went off to locate Golāl Bibī. In no time his search had taken him deep into the jungle, and only after some indeterminate number of days did he finally track her down. When he encountered Golāl Bibī, she was sitting at the foot of a tree with Jaṅgali. They were slumped down to the ground, malnourished and weak, forlorn and despairing. Berāhim wept as he swept them into his arms. He confessed: "My transgression, my culpability in this affair is monstrous, but it was written in the ledger of fate by Khodā's direct command. Listen, my beloved Bibī, please forgive my sin. I have been searching for you for many long days, but nowhere had I found any trace of you. There is no remedy for what has transpired. Please get up, Bibī, and let us return to our home."

Golālbibī sharply replied, "How can you utter such lies? I learned all too well the workings of your heart and mind: you are the man who abandoned his wife in the forest, while returning home to live in comfort. You turned out your pregnant wife in the forest, and then, after an inordinately long time, you claim that you have been looking for her!"

Berāhim implored her, "Let me say again to you: Who has the power to abrogate what Khodā has penned? What was written in our fate has come to pass. Come now, bring the boy and let us go back home." With this explanation, Bibī was mollified, so she held Jaṅgali close and headed out of the forest.

Look, who is able to fathom Āllā's drama?

Bonbibī was still living in the jungle. As Golālbibī was moving along the road with Jaṅgali by her side, Bonbibī caught sight of them and ran after them. She caught up and said, "Brother Śājaṅgali, where are you going? You no longer need to be attached to our mother and father. Previously we were with one another as brother and sister. Our mission, our fame and glory will be found in the low-lying lands of the eighteen tides, the Āṭhārobhāṭī. It was Khodā's command that brought us here. Come on, let's just the two of us enter the mangrove swamps together!" When Jaṅgali heard what she said, he quickly pulled free of his parents, and made his way over to Bonbibī. After such a long, long time, the twins, brother and sister, were reunited. Then they tried to make their mother and father understand: "It is by Khodā's decree that we must go into the mangrove swamps. It was for this reason alone that we took birth in your family. We will now seek out a teacher, a *murśid*, to achieve appropriate respect and recognition for our mission."

As Golāl Bibī listened to this, tears streamed from her eyes, she fell to the ground, writhing in grief, crying out "My son, my son!" She continued, "My son, are you leaving me behind after all this time? For ten months and ten days I carried you in my womb. Is there anyone in this wide world more unfortunate than I? At the time of my death, who will recite the *kalemā*, the declaration of faith? When I die who will wrap me in the white funeral shroud?" And in this vein Golāl Bibī and Berāhim both vented the acute sadness that gripped them.

Bonbibī tried with some difficulty to make them understand and said, "Go back home now and weep no more. Were I to forget my love for you, what possible response could I give when the accounts are reckoned at the end of time?" And with these words they took their leave of their mother and father. The twins departed for Madinā in search of a qualified teacher, while Berāhim ushered a weeping Golāl Bibī back to their home.

At this point Bonbibī took Jaṅgali along, and after an uncounted number of days they reached Madinā. They were initiated as the pupils, *murids*, of the son of Hāsen,[6] after which paid their respects at the tomb of Phātemā. Tearfully, they requested, "Mother, please show your beneficence. By the power of your grace we will go to the paradisiacal splendor of the low-lying regions. Please wrap us in your mercy, dear Mother, to protect us from the vexations that abound through those forests."

In response, an oracle, a disembodied voice emanated from the tomb: "Listen, Bonbibī, to what I have to say to you. You must follow my instruction precisely, then afterwards take yourself to the low-lying lands of the eighteen tides, the Āṭhārobhāṭī. Āllā, the Exalted One, has populated the Āṭhārobhāṭī with eighteen thousand people, but they have become wayward and given to deceitful behavior. When they call out to you as Mother, begging for your blessings, be compassionate and lift them up, save them."

Bonbibī replied, "Oh blessed Mother, I promise to do precisely what you bid me do. Please cover me with your grace!" With these words, blessings issued from Phatemā's grave, and Bonbibī successfully completed her formal visit to the tomb, her *jiyārat*, in a state of pure joy.

6. There is no indication who this individual might be, though the Bangla spelling Hāsen would point to someone named Hashim and not Hāsān (Ḥasan); see the opening to Ohāb's *Gāji kālu o cāmpāvatī kanyār puthi*, p. 142, and n 1, p. 143. above.

And so the brother and sister together headed for the settlement in the low-lying regions.

Mohāmmad Khāter says: I am temporarily living in Hābaḍā District,[7] *but my permanent address is in Bāliyā Govindapur; Mohāmmad Mechām-uddin is the name of my respected father.*

BONBIBĪ AND ŚĀHJAṄGALI LEAVE MADINĀ AND ARRIVE IN THE MANGROVE SWAMPS

Bonbibī and Śājaṅgali, brother and sister, took formal leave from Phātemā's burial place. They soon arrived at the blessed garden tomb of the Prophet. Performing the *jiyārat*, the traditional ritual prostrations at the tomb to elicit favor, they raised their arms in solicitation and ceremonially submitted their request. "O revered Prophet, *nabī*, we declare ourselves: we have come to you to be sanctioned as your representatives, your *khelāphat*. As the *guru* of *phakir*s, be pleased to bestow your imprimatur. Then pray grant the two of us proper leave." After listening, the Prophet honored their request, and at that precise moment, they received traditional patchwork cloaks and black hats. When they experienced this confirmation, the hearts of both the sister and brother sang with pleasure. They placed the hats on their heads, uttering *bichmillā*. Bibī said to Jaṅgali, "We have received a sign that the grace of Khodā has fallen upon us, so from this point forward we should have no fear of any situation or any person. Come, let us leave this place and head to the low-lying regions." With these words, the twins made thousands upon thousands of prostrations, salaams, for receiving the beneficence permeating the tomb of the Chosen One, Mostaphā, the Prophet. With an unrestrained joy, they took their prayer beads, *tasbi*, water pots, and other paraphernalia and began their journey.

They left the holy station of Madinā and after only a few days reached their designated territory within Hindusthān. When they crossed the Gaṅgā River, they felt a great satisfaction and joy. Arriving at the eastern regions, they avoided entering the waters directly, rather skirted around their banks.[8] While they were following the course of

7. Hābaḍā is modern-day Howrah.

8. Following the bank of the Gaṅgā, after it turns south, it takes them straight into the Sundarbans.

one large stream, they encountered a man named Bhāṅgaḍ. When he saw them, Bhāṅgaḍ Śāhā stood tall. His hands pressed together in respectful greeting, he spoke, "Please tell me, where are you coming from? Please introduce yourselves because I do not recognize you."

Bibī replied, "We are twins, brother and sister, and we have just arrived here from the city of Madinā. At the tomb of the Apostle, the *rasul,* we received his imprimatur to represent him, his *khelāphat.* Khodā has been most gracious to us and has granted the low-lying lands of the eighteen tides as our land-holding, our *jāygīr*. So now we are headed into the mangrove swamps to pacify them and their inhabitants. Please tell us now, in which direction should we go? After traveling so far, we are anxious to reach the low-lying lands."

Bhāṅgaḍ said, "My dear Mother, listen and take this to heart. You have almost reached those very low-lying lands. Here the ruler and landlord of the low-lying regions is one Dakṣiṇā Rāy. He has large numbers of disciples throughout the forests. He has vast stores of salt, beeswax, cowries, and other items. He has established honey markets in any number of places. If you should begin by cutting down the trees of the forest, then, dear mother, you will gain control of the low-lying lands. Following that, take the settlements called Rāy Maṅgal, C̃ād Khāli, and Śibādahe, after which you can establish your legal jurisdiction. You can then discipline and calm your subjects, but you should not expand further outward from that region. In the city of C̃ād Khāli, there is a man appropriately named C̃ād. You should search him out, for he is well-informed and experienced. He enjoys legal jurisdiction up to Andhār Mānik, so do not attempt to establish your own authority there." After Śāhā Bhāṅgaḍ had explained things to them in detail, Bonbibī begged his leave to proceed further.

This lowly subject says: Wherever the friends of Khodā go, everyone approaches them with honor and respect.

BONBIBĪ ENTERS THE LOW-LYING LANDS AND ENGAGES NĀRĀYAṆĪ IN BATTLE

As she listened to Bhāṅgaḍ's words of advice,
the good-natured Bonbibī
  was in high spirits.
She politely bade farewell.

Then she took Jaṅgali along with her
to establish her authority over the mangrove swamps.
First, to initiate action, they entered the forest,
established a home base and settled in
to formally execute the ritual of prayer.
Jaṅgali issued a resounding call to prayer
that rolled across the skies like thunder, so loud
that even Rāymaṇi could hear.
Sitting there on his high seat,
Rāy was shaken, momentarily at a loss, then mumbled,
"What warrior issued that mighty cry?"
Rāy turned to address Sanātan,
"This is worrisome, so please go quickly
and find out what *phakir* has come.
That cry was not at all
that of our friend Barakhān,
so who else has shown up here?
Go quickly! Pay my heartfelt compliments
and drive him away,
back to wherever he came from!"
When he received his marching orders,
Sanātan quickly sped off,
and soon found the twins sitting calmly,
black caps on their heads, and in loud voices
chanting, "Āllā, Āllā," their staves of aspiration[9]
firmly planted in front of them.
As Sanātan watched, he was truly frightened
and did not dare approach them, rather
he returned and reported back to Rāymaṇi.
"There are a young woman and a young man,
both of them sitting, their faces upturned,
their arms raised, repeating, 'Āllā, Āllā.'
As soon as he heard this, Dakṣiṇ Rāy was enraged,
as if smoldering embers had suddenly burst into flames.
So he summoned all of his advisors and friends.
He asked, "Why has a barbarian *jaban* come
to the low-lying regions, to my forests?

9. The term *āśā* (alt. *āsā*, *āṣā*) is the mendicant's staff and it also means "hope" or "aspiration"; it is not uncommon for authors to play on this double-meaning of this homophone.

Go and fetch him to me right away!
Ghouls, hungry ghosts, spirits, and demons—
summon them all,
for today we will engage them in battle.
I will personally engage the *phakir*
and anyone else they may have brought here to fight.
I shall defeat them and have them bound."
After announcing his intention, Rāymaṇi
fitted himself out and left,
taking his demons and ghostly spirits with him.
As this was happening, Nārāyaṇī,
Rāymaṇi's mother, inside the house,
had heard the news.
She hurried out and said, "My son, my dear one,
there are no good grounds, no reason,
for you to fight against a woman.
If you are victorious, no advantage accrues;
if you are killed, it will be disgrace;
our honor, our standing in the region will evaporate.
You must hold back and stay put; I will go.
Whether I win or am wounded, does not matter.
It is best for a woman to fight against a woman."
After Nārāyaṇī had made her case,
she took the spirits and demons with her,
as well as all the disciples present.
Hungry ghosts, *bhūt*s, emerged from the cremation grounds,
appearing as so many messengers of death;
more than 156,000 issued forth from secret places.
Witches, *ḍākinī*s—all fierce viragos, numbering 360,000,000—
fanned out over the low-lying lands of the eighteen tides,
screaming, "Kill! Kill!"
Once they were assembled,
Nārāyaṇī prepared her battle dress,
covering herself with glittering ornaments of war.
Arming herself with a myriad of weapons,
puffed up with pride, confident of victory,
she arrogantly sashayed down the road atop her royal chariot.
Small *kāḍā* and large *ḍhol* drums thumped an ominous beat,
which had reached a strident and dissonant din
by the time they reached the center of the city.
All around they assembled, scampering here and there

in their self-important brazenness till the earth quaked.
Bonbibī looked on, taking their measure.
She then instructed Jaṅgali, "Brother,
look, there is no reason to be afraid,
for God is the Pure and Wondrous.
All the ranks of witches and hungry ghosts
will clear out of this swampy forest
as soon as you let fly your powerful call to prayer."
Jaṅgali heeded her words,
meditated momentarily on Āllā the Pure,
then let a mighty call to prayer peal forth.
The spirits and hungry ghosts heard it
and in a heartbeat were rattled;
suddenly skittish, they fled the scene in terror.
When the spirits and hungry ghosts took flight,
vanishing from the place in a wild rush,
Nārāyaṇī herself grew apprehensive, indeed afraid.
She called out to the witches, the *ḍākinī*s,
"Come, we must fight!
They heard and returned in orderly ranks.
With a blood-curdling cry of "Victory, victory!"
it seemed the sky itself had initiated the sound as it reverberated
from the highest heavens to the furthest depths of the underworld.
To counter, Bonbibī emitted a deafening roar
that encircled them on all sides,
paralyzing them, fencing them in with a magic net.[10]
She wielded her staff as a paddle,
and charging it with words, sent it off
flying to the skies above.
It rained down destruction on heads of the witches
like a thunderbolt shattering a mountaintop—
the direct result of Bonbibī's majesty and virtue.
It was at the command of Khodā
that the staff flew up, riding the wind, and
battered them this way and that, smashing their heads.
The *ḍākinī* witches and sorceress *jogini*s
that had engaged there in the hundreds were,

10. I have translated *echamer jāl* as "magic net"; literally, the "net of the Lord on High," it seems to be a direct translation of, or at least an allusion to, the ancient Vedic concept of *indrajāla*, "Indra's net," the illusory or magical nature of the world.

without exception, all killed in the battle.
Those few who chose not to confront Bonbibī
escaped pell-mell from the scene.
Nārāyaṇī shook with fear as she witnessed the carnage:
all the spirits, wraiths, and hungry ghosts that had assembled
were dispersed by a single ear-splitting roar,
while the *ḍākinī* witches and sorceress *jogini*s were slain.
Realizing the extent of her danger,
Nārāyaṇī screwed up her courage
and calmly steeled her heart.
She nocked arrows in her bow,
pulled taut the bowstring, and let the shafts fly.
But Bonbibī saw them slicing the air toward her.
The arrows flew at her from all directions, but
wetting her lips with the words of the *kalemā*,
they passed through her body as if she were made of water.
Nārāyaṇī saw clearly that
the arrows had no effect on Bonbibī's body
and she cursed the arrows for their worthlessness.
She followed this with fearsome arrow-missiles,
drawing her bowstring even more forcefully,
releasing the projectiles toward Bonbibī in quick succession.
She fired three fabled arrows: first was *ṣaṭcakra*,
followed immediately by *gadācakra*,
and finally the *dharmmacakra*.
When they were discharged, their intense effulgence
was like a flame that had suddenly ignited;
but Bonbibī again was able to intercept them.
Reciting the *kalemā* a second time, affirming the unity of God, *taohid*,
she vigorously raised her staff and
drove it forcefully into the ground.
When those arrow-missiles fizzled out, neutralized,
Rāymaṇi's mother's frustration erupted in unmitigated fury,
so she vented by beating a magical pot with a metal bar.
Soon the clanging sounds of metal on metal
reverberated around Bonbibī on all sides,
then arrow-weapons began to rush at her from all over.
Bonbibī realized she was in grave danger
and was speechless as she
contemplated her demise.
A small bag for counting auspicious recitations hung from her neck,

so she uttered a prayer over the beads and blew on them:
    the beads instantly shattered the arrow-missiles into fragments.
When Nārāyaṇī's weapons were exhausted,
It was her turn to contemplate impending doom,
    which left her utterly flummoxed.
She picked up a thin, stiletto-like dagger,
jumped down off her chariot,
    and set upon Bibī.
By the power of the grace of Phātemā,
the knife never touched Bibī's body; rather
    it magically transformed into a flower which flew off.
Nārāyaṇī watched in amazement and exclaimed,
"I have never seen anything like this!
    Nothing so much as even grazed her face.
This is alarming in the extreme!"
What's to be done? What she did was pick up her club,
    her anger propelling her forward.
Nārāyaṇī ran toward Bibī and
pummeled her head.
    She raised the club and struck repeatedly.
But those too failed to leave a mark on Bibī's body.
When Nārāyaṇī realized this,
    she redoubled her rain of blows.
Many times over did she thrust the whetted tips of pikes
into Bonbibī until that cache of arms was exhausted,
    and there simply were no more weapons left.
As a last resort, she lunged at Bonbibī,
tackling her around the waist,
    and engaged in hand-to-hand fighting.
In a vicious rage the two locked in combat,
coming together as one,
    the clashing of two unyielding mountains.
For the whole day they waged war,
with neither one able to gain the upper hand,
    until Bonbibī felt herself giving way.
She called out, "All-beneficent Mother!
Please rescue me,
    and help me beat down Nārāyaṇī!"

The Beneficent One, Phātemā,[11] was in heaven,
and Khodā commanded her:
    "Bonbibī has fallen into serious peril.
Use the power of your grace
to rescue her from this danger
    so that she is not slain!"
The venerated Beneficent One listened,
and with a happy heart bestowed that grace,
    revitalizing Bonbibī's body to continue to fight.
She immediately grabbed hold of Nārāyaṇī,
tossed her high into the air,
    only to fall, crashing back onto the hard earth.
Bonbibī grabbed her by the hair,
sat on her chest, squeezing out her life-breath,
    and brought the sharp end of her staff to her throat.
Nārāyaṇī watched in horror,
and struggled to grasp Bibī's feet in submission.
    She spoke, invoking her as beloved friend.
"Spare me my life,
please do not kill me.
    I will ever be your loyal servant.
Through the low-lying lands of the eighteen tides,
all those who exercise power
    will become your loyal and obedient followers.
From this day forward you will rule as *rājā*
and we will be your subjects.
    You have become the master.
Please pledge to forgive and protect us
and we will be your loyal vassals.
    We will flawlessly execute your every order."
As she listened to this prayer of heartfelt contrition,
Bibī, being naturally beneficent,
    did not crush and dismember her, but spared her.
Contemplating the nature of the Mother's grace,

11. There are two ways to read *barakat*, or power of beneficence, in these triplets. I have chosen to render it as an epithet of Phātemā, the Beneficent One, Bonbibī's preferred intercessor. The alternate reading would be to personify *barakat* as a general aura of power (in contrast to *kerāmat*, power wielded to gain a very specific end, usually to convince infidels), but I have not seen that personification elsewhere, though it is grammatically feasible.

Bibī lifted up Nārāyaṇī
  and pulled her close, hugging her.
Relieved to have survived the battle,
Nārāyaṇī came forward and sat down by the throne,
  assuming her new position as attendant.
The time arrived for the prescribed evening prayers, *nāmāj*,
so Jaṅgali gave the call, the *ājān*,
  with Rāy, lord of the low-lying regions, in attendance.
When the residents of the forest heard that sound,
they, too, came to join the gathering,
  bringing food and the requisite fees for using the land.
Serving the feet of Bonbibī,
the lowly Khāter observes:
  The forest was now under her control.

Nārāyaṇī praised her, "You are now the revered queen of this land, collecting all the revenue from it. You are now the master, the *karttā*, of the low-lying lands of the eighteen tides. You should do whatever you feel you must. How can I object?"

Bonbibī replied, "My friend, listen and take this to heart. To one and all will I parcel out the low-lying lands of the eighteen tides to ensure that no one ever suffers any misery. Now, you are free to return to your home." With this pronouncement, Bonbibī embarked from that place to tour the Āṭhārobhāṭī and establish her administration.

As the ruler of the low-lying lands, she systematically inspected each and every place. Bibī eventually landed up in a station called Bhurkuṇḍa. She paused to sit at the base of a large tree and when she looked around, her heart thrilled at the natural abundance of the forest. This prompted Bibī to instruct Jaṅgali: "Listen, brother, out of my love for you, I want you now to remain with me, serving as my personal assistant and deputy. Make my dream come true: let us clear the marsh and stake out the perimeter of a settlement and build it here in the midst of this lush forest." After she finished speaking, Bibī meditated on God the Almighty. Then she set out meticulously to survey the mangrove swamps in order to clear the land and establish settlements. Jaṅgali, in his capacity as her chief deputy, followed up after her. In the south, they surveyed and laid out Eḍojol. Then Bibī reached Bhāvānīpur. Crossing over the mouth of that branch of the river, they came to Rājpur. Next they arrived at Birāḍi and from there doubled back to Mākhālgāch. They erected Āsaḍi in the forest swamp. Maynāḍāṅgā was set up as the administrative center for the whole lot. They then ventured into the Hāsnā wetlands. Afterwards they cut a canal to mark the boundary of Pāṭhāligrām, then measured out, clear-cut the trees, and fixed the settlement in the midst of the muddy forest. As she made her way back, Bibī was very pleased. When she returned to the station of Bhurkuṇḍa, she ascended her throne, having established her righteous sovereignty over the domain. Soon beeswax and honey began to be harvested. Bibī ceded Kēdokhāli to Dakṣiṇā Rāy, without having to go there to contest it. And in a similar fashion Bibī apportioned the land among all those who counted as headmen, her new vassals, in the forest communities. There was no attempt by anyone to exceed the set boundaries. Each of the local chieftains, the *sāheb sarddārs*, cooperated by staying within their assigned parcels.

This was how the story unfolded. Now listen everyone, for now I will relate the saga of Dhonā and Dukhe. Mohāmmad Khāter, whose home is in Bāliyā Govindapur, says: Āllā is the essence of all things.

DHONĀI THE HONEY COLLECTOR TAKES DUKHE TO THE MANGROVE SWAMPS ON A BUSINESS VENTURE

In the month of Caitra—March-April—the production of honey surges, and people swarm the area to collect it. There were two brothers, Dhonāi and Monāi, who had regularly exploited the mangrove swamps. They made their home in Bārij Hāṭi. Dhonā nurtured a strong compulsion: "I shall head back to the mangrove swamps for another commercial venture, to collect beeswax and honey." And so he began to formulate a meticulous plan.

One day Dhonāi finally broached the subject with Monāi, "Please charter and fit out seven ships for me. I shall go to the low-lying lands in my quest for trade, to set up an outpost."

When Monāi heard Dhonā's request, he was incredulous, dumbstruck, as if a lightning bolt had suddenly smacked his head. He said, "God, the Pure, has blessed us with incredible wealth. Why should you again risk going on this trip for more trade? As we have heard, in those swampy forests there is a great fear of the tiger, and for good reason.

Who knows, if you go there, you could be killed! If that horrible fate befell you, I would simply die of grief. Stay here in your own home, brother. If it is money you need, I will give you whatever you want."

When he heard his response, Dhonāi said to Monāi, "I don't want any of your money. A king's treasury is soon depleted if he remains idle. How can anyone revoke what fate has written? I'm destined to go. Do not try to dissuade me for I am going to go on that trading venture. So please now secure a pilot and oarsmen and make the preparations. Be quick and secure the ships and have them fitted out." Dhonāi stubbornly refused to listen to any objections.

With a feeling of helplessness, Monāi then weakly countered, "Where am I going to get enough sailors to man seven ships?"

Dhonāi replied, "Don't you worry yourself about that!" and with those parting words, off he went. In no time at all, he had rounded up and hired enough crew for all seven ships. He made generous offers of compensation that quickly and satisfactorily settled matters. When he reckoned the final numbers of the crews, he was just one deckhand short. Dhonāi mentioned it to Monāi, "Load the boats with all the provisions of rice, lentils, and other foodstuffs. We are short one person; so I need to lay hands on someone and bring them aboard. After that, I am all set, and with meditations on Khodā, we can launch."

With these words he took off and headed straight for the home of poor Dukhe, his name appropriately signaling "long suffering." Standing outside the house, he called out "Dukhe, Dukhe! What are you doing, little father, please listen, come outside." Dukhe did hear his call from inside the house, so he came outside and reverently made obeisance to his father's brother. Dhonāi said, "When your father passed away, he enlisted me to watch out for you. That is why I am here, to inquire of your well-being. How are you managing, are you getting enough to eat?"

Dukhe replied, "I don't have any satisfactory work, but I do take care of the cattle for a local householder."

When he heard this, Dhonā responded disparagingly, "You, such a grown-up young man, tending cattle to make ends meet? Come, join me in my business venture. You can stay put safely aboard the boat, and the work will not be particularly hard. After we have established our trading post—if Khodā desires it—you will have earned enough money upon our return that I will be able to arrange your marriage. So now, I will give your mother money sufficient to support her and enable her to eat comfortably while I take you under my wing."

Hearing the promise of marriage made Dukhe very happy indeed, so he spoke to his mother. "Listen, my dear mother, Dhonā Uncle is going on a business expedition, and he wants to take me with him. Were I to stay here in this house, there would be no end to our poverty and distress. Please say that I can go on this venture with Dhonā Uncle."

When she heard Dukhe's request, she said to him, "Little one, you are my only child, my only treasure in this world. Apart from you, I have no one else. How can I send you off to some strange foreign land? We all know that the threat of tigers pervades the settlements of the low-lying regions. Please do not go there, my dear child, stay here at home. We don't need the extra money you'd make, my child. I can manage well enough to feed you just by begging."

Dukhe pleaded with her, "Please don't forbid me, dear mother, surely I am destined to go with Uncle. Who hears of any young man remaining at home for so long? People are always finding reasons and ways to travel to other lands. I cannot bear to stay at home when I could be going. If I do as you ask, what will become of me in the end? It is inevitable. I am destined to go, so please do not hold me back. Khodā has already written that this is my destiny."

When she heard his argument, the miserable old woman was resigned. She said to Dukhe, "Call Dhonā and bring him here."

As soon as he heard, he went outside and called Dhonā to come in: "Come in, Uncle, Mother wants to talk to you about the proposed trip."

Hearing him, Dhonā wasted no time presenting himself to Dukhe's mother. He made his obeisance of salaams and acknowledged her as his respected elder sister-in-law, his *bhābi*. The old woman, Dukhe's mother, said, "Listen, Dhonāi, what did you say to Dukhe? As soon as he heard your proposal he wanted to go. How can I stay here in this house all alone? I do not have five or ten children, I only have my one Dukhe. How can I manage when he is not here?"

Dhonā replied, "My dear *bhābi*, you have no cause for worry. I will look after Dukhe as if he were my own son. After we return from our trading mission, I will provide money sufficient for Dukhe to get married." When she heard that, Dukhe's old mother started to cry and acquiesced.

Weeping pitifully, she took Dhonā's hand and said, "Go ahead, my brother, and take my Dukhe with you. I gratefully place him in your hands. Keep him in good health. Speak to him and encourage him, but may Āllā have mercy should you berate him or abuse him with words, or show contempt for him." With these parting words, she entrusted Dukhe to Dhoṇāi. The old woman wailed as the tears flowed freely.

And that was how Dhonāi came to bring Dukhe along.

They went and boarded the ship and got everything squared away. Dhonāi issued instructions to all the pilots and oarsmen. The hawser of his ship was loosed, and the ship launched into the stream. As soon as they got the signal, all the other helmsmen and their crew likewise launched their ships. The downbound convoy of seven ships sailed with the current in a neat, straight line astern. Dukhe's mother watched and wept. With urgency she cried out, "Listen carefully to what I'm saying, Dukhe. Deep within the forests Bonbibī is the Mother of Mercy. If you fall into trouble, call on her as Mother. She will grant you her grace, protect you, when you call out 'Mā!' She will guide you through any adversity and lift you to safety. I cede you to the protection of Bonbibī Mā. May Bonbibī, Mother of the Forest, escort you back upriver quickly!" Calling out, "Be safe!" that old Bibī wailed her farewell.

Dukhe called out to her, "Don't cry, Mother, please go back home. What good does it do to shed tears?" Eventually the old woman returned to her home where she could never stop weeping, long and hard, for her beloved son. Though she cooked a little food, she could never manage to eat it. And this is how the old woman kept to herself at home: sobbing and worrying constantly over what danger might threaten her beloved son.

Meanwhile the crews, bent to their oars, propelled the ships steadily downstream. After some distance they reached Baruṇhāṭi, after which they glided right past Santoṣpur. By evening they had gotten as far as Dhuli. They moored their ships there and passed the night. After cooking and eating, they were quite contented. In the early morning they pushed off and the relentless churning of their oars carried them further downstream. They paused at Kānāi Kāṭhir Gaṅgā before sailing on. They soon passed Rāy Maṅgal and Rāymā Talā, then they skipped past Heḍo Bhāṅgā, and Phalatali. A short time after leaving there, they crossed over to the opposite bank of the Gaṅgā. They carefully scrutinized the mangrove swamps lying on the left bank, but they spotted no honey or beeswax deposits at all, which made Dhonāi worry if he had committed some grave sin that might prompt this bad luck. After leaving that place they next sailed to Gaḍakhāli. He then gave orders to the helmsmen and oarsmen, "Let's put in here, and moor the boats so that we can enter the forest in search of honey." Hearing their instruction, the sailors wasted no time in berthing the vessels, neatly lashing them together along the shore, tiering them. After that, Dhonā picked some men and went ashore to enter the forest to search out honey. Before disembarking, he said to Dukhe, "Stay put aboard the boat. Remain alert and do not venture anywhere off the boat." With these words of warning to Dukhe, the men entered the forest.

From the estuary Dakṣiṇā Rāy was able to catch sight of them. Watching them, he commented to Biṣam Rāy, "Take a look, brother, Dhonā has come into our territories without showing me honor or making a proper animal sacrifice. He is trying to evade me and steal the honey. But when he reaches Gaḍakhāli, I will work some magic and trick him instead. I will conceal the beeswax and honey so that he can find none of it. He will get his just deserts unless he performs a *pūjā* with a human sacrifice. I will take great delight in giving him neither beeswax nor honey." The more Dakṣiṇā Rāy talked, the more his anger welled up, so he headed off to Gaḍakhāli, where he camouflaged all the beeswax and honey.

Where Dhonā had gone into the forest, he immediately spotted an abundance of honey, which pleased him enormously. But every place he spotted it, as soon as he drew near enough to break off a honeycomb, it would disappear. It vanished from sight every time. Dhonā muttered to himself, "What have I done to cause this torment, to vex me so? I imagine that it can only be the play of some god, a *devatā*. No matter where I looked in the forest, the honey was plentiful, but as soon as I drew near, it disappeared, and I could no longer see it." Remaining in Gaḍakhāli with his men for three more days, he continued to grumble and rant. They combed the area, searching all around, back and forth, in their eager search for the honey, but they did not manage to taste a single drop. In the end, Dhonā was beating his head in distress and weeping. "I came to this barbaric land with the desire to make a profit, but all my profit and my original investment both are slipping away through some horrible fault of fate." The tears flowed as Dhonā bitterly complained. He repaired to his boat, and, without eating, lay down. He concluded that if this was the work of some god, then surely that god would show himself in his dreams. But if it were the result of his own fate, then good or bad, that at least would be fathomable.

As he lay there pondering the possibilities, Dakṣiṇā Rāy slipped into his dreams and said, "Why, Dhonā, are you lying here in my territory asleep, going without food? Tell me, what misery has befallen you?"

He remonstrated with a certain petulance, "Just who are you magically appearing before me? Make yourself known!"

When he heard this, Dakṣiṇā Rāy explained the matter this way, "I am the one who creates the honey and the beeswax in these swamps and forests. A sage, *muni*, who was a strong-willed arbiter of justice used to be the chief in the low-lying regions. I am his son, Dakṣiṇā Rāy."

Dhonā replied, "If you are indeed really the great lord of this low-lying land, then why can I not find any beeswax or honey?"

Rāy responded, "Oh, Dhonā, it has been many long days since anyone offered me human sacrifice in worship. Should you manage to perform a human sacrifice for me, I will fill your seven ships with beeswax."

But when he heard this demand, Dhonā could only exclaim in distress, "Argh, aiee!" It was as if the sky itself had shattered and fallen on his head. He quickly improvised, "The only people I have brought with me are low-born. Tell me, how can I supply someone suitable? I can do without your beeswax and honey. We will row our boats back to our own land."

Rāymaṇi patiently heard him out, then, his anger welling up, he retorted, "I'll feed all of the sailors that man your ships to the crocodiles, and then we'll see how you get back to your homeland, you impudent rube!"

Dhonā was terrified, shaking, utterly speechless. He put his trembling hands together in a gesture of supplication and begged, "Please forgive me."

Rāymaṇi said, "If you want something good to come out of this, then hand over Dukhe and you can haul away the honey."

Dhonā replied, "I cannot give you Dukhe. Dukhe's mother placed him in my hands for protection, and my hands only. Please listen, respected sir, they are poor in the extreme. Apart from Dukhe, she has no one else to call her Mother. Rather, if a human sacrifice is the only thing that you will accept, then take me and send all the others home."

Rāy countered, "My eye has landed on Dukhe and on Dukhe alone; no one else will do."

Dhonā was filled with dread when he heard that demand. In the end, he acquiesced, so he began to negotiate. "Please tell me where I am to deliver Dukhe?"

Rāy said, "Deliver him to me at Kẽdokhāli, but first load your ships full of honey and beeswax. Then when it is time for you to return home, you can hand him over." And with these final words, Rāymaṇi took his leave.

Dukhe had been awake and had overheard the entire exchange. He realized, "Dhonā Uncle is going to trade me, pawn me to Rāy, while Uncle himself will fill the holds of his ships with beeswax and honey and head home. When Uncle makes his way back to our homeland, he is going to be fabulously wealthy, while my mother, without a man around, will have to beg food just to survive. She will go blind with grief for her young and only son, will stumble in the mud at some landing ghat, and in the end surely die. In this and other matters, Dhonā Uncle deceived me. He tricked me into coming to the settlement of the low-lying regions." Reasoning to himself and working out the ramifications, Dukhe wept, but not a sound leaked from his mouth. Then he called out, "Where are you Bonbibī? Show yourself to me. I have heard with my own ears that you are the one to guide me through dangerous times. I have come to the forest keeping you, my dear Mother, foremost in my mind." Three times like this did he call out, "Mā!" Then Dukhe slumped in a heap, his head down, and wept bitterly.

Dukhe's lament jolted Bibī's throne, tilting it off center. Looking inward through meditation, Bibī then understood. "To be sure, someone has entered the forest and has fallen into danger and they are summoning me, calling out 'Mother!'" With this realization, Bibī spoke to Jaṅgali, "Let us go find out who is seeking me by calling for Mother."

Jaṅgali replied, "Big sister, listen to what I'm telling you. Why should you go in search of someone just because they called for you?"

Bonbibī, the Mother of Compassion, said, "Whenever anyone in this forest calls me Mother, I must fly to their rescue. You do not understand the responsibility, the implications of wielding the power of *barakat*. In the low-lying lands of the eighteen tides, I am the mother of each and every one." And with these words, Bonbibī assumed a magically created disguise. For Dukhe's sake, she took off and instantly reached him. Standing by his head, she gently spoke, "Open your eyes, my little man, and stop your crying. It is I, your very own mother, who has come. What is it that makes you cry, please tell me, make me understand."

When he heard her, Dukhe slowly opened his eyes, but what he saw was his own mother's form. Utterly astonished, he exclaimed, "Where have you been during the three legs of our journey through the *bhāṭi*? How could you, Mother, possibly have landed up here?" Then he remembered her words: "Whenever you are in danger, I appear for your protection."

"I have come in the bodily form of the one filled with compassion."

Then Dukhe said, "Listen, my dear Mother, tell me exactly who you are to be appearing here in this magical form. Please tell me, I want to hear the truth. Swear to God, to Khodā, that you are not telling a lie."

In response the Mother of Mercy then reassured him, "Listen, my dear child, my name is Bonbibī, the Matron of the Forest. Why, my child, have you called out to me? Tell me what danger has befallen you."

He replied, "My uncle deceived me, brought me here under false pretenses. He is going to hand me over to Rāy as a sacrifice in exchange for honey. Rāymaṇi will shape-shift into a tiger and will eat me. This is my miserable fix and why I am calling you, O Mother!"

As she listened, the Mother of Mercy took his plight to heart. Calling him her son, she picked him up and placed him on her lap. She promised, "You have become my own son. From this point forward, no one will have the power, the wherewithal, to kill you. When Dhonā goes to hand you over to Rāy, you simply call me by uttering my name and instantly will I be at your side. I will pluck you from Rāymaṇi's grasp and save you." After reassuring Dukhe, Bonbibī bade him farewell and returned to her own place. And not too long later the night had passed.

Dhonā called out for all the pilot and crew to get ready, "Let us quickly launch and head out to Kēdokhāli. We will gather honey and beeswax as we work our way down." As soon as the helmsmen and other sailors heard this, they wasted no time in loosing the hawser, pushing off, and getting under way. The seven vessels glided forward, running in orderly intervals, one just aft of the other.

Onshore, Rāymaṇi said to Sanātan, "Here comes that honey merchant Dhonā, desperate for his beloved honey. I am going to set up the honey market there in the forest." And with these words, Rāy then took off for Kĕdokhāli. He issued an order to all the bees, who by Rāy's command rose up in massive swarms. They turned the forest into a veritable commercial warehouse of honey strung along both banks of the river. In the fissures of every tree trunk and hanging from the branches of every tree they generated hundreds of hundreds of thousands of hives with their honeycombs. As Dhonā floated down the river to this place, his heart was thrilled with what he saw, and they soon hove to on a silty sandbar at Kĕdokhāli. He commanded the pilot, "Let us put in right here. Then let us go ashore and enter the forest to harvest the honey." With these instructions, they made fast the boats and set off into the forest. What they beheld was honey beyond any calculation. And after they had sized it up, they returned in high spirits. They feasted and drank that night, then lay down to sleep.

In the middle of the night, Rāymaṇi returned and in Dhonā's dreams spoke to him along these lines: "When you enter the forest to harvest the honey, first remember me, uttering my name. After that, place your hand on the honeycombs filled with honey and the swarms of bees will not bother you, but will rise up and vanish. And I am giving you further instruction, so listen up. Take with you one person and one person only when you venture up the canals. You will not have to harvest the honey and beeswax yourself. You should just roam around the canals and watch the spectacle. I will enlist hordes of spirits and demons to harvest the honey, which I will ensure reaches your ships, where you should then wait to receive it. But do not forget our agreement, my good father: at the time you take final possession of the honey, you must hand over Dukhe." With this reminder, Rāymaṇi departed.

After everyone assembled following morning prayers, Dhonā said, "Let us go into the forest to harvest the honey. Dukhe, you stay here and keep watch over the fleet." And with those words, he then stationed Dukhe on his boat. With every hand mustered, they shoved off to harvest honey. Dukhe was beside himself, and through his sobs he challenged Dhonā, "Listen, Uncle, I know your intentions. I was awake and I heard everything you discussed with Rāymaṇi." Dhonā tried to cover, "Why do you cry over something that is untrue? I promised your mother directly that I would bring you back. You only need to stay here on the ship and busy yourself cooking some lentils and rice." With these words he attempted to mollify Dukhe, to calm him. So when the entire crew headed into the forest, Dukhe remained on the boat directing his thoughts toward Elāhi, God. Misery flooded his mind, and with that matching floods of tears followed.

There in the forest, Dhonā looked all around; the quantity of honey was incalculable, the honeycombs numbering hundreds and hundreds of thousands. Meditating on Rāy, he reached out and touched a hive with his hand, which instantly flushed out the bees; they rose up, gathering in thick seething swarms that numbered in the hundreds of thousands, then they up and flew away. Dakṣiṇā Rāy watched knowingly, so he mobilized his hordes of demons and spirits, which quickly reached the spot where Dhonā had landed in the forest. He said, "Just stand there rooted to the spot and take in the spectacle. I will have the beeswax and honey delivered directly to your ships." After he said this, Rāymaṇi instructed the throngs of demons and spirits to harvest the honey and beeswax, and no sooner was the command issued than it was executed by all.

It is not documented in the written record exactly who harvested and who hauled and stored, but within the hour all the honey and beeswax was efficiently gathered and transported.

Soon all seven of the ships were fully laden. Then Rāy said to the obviously satisfied Dhonā, "Check it out, is it possible to stow anything more on any of your ships?"

Dhonā immediately surveyed them. The holds were so heavily overloaded that each of the ships sat low in the water, to the point where only a single plank, the top sheer strake covering the gunnels, was visible. Surveying them, Dhonā spoke formally to the honorable Rāy, "Indeed they are absolutely packed to maximum capacity; they can accommodate no more."

Rāy heard him out and then baited Dhonā, "Hey, Dhonā, the value of beeswax is high compared to honey which fetches a lot less, so why don't you heave all the honey overboard and fill the remaining space in the ships' holds with beeswax." Hearing him out, Dhonā happily concurred and so he duly dumped most all of the honey overboard into the river Gāṅga[12]—and the place where he jettisoned the honey into the Gāṅga from that moment on became known as the Madhukhāli—the "honey channel."[13] Even to this day the water from that part of the Gāṅga is especially sweet, while all the waters in the surrounding area are briny. And so after dumping the honey into the stream, they took on the beeswax, once again loading all seven ships to the brim.

Dhonāi grew even happier as he watched activity. Then he announced to Rāy, "I want nothing more."

Rāy responded, "I have supplied you with an extraordinary amount of saleable commodities, which in turn will generate an equally extraordinary amount of riches. You will live like royalty, comfortable in your own home. I provided that wealth to you for a particular reason, so do not conveniently forget the conditions of our agreement: at the time of your departure, you must hand over Dukhe. If you do not give him up, then you squander not only your wealth, but your life. I will scuttle you and your boats in the middle of the Gāṅga with no hope for recovery." And with these parting words, Rāymaṇi took his leave.

Meanwhile Dukhe was back on board trying to cook rice, but a fire is nearly impossible to ignite with green wood. As he blew harder and harder, the smoke made his eyes red and soon they were watering, then the tears welled into a flood. He said, "Mā Bonbibī, where are you? Come to me quickly! I am calling out to you as 'Mother' because I am in grave danger."

Bibī was in Bhurkuṇḍa when she heard his call. Bibī said to Jaṅgali, "Listen my brother, I am going off to Kēdokhāli to find out why Dukhe has called." And with these words the Mother of Compassion flew off

12. The normal spelling is Gaṅgā, so it would seem that this is a typesetter's misspelling; but it should also be noted that the river is generally not referred to as the Gaṅgā in the Sundarbans, except in a generic way meaning any large river.

13. *Madhu* means both "honey" and synecdochically "sweet," but it should be noted that the second half of the compound name *-khāli*, which can mean a "channel," a "current within a stream," and a "canal," also means "emptiness" or "void," with the implication of emptying out, hence the act of emptying the honey into the channel certainly resonates as well, giving a richer meaning to the construct, a place and an act.

in a speedy wind and in no time at all she reached Dukhe. "Tell me, my child, for what reason have you called out to me?"

Dukhe replied, "Mother, please hear out my request. Dhonā Uncle tasked me to cook the food. But the wood is wet and will not light, so I am unable to cook."

Bibī replied, "My child, do not worry yourself. Through the power of providence I will cook the food right away." With these words, Bibī placed her hand on the kindling and without a flame the rice was instantly prepared. Bibī said, "Take the food and feed everyone, and now I will depart."

Dukhe then made another request, saying, "I know that tomorrow Dhonā Uncle will launch the boats. He will offer me to Dakṣiṇā Rāy to sacrifice. Please, my dear Mother, come back and save me!"

Bibī replied, "Do not worry, be consoled, and rest easy: I promise you that Rāy is not powerful enough to eat you." And saying this Bibī decamped and went on her way.

After tidying up all the business details, Dhonā returned to the boat. He queried Dukhe, "Tell me, on which boat did you prepare the food, where have you kept it?"

Dukhe replied, "Uncle, I have prepared the food here on this boat. Everyone should come and eat."

When they heard that, everyone crowded onto the designated vessel. They all sat together, mixing freely as they consumed the food. The food they ate was exquisite, like immortal nectar. Whispering among themselves, someone said to Dhonā, "Look, this food is so pleasing, so satisfying, that it is troubling and cause for real concern. We don't think it possible for this food to have come from Dukhe's hands. It seems to us that the great ocean of compassion, Bonbibī herself, must have come and befriended Dukhe."

Dhonā scoffed, "That little boy does not even wash properly after taking a shit. Will Bonbibī come and associate with the likes of him?"

And with this everyone continued to prattle and gossip, to whisper among themselves until the day had passed and night made its arrival. They all boarded their respective boats and bunked down, while Dukhe sat alone, the tears swelling from his heartache and misery. "Tomorrow the ships will cast off and Dhonā Uncle will return home. He will surrender me to Dakṣiṇā Rāy to be mauled to death. Dakṣiṇā Rāy will shape-shift into a tiger, a man-eater, and devour me. In exchange for my life, uncle will have made himself a rich man. My mother will be heartbroken, and already an impoverished beggar, she will be reduced further. When all the crews return to their homes in our native land, my mother will hear that her Dukhe has been eaten by a tiger. She will simply cry herself to death from her grief for me. Apart from me, there is no one else to look after her, to call her Mā. Alas, Fate wrote that this was my allotted destiny: to be brought to the forest and devoured by a tiger." In this and other equally pitiful ways Dukhe wailed and gave vent to his bitter plight.

Mohāmmad Khāter says: Do not cry, for Bonbibī, the Mother of Compassion, provides a safe haven; her care and solicitude circulate throughout the settlements of the low-lying lands. What will Rāy be able to do in the face of that, my son? Worry after worry panics your overwrought heart, but by the grace of Bibī all of your suffering will be transformed into happiness.

DHONĀI, THE HONEY COLLECTOR, GIVES DUKHE TO DAKṢIṆĀ RĀY AND BONBIBĪ SHOWS HER COMPASSION AND RESCUES DUKHE

After eating and drinking, everyone lay down and slept until the night came to a close and dawn broke. Dhonā announced, "Helmsmen and crews, everyone listen up. Loose the docking lines, cast off, and head back to our homeland." When they got their orders, six of the ships loosed their hawsers and pushed off, but Dhonā and Dukhe did not unmoor and so did not put out into the stream. Dhonā asked, "Why does our ship delay in loosening the lines and casting off?"

One of the crew volunteered, "There is no firewood, so how are we going to eat?"

When he heard this, Dhonā ordered Dukhe, "Go and gather some wood, my child, and be quick about it!"

Dukhe replied, "Uncle, sir, please forgive me, but there are so many others around, please send someone else."

Dhonā retorted, "My son, all you do on the boat is sit here doing nothing and now, the one time I ask, you refuse to follow my order?"

One man came forward, grabbed him by the scruff of the neck, and said, "Beat this insolent, cheeky, insubordinate and toss him overboard.

His manner is uncouth, he is low-born, and he does not listen to what he is told. Give him to me and I will cut him to pieces."

Dukhe pleaded, "Dear Uncle, I know fully well what's going on, I was awake and heard everything you discussed with Rāy. I know all about what you intend to do. You will hand me over to Rāy, while you make good your escape. You dangled promises to bring me here, you gave me hope, but instead you deal disaster. Your plan to abandon me on one of the silt embankments in Kēdokhāli will be the end of me!"

Dhonā said, "You ungrateful little bugger, why do you make up such lies? If you know what is good for you, you had better gather some firewood and fast! And if you don't do it right this moment you are going to see the ugly consequences: my men will collar you and fling you overboard!"

Dukhe pleaded, "Why do you lie and heap abuse on me with such scorn? Whatever happens to me is what is destined by my fate. I am going, I am getting off this boat of my own accord. Tell me clearly so that I can understand, make no mistake: where am I to gather this wood?"

Gesturing, Dhonā replied, "There is dry wood to be had in that garden-like plot over there. Now hurry up and fetch it."

Dukhe listened and in the end he realized he had no choice, so he capitulated. Weeping all the while, he stepped off the boat. After Dukhe had wandered along the edge of the river for some time, Dhonā ordered his men, "Cut loose the mooring line and push off, be quick about it!" The helmsman and his ready crew heard and nimbly cast off. Dhonā then said, "Rāymaṇi, I have gifted you Dukhe, now take him. No fault can accrue to me now in the divine ledger. I am headed back to my homeland and take my leave straight away." With these parting words, they decamped and plunged forward.

Abandoned in the forest, Dukhe was now utterly alone. It did not take long for him to find and gather the firewood. When he returned, he watched as Dhonā's ship slipped away, receding in the distance. Dukhe erupted in tears at the disaster that had befallen him. From where he was standing in the estuary, Rāymaṇi watched. This son of a demon *rākṣas* suddenly transmogrified into a tiger. He advanced at a lope, making straight for Dukhe. With terrifying and predictable menace, the tiger came to devour him. When Dukhe spotted him, he screamed "Mā" and slumped to the ground. He cried out, "Mā Bonbibī, where you are now? You must come quickly because your Dukhe is about to die! You gave me your promise, dear Mother. If you do not honor it, then your reputation throughout the low-lying lands will be stained and no one will call you Mother ever again!" With this frantic gasp, an enervated Dukhe lost consciousness.

Bibī was in Bhurkuṇḍa and heard his call. She said to Jaṅgali, "Brother, Dukhe is about to be killed. We must move quickly to protect him so that the *rākṣas* demon does not manage to eat our little boy!" And with these words, brother and sister flew like the wind. They reached Dukhe in a split second. They found Dukhe right where he had fallen, unconscious, and in a wretched state. With affection she murmured, "My child, my child." Then Bibī, Mother of Compassion, scooped him up, dirt and all, and hugged him onto her lap. Placing her mouth next to his ear she whispered to him, "Dukhe, Dukhe." But Dukhe heard nothing for he was completely insensate. He could say nothing, he was unable to open his eyes.

Jaṅgali then said, "Bibī, look, I think I know what has happened: Dukhe knew he had fallen into a fatal fix, and he simply died of fright."

"If Dukhe dies in my lap, here in my embrace, I'll be compromised, my character besmirched forever and ever throughout the low-lying lands of the *bhāṭi*."

Ever vigilant, Jaṅgali moved decisively. He blew his breath across Dukhe's body, repeating the name of God, Echam, then poured some of the everlasting waters of paradise into his mouth. Dukhe came to his senses and opened his eyes, fully alert, revived. As she watched, Bibī was thrilled at heart. As she searched about, her gaze landed on Dakṣiṇā Rāy and her anger erupted. She said to Jaṅgali, "Brother, listen with all your heart. Look, that bastard *rākṣas* demon is standing right over there. Take hold of him and punish him severely. He has come to devour the boy I've accepted as my own. Chastise this low-life severely! Deliver a punishment to match to his blood-lust!"

When Jaṅgali received his instruction, his temper rose, and he ran after Rāy. He struck him full in the face with the force of a lightning bolt. Eating this colossal blow, Rāy's face immediately began to swell. Dakṣiṇā realized he had just cheated death from that closed fist punch and slipped away in a sprint. Jaṅgali gave chase, hot on his heels, then he yelled, "You're running away, but just how far do you think you can go? I will send my staff through the air to flail your head!" Yelling like this made his anger well even more and he screamed, "Kill, kill!" He took his staff in his hand and hurled it at that figure looming large as a mountain that was laying waste to hundreds of trees as he crashed through the mangrove swamp. Rāy suddenly found himself facing a fathomless waterway, but by his superhuman powers he hurdled across to the opposite bank, completely clearing the river. He wondered aloud, "Will that brazen upstart have the power to follow me here?" But in no time Jaṅgali had already caught up. Standing on the bank opposite Rāy, Jaṅgali Śāhā invoked the name of Āllā, which resounded straight to Elāhi, God, like a cannon shot, and, as he stood there, the waters of that seemingly bottomless river suddenly dropped to less than knee-deep.

Witnessing this miracle, Rāymaṇi was genuinely rattled. He muttered to himself, "There is no way I can shake this man, but now I do have some advantage while he is in the water." With this assessment, he summoned the sharks and crocodiles. "That son of a bitch is wading across the river to this bank. All of you go! Catch him!" When they received Rāy's orders, crocodiles by the hundreds set off in pursuit, jaws snapping, intent on devouring Jaṅgali. Some whipped him, wildly cracking their tails, others raised their heads just above the waters and champed at his legs. To counter this, Jaṅgali Śāhā began to thrash their bodies. From all sides, the entire float of crocodiles lunged at him. Even though they numbered countless hundreds, he proceeded to grab them by their tails, swing them round and round, and fling them away. How many times his staff flew up and fell on them with blows from above! It was a slaughter. How many times the sheer force of his pummeling killed them outright! In this way he systematically rained destruction on the crocodiles, slaying them all. And so he eventually managed to wade across to the opposite bank of the river. Watching this scene unfold, Rāy was doubly frightened and fled.

Eventually, Rāy made his way to Baḍa Khān Gāji. Gāji observed, "Rāymaṇi, Lord and Overseer of the Bhāṭi, please tell me where on earth you have been! What have you been up to? I am anxious to hear, because you seem to have arrived here in a terrible state. Why are you shivering so violently? What has happened to your face?"

Rāy replied, "Listen, Gāji, I am telling you exactly as it is. A honey trader by the name of Dhonā, who makes his home in Bārij Hāṭi, had come to the low-lying lands with seven ships. I furnished him with honey and beeswax, and in return he handed over a poor ruffian named Dukhe. I was set to take him on a silt embankment at Kẽdokhāli. Suddenly, a boy and a girl came out of nowhere and blocked me from taking Dukhe away. The young woman has a beauty that cannot be described—the splendor of her form illuminated Kẽdokhāli with its glow. As for the young man, what can I say about his incredible presence? He is able to take on any form he chooses. Sometimes this young man takes the form of a *phakir*, sometimes he takes up his staff and fights like a warrior. How else can I describe him, he is a dangerously powerful young man. With but a single slap, he knocked me absolutely silly, leaving me powerless."

Gāji replied, "Rāymaṇi, are you not aware of the news. Bonbibī is her name and she is the *īśvar* of the *bhāṭi*, supreme ruler, the goddess of the low-lying lands. You were obviously unaware, so you have blundered by tangling with them. You will never be able to match them in a fight. Bonbibī is exceedingly pious and blessed with a great fortune. She is numbered among those known as the friends of God, Nirāñjan, the Stainless One. Do you not recall how Nārāyaṇī fought her and lost. In the end, Nārāyaṇī managed to save herself only by formally invoking her as her dear friend and close companion?"

Rāy responded, "Gāji, my brother, listen to what I say. I honestly did not know that this woman was Bonbibī." And in this way Śāh Gāji gently interrogated Rāy, asking him questions until they had touched on every single detail.

About this time Śā Jaṅgali arrived hot on the chase, wielding his staff and screaming, "Kill, kill!"

Seeing him Rāy was terrified and said to Gāji, "Please protect me this time, Gāji brother!" As he said this, he maneuvered himself so that he crouched behind Gāji.

Gāji stood up just as Jaṅgali reached. Gāji greeted him, saying, "*Sālām ālek*, may peace be upon you!" as he firmly grasped Jaṅgali's hands. "Against whom are you venting such incredible anger? Won't you please tell me?"

Jaṅgali snapped at Gāji heatedly, "As one who practices *ichlām*, have you no fear of God, the One Whose Nature is Pure? You are sitting there together as friends with one who is vile and depraved."

Gāji gently replied, "Śā Jaṅgali, please sit down now, and when you have cooled off, please explain the situation to me." And after seating Jaṅgali, he continued, "The *brāhmaṇ* here is my friend."

Jaṅgali retorted, "You are a *phakir*, how is it you can befriend this demon, this *rākṣas*? The moment I can get the order from Bonbibī, I will beat him to death and send him to Yam's abode, to hell!" As Jaṅgali spoke, his words fueled his anger.

"Please sit, calm down," Gāji said gently as he held his hands.

Jaṅgali retorted, "I am not going to sit down here! Let us go now and quickly, for Bonbibī has summoned us."

Rāy interjected, "Gāji brother, I am not going to go. I am sure to be utterly humiliated if I go just because a woman, the Mother, commanded it."

Gāji said, "You have nothing to worry about. Come, let's go. Brother, I will go with you." And with this reassurance, Gāji took Rāy along. Gāji and Rāymaṇi accompanied Jaṅgali to go to meet Bonbibī, and they soon arrived and presented themselves. They placed their hands together in the traditional gesture of respect and made salaams.

Bonbibī inquired, "Tell me *miyā*, my good sir, what is you name?"

Gāji replied, "Barakhān is my name. My father's name is Śāhā Sekandār. The Holy Prophet Himself showed his grace by personally making my father Śāhā the Sultān. When I was awarded my patrimony, that *jāygīr* land-grant was the kingdom of the low-lying regions, the *bhāṭi*, so here I came. You were fully aware of me, but you did not acknowledge me."

When she heard his reply, Bibī was incensed, "Tell me, Barakhān Gāji, if you are the resident *oli* here, the saint of Āllā, then how is it that a human can be allowed to be eaten by a demon, a *rākṣas*? If the Lord conferred on you sainthood, *āuliyā*, and sent you, then your work, your commitment must always be to the welfare of all creatures. But you are not doing that when you mix with hungry ghosts, *bhūt*s, for they kill humans and cows here in the forests."

Gāji respectfully replied, "Listen, my dear Mother, to what I humbly submit: You should not use such disrespectful terms, calling him a *bhūt*, a hungry ghost. You must understand that resorting to this kind of speech is offensive, in fact, caustic in the extreme. The one you call the hungry ghost is actually your own son."

When she heard this Bibī said to Barakhān, "How is it possible that Dakṣiṇā Rāy is my own son?"

Gāji replied, "Tell me, when you first arrived in the low-lying regions, whom did you engage in battle?"

Listening, Bibī then chuckled and said, "Initially, it was with Nārāyaṇī I fought, and when she lost the battle, she reconciled by calling me her dear sisterly friend."

Gāji closed in saying, "Now, what you just said Bibī is good and true. Now please consider this, Rāymaṇi is the son of your 'sister,' so your son, too. Since you are his mother, it is deplorable to talk of your son this way. You should not speak like that."

Listening to Gāji's gentle chiding, Bibī lowered her head in embarrassment and the anger she had felt in her heart slowly dissipated. Bibī then said to Gāji, "What I now realize deep in my heart, is that my one son, Dukhe, is in reality only one of three sons. You three are brothers, so you should come together in embrace."

As soon as he heard this, Gāji stood up and pulled the other two into an embrace. Gāji hugged Dukhe, then said to him, "Be happily reconciled to Rāymaṇi and embrace him as your brother." When Rāi heard this, he stood up and embraced Dukhe. In their mutual embrace each addressed the other as brother.

Bonbibī then interjected, "Gāji, if Dukhe has indeed become your younger brother, while you are here standing in front of me, please declare what provision you will make for him."

Gāji replied, "The Pure and Holy One has blessed me by making me master of enormous wealth, so I will bequeath to him seven baskets of those riches. I make this pledge in your august presence, Mother."

Bibī followed up, "When the time comes to hand over these riches to him, tell me how you plan to convey them to Dukhe."

Gāji answered, "You need not trouble yourself with that. When Dukhe goes back home, I will make the provision to transfer it."

Hearing this left Bonbibī quite satisfied. Then she turned to Dakṣiṇā Rāy and asked, "Listen, Rāymaṇi, if Dukhe is truly your brother, I want to hear what will you do to make him happy."

Rāy said, "I can generate beeswax and honey, for that is the source of my wealth in the low-lying lands of the eighteen tides. Whenever he desires any wealth, I can supply it effortlessly. When he has reached home and is settled, I will send it along as his nuptial present."

After these pledges were tendered, Gāji and Rāy, feeling quite satisfied, bowed, and made their salaams to Bonbibī's feet. They took their leave and headed back to their respective domains. Bonbibī hugged Dukhe closely and resumed her tour of the lands of the Āṭhārobhāṭī, where she showed him all the mangrove swamps, canals, and creeks. Eventually, they returned to her place, the Bhurkuṇḍa station. And so it was with great joy that Bibī took her seat on the throne. The abject misery of Dukhe was fully relieved by Bibī's kindness. Dukhe remained with her, personally serving her with befitting reverence.

Mohāmmad Khāter says: Dukhe was comfortably settled in there, but listen, everyone, to the saga of Dhonā.

DHONĀI THE HONEY MERCHANT RETURNS HOME, TELLS DUKHE'S MOTHER THE BAD NEWS, AND SHE GRIEVES

Dukhe was relieved, indeed joyful
staying close by Bonbibī,
    and he served her with great pleasure.
Meanwhile, Dhonā had already boarded his boat
and turned sail toward the homeland,
    docking at his own designated ghat when he got there.
Crew, pilots, helmsmen, and oarsmen all
were jubilant upon arrival,
    and quickly scattered to their own homes.
The news that Dhonā had returned from his venture
spread quickly throughout the town,
    and the beeswax and honey was quickly loaded on carts.
Dukhe's mother was in her house
but the old woman caught wind of the news
    that Dhonā had returned from his trading trip.
The moment the old woman heard,
she took herself to Dhonā's home
    to inquire of him.
"Hey, Dhonāi, where is my Dukhe?
Please call him right away,
    so that I may bask in the glow of his moon-like face.
So many days have passed,
what is his condition, how is he?
    I have heard nothing, good or bad."
When he heard the old woman's query,
Dhonā lowered his head and

did not comment in any way, good or bad.
The old woman pressed him, "Why, brother,
do you not say anything at all?
Where is Dukhe? How is he?"
Dhonā replied, "Sister-in-law,
How should I say it?
To explain absolutely breaks my heart.
After he went into a field
to gather firewood,
a tiger hunted him down and devoured him."
When she heard Dhonā's fateful words,
she beat her head with her hands,
and with a groan, slumped to the ground.
With screams of heartbreak,
she pounded her head in the dirt,
tears streaming from her eyes.
"Oh, Dhonā, what you just said
turns my liver black as ink,
the arrow of grief has pierced my breast and
taken the only wealth that matters, leaving me destitute.
Where did you lose him?
Who now will call me mother?
Alas, O star of my eye,
where have you disappeared?
Come and show yourself to me, this desolate woman.
When you come running, calling 'Mother, mother!'
into whose lap will you climb, who will call you 'My son'?
Please soothe my eyes by letting them see you."
Out of grief for her son, the old woman wept bitterly,
She writhed on the ground, pounding out with her head
her desperate cry of "My son, my son!
Oh, poor Dukhe, son of this miserable old woman,
come to me, show yourself,
be the soothing waters for my smoldering liver.[14]
In my old age, who will look after me—
be present for me, listen to me—
for I have no one else.
To whom will I turn?

14. Literally, "my liver kebab," the liver as the locus of emotional trauma and pain. Cf. the general Introduction above, p. 23.

Who will love me?
    Without you, everything grows dark."
Dhonā callously observed,
"What will you gain by crying?
    Why do you go on sobbing for nothing?
Whatever has happened, happened,
and there is no point in crying about it.
    Now calm your heart and compose yourself.
For as long as you live,
I will provide food, clothing,
    anything you desire, just say."
The old woman rejoined, "Alas, Dhonā,
what do I need of food and drink
    when the fire of grief is burning up my liver?"
After saying this, the old woman howled and thrashed;
she bawled and continued to yell,
    "My son, my treasure, where have you gone?
Come to me just once more!
Don't delay, show yourself, show yourself!
    You are the very life of this miserable woman!"
With words of mourning, the old woman wept
and writhed in the dirt,
    her grief so violent that she cracked some ribs.
As the people of the town looked on,
one and all felt her anguish,
    and commiserated with the old woman.
As time wore on, she would not be consoled,
and she wept so incessantly that she
    literally cried her eyes out, making her blind and deaf.
Because she would not eat, she grew thin,
nor was she able to hear anything, so
    she lived wherever she wandered, in a field or ghat.
Sometimes she could be heard saying, "Oh, my Dukhe,
at the time of your leaving,
    I entrusted you to Bonbibī Mā.
When she is there for you,
how can a tiger eat you?
    Did you not understand you were to call her?"
The old woman faulted Bonbibī.
She wept without respite,
    the flow of her tears never abated.

The heart-rending sobs of that old woman
finally shook Bonbibī's throne,
    prompting the Mother to search in her mind's eye.
Recognizing the grief of Dukhe's mother,
she herself was moved to sorrow,
    so Bibī turned to Dukhe and said,
"Your mother weeps for you without respite,
so you must go back home.
    There is nothing to keep you here.
When Dhonā returned, he told her
that you had been devoured by a tiger.
    To hear it turned her into a homeless mendicant.
She does not eat, she does not drink,
all she does is weep.
    Tears stream from her eyes day and night."
Dukhe said, "Oh, dear Mother,
I cannot, will not go back,
    I will live here as your servant.
What shall I do when I return home?
Who is there for me?
    Who will save me when I am in danger?
With you as my mother,
I am content to live right here, and
    no tiger will ambush me and eat me.
Were I to go home,
would I find my mother there?
    Please tell me, dear Mother.
Beloved Mother, please tell me how this could be,
for were it possible to leave here,
    I would no longer be able to count on you."
Bibī replied, "You must return home,
and I give you my solemn word that
    I will come to you there.
If you fall into any danger or difficulty,
summon me right that moment
    by simply calling out 'Mā,' and
I will fly to you in a trice,
lift you up and protect you.
    I shall never forget you, not for a moment.
Were you to call and I not go,
may I eat Jaṅgali's head—

and I do not say that lightly.[15]
And listen to another thing:
when you go home,
do not be angry with Dhonā.
Do not engage in any abusive talk,
quarrel, or conflict of any sort with Dhonā—
there is no call for ill will.
Because what he did when he came here
afforded you direct access to me;
otherwise you would not have gotten my *darśan*.[16]
That solemn pledge that
he made to you,
can now be fulfilled.
Go home, my darling son,
marry his young daughter,
and may your heart be filled with joy."
Dukhe replied, "Oh, beloved Mother,
how will I manage to get home?
I know nothing about the roads and ghats.
It took three days to make the trip here,
but through the mangrove swamps of the low-lying kingdom
weave hundreds upon hundreds of canals and waterways."
Bibī assured him, "I shall
send you home
mounted on the back of a crocodile."
Dukhe quickly countered, "O dear Mother,
don't say that! Surely
the crocodile will lay hold of and eat me.
You saved me once
from the hands of the demon *rākṣas*,
only to be eaten by a crocodile!
I will not go home.

15. The oath to "eat someone's head," invariably that of someone who is dear to the speaker, is perhaps the strongest promise one can make because of the perceived danger to the person named; it is the most serious of guarantees or promises.

16. *Darśan* is an auspicious devotional act of viewing of a deity or prominent person, but it works both ways, to look at and be seen by, making a lasting connection, in this case with Bonbibī. It also implies simply being in someone's, especially divinity's, presence.

I will live here and serve you,
    which will make me happy no matter what."
Bibī consoled him, "Listen, Dukhe,
the crocodile will not devour you.
    Have no qualms about that.
If you are afraid to go
seated on the back of the crocodile,
    then I will scoop you up and carry you myself."
When Dukhe heard that, he said,
"If I am comfortably seated in your lap, Mother,
    what is there to fear?"
The lowly poet says:
Who could enjoy such an incredible fate—
    to be called the favored son of Bonbibī.

BONBIBĪ'S DECREE AND DUKHE'S RIDE HOME ON THE BACK OF A CROCODILE

When he heard the conditions of Bibī's order, Dukhe asked, "Can you show me which crocodile it is?" Bonbibī then summoned the one named Seko, who immediately floated up to the river's edge. As Dukhe watched, he began to wonder just what this leviathan was, this monstrous creature on the bank of the river, for they almost never crawled up on the land, save in the dark of night. "I have never seen such a monstrous crocodile anywhere, nor have I even heard tell of such a one. How can I possibly ride on its back?" As he watched, Dukhe began to speculate as to what kind of grave sin he had committed for it to come to this.

The crocodile respectfully addressed Bonbibī, "Why, O Mother of Mercy, have you called me?"

Bibī replied, "Seko, my son, this is why I summoned you: Your younger brother, Dukhe, is stuck here in the forest. There is no boat anywhere to ferry him away. Please carry him on your back to his home."

Seko responded, "I will certainly fetch him there and I will deliver him within three quick measures of time."

When she heard his promise, Bonbibī turned to Dukhe and said, "My dear child, go now and do not waste any time."

Dukhe replied, "O dear Mother, I ask your leave. And may I receive your *darśan* whenever I fall into trouble."

Bibī reassured him, "My son, Dukhe, never worry. Whenever you call out 'Mā', I promise to show myself."

With these words, Dukhe began to cry, repeating over and over, "O Mā! O Mother!" He kissed her feet and then made obeisance, his salaam. Uttering the *bichmillā*—In the name of God—he closed his eyes tightly and she lifted him up and seated him on the back of the crocodile. The crocodile whisked Dukhe away, gliding quickly through the waters, while Bonbibī, the Mother of Compassion, stood and watched. With the wind at their back, they practically flew, and in no time at all reached Dhonā's landing ghat.

Seko said, "Brother Dukhe, get your bearings. Have we arrived at the right landing?"

Dukhe heard and opened his eyes and was delighted. He instantly caught sight of Dhonā's ship. Looking around, Dukhe heaped praise on the crocodile. "What took us three days before, you navigated in three quick clicks. Your stature and strength are truly extraordinary to have done this, my good sir. There cannot possibly be any creature in the rivers to equal you in strength."

Seko said, "Now set aside such talk and quickly scramble onto shore. Bonbibī sent me to deliver you, and now she is impatiently waiting for me to return."

As he listened, Dukhe earnestly called Bonbibī Mā to mind, then he made his obeisance of salaam to the crocodile. After he had clambered up the banks, he gave permission, "You may go now, my brother! I am going to go search out my mother, wherever she might be." And with these words he bade farewell to the magnificent crocodile and, weeping a little in his excitement, he ran toward his house, repeating "Oh, Mother, Mother." He soon found the old woman: she had fallen and was in sad condition, delirious. Distressed, Dukhe lovingly called "Mother, Mother! Get up, get up, Mother dear, don't cry any more. Open your eyes: your Dukhe has returned!" As he said this, a pain rent his heart, and the tears began to well up, for the old woman could neither see nor hear. As Dukhe examined her he lamented, "Aiee, such is my fate. My mother cannot hear or see out of her grief for me. Were she to die from her anguish over me, then my life would not be worth living." Weeping, and with worrying thoughts like these, Dukhe called out to Bonbibī. "Where are you my dear Mother of Compassion, for I am in dire straits!"

Bibī was in Bhurkuṇḍa, seated on her throne. Dukhe's cries of distress shook her throne, and when she looked through her mind's eye, she divined everything. In a flash, Bonbibī appeared at Dukhe's side, but this time she had taken the form of a white fly and landed on Dukhe's ear. She gently asked, "Tell me, why have you called on me?"

Dukhe replied, "Dear Mother, I called out because of this crisis: The old woman has gone blind and deaf. What can I do? She cannot hear anything, nor can she open her eyes to see. When I call her Mother, over and over again, she simply does not respond."

Bibī said, "My son, place your hands over her eyes and ears and gently rub, all the while taking my name. Instantly she will be able to open her eyes to see, and that lock which has closed her ears will be opened." As soon as she had delivered this instruction, Bibī disappeared. Concentrating his memory on Bonbibī, Dukhe rubbed his hands back and forth across the old woman's eyes and ears. Simultaneously she opened both eyes and suddenly could hear. She looked up and saw Dukhe right in front of her. "My son, my son!" she cried and pulled him to her lap and hugged him tight. "Tell me, my little boy-child, where have you been? Please, I want to hear the full story. Without you I could hardly survive, like the walking dead, a corpse. That pitiless Dhonā returned and reported to me that a tiger had devoured you back in Kēdokhāli. When I heard this I was so lost in grief that I fell and broke my ribs. My ears suddenly locked tight and my eyes went dark. Today marks ten long days since I laid eyes on you. In the dark, I stumbled around from field to ghat, weeping without end. I could not sleep, nor could I eat, so my body quickly grew thin and frail. The fires of grief raged through my heart day and night. It is my great good fortune that you have returned to me. Please soothe and cool my smoldering grief by calling me Mother."

Dukhe said, "Mother dear, what can I tell you? What Dhonā told you was not entirely false. Convincing me with promises of family and status, he took me along. He procured beeswax and honey from Rāymaṇi. But it was me he gave to Dakṣiṇā Rāy in return for the beeswax and honey he brought home. Rāy then transformed himself into a tiger and bounded forward to eat me. The Mother of Mercy, Bonbibī, had also come to that forest, and she granted me grace and rescued me. That is the reason I am still alive and have returned home." And so to his mother Dukhe narrated his saga in great detail, item for item, all that had transpired.

The old woman finally said, "My son, for receiving the gift of your life from Bonbibī's compassion and surviving to return home, drape a mendicant's net bag around your neck and go begging in seven different villages. Donate what you collect to those in need. Do it quickly."

Listening to this advice, Dukhe hung the net bag from his neck, and went begging for alms, constantly chanting, "Bonbibī, Bonbibī." He wended his way through seven local villages, skipping no neighborhood. When people saw him, they asked, "Dukhe, where were you? We had heard directly from Dhonā that a tiger had eaten you. So how is it that you have now returned home? Why are you now dressed for begging with your net bag and asking for alms?"

Dukhe always replied, "I will tell you, so listen to my tale." And with these words he recounted in detail all that had transpired. He narrated to all who would listen exactly how Bonbibī had saved him and how being a fount of mercy, she managed to restore him back to his home. He related every single detail, then he would say, "Brother, I am begging door to door, and with the food I beg, I shall cook some sweetmeats in the name of Bonbibī Mā, and that ambrosia will fulfill one's wishes and needs." As soon as the locals heard, they offered him rice and sugar, each one proffering these alms in the name of Bonbibī. After he had completed his begging rounds, Dukhe returned home.

Meanwhile, Dhonā heard the news from all the locals that by the grace of Bonbibī Dukhe had safely returned. The more he heard, the more he quaked in fear. He wondered aloud what torments Bonbibī would bring down on him. Worrying himself sick, Dhonā contemplated the full extent of his quandary.

When Dukhe finally returned to his own home, he handed over to his mother the rice, sugar, and ghee. "Please make the sweetmeats right away, and I'll be back shortly. I'll let all the village boys know and fetch them back here." The old lady heard and prepared the sweetmeats within the hour, and Dukhe summoned the boys, who quickly appeared. In Bonbibī's name, the sweetmeats were distributed to those needy boys. With a great commotion everyone began to eat. After they had consumed their food and drink, they dispersed, heading back to their own homes, reciting over and again, "Bonibibī, Bonbibī."

All because of Dukhe, the glory of Bonbibī began to spread by his simple act of distributing alms of milk, sugar, and sweetmeats to the needy. And in this way Dukhe repaid her.

Dukhe then spoke seriously to his mother, "Listen, Mother dear, as I speak frankly to you: Dhonā caused me an incalculable amount of misery when he deceived me then handed me over to the *rākṣas* demon, while he returned safely home with his honey and beeswax. I shall file a complaint against him with the local judge. Once I have received that official favorable ruling, I shall have him shackled."

The old woman responded, "There is no advantage to fighting with him. Where will we get the money when there isn't even enough to buy food?"

Dukhe said, "Pay attention, Mother, and I will tell you: By the grace of Bonbibī I have received the promise of great wealth. In the presence of Bibī, Gājī made a formal pledge that he would supply me with enough riches to fill seven cart baskets." And with this reassurance, Dukhe raised the hopes of his mother. He went outside and issued a call to Barakhān. "O brother Barakhān, where are you? Please honor my request. Please come and appear before me just this one time."

Barakhān Gājī was deep in the labyrinth of creeks, but as soon as he heard Dukhe's plaintive call for help, he appeared instantly and addressed him: "Why have you summoned me, brother, tell me your predicament."

Dukhe replied, "Previously you made a solemn vow to me: I am requesting you now to make good and supply me with the riches you promised. When I receive that wealth, I shall build a proper home."

Gājī said, "You cannot take the wealth right this moment, brother. Lying just to the east of your current house there is a tree, a fan palm. Beneath that tree are buried seven baskets of treasure. My father was Śāh Sekendār and there is almost no place where he did not bury valuables. Those riches I will hand over to you. Tonight you should show up to retrieve them. You will not have to dig them up yourself—they will simply show up outside your house. But when you are going, you must take precautions, for if you are not careful, what you desire will not transpire." And after saying this, Gājī departed.

After dark that evening, Dukhe took a spade then headed out to find the fan palm. There he saw the faint outlines of seven cart baskets of treasure lined up in a neat row, one after the other. With joy he dug, attacking the earth with his spade, but he repeatedly hit hard rock, making his spade ring *thon thon*. Unable to penetrate the unyielding soil, he abandoned his caution and fear, and—clearly annoyed—he vowed, "Gājī deceived me. In the morning I shall report him to Bonbibī Mā." And spitting out these words, he took his spade and left. As he was going along the path, there were seven thieves who had witnessed this event and sized up everything. They accosted Dukhe and relieved him of his spade. When Dukhe caught sight of the approaching bandits, he fled, while the seven dacoits headed straight for the treasure, which they quickly unearthed, all seven baskets. As they inspected each of the seven baskets in turn they began to speculate, "I wonder what kinds of treasures are locked in these baskets?" As they discussed and imagined the possibilities, they began to pry open the lids of each basket. When they lifted the lids, great serpents reared up from inside and hissed angrily. The sight rattled them, in fact, scared them to death, and in fear they fled to a safe distance. Then they began to jaw, "What grudge do we have with Dukhe that he would lure us here to feed us to snakes? We'll follow that son-of-a-bitch Dukhe and dish out the same treatment." They declared their course: "Let us take the snake-filled baskets and deliver them to Dukhe's home. In the same way that he endeavored to murder us, we shall feed him to those selfsame serpents." With this decision, they picked up all seven baskets and carried them to Dukhe's home. With scurrilous language they cast endless aspersions on Dukhe, "Here, we've hauled your seven treasure baskets for you, you little son-of-a-bitch." With this parting shot, they slammed down the baskets and, terrified of the now-agitated serpents, they ran away as fast as they could.

Later, when Dukhe went outside, he saw that someone had carried the seven treasure baskets straight to their home. When Dukhe's mother got sight of them, she was thrilled beyond measure. The seven cart-baskets were brimming with gold and gemstones. In a flurry of activity, they hauled them into the house for storage. They spread out straw and cut grasses on top to conceal them. The old woman said, "And to think that I used to beg from door to door to scrape together enough food, yet now, seeing how destitute I am, Fate has bestowed fabulous wealth on me. It seems that the Protector Himself has now decreed my happiness, after doling out long bouts of misery before. That was then, but now I want to build a house." Imagining her future along these lines, the old woman discussed everything with Dukhe.

Hearing this sent a thrill of pleasure through Dukhe's heart. He immediately headed for the banks of the river. He called out to Dakṣiṇā Rāy in a booming voice. Though he was deep in the backwaters, Rāy heard clearly. In an instant he appeared before Dukhe. "Why have you summoned me, Dukhe, my brother?"

Dukhe replied, "Listen, my brother and overseer of the low-lying regions, I have decided to build a house, a grand house. Please supply me with the wood that you promised, brother!"

Rāymaṇi responded, "Dear brother, in my part of the jungle I have stockpiled three hundred thousand logs, all fine timber. By the time you reach home, it will all have been dispatched." And with this promise, Rāymaṇi took off. He summoned a crowd of hungry ghosts, spirit beings, and semi-divine figures from all over and instructed them: "Collect and bring the wood to build Dukhe's house." When they heard Rāy's orders, they floated the logs, miraculously driving the cut boles upstream against the strong currents of the low-lying regions. In no time at all, they arrived at Dukhe's landing. The timber was hauled from the waters and off-loaded beside Dukhe's house. After they had secured the delivery, they took their leave.

Dukhe then began to worry, "Now that I have amassed this stockpile of wood, where shall I find carpenters and day laborers? As I think through the issue, I realize that I have no clue how to go about it." So the young man once again called out for Bonbibī, "O dear Mother of Mercy, where are you? Please show yourself to me! I am faced with an enormous problem."

Bonbibī was comfortably settled in Bhurkuṇḍa when Dukhe's call shook her throne. Within the moment, Bibī appeared in Dukhe's presence. "Tell me, my son, why have you called on me?"

Dukhe responded, "Beloved Mother, here is why I called: I have decided to construct a mansion, but how do I procure the necessary carpenters and day laborers? Please tell me, dear Mother, what is required."

Bibī replied, "There is a man, Jadurāy, who is very knowledgeable. Put him in charge, and he will come and build your estate house. Decide what you want, and he will execute your orders. I will visit him in his dreams tonight and speak to him. He will be amenable and will arrive in the morning." And with these words Bibī took her leave and departed.

That night Jadurāy had a dream. Someone said, "There is a poor boy living in this particular village. As his friend, I bestowed on him seven cart baskets of riches, and I have designated him as the *caudhurī*, the chief revenue collector and headman of this region. You should present yourself to him and serve as his overseer and estate manager. Whatever he wants—be it a hut or a mansion, a garden, or a pond—agree to construct it and place it wherever he wants. Understand that you are to build as if you were fashioning a king's palace, so listen carefully: execute all aspects of the construction fully and don't cut corners. Have no reservations about Dukhe's low birth and social standing. If you do not wish to work in his service as paid labor, then in the end I will have a tiger devour you and your wife, together with your children."

As he looked at her in his dream, he asked, "Who are you exactly, dear lady? Please reveal that to me." Bibī then disclosed her identity. The magical spell of his sleep was soon disrupted, he woke up, and immediately got up. After the time for early morning prayers, he suitably presented himself to the service of Dukhe, explaining everything that had transpired in his dreams. Dukhe's spirits lifted as he listened to what Jadurāy reported. "As my estates manager, take whatever money you need to build the things I want—an imposing mansion, a pond, and whatever goes with it. Do it as you see fit. Go out and hire servants male and female, domestic staff, peons, guards and gatekeepers, carpenters, and day laborers. Appoint and oversee the necessary agents, accountants, rent and revenue collectors, and constables."

Jadurāy took note and then took the money and sent first for carpenters, day labors, and others to construct a grand cut-stone dwelling, with paved walkways to a tank, a mosque, and luxurious gardens replete with terraced floral beds. Agents, ceremonial staff, and all the other requisite personnel, such as messengers and constables, female servants, domestic staff, and hundreds of others were assembled. The night watchmen kept a keen eye at night and the gatekeepers began to patrol the site during the day.

Proclamations publicizing Dukhe's authority were sent around the area, and everyone soon came to know that Dukhe was the *caudhurī*. Ryots and tenant farmers were moved into the area and settled. Widows who counted among the poor were given cash and had houses built for them. Villages, one after another, were systematically provided with access roads and tanks or ponds. So many hundreds of construction projects were completed that they exceeded count. Under Dukhe's ruling control, all the peasant farmers were made quite happy for he suspended the collection of tax from small tracts.[17]

When they heard Dukhe's name, so many *munśīs*, *maulvīs*, and *kājis*—well-lettered scribes, religious guides, and judges—and many other learned persons congregated there. Some laughed, some played, and some sang songs, expressing their pleasure in the service of Dukhe, the ruler of the land. Seated on a soft cushion, Dukhe received people in his audience hall, where he made decisions and dispensed justice after consulting the appropriate texts. Secretaries, accountants, and clerks, untold numbers of good people were present, some seated, others standing, ordered according to their duties. Smartly wrapped in their cummerbunds, footmen stood at the ready, motionless until receiving their orders, so too the gate keepers and porters, guards and couriers. All those assigned duties worked diligently at their callings. Grandeur and dignity prevailed, and there was no opposition to them. If money were found lying around outside, no thief would think to touch it.

When Dhonā heard all of this, he quaked all the more with fear. "People say everywhere throughout the countryside that Dukhe has become the most powerful person in the realm. It seems inevitable that he will remember the exchanges we had back then, so at any moment he might come and arrest me." Along these lines, his heart ached over his offenses, causing Dhonā to live in a constant state of agitation.

Mohāmmad Khāter says: By the fruit of Fate and the fortune of sinful acts, the son of Dhonā's poor sister-in-law came to rule the land.

DUKHE ŚĀHĀ'S MARRIAGE

One day as Dukhe sat discharging his duties, his entire entourage of attendants stood crowded around. Some were local, while others came

17. A small tract was called a *basbās*, a term going back to Mughal times, found in Abu'l Fazl's *Āʾīn-i Akbarī*, or "Chronicle of Akbar." A *bīgha* was a measure of land approximately sixty *gaz* or eighty cubits square, of which one twentieth part was call a *biswa*, and a twentieth part of a *biswa* was a *biswānsa*; see Abu'l Fazl, *Āʾīn-i Akbarī*, trans. H.S. Jarrett, 2 vols. (Calcutta: Asiatic Society of Bengal, 1891), 2: 62. Given the phonetic shifts in pronunciation between Persian, Urdu, and Bangla, the phonemes *b/v/w* are often equivalent, so we have here the smallest tracts of land.

from afar, but they all were pleased to meet with him. The rich and famous similarly made their appearance. Out of his deep-seated fear, only Dhonā failed to show. Everyone had made their way to Dukhe to pay their respects; the only one in the entire land not to approach him was Dhonā. His patience at an end, Dukhe finally ordered, "Chief minister, please listen. No doubt, in anticipation of some reprisal, Dhonā has failed to make an appearance. Send a courier and sentries right away, seize him, and haul him back here."

When the minister received his orders, he issued a formal proclamation, a *pharmān*. All at once, ten or twenty sentries were dispatched, wearing their cummerbunds, signaling official business. The courier informed Dhonā that Dukhe, the local ruler, had issued a summons. Terrified, shaking, quaking violently in fear, Dhonā collapsed on the road as he made his way, but they dragged him along and ushered him into Dukhe's presence. He offered his salaam and dropped his head. Dukhe addressed him, "Dear Uncle, why do you have your head down? Perhaps you are remembering what transpired at Kẽdokhāli? It was my good fortune that Bonbibī bestowed her grace so that I survived and could return to meet you. There really is no one as pitiless and cruel in the triple worlds as you, but this time the tables are turned, and the displeasure is directed toward you."

Dhonā heard him out and was seized with an uncontrollable terror. Falling down and grasping Dukhe's feet, he cried out, "Please forgive me!"

Watching this spectacle play out, the chief minister, Jadurāy, on behalf of the accountants, the clerks, and all the other officers of the court, humbly submitted a request to Dukhe: "Please forgive Dhonā regarding this issue. That which Fate had written has transpired. Do not dwell on that past matter, forget it, for you do realize that because doing what he did back then allowed Bonbibī to intervene with her grace and, as a result, she made you a *caudhurī*." They all pressed this kind of reasoning on him until Dukhe Śāhā finally grasped the truth of it deep in his heart of hearts. He said to Dhonā, "Go back to your own home. There is no further cause for you to remain here." Dhonā heard, made his salaam of obeisance, and without wasting any time, stood up and headed back home.

After he returned home, he began to worry along the following lines. "My culpability in all that happened now lies completely in the hands of Dukhe and what he desires. At any moment he could detain me for any thing that may have transpired and then kill me to expiate his anger. Today he let me go because of the arguments made by those in the assembly, but the next time he may not let me off in the same way. Now I am really in a bind. What will happen now? Where shall I go? To whom can I petition for help?" Brooding over his perfidy, he could envision no way out. Anxiety-ridden and in desperation, he yelled out, "Bonbibī Mā! Where are you my dear Mother Bonbibī, please shower me with your grace lest I die at the hands of Dukhe!" Uttering this, he began to fast, so that the Mother of Mercy, Bonbibī, came to know of it.

That night she came and spoke to him in a dream. "Listen up, Dhonā, you imbecile. If you really want to avoid being chastised at the hands of Dukhe and escape with your life, then gift him your daughter in marriage. You took Dukhe along with you with that promise, so honor that pledge and arrange to give your daughter in matrimony. If you do not make good on that promise, you will come to realize just how completely your life lies in Dukhe's hands." And with this warning, Bonbibī vanished. After the warning had been issued, Dhonā awoke and got up.

Bonbibī then made her way to speak to Dukhe. "Listen carefully to what I am saying, my dear son, Dukhe. At some point tomorrow, Dhonā is going to come to you. Do not ignore him, my child, but acknowledge him graciously. He has a daughter by the name of Cāmpā, and he will give her to you in marriage." Informing him thus, Bonbibī disappeared.

When the night finally passed, Dukhe got up in time for morning prayers, then sat in his audience hall. At that same time, Dhonā was making plans in his own house, "I will give my daughter Cāmpā in marriage to Dukhe. Then the antipathy between us will be nullified and turned into loving affection." Declaring that intention, he gathered together all his friends and relatives, and took along a number of very prominent and well-known people as well, and went forward to present himself at Dukhe's court. He made his salaams of obeisance and formal greetings with his head bent low. Acknowledging this gesture, Dukhe motioned for everyone to sit.

Sitting beside him, Dukhe questioned Dhonā, "Tell me, Uncle, what do you have in mind that brings you back here?"

Dhonā replied, "Please listen to what I propose to you. I had given my solemn promise to you that when we returned, I would arrange for your marriage. To make good on that pledge, Bonbibī has sent me to your honorable presence. I have a daughter by the name of Cāmpā. It is Bonbibī's decree that you agree to the marriage."

Dukhe listened and consented and immediately said, "Let the preparations begin from today. On the day calculated to be auspicious, we shall arrive with a large retinue and have the wedding ceremony."

Taking his leave, Dhonā returned to his home. All of his worries and fears were assuaged and he busied himself making all the arrangements for the wedding. Meanwhile Dukhe ventured into the interior of the house looking for his mother. He informed her of the wedding plans and everything that had transpired that led to it. To hear of it gladdened the heart of the old woman, and she immediately spread the word to her cooks and other female servants. When they heard, all of them were suitably and genuinely pleased, so much so that they immediately broke into a raucous celebration, laughing, joking, and singing bawdy songs. After he had shared the news with his mother, Dukhe escaped back outside. He sent for his personal servants and gave each of them orders to take all appropriate measures to prepare a wedding suitable for nobleman or prince. The moment they heard, the set out to transform the streets and ghats in a manner befitting royalty, erecting shops and snack stalls in neatly ordered rows.

The revelry was extravagant and lasted throughout both the days and the nights. Skilled chefs prepared food in large tents which were dotted around here and there. Some came for seated dining and others took their food away. In these ways were the wedding grounds made lavish. The pleasure and merrymaking went unabated among groups of those of both high and low station alike.

Dukhe Śāhā then issued invitations requesting the attendance of both close and distant relatives and they soon descended from many different villages in all parts, near and far. Arrangements were made for anyone who came. On the day of the wedding, the crowd swelled excessively, the roads jammed as people by the thousands traveled from their villages. Being dressed as the groom made Dukhe Śāhā very pleased. He mounted and took his seat on a colorfully decorated golden litter. The people carried Śāhā with great commotion until they finally reached Dhonā's house. To see all of this taking place gratified

Dhonā in the extreme. He respectfully had everyone seated, while Dukhe was installed on a low dais woven with gold thread. Some people were fanning and others waving fly whisks. After that, food and drink were provided and the eating and drinking lasted throughout the night, until dawn finally arrived. After morning prayers, Dukhe sent for the judge, the *kāji,* and the law specialist, the *mollā*. The *kāji* arrived, and after he had sat down, he consulted his text. Donning his turban, he inquired into and confirmed the couple's intentions and had them repeat the wedding vows. Putting their hands together, he blessed them with the words of beneficence. Feeling great joy, Dhonā then offered his own unrestrained blessings, "May your hearts remain happy, my children, for as long as you live." Dukhe Śāhā then stood up with a heartfelt joy and offered reverent salutations to Dhonā's feet. Dhonā in turn raised up his son-in-law and hugged him hard to his chest, an act that filled both Dhonā and Dukhe with joy. Then Dhonā brought out and presented all the items of the dowry, after which he took leave of his daughter and son-in-law. With the conclusion of the marriage festivities, Dukhe Śāhā returned to his own home, where he made formal salutations at his mother's feet. The old woman offered her blessings and said, "I have suffered so much pain and misery, but now, gazing at your bride's lustrous face, that misery has passed." With these words, she embraced her son and his wife, showering their beaming faces with thousands of kisses. All of the serving staff, everyone from the most senior retainers to most junior slaves, were thrilled, indeed, enchanted at the way Dukhe himself was so obviously happy. He charitably distributed great sums to the poor and indigent. He issued a decree that for the next three years, all farmers, from the largest to the smallest, would be exempt from taxes sent to the treasury. When they heard it, everyone was jubilant, and they feasted on the lavish food and drink before taking their leave and heading back to their homes.

After they had left, Dukhe had prepared large quantities of rice, beef curry, and rice pudding, which he had distributed as charity in the name of Bonbibī. Then Dukhe called somewhat anxiously, "Mother, O Mother!" and Bonbibī instantly arrived assuming the shape of a white fly. Dukhe said, "Dear Mother, everyone acknowledges me as the reigning *caudhurī* of this land only by dint of your virtue and intervention. It was you who arranged for me to marry Dhonā's daughter.

Please now come and meet my bride, O Mother, and give her your blessings." Bibī then met his bride and sanctified their liaison, blessing them as a couple. Having given her benediction, she bade farewell to Dukhe. Afterwards Dukhe returned to take his seat in his audience hall, where he resumed his activities, adjudicating conflicts and administering justice, so that the people's troubles disappeared and happiness reigned.

And now this book is completed by the grace of Khodā in the year 1287 BS on the seventh day of the month of Kārttik *just after the weekly assembly.*[18]

Mohāmmad Khāter says: All of you good and pious people, I beg you not to hold anything against me for any faults in my composition and please overlook any and all mistakes. I have not enjoyed particularly good health during the writing, but I composed it in response to the demands of an eager public. The pen now has stopped its writing of words. At the foot of every person I say, may peace be upon you.

18. Saturday, 23 October 1880.

Wayward Wives and Their Magical Flying Tree

Wayward Wives and Their Magical Flying Tree

Introduction to the Satyanārāyaṇer puthi of Kavi Vallabh

Kavi Vallabh is one of over a hundred authors who have composed tales narrating the sagas of Satya Nārāyaṇ, this late seventeenth-century story edited and published a little over a century ago simply as "The Tale of Satya Nārāyaṇ," or *Satya nārāyaṇer puthi*.[1] The sheer number of compositions dedicated to this figure, today much more commonly known as Satya Pīr, constitute the second-largest body of thematically related Bangla texts from the early modern period. The earliest of Satya Nārāyaṇ's tales were composed in the sixteenth century by Phakīr Rām, Ghanarām Cakravartī, Rāmeśvar, and Ayodhyārām Kavi.[2] These and all subsequent authors sought to equate the traditional Indic deity Viṣṇu, or Nārāyaṇ, with a *musalmāni* saint, the mendicant called Satya or, on occasion, the Prophet Muhāmmad

1. Śrī Kavi Vallabh, *Satyanārāyaṇer puthi*, edited by Ābdul Karim, Sāhitya pariṣad granthāvalī no. 49 (Kalikātā: Rām Kamal Siṃha at Baṅgīya Sāhitya Pariṣat Mandir, 1322 BS [ca. 1915]).

2. For quality editions of these texts, see Ayodhyārām Kavicandra Rāy, *Satyanārāyaṇ kathā*, edited by Vyomakeś *Mustaphī, Baṅgīya sāhitya pariṣat patrikā* 8, no. 1 (1308 BS [ca. 1901]); Ghanarām Cakravarttī, *Satyanārāyaṇ ras sindhu*, edited by Praphullakumār Bhaṭṭācāryya and Kālīpad Siṁha (Barddhamān: Barddhamān Sāhitya Sabhā, 1353 BS [ca. 1946]); Phakīr Rām, *Śrī śrī satyanārāyaṇer phakīrānī kathā: pūjā paddhatti o śabdārtha sambalitā*, edited by Raghunandan Śatapathī (1282 BS [ca. 1975], reprint, Bāṅkurā: Vikrampur Jagadbandhu Catuṣpathī, 1978); Rāmeśvar, "Satyanārāyaṇ vratkathā" in *Rāmeśvar racanāvalī*, edited by Pañcānan Cakravarttī (Kalikātā: Baṅgīya Sāhitya Pariṣat, 1964), 509–28.

himself. The semantic field of the designation *satya*—a word of Sanskrit origin in the Indian subcontinent—stretches from the concepts of "true," "real," "pure," and "virtuous" to "effectual" and "valid."[3] Satya Nārāyaṇ was, in short, someone who could be counted on to make one's life better. All of the texts assert that Satya Nārāyaṇ and Satya Pīr were more than synonymous—they were simply two names for the same figure and were used interchangeably. No matter the name, Satya Nārāyaṇ was God. Vallabh invokes both names throughout the text, notwithstanding the title given it by the editor.[4] This most famous of *pīr*s retains his popularity today, though a devotee might prefer one name over the other because of the shift in political climate that has tended to separate the communities. As a presumably Hindu twentieth-century author named Prāṇkiśor Ghoṣ wrote,[5] using the term *jaban*, or "foreigner," for *musalmān*, but retaining the original sense of Satya Pīr as Satya Nārāyaṇ, differences of name only:

> No matter if one is rich or poor,
> no matter *hindu* or *jaban*,
> each and every one is rescued. . . .
> Whenever disaster grips one in fear,
> he suffers misery no more
> if he seeks the refuge of His name.
> Listen brother, *hindu* peoples
> call on Satya Nārāyaṇ,
> while the *jaban* calls on Satya Pīr.
>
> Prāṇkiśor Ghoṣ, *Śrīśrīsatyanārāyaṇer puthi*, 34

3. Tony K. Stewart, "Alternate Structures of Authority: Satya Pīr on the Frontiers of Bengal," in *Beyond Turk and Hindu: Rethinking Religious Identities in Islamicate South Asia*, edited by David Gilmartin and Bruce B. Lawrence (Gainesville: University of Florida Press, 2000), 21–22, and passim.

4. Since hand-written Bangla manuscripts seldom have titles, modern editions generate them from the signature line (*bhaṇitā*) embedded in the text; Vallabh tends to use "Satya Nārāyaṇ" more commonly in the *bhaṇitās*, but "Satya Pīr" almost exclusively, and much more frequently, in the body of the narrative.

5. Prāṇkiśor Ghoṣ, *Śrīśrīsatyanārāyaṇer punthi*, ed. Kumudkānta Devśarmmā (Kalikātā: Aśīm Kumār Ghoṣ at Jayaguru Prakāśālay, 1375 BS [ca. 1968]); quoted in Stewart, *Witness to Marvels*, 202 (for a survey of the vast canon of works dedicated to the stories of Satya Pīr and Satya Nārāyaṇ, see ibid., ch. 6).

The initial sixteenth-century compositions included three distinct stories, which have become a template for the majority of authors and formulaic for the domestic *vrat*s, rituals performed by the women of a household to ensure the health and prosperity of the family. They are the story of the poor *brāhmaṇ* who gets rich worshiping Satya Pīr, of the woodcutters who benefit from following the *brāhmaṇ*'s lead, and of the *sadāgar*, the oceangoing merchant who undertakes perilous trading voyages at the behest of a local king or *rājā* and eventually returns triumphant aided by the *pīr*. Significantly, the protagonists of these three tales seem to index the majority of the populations of early modern Bengal: they embrace the ritually pure priests and scholars, the lowest castes and outcastes living in the forests or dealing directly with the land, and those wealthy powerbrokers who land in-between those high and low social classes: merchants, scribes and other professionals, and kings. The stories signal a consistent message: Satya Pīr will provide for individuals of all stations, because penury is a detriment to living an ethical or pious life; distinctions of social rank or religious orientation are to be dissolved among his followers, a recurrent theme in the stories in this anthology.[6]

The third tale, the merchant's adventure, historically has taken a substantially longer form than the other two, in large part because of the detailed narrations of travel through Bengal and beyond. It is here where the narratives of the *pīr*s, their *kathā*s, can be seen overtly to parody the *maṅgal kāvya* genre of semi-epic poems about Bengali gods and goddesses, mainly through positive mimicry, and, as has already been suggested, through trenchant satiric critique. A number of tales spin out the narrative of the trading voyage, often serving as a basic frame or backdrop for other adventures. This is precisely where the current translation of Vallabh's text of the *Satyanārāyaṇer puthi* can be located in this complex literary history. Tales that involve the uprooting of the protagonists, leading them to distant lands, often

6. For those interested in a representative selection of those three tales, see Tony K. Stewart, trans., "Satya Pīr: Muslim Holy Man and Hindu God," in *The Religions of India in Practice*, edited by Donald S. Lopez Jr. (Princeton, NJ: Princeton University Press, 1995), 578–97. Those translations include tales from Dvīja Rāmbhadra, Bhāratcandra, and Ayodhyārām.

shift their focus to female protagonists left behind, or, in the case of Vallabh's narrative, twin antagonists. The stories tend to take one of two tracks. Some feature resourceful women who find themselves utterly compromised by the questionable, if not downright mindless, decisions made by the men around them, which in turn lead to chaos in the world that must be and can only be set right by the actions of these heroines, who alone manage to keep their wits about them. Stories of that type lend themselves to a mocking humor that plays on and manipulates gender stereotypes. In other tales, the wives or daughters of the merchants are vouchsafed to the care of their younger brothers or sons, who upon maturity realize that they must undertake perilous ventures of their own to rescue their fathers or sisters or sisters-in-law—we have already seen that trope in Kṛṣṇarām's *Rāy maṅgal*. Both of these types can be found among the eight tales I have translated in *Fabulous Females and Peerless Pīrs*.[7] The story of Bonbibī translated in chapter 3 above is a distant variant of the latter form, but Vallabh's tale is an inversion of it, because the women are not in trouble as a result of the machinations of some miscreant or otherwise misguided man, rather, they have brought their woes on themselves. Madansundar, the younger brother of two merchants, finds himself in the unenviable position of watching over his cunning and duplicitous sisters-in-law—Sumati and Kumati—while their husbands are away trading. And in keeping up with them, he suffers his own adventures.

The primary manuscript of Vallabh's tale was copied in 1755, but probably composed in the second half of the seventeenth century, and it goes as follows. Two merchants named Sadānand and Binod Sadāgar set out to trade and, for many long years, their wives dutifully worship Śiv every day in hopes of securing the return of their husbands. As they call out for help, Satya Pīr assumes the form of the god Śiv, accosts them, and grants them a boon: the ability to make a special tree magically fly them to find their lost husbands. The women are easily distracted, however, and take a side trip instead to attend the ritual choosing of the groom for an anticipated wedding of a prominent princess named Kuntalā, about whom they are curious. The merchants' younger brother Madan overhears their plan, and knowing he is responsible for

7. Tony K. Stewart, trans., *Fabulous Females and Peerless Pīrs: Tales of Mad Adventure in Old Bengal* (New York and London: Oxford University Press, 2004).

them, tags along, hidden in the trunk of the flying tree. He is soon embroiled in his own affair with the princess, for even though he is dressed in cast-off clothes and sitting in the back of the audience hall with the servants, with a little guidance by Satya Pīr, Kuntalā unexpectedly chooses Madan as her groom. The rest of the tale follows the merchants as Satya Pīr helps them to find their way home, while their wives attempt to cover up their own actions out of fear of being punished, if not killed, by their husbands. In a parallel narrative trajectory, Princess Kuntalā searches for the merchants' younger brother, Madan, who has abandoned her on their wedding night, but left instructions on how to find him. Eventually, Madan, whom Satya Pīr has transmogrified into a falcon to avoid his certain death at the hands of the two evil women, is magically returned to his princess bride after she has fed him the sacred *śirṇi* offering in his golden cage as part of her worship of Satya Pīr. Significantly, the bird is fed because "No one was to be left out of Satya Pīr's beneficence." The surface narrative demonstrates how Satya Pīr watches over his devotees, while the many reversals suffered by the characters point to the vagaries of fate and the need for resourceful responses to its predicaments. Satya Pīr is there to help, but it is up to his devotees to bring about a satisfactory conclusion to life's challenges.

Versions of the Text. More than other tales in this anthology, Vallabh's tale of Satya Pīr shares certain tropes with other Bengali folktales, but like its more literary counterparts, it adopts a neutral position regarding the promotion of religion: regardless of who you are, you will benefit from worshiping Satya Pīr. I have located two other versions of the tale that seem to move the stories toward uneasily sectarian orientations in the nineteenth century. The poet Kavikarṇa, who likely wrote in the second half of the seventeenth century in Bangla inflected with grammar and lexical items from neighboring Oḍia language, follows Vallabh's plot line very closely.[8] But the text as it is reproduced today

8. Śrī Kavi Karṇa, *Madansundar pālā* in *Pālās of Śrī Kavi Karṇa*, translated and compiled by Bishnupada Panda, 4 vols., Kalāmūlaśāstra Series, vols. 4–7 (New Delhi: Indira Gandhi National Centre for the Arts. Delhi: Motilal Banarsidass, 1991), 4: 144–233. All twenty-one texts in this four-volume set are transcribed in Bangla and Nagari scripts, with a loose translation in English.

shows an unmistakable heavy-handed intervention that bears the mark of nineteenth- and early twentieth-century Hindu politicizing. Scores of intertextual references to classical Indic mythology make it clear that God is Nārāyaṇ and the *pīr* is only an unfortunate, but expedient disguise, useful in the Kali Age of degradation, but making *musalmān*s the allies of *śākta*s and *tāntrik*s, caricatured as bloodthirsty. The tale thus tips in favor of overt religious propaganda and by that measure seems to pale as a literary work.

Similarly, the version of the tale by Śāh Garībullāh[9] adopts a different demonizing tactic. In the opening stanzas he immediately declares the wives of the two merchants to be *ḍākinī*s, ghoulish witches, worshipers of the goddess Kāmikṣyā in the Kāmrūp area of Assam. Another printed edition of the very same text has attributed authorship to one Oyājed (pronounced Wajed, from Arabic Wājid) Āli, yet it is identical in every letter and word.[10] Several prominent scholars, including Muhāmmad Śahīdullāh and Ānisujjāmān, have argued that the text was composed by Śāh Garībullāh and not by Oyājed Āli.[11] Were that attribution to hold, the date of the text would be mid-eighteenth century, but in my reading of the text we have today, the perspective is all-too redolent of nineteenth-century vilifications of women as sources of evil for god-fearing Muslim men, a theme common among conservative commentators of that period. And for this reason, it makes both attributions of authorship suspect. For those commentators, women were deemed to be lacking in intelligence, their natural lasciviousness making them unpredictable, untrustworthy, and immoral—and, as if in confirmation, in the Śāh Garībullāh / Oyājed Āli version of the story, the two wives of the merchant succeed in slaying their young brother-in-law Madansundar on three separate occasions, only to have Satya Pīr revive him each time. When their husbands return and consult with Madansundar, they realize that their

9. Śāh Garībullāh, *Satyapīrer kathā* in *Jege uṭhilām: Baṅgīya musalmān sāhitya samiti suvarṇalekh*, edited by Āmjād Hosen et al. (Kalikātā: Viśvakoṣ Pariṣad, 2019), 370–88.

10. Munśī Oyājed Āli Sāheb, *Satya Pīr pūthi: madan kāmdever pālā* (Ḍhākā: Mohāmmad Solemān eṇḍ sans, n.d.).

11. Muhammad Ābdul Jalil, *Śāh garībullāh o jaṅganāmā* (Ḍhākā: Bāṃlā Ekāḍemī, 1379 BS [1999 CE]), 26.

wives are irremediably evil, so they trick the women into thinking they are helping store immense treasures in a pit in the inner compound of the house, banking on their greed, and the women jump in and are quickly buried alive. It is a somewhat ambiguous ending, which leaves the two older wealthy merchant brothers widowers and the younger brother happily married. It is his wife, Kuntalā, the young princess, who afterwards initiates the worship of Satya Pīr in the community.

Satya Nārāyaṇ as an epithet is absent in the Śāh Garībullāh / Oyājed Āli text; all references are to Satya Pīr, suggestive of an increasingly vocal Sufi counternarrative to criticisms from conservative factions that sought to vilify any connection to the Hindu community. In this text, it is only by following the lead of *phakir*s in general, and Satya Pīr in particular, that men can hope to break and tame the power of women, a common refrain in nineteenth-century reformist *nasihat nāmā* polemical literature, where women are blamed for everything from storms and earthquakes, pestilence and crop-failure, to corrupting men through their physical charms. Taken together, these two tales seem to illustrate the gradual disaggregation of the narratives of Satya Pīr from a synthesizing position into one of sectarian stands in opposing directions. But Vallabh's story, translated here, points to a premodern period when accommodation and collaboration were the operational norm, and it is the story of that success, not the ethics or the political theology, that is important.

Vallabh wrote in a style that stretches the concept of Bangla's tendency to economy of expression as described in the general Introduction to this volume. He repeatedly relies on the reader to supply context and intertextual references, offering only the barest of clues. He seems to have assumed that the reader or auditor of this tale would already be familiar with the contours of this literary genre and so wrote in an unusually abbreviated style. Causality is routinely determined simply by an agentless sequence, and the usual markers of attributed speech ("he said," "they argued," etc.) are frequently absent altogether. Given these tendencies, the narration on occasion abruptly changes direction without the smooth transitions found in our other authors. But the fits and starts of the grammar and diction of this remarkable tale document a Bangla that is still coming into its own as a literary language and, in that, is a translator's delight.

PRIMARY CHARACTERS, HUMAN AND DIVINE

Barṇṇeśvar – king of Kīkaḍā in Pāṭan

Bharasil – king who is father of Kuntalā

Bijaydatta – grandfather of Madan, father of Jaydatta

Binod Sadāgar – merchant from Saptagrām who engages in maritime trade with his brother Sadānand

Deoyān – the Summoner, Satyapīr

Jaydatta – father of Madan

Khodā, Khudā – God; Satyapīr

Kumati – wife of the merchant Binod

Kuntalā – princess, daughter of Bhadrasil, Mahārāj Cakravartī; also Sundarī, q.v.

Madan, Madansundar – son of Jaydatta, grandson of Bijaydatta, and younger brother of merchants Binod and Sadānand

Pekāmbar, Sāheb Pekāmbar – see Satyapīr, q.v.; in other contexts Pekāmbar would refer to Mohāmmad the Prophet or other Messengers, but is conflated here with Khodā or Satyapīr

Phakir Gosāṅi or Gosā̃i – see Satyapīr, q.v.

Prabhu – lord, master; see Satyapīr, q.v.

Rājā Ratneśvar – wise king capable of adjudicating the most difficult of problems

Sadānand Sadāgar – merchant from Saptagrām who engages in maritime trade with his brother Binod

Sumati – wife of the merchant Sadānand

Śiv, Siv – deity also called Paśupati, Śaṅkar, Bhūtnāth, Mṛtyuñjay, Śulapāṇī, Trilocan, Har, Māheś Ṭhākur, and Maheśvar Bholā

Satyapīr Nārāyaṇ, Satyanārāyaṇ, Sāheb Satyapīr, Sāheb Pekāmbar, Phakir Gosāṅi, Deoyān the Summoner; see also Khodā, q.v.

Sundarī – Kuntalā, q.v., as the "beautiful one"

OTHER CELESTIALS AND EPIC FIGURES

Ambikā – goddess who is a slayer of demons, also called Caṇḍī or Bhagavatī

Arjjun – greatest warrior and archer of the five Pāṇḍav brothers in the *Mahābhārat* epic

Bāṣuli – threatening form of the goddess who receives blood sacrifices

Basumati – Mother Earth

Bhūtnāth – Śiv in the form of lord of hungry ghosts (*bhūt*)

Bidhātā – god who inscribes fate on one's forehead

Brahmā – the creator god

Caṇḍī – form of goddess, spouse of Śiv

Draupadi, Dropadi – shared wife of the five Pāṇḍav brothers in the *Mahābhārat* epic

Dusvāsan – antagonistic cousin of Pāṇḍav brothers in the *Mahābhārat* epic, Kaurav prince who drags their common wife, Draupadi, by the hair and attempts to disrobe her

Gaṇeś – elephant-headed son of Śiv and Pārvatī, leader of Śiv's armies

Gaurī – form of goddess also called Caṇḍī, spouse of Śiv

Govinda – Kṛṣṇa

Har – Śiv; the name of the servant guarding Kuntalā's door

Hari – Nārāyaṇ, Kṛṣṇa

Indra – Vedic king of the gods

Jagannāth Ṭhākur – the distinctive form of Nārāyaṇ in Puri, a wooden image with enormous eyes, flanked by his sister Subhadrā and brother Balabhadra or Balarām

Kālī – the daughter of the goddess Durgā, who has no father and emanated solely from Durgā's mind

Kāmikṣyā, Kāmākhyā – a tantric goddess of Assam or the mountainous northeast; her temple marks the site where the goddess Satī's *yoni* (vulva) fell when she was dismembered, and so this form of *śakti* (feminine power) is synonymous with unbridled passion and desire

Kṛṣṇa – deity also called Śyām, Śyāmrāy, Hari, Viṣṇu, Śrī Nandanandan, Govinda

Lakṣmaṇ – brother of Rām in the *Rāmāyaṇ* epic

Lakṣmī – goddess of wealth and prosperity

Maheś Ṭhākur – Śiv, the supreme lord

Min – Mīnanāth, the first *guru* of the Nāths

Menakā – one of the most beautiful celestial nymphs or *apsarasa*s

Mṛtyuñjay – the old Vedic Rudra form of Śiv, the Conquerer (*jay*) of Death or mortality (*mṛtyu*)

Nanda – Kṛṣṇa's foster-father

Nandanandan – Kṛṣṇa, lit., "son of Nanda"

Pāṇḍav brothers – five heroes of the *Mahābhārat* epic: Yudhīṣṭhir, Bhīm, Arjjun, Nakul, Sahadev

Parīkṣit – in the *Mahābhārat* epic, king who succeeds granduncle Yudhīṣṭhir to the throne

Rādhā – Kṛṣṇa's favorite cowherd girl

Rām – hero god of the *Rāmāyaṇ* epic who fights Rāvan over Sītā

Rāvaṇ – ten-headed enemy of Rām who captures Rām's wife Sītā in the *Rāmāyaṇ* epic

Ravi – the Sun god, also known as Sūrya

Rukmiṇī – wife of Kṛṣṇa

Śacī – Vedic goddess Indrāṇī

Saṣṭhī Mātā – goddess of children

Satyabhāmā – wife of Kṛṣṇa

Śukdev, Ṣukdev – a sage, son of Vyās and main narrator of *Bhāgavat Purāṇ*

Śulapāṇī – Śiv as the trident-bearer

Śyām – the dark lord, a particularly alluring form of Kṛṣṇa

Trilocan – the three-eyed Śiv

Tripurāri – Śiv as the destroyer of three cities in Vedic and epic lore

Usāvati – the Vedic goddess of dawn

Viṣṇu – ancient form of Nārāyaṇ or Kṛṣṇa

Yudhiṣṭhir – eldest of Pāṇḍav brothers in the *Mahābhārat* epic, known as the *brāhmaṇ*-king by reason of his sagacity

Wayward Wives and Their Magical Flying Tree

Satyanārāyaṇer puthi of Kavi Vallabh

At the request of the king, the merchants Sadānand and Binod Sadāgar prepped and outfitted their flagship, the Madhukar, for a trading voyage, entrusting their two winsome wives to their younger brother, Madansundar. After placing them in Madan's care, one of them, Sumati, requested of her husband, "You, who are the lord of my life, please bring back gold bracelets to adorn my arms." The other, Kumati, similarly spoke to her husband and submitted her wish, "And for me, please bring a golden diadem to grace my head." After those requests, Madan addressed his brothers, "For me, older brothers, be pleased to bring me a *saycān* falcon."[1] The merchants dutifully noted what each of the three had requested, recording it in their logbook, which they kept safe in their private cabin. Then in good spirits, they settled in for the voyage.

One of the merchants called out the order, "We're ready to set sail! So let's row, row!" and the sailors dipped their oars and shoved off. The merchants sailed to Saptagrām and eventually reached the Tripīni confluence,[2] where they beat across the rough chop and entered the Hugli. Settled comfortably on their ships, the merchants engaged in

1. *Saycān* < *śyen*, the latter spelling, which is much more common in Bangla, indicates a generic term for a raptor dating back to the Sanskrit of the *Ṛg Veda*. The falcon is generally the smallest of these and therefore more suitable for a pet to be caged, as occurs in this tale.

2. *Tripīni* is *triveṇi*, the confluence of the three rivers at the mouth of the Gaṅgā.

various pleasantries as they sat back and enjoyed the scenery for the next three days until they finally reached Digaṅga. No one issued the order to rest, because the merchants insisted that they keep pushing forward. They soon spotted Pāhan to starboard, then to port Khaḍadaha. After they cruised past the confluence, they caught the current downbound along the Magarā Sāgar, the Dolphin Seawaters, and soon reached the Kahar River. It was then that God, Khodā, mischievously teased the merchants by floating a tomb in the middle of river channel, directly in their course! Heavenly dancers cavorted on top of it, while celestial musicians played and sang their songs. This unprecedented spectacle appeared midstream, where four mendicants, *phakirs*, had rolled out their deer skins on the waters and were praying, prostrating themselves with their faces turned to the west. A wild motley of flowers bloomed atop the tomb. Witnessing this marvel left the two merchants stunned. The captain and pilot—though unable to read and write[3]—bore witness, for he, too, had gazed at this unimaginably grotesque vision circling round a whirlpool in the channel. The merchants, however, diligently recorded the details in their logbook.

Afterwards, they slowly worked their way along the Vaṅga coast for two or three days until they reached Pāṭan. The ships advanced as the chained oarsmen rowed to their rhythmic chants. They eventually put in at Kīkaḍā, hove to, and dropped anchor in the shallows. The king in that place was Barṇṇeśvar, and as he sat comfortably on his throne, he heard the pleasant rhythmic sounds emanating from the landing ghat. He quickly summoned his experienced, hard-nosed constables and instructed: "Quickly find out by what order those ships have been given permission to dock. If you find them friendly, then treat them with dignity; if they are ill-mannered ruffians, then shackle them and haul them in."

Śrī Kavi Vallabh sings a mellifluous song, his mind ever immersed in the presence of Satyanārāyaṇ.

3. The term is *bāṅgāl*, which in the dialect common to Chittagong of the eighteenth century meant "bumpkin" or "unlettered," but not necessarily someone from eastern Bengal, as it can signify today, especially when used derogatorily. It should be noted that ship captains and crews frequently did hail from the eastern regions.

At the command of the king, the two seasoned constables armed themselves with sharp spears, strapping shields to their backs. They cinched their girdling cummerbunds extra-tight, just as Rāvaṇ did to prepare himself to engage Rām in battle. They surrounded themselves with reinforcements in the same manner that Indrajit marshalled the planets and stars to fight Lakṣmaṇ.[4] The uncle of two of the constables, their mother's brother, made sure that arrays of reserves were visibly on standby, fanning out like the brilliantly powerful rays of the sun. The uncle tied up his whiskers and belted out the order: "If you have to attack, strike to kill!" just as Arjjun had powerfully called out in his war battles. Meanwhile, the sons-in-law of the constables sped to the Bhagīrathi River as impetuously as Sudharmmā drove his chariot to engage Arjjun in battle. Some pounded large kettledrums strapped to the backs of low-caste bearers, while others blasted horns. Indigenous Odisha footmen assembled, their bodies smeared with a distinctive red dust—anyone who witnessed their tetchiness was left quaking, lips trembling in fear.

The two constables then mounted the backs of elephants, and just a short time later, they arrived at the landing ghat. One of them called out, "O merchant, from what land do you hail?"

The good merchant replied, "I make my home in the northern country. As a merchant, I come for trade, so there is no reason for anyone to be alarmed. If it pleases you, then I shall engage in my trade here; if not, then I shall ship out for some other locale."

The constables bowed respectfully and reassured him of their good intentions and quickly escorted him to the presence of the king. The merchant made the customary gifts to that ruler, then formally put before him his request. The king proceeded to query him about his particulars. The merchant answered, "I make my home in the northern regions and, your highness, I have come flush with cash money to

4. Based on the intertextual references, the author was clearly conversant with the Bangla versions of the epics, the *Rāmāyaṇ* of Kṛttibās and the *Mahābhārat* of Kāśīrām Dās, as well as with some stories from the Sanskrit *Bhāgavata purāṇa*. See the standard editions, which have been frequently reprinted: Kṛttibās, *Rāmāyaṇ*, edited by Subodhcandra Majumdār (Kalikātā: Śrī Aruṇcandra Majumdār, 1985), and Kāśīrām Dās, *Mahābhārat*, edited by Maṇilāl Bandyopādhyāy and Dhīrānanda Ṭhākur (Kalikātā: Tārācād̃ Dās eṇḍ Sans, n.d.). Reference to well-known stories are unmarked here, but unusual tales or incidents unique to the Bangla tradition are noted.

undertake trade. When we boarded our ships, we first plied the waters of the Gaṅgā, then floated through various regions until we gained sight of the river's mouth at Sāgar. We soon reached the Kahar River and were cruising there when we encountered, O king, the most fantastic and mystifying scene: right in the middle of the river's fairway, the deep river channel, floated a stone tomb, with dancers cavorting on it, accompanied by celestial musicians, who were singing and playing. Four *phakir*s had thrown down their tiger skins on top of the water and were bowing down toward the west, performing their prayers."

The king quickly chimed in, "If what you say is true, I will bestow on you gifts of horses and elephants, fly whisks and sandalwood. But if this proves to be false, my good merchants, then I will have you and your sailors bound in chains, impaled on tridents, cut into pieces, and offered in worship to the goddess Bāṣulī!"

After the king and the merchants had concluded their agreement along these terms, the military entourage moved everyone forward. When the king finally reached the designated area in the Kahar River, the Prophet, Pekāmbar, vented his annoyance with the merchant by hiding the vision. When the king said, "My good merchant, listen to me carefully: show me this stone that floats," the merchant cast his gaze around all four directions but caught no sight of a rock slab tomb anywhere floating on the deep waters. Getting no response, the king grew testy, indeed livid. "Produce witnesses and you can be absolved!" And so the king issued the order to fetch the helmsman and pilot to bear witness. First the king explained the difference in doing one's duty, what was right, as opposed to doing what was wrong, that is, covering for the merchant. Then he questioned him, "Face the east and then speak truthfully, helmsman. You have ninety-seven men eagerly watching your face for the truth. If you tell the truth, then the gods will reward you with heaven; if you lie, then you will be chastised in hell."

"O great king, here is my confirmation which I submit to your royal presence: I heard the event being described, but I did not see with my own eyes."

The king then turned to the merchant and said, "You privileged twice-born, now take this under advisement: You are a miserable scoundrel, and your eyewitness has tossed you overboard."

The constable wasted no time trussing them up and proceeded to loot all the goods from the ships' holds and remove them to the treasury. Some of the simple *bāṅgāl* sailors held their heads in their hands and wept, while others jumped ship to swim away. Some of the deckhands cried and beat their heads in anguish, "What little I've got—my small rice plate, my necklace—all of it is lost, washed away in these waters," one sailor wept openly in the hope of clemency. "Surely some evil magic has afflicted the ship, for we are stripped of all but our loincloths." Another *bāṅgāl* sailor blurted out, "I am already the bastard son born of a remarried widow, so why has the god of fate, Bidhātā, chosen me for this new misery?" Yet another *bāṅgāl* sailor lamented, "Brother, I see no way out. Never again will I lay eyes on my aged mother or father." And without time even to put on a shirt, the galley slaves and crew abandoned ship and scattered in all directions, while the constables, those terrors of the night, bound and hauled off the merchants.

"I shall offer you as human sacrifice to Bāṣuli," the king promised, but Satyapīr Nārāyaṇ called out to him, "Incarcerate those two brothers in your prison! Do not be so quick to chop to pieces those merchants, who are in trouble now because they previously failed to show me proper respect."

When they heard this oracle, they took heed; the constable bound the two merchants and remanded them to prison, where they languished for twelve long years. Meanwhile back home, the two wives, Sumati and Kumati, kept track of the worrisome delay and went daily to bathe in the Gaṅgā to perform their worship of Paṣupati, Śiv.

Śrī Kavi Vallabh sings a mellifluous song, his mind ever immersed in the presence of Satyanārāyaṇ.

While the two merchants remained in detention in Pāṭan, Sumati and Kumati continued their regular daily worship of Saṅkar, offering to the head of Har, Śiv, flowers of the swallow wort and leaves of the wood apple:[5] "Pray please bring our two merchants home now. You

5. Swallow wort is *Calotropis gigantea*, the crown flower, a poisonous plant in the Apocynaceae family, with clusters of small star-shaped, whitish and lavender flowers well-known in Hindu mythology as a favorite of Śiv, the offering of which grants the devotee his favor. Wood apple is *Aegle marmelos*, known as *bhel* in Bangla; other common English names include Bengal quince and stone apple; the use of the wood apple in sacrifices dates back to the *Ṛg Veda* and is alluded to in early Ayurvedic texts.

are Prabhu, our Sovereign Master. You are Bhūtnāth, Lord of Hungry Ghosts. You are all knowing. Apart from you alone, who else is immortal in this triple world? We humbly bow at your holy feet, O Lord. How many more days before you bring home our husbands, the lords of our lives?" And in this manner the two worshipped Mṛtyuñjay every day—and Satyapīr Nārāyaṇ was well aware of it.

A black turban on his head, his body wrapped in a torn patchwork cloak, Khodā, Satyapīr, materialized, standing there on the Gaṅgā water's edge. Sumati said, "Look sister, take a good hard look. There is an extraordinarily handsome *phakir* standing there. He is young, not at all grown, perhaps twelve years old, looking as if he were Kṛṣṇa, the adolescent son of Nanda, with the complexion of a newly blossomed Śyām. This *phakir* has such presence, such a subtle clear color, unblemished, as if he were Śiv, the trident-bearer Śulapāṇī himself, come to wipe away our miseries. Come, let us go over and make our prostrations of obeisance and, if he be Śiv, we will ask him for a boon to grant our heart's desire." And with these thoughts, the two hastily went forward and quickly reached the place where Satyanārāyaṇ stood. They both bowed down, offering their obeisance. The Summoner, *deoyān*,[6] said, "May both of you have sons."

When they heard the *phakir*'s pronouncement, the two women lapsed into gales of laughter. "That would be a some wonderful boon indeed, my lord, except our husbands are not here at home."

Khodā replied, "This prediction is irrevocable. Trust in me, have faith, and you will surely bear sons."

The two flippantly replied, "And just how will we fulfill such erotic desires? Will Bhagīrath take birth from the copulation of our two vulvas?"[7]

When he heard their sassy rejoinder, Satyapīr laughed mischievously and said, "Come on, tell me to what lands have your husbands gone to trade."

6. The title refers to the person who calls out the *da'wa* (Arabic) or *dāoyā/dāoā* (Bangla), which summons people to join the *ummā*, the community of *musalmāni* practitioners.

7. There is a tradition in Bengal that in order to ensure a proper male heir capable of restoring the lost Sagar sons, Bhagīrath was born from the copulation of his mothers, the two widows of Rājā Dilīp. The story is attributed to the Bangla recension of the *Padmā Purāṇa*, but is better-known through the first major Bangla composition of the *Rāmāyaṇ* by Kṛttibās; see Kṛttibās, *Rāmāyaṇ, Ādi kāṇḍa*, 37–38.

They replied, "The two of them headed to the city of Hiṅgunāṭ and after twelve years, they have still have not returned home."

Khodā then said, "Both of you, listen carefully to what I am about to say: go right now and make an offering of *siriṇī* to Satyapīr."[8]

The two women immediately covered their ears with their hands so as not to hear and started repeating "Rām, Rām!" Then three times they silently uttered the formulaic chant for Jagannāth Ṭhākur. "You should consider this: to offer the *pīr*'s *sirini* to some random *phakir* who happens to come along is to hanker after the loss of our social standing, our *jāti*. We have never listened to any part of the *kālām kitāb*, the holy writ of Korān, lest we of the caste of perfume merchants, *gandhabāṇiks*, be made *muchalmāni*."

Khodā then said, "You two listen to what I am asking you: to whom within this universe do you make offerings?"

"How could we offer worship to any other being than to Siv?"

Khodā then proposed, "When you exhibit great devotion toward and perform worship for Siv, that Siv is actually me: I am that Siv."

Hearing this left the merchants' wives nonplussed.

Śrī Kavi Vallabh's song generates waves of the nectar of immortality.

The two women looked long and hard at the *phakīr*: "Look, this stray *phakīr* wants to be Siv. The Vedas teach that Har and Hari are united in a single body, and now this *phakir* says, 'I am that very Mṛtyuñjay.' Let the moon and sun, the trees and creepers together bear witness that if we see Trilocan offering us the boon of a son, may lightning strike us!"

Suddenly, Har and Hari materialized in single body, while Brahmā accompanied him, singing the name of Rām in sweet song from all five of his mouths. Horns announced the name of Rām and the small tom-tom played to the name of Hari, as attending wives of the temple's deity danced in the archway housing Śiv Tripurāri. Shedding his black turban and the patchwork cloak that had wrapped his body, it was Satyapīr who became the granter of boons to the two women. Those two grasped Prabhu's feet and exclaimed, "After, oh, so many days, a

8. *Siriṇī* (also spelled in this text as *sirini*, but more usually spelled *sirṇī*, *śirṇī*, *śinni*)—a mixture of uncooked rice flour, banana, milk, and some spices, such as cardamom—is the preferred offering to Satyapīr.

blessing has settled upon us. The misery that has plagued us for so long is now made distant."

The *pīr*, who had just manifested himself as Śiv, Maheś Ṭhākur, then reverted to his previous form of *pīr phakīr*. When they beheld this transformation, the two beautiful women were dumbfounded. The Summoner, Deoyān, said, "Pay close attention to what I'm telling you. Go quickly and offer *siriṇī* to Satyapīr. Worship Sāheb Satyapīr with heartfelt devotion and your two merchant husbands will be back in their homeland within ten months."

In response, they said, "Listen, O revered Khodā, our bodies have been neglected, wasted away, as if pricked by the arrow of Harisuta, Arjun. How can an attractive young woman filled with longing and desire hang on to life without her lover? Please bring back our merchant husbands within a single month."

When he heard them talk in this vein, the Deoyān again laughed knowingly and said, "Whoever said that *hindu* wives were known to be chaste and forbearing? Normally, it takes a year to follow that road down and back, so how can I bring them back within a month?"

One quickly replied, "Please listen, Phakir Gosāi. Fashion some wings and turn us into birds so we can fly there. It is entirely possible, if not likely, that were there some lavish wedding festivities for a daughter of the king in Pāṭan, we will find that our two husbands have gone and taken up with some attending prostitutes. I will take my sister-in-law to check, to see whether those two are alive or dead. We can simply perch on the branches of a tree and see everything for ourselves."

Khodā thought, "I can certainly fashion wings, but my fear is that a fowler will trap them as they make their way to Princess Kuntalā's wedding. Therefore I will share with these two sisters-in-law the *ḍākinī mantra*, the magic incantations used by witches." It was along these lines that Khodā mulled his options. And this is how the two sisters-in-law came to learn the *ḍākini mantra*, the magical spell of witches.[9]

9. The *ḍākinī mantra* is associated with witchcraft and the practice of *tantra*, but more normally associated with Tibetan forms of Buddhist practice, which were and still are familiar to people in the mountainous areas that ring the north and eastern areas of the Bangla-speaking world, including Chittagong, where this text appears to have been composed.

"When you shake the tree, it will go places and carry you along. But you must enter the cremation ground at the darkest part of night, and only by walking upside down—feet up in the air and head down toward the path—wearing no clothes. You can only effect this action in the cremation grounds." When they received the *mantra*, Satyapīr accepted his offering and left.

The next day the two women went back to the Gaṅgā to bathe, and here is what they saw. It turns out that the king's daughter, Kuntalā, was in fact holding a traditional bridegroom choice, and the matchmakers had summoned a hundred suitors, would-be grooms. One passing by sported a golden crown he had jauntily perched on his head, with thick cords of a solid-gold necklace casually draped around his neck. One rode up on horseback, another arrived carried in a litter, but one man passed by tricked out on a highly spirited bull elephant.

Sumati said, "Sister, seeing this parade is rather intimidating. The crew and soldiers of someone's ship must have come down the Gaṅgā River and they are kitted out with all manner of weapons as if they were preparing for war. Let us check out the various endearing qualities of these suitors, such as they are. Being women, we should naturally be shy and diffident, but it would truly satisfy our curiosity only if we questioned all of them. But were we to question some strange man, one not known to us, then seeing us as two beautiful young women, there is no telling what amorous thoughts that might arouse." Sumati continued, "Sister, listen to this: We will do nothing until the various important personages have passed us by. Following them will be the servants, so let us waylay the ones that follow. Come on, let's go and find out what's what." And so, after all the important men and their retainers had passed, there was of course one last servant bringing up the rear.

Sumati accosted him, "Please listen, you who are clearly the servant of a great king. Who has marshalled all of these soldiers and from where?"

The servant replied, "Listen, my mesmerizing beauty, the beautiful virgin, Kuntalā by name, a princess, the daughter of the king, is having a traditional bridegroom choice where she will choose the man she fancies. So a hundred suitors, warriors, have come, each in the hopes of marrying her."

The hands of both women instantly flew to their noses in astonishment. "Oh, Mother, it is unthinkable that a woman should be the one to indulge so frankly and crassly in the sensual matters of this world. We have never heard such talk before, anywhere or any time. One hundred would-be grooms fighting over a single beautiful virgin!"

The servant replied, "Do take note. After all one hundred suitors have been seated in the assembly hall, that beautiful moon-faced woman will choose by placing a flower garland on the man her heart desires."

Sumati continued to ply him for more information, "Have you personally seen this sweet virgin girl? Just how beautiful is she?"

The servant replied, "No, I have not seen her in person, but I have heard directly from the mouths of the matchmakers that she is exceptionally beautiful."

Śrī Kavi Vallabh sings a mellifluous song, his mind ever immersed in the presence of Satyanārāyaṇ.

When they had ferreted out this piece of intelligence, the two women were giddy with excitement. "But sister, how can we go attend the wedding of Kuntalā? To witness that wedding we would have to travel all the way to the banks of the Bhadrāvati River."

"But using the protective power of the *mantra,* we can fly there to see the man she chooses."

That course of actions was quickly settled, so the two women headed back home to begin their preparations. They hastily entered the house and prepared their food. They had young Madan stretch out comfortably on a sumptuous bejeweled divan and served him lavishly off of gold plates, after which the two prepared and ate their own meals with the satisfaction of anticipation. Finally one said, "Let's go and witness this wedding!" So they rinsed their mouths and wrapped themselves in heavily pleated fancy saris. They ran briskly to the tree, mounted it, and recited the *mantra*. The two women executed their plan perfectly and were off.

As he was stretched out on his cot, Madan had overheard everything. He muttered to himself, "I do not see any alternative. These two women have learned the magical *ḍākinī mantra* of witches and goblins. If I restrain them from an act that will utterly destroy their social standing, their *jāti*, I foresee that the hour of my own death hovers close at hand. When my two brothers left for Pāṭan, they turned these two women over to my protection. Everything these two women do is my responsibility, but if they have mastered a black magic, the most evil of *mantras*, they will, when they return, eat me alive. So I will go and hide myself in the hollow of that tree and see how we manage to fly to Kuntalā's city." So reasoning like this, Madan shed his ornaments, put on a torn loincloth, and wrapped his upper body in a threadbare rag. And this is how Madan ended up hidden in the hollow of the tree. Not long after the two women mounted the tree and, by the power of the *mantra,* flew that tree to Kuntalā's city. In the twinkling of an eye the tree made that journey to Kuntalā's hometown, where all manner of preparation for the princess's wedding were under way. The two women parked the tree some distance away and dismounted, then they made their way into the women's quarters.

In the public hall, one hundred prospective grooms had been assembled, while Madansundar found a place strategically behind the lowest retainers. The princess picked up the garland by which she would signify her choice. That moon-faced beauty systematically searched for the man who would be her heart's lord, but alas, she did not fancy anyone in the audience hall as her husband. This woman, who was a stunning embodiment of beauty itself, grew increasingly distressed.

If the pīr *fails to bring forward Madansundar, then I will hold him responsible for femicide!*

When they saw the alluring beauty of this virgin girl, the suitors grew anxious with desire, and each of them recalled his personal tutelary deity. The would-be grooms who counted as devotees of Viṣṇu, muttered, "O Supreme Lord who rules over the triple qualities of the universe, be favorable!"

Those among them who were devotees of Śiv, could be heard praying, "O Maheśvar Bholā, please share your grace! I will pour one hundred pots of ghee and one hundred pots of honey over your head. Please impel the king's daughter to proffer the garland to me!"

And there were among the suitors devotees of the goddess Caṇḍī, who similarly prayed, "O Bhagavati, please be merciful to me! I shall collect the blood of buffaloes and rams and offer it in a skull, if you would but ensure the king's virgin daughter places the garland on me!"

Every single suitor said something along these lines as they stared longingly at her radiant countenance, but as she made the rounds, the moon-faced beauty was unable to identify who could be her life's love. When she could identify no one suitable to be her husband among those assembled in the king's court, this alluring beauty grew increasingly apprehensive. The young daughter of the king was overwrought when she failed to see who would be the lord of her life, the same emotion Rukmiṇī experienced when she searched for but failed to find Kṛṣṇa. Satyanārāyaṇ well understood the young virgin's desperate seriousness and desire to do the right thing, so he proceeded right then to take on the garb of one of the king's personal priests, his *purohit*. In his *brāhmaṇ*'s garb, he spoke to her, "Listen, my dear woman, I know the one who is to be your husband, the love of your life." That best of twice-born then moved quickly ahead, while the king's daughter ran behind, close on his heels. In his role and dress as a twice-born, he said, "Please accept my blessings. Here is the one who will be lord of your heart. Garland him." And she did, placing the garland around the neck of Madansundar, whose name appropriately meant "the enchanting embodiment of the god of love."

All one hundred of the suitors were flabbergasted and smacked their heads in shame and disbelief, while all the women present put their hands to their noses in bewildering shock, the vulgar profanity that erupted was enough to burn the ears. Sumati said, "Sister, let's go home. May a lightning bolt strike the head of that girl for choosing that groom! Maharāj Cakravartī would have been a heavenly choice, but she passed over everyone in the group, and slipped the garland on that wretched beggar."

Kumati replied, "Sister, yes, let's go, but didn't we come here to look for our own husbands?"

Sumati said, "Sister, that can wait a bit longer; let us linger to see if the king really will give his daughter in marriage to that indigent."

And so all the women cast aspersions on Kuntalā in the pleasing episodes of Śrī Kavi Vallabh's song.

The ladies all bitterly denounced Madansundar. "How could she have been so utterly blind as to garland him? His dhoti was torn and his upper body was wrapped in a threadbare rag. What cheek, shouldn't she be ashamed to place the garland round his neck?" Another one observed, "The mendicant *phakir* must have offered *sirini* to Satyapīr, which landed him the boon of becoming the groom."

One particularly devoted and chaste, wiser and more reflective, woman among them, said, "Do not deride Kuntalā's husband. He must be the son of a king disguised in the rags of a beggar, so that is why the beautiful Sundarī gave him the garland."

"He cannot be very accomplished in the ways of the world, for he appears to be but twelve, just pubescent, a fresh raincloud like the son of Nanda, Nandanandan."

One stupid woman added, "He is no great sovereign. Whatever you may say, he is just a simple cowherd."

Another chimed in, "Hear what is said in *Bhāgavat purāṇ*. Be assured, birth, marriage, and death are written on the forehead":

> There was once a *brāhmaṇ* named Viṣṇu Dev resident in Ayodhyā, whose wife was five months pregnant. The pregnant *brāhmaṇ* woman was kept back in their residence while the twice-born remained away for twelve long years performing austerities at Tapavan up in the mountain forests. Meanwhile, the goddess Lakṣmī herself took birth from that *brāhmaṇī*'s womb. Much advice and numerous marriage proposals had been advanced for giving away this now twelve-year old virgin—who was actually Lakṣmī, Kṛṣṇa's wife—but who was a suitable groom?
>
> When the twice-born had completed his austerities, he returned home feeling quite satisfied. After offering water to her father, the virgin girl stood before him, disheveled, her hair unkempt. The *brāhmaṇ* examined her and asked, "Who exactly is this unmarried girl in my house?"
>
> The *brāhmaṇ's* wife replied, "Lord, listen, and I shall tell you. She is your daughter, born from my womb."
>
> The *brāhmaṇ* immediately responded, "Whatever I have achieved in my austerities, this cursed virgin girl has destroyed. For the father who gives his virgin daughter away at two and one-half years of age, Śacī blows her auspicious conch and Indra sings his praises. Mother Earth, Basumati, ripples with the thrill of bearing such a moon-faced beauty, and that auspicious daughter of the gods rains down flowers from heaven on the virgin girl and her groom. If a father gives away his daughter at five years of age, the gods bless that man with extreme fortune. When a father gives away a virgin daughter at seven years of age, he claims the merit equivalent to the gifting of seven lakes. When a father gives away a daughter at nine years of age, neither transgression nor merit accrue for they perfectly balance out one another. At twelve years of age, the daughter is timeworn, no longer suitable for having intercourse, and ninety-seven generations of the father's forebears fall into the depths of hell. If a father has failed to fix his daughter's marriage at the expedient time, it is not inappropriate to consider him to be his own worst enemy. Tomorrow morning I will give away my

daughter to the first man I see, regardless of his social standing, his *jāti*."

When the *brāhmaṇ* swore this monstrous vow, Lord Kṛṣṇa, Śrī Nandanandan, assumed the form of someone of the lowest caste, a *hāḍi*. The very next morning he arrived at the door of that *brāhmaṇ*, accompanied by his dog, and the twice-born did indeed make over his daughter in marriage to that groom. It was the great good fortune written on the forehead of this virgin girl that it was Śrī Nandanandan himself assuming the body of a *hāḍi*.

In just this same way the virgin daughter of the king recognized her husband, the one some have called a rustic cowherd, when in fact he is genteel and no doubt skilled in amorous sport.

But here, the queen, the *mahārāni*, would have none of it. "A curse on the harshness of Bidhātā, the god of fate! What horrible fault must he have written on my forehead to have a country bumpkin as a son-in-law? I will never give my virgin daughter in marriage to that would-be groom. I would rather tie a rock around Kuntalā's neck and drown her!"

On the occasion of Gaurī's wedding, can you just imagine what aspersions spewed from the mouth of Menakā when she saw the ascetic Śiv? It was in just this way that the king's wife remonstrated against her new son-in-law. But the young bride—who would soon place the vermillion mark of marriage in her hair's part—consoled her mother, "Father is the progenitor, my dear mother, but it is Fate itself that determines one's action, one's *karma*. I have served and worshipped this cowherd in the past; where will I find anyone better?"

There was no anguish whatsoever in any corner of this virgin girl's heart. Śrī Kavi Vallabh advises: Make yourself ready to start the wedding ceremony.

At the most auspicious time for the marriage,
the groom was seated properly, and
  the preliminary *adhibās*[10] ceremony was redolent with joy.
The men and women of the town,
like an endless stream of heavenly figures,
  arrived making great merriment.

10. For details of the *adhibās* ceremonies preparatory to the wedding proper, see Kṛṣṇarāmdās, *Rāy maṅgal*, §45, pp. 115-116 above.

The double-headed *dundubhi* drum beat out a rhythm
accompanying the play of horns and other instruments,
    while the women were awash in celebratory cries of joy.
The text of the Veda was intoned aloud,
A pot made of gold was formally installed.
    The priests ritually purified their bodies, ending with the tongue.[11]
The goddesses Ambikā and Saṣṭhī Mātā
were then worshipped according to script,
    along with Gaṇeś, Ravi, Hari, and Har.
They performed their worship of the many gods,
bowing with hands reverently pressed together,
    their minds earnestly focused,
honoring Viṣṇu's sacred stone with earth and incense,
the finest white rice, and garlands of various flowers.
    Bracelets of fine *durbā* grass[12] were tied around the couple's wrists.
They offered vermillion, fruits, curd,
ghee, and other foodstuffs in abundance.
    Singularly crafted conch bangles adorned the couple's arms.
They assembled profusions of collyrium, purifying cow's urine,
a smooth, flawless mirror, a small hand mirror,
    betel nut, and fly whisks.
Sweet-smelling turmeric filled
vessels of gold, silver, iron, and lesser bell metal,
    all perfect, just like the beguiling bridegroom.
Hosts of deities gave voice
to auspicious cries of approval
    for that bride and groom, now a perfect couple.
As she turned to face her groom,
the women attendants placed the groom's hand
    on the head of the winsome Kuntalā.
    Being a servant to brāhmaṇs,
Vallabh sings the song
of the adhibās *rituals perfected, performed*
    fully in accord with Vedic prescript.

11. Though not identified by name, the purification ritual is most likely *nyāsa*, where purifying *mantras* are recited as each part of the body is touched, a preliminary rite (*upacāra*) for significant rituals, such as *pūjā* or marriage.

12. For *durbā* grass, see above p. 251, n. 60.

Bowing your head, may you repeatedly praise Satyapīr. Alas, what an unprecedented glory he brings to this last dreadful age of humanity, the Kali. Listen, all you good people, to the singular story of the Satyapīr vratkathā, *in which he is comparable to Nārāyaṇ.*

By way of personal rebuke, the ruler agreed only to furnish a very expensive dhoti for the wedding dowry. "If the groom had been a *mahārāj* or a king of kings, I would have given horses, elephant cows, and a rutting bull elephant. I would have furnished clothing so exceptional as to be envied by the gods. And I would have gifted those traditional five gemstones that dazzle the mind and heart."[13] With all this racing through his mind, the king stayed silent throughout the entire wedding ceremony, and only reluctantly handed over his daughter.

The officiating *purohit brāhmaṇ* looked over the face and overall appearance of the groom and thought: "Will the gratuity I receive from this be sufficient to allay my misery? If the groom was the son of a king, then all would be good, for he would provide more than satisfactory gratuity for all the *brāhmaṇ*s. But when the groom is of this type and station, I shall have to hire him to herd cattle to pay the fee."

Going through the motions, the ruler handed over his daughter, yet all the requisite vows that must be witnessed by the *homa* fire were executed according to scriptural writ. The groom and virgin bride then blissfully repaired to the flower-room, where the two engaged in games of dice with spirited intimacy.

Śrī Kavi Vallabh sings a mellifluous song, his mind ever immersed in the presence of Satyanārāyaṇ.

The princess rolled the dice with the lord of her life, while the servant girl listening near the door smiled and giggled to herself.

"Three! Four! *Caubāñc*! Take that!" cried the groom.[14]

13. Diamond, emerald, sapphire, ruby, and red coral.

14. They appear to be playing a version of the traditional Indic cloth or board game called *caupaṛa*: *cau* from Sanskrit *catur* "four" and *paṛa* from Sanskrit *paṭa* or cloth, which references the four radiating arms of the board. The exclamation "*Caubāñc*!" would be a Bangla variant. The dice can either be rectangular stick or cube-shaped dice, which would likely be the case here, since they are made of silver, or the dice can be cowries, which, when rolled in sets of five, six, or seven, are calculated by the number of "mouths" facing up, in some cases multiplied by five or some other number, so that a roll

The virgin bride rejoined, "Eighteen, now that keeps the clever guy in check!"

Using the silver dice, the couple played, just as Rādhā and Kṛṣṇa had played in Bṛndāvan. The beautiful woman prevailed three straight times, then she began to realize that her husband was getting annoyed. The young virgin girl said, "My beloved, if I win this time, I shall snatch away your worn-out old dhoti and tear it in two."

The groom replied, "My lovely moon-faced bride, don't be so presumptuous! I shall trounce you and bring you down to the level of your villain husband! And I shall strip you of your stunning bridal vestments and wave them before your face like a jewel-studded lamp."

Kuntalā replied, "O my beloved, I would submit this one request. When the royal Yudhiṣṭhir lost at dicing, the reigning king granted Dusvāsan permission to strip Draupadi naked in the public assembly hall. Terrified, the pure and faithful Dropadi called Kṛṣṇa to mind: 'My lord, as the wishing tree with the power to grant all desires, please be merciful to me.' At the time, Kṛṣṇa was playing dice with Satyabhāmā, but Govinda was instantly aware the moment Dropadi had called him to mind. Just as Satyabhāmā rolled her stakes and defeated Kṛṣṇa, Śyāmrāy yelled out, 'Wait! Stop!' Satyabhāmā curiously asked, 'My lord, may I enquire, just whom were you protecting as the Lord Śrī Nandanandan?' The Lord Nārāyaṇ smiled and gently replied, 'I just saved Dropadi, that pure and chaste woman.' Rukmiṇī, the daughter of Kṣirod, and the righteous Satyavati, rushed to the assembly hall to see what had transpired. Dusvāṣan was unable to unravel Dropadi's garment, because Nanda's son kept making it longer. In that very same way, were I to lose to you, lord of my life, you should be my Kṛṣṇa and I your Dropadi. If, on the other hand, were I to manage somehow to win, I shall mount your shoulders this one time here in our wedding bedroom."

Madan stared at his virgin bride with growing consternation. It rattled him when he heard that she, his wife, might sit on his, her husband's, shoulders.

---

of five would be twenty-five, which in Bangla is *pāciś* (Hindi *pacīs*), from which the game Pachisi takes it name, and in its anglicized derivative, Parcheesi. For more on this and the relationship of these dice and board games, see the brief article by W. Norman Brown in the magazine of the University of Pennsylvania Museum; Brown, "The Indian Games of Pachisi, Chaupar, and Chausar," *Expedition Magazine* 6.2 (1964): 32–35.

Kuntalā continued, "My beloved, I only lay this one request at your feet because when Rādhā and Kṛṣṇa played with the dice in Bṛndāvan, Śukdev conveyed to Parīkṣit that Śrī Nandanandan lifted the revered Rādha onto his shoulders. A husband and his wife are but a single body, there is no distinction between them. Knowing this to be true, why, my master, would you object?" And in this manner the evening progressed into the second watch.

But worry about his two brothers' wives nagged at Madansundar. He calculated just when they would fly the tree back to their home and he knew they would not see him for those two sisters-in-law were instructed not to turn and look behind them.

Madan then said, "Listen, you who are the beautiful daughter of the king, by the will of Khudā, I am famished, struck suddenly with hunger pangs." So that moon-faced beauty scavenged the grains of the auspicious rice that had been scattered and began to cook for the lord of her life. The moon-faced one said, "How will I manage? How can I serve the food when there is neither leaf nor plate?"

The winsome Kuntalā was weeping when she said this, just as Śrī Kavi Vallabh's song generates waves of life-giving nectar.

Madan spoke, "Listen my princess, we have our veiling canopy right here at hand from which we can fashion makeshift plates. My beautiful woman, now why don't you serve the rice in those." Fashioning the plates, she served the food to the lord of her life, just as Lakṣmī had served special delicacies to Govinda. When he had finished eating, the son of the merchant was sated: "The food you have cooked would be rare even for the gods." He rinsed his mouth and then reclined on the elegant divan. "Lest anyone later spot the evidence of our eating, please don't be slow to clear up, good woman, do pay attention. Hide everything, and especially watch out for your girlfriends and companions." So the woman excavated a small trench with the pot used for her mascara, then gathered up all the evidence of this meal so uncharacteristic for the bridal chamber—the cooking pot, the plates, and even the ash—and buried them in the northeast corner. Then she stretched out with the lord of her life on that same elegant divan, just as Rādha and Kṛṣṇa relaxed together in Bṛndāvan. They soon embraced, breast to breast, mouth to mouth, coupling—one whose body was dark enmeshed with one whose body was the color of gold.

Afterwards, Madansundar fell into a deep sleep, which made the Lord, Sāheb Pekāmbar fume. "Listen to what I tell you, you mindless, faithless *hindu*! How long are you going to sleep here in your nuptial bedroom?"

As Madan held the king's daughter close, something stirred deep in his subconscious dreamworld, "Listen, I will break the neck of your little sweetheart . . ."[15] What he witnessed in that dream woke the merchant, forcing him up. As he sat on the elaborately decorated divan, he worried through the problem: "If I awaken the gorgeous Kuntalā, then will my princess allow me to leave? If I slip away without giving her my details, I fear that not seeing me may well cause the death of her who is the very image of beauty." The groom then picked up the endpiece of her sari and using as a pen the twig that served as her mascara applicator, he sat and wrote in black everything she needed to know. "If you are truly a *satī*, a devoted wife, you will seek and find me. My name is Madan and I make my home in Saptagrām. My two sisters-in-law have knowledge of a *ḍākinī mantra*. Their bodies rippled with wonder and excitement when they saw a hundred prospective grooms making their way along the Gaṅgā. That generated a compelling, insatiable urge to witness the wedding in person. Using the power of the *mantra*, they magically flew in a tree to Kuntalā's city, and I followed by worming my way into a hollow of that tree. As the hundred suitors took their places in the assembly hall, I hid in the back among the servants, but you, virgin woman, passed over everyone in the assembly and placed the garland on me. All the beautiful women who were there laughed at me, but the king reluctantly but dutifully gifted me the expensive marriage dhoti. Raising the flower canopy, we entered the nuptial bedroom. Three times I lost at dice there in the bridal chamber. At my request, you, my devoted wife, cooked. I ate and was extremely satisfied, and beginning to feel amorous. Then the two of us lay down on the bejeweled divan. Later, my two sisters-in-law visited me in my dreams, and this is why I am leaving you behind and heading back to my own home. If you are truly a *sati*, a devoted wife, you

15. The last two-syllable word of the couplet is missing in the manuscript, but the threat seems to be from Satya Pīr, Sāheb Pekāmbar. In this context, the term *beṭī*, which I have translated as "little sweetheart" in this context may well carry much more derogatory connotations.

will find me along the banks of the Gaṅgā. I am the son of Jaydatta, grandson of Bijaydatta. My beautiful woman, I go, leaving you with these personal particulars. I have not inflated nor deceived you in what I have said; I have spoken only the truth so that you and I may be reunited again in this birth."

Madan then went and hid himself in the hollow of that tree that the two women flew back home following along the banks of the Gaṅgā. Each woman then retired to her respective house. But when the beautiful bride awoke from her sleep, she wept inconsolably. This lovely woman frantically searched everywhere, every nook and cranny under the flower canopy, but this moon-faced beauty could not find any trace of the lord of her life.

Śrī Kavi Vallabh's song generates another wave of life-giving nectar as the beautiful Kuntalā beats her forehead in anguish.

"The lord of my life was sleeping on our bejeweled divan. He has deserted me! Where has he gone? How have I offended you, what fault accrues to me, my beloved? What you have done to this defenseless woman because of a dice game is a violation of morality, of *dharma*. Male and female bees consume their honey together as a couple—my heart burns to see their loving play. I'd have preferred to be turned into simple anklets, adorning your feet, had I known how incredibly hapless and star-crossed I was to be rendered." Lamenting in this vein, she slumped down and groveled, rolling back and forth on the ground, just as the beautiful Rādhā did when Kṛṣṇa left Bṛndāvan. In her distress, this image of perfect beauty violently pounded her forehead with her fists, just as Usāvati did when she was worried about Govinda's grandson. When the daughter of the king could not find her husband, the lord of her life, she was worried sick, just as Rukmiṇī was when she could not find Kṛṣṇa. "Alas, my beloved, why have you rendered me husbandless? Here in my youth, my life is without meaning apart from you. What will those one hundred would-be grooms say now that my beloved has publicly humiliated me before the whole world, has saddled me with this indelible stain?" Tears poured from her eyes like the monsoon rains of the month of *srāvaṇ*.[16] Then she discovered the

16. Mid-July to mid-August.

unexpected handwriting on the end of her sari: On the border were written the personal details of the lord of her life. That treasure made her giddy as if she were drinking spirits, just as Rādhā's mind filled with bliss upon finding Kṛṣṇa's flute Murulī. "I shall head for the banks of the Gaṅgā the moment night gives way to day. By the strength of my affection I will again see the feet of my lord."

Madansundar had departed toward the end of the night, but by mid-morning all the suitors had heard about it, which generated a raucous commotion. It was the servant girl who had come at dawn who provoked the furor. She told everyone she saw that that beggar had abandoned Kuntalā. The matchmakers went to their various prospective grooms and advised them, "That son-of-a-bitch beggar is nowhere to be seen in the house. Go, now, right now, bearing jewelry! Whoever manages to get into Kuntalā's rooms first is likely to be accepted as her beloved and will become her husband." When they heard this, the various suitors headed off, jewelry in hand.

"Listen, my dear princess, please accept my bejeweled ornaments. Yesterday you placed the garland on me, so please open the door."

The young woman said, "Har, stand guard right here and swear on your *guru* that if anyone comes to my rooms, only the one who knows precisely what happened and what conversations I had with my husband toward the end of last night should be admitted." Alas, no one was able to repeat the affairs that transpired in the bridal chamber. Of the one hundred suitors, not one was able to report precisely what was said.

There was one among the lot who was particularly enterprising and he contrived to secrete himself in the rooms of the old woman garland-maker. "Listen, my dear old garland-weaver, please accept a generous amount of cash—one hundred thousand *ṭākās*—to go and find out and then report back to me the conversations the groom and his bride had."

So the next day the garland-weaver concocted a ruse, taking ten garlands in hand. As she handed over the garlands to the bride, the old garland-weaver commiserated. "Truly, you are as dear to me as I am to you. No one is around, so you can tell me, just what did you and your new husband talk about toward the end of last night?" A flurry of fast talk fooled the naïve, sincere girl, and she was momentarily deceived, just as Mīn in the womb overheard Gaurī conversing with Ṣukdev.[17]

"Listen, my dear old garland-weaver, to what transpired. My husband lost three times playing dice with me. My husband was famished, so I cooked for him and I fed that lord of my life right in the bridal chamber."[18] Then the legend of Har and Gaurī suddenly came to her mind. She had thought of four different things to relate, but told only two of the stories, lest anyone else be lurking in the vicinity of the marital chamber. Then she bade farewell to the old garland-maker.

When the old garland-weaver's had gleaned the information, her arms trembled with anticipation as she thought to herself, "I am going to collect one hundred thousand *ṭākā*s from that prince and to be sure I shall personally count every bit of it." To the prince, she said, "Listen up, prince, I have brought back reliable intelligence regarding the conversation and activities of the bride and groom, so please hand over the one hundred thousand *ṭākā*s! Go and convey to Kuntalā this string of events: You lost three times playing dice with that maiden. Then you, the son of a king, grew hungry and at your request, that virgin bride cooked for you. You ate right there in the bridal chamber."

May the song of Śrī Vallabh bless each and everyone of you.

17. This reference is to a foundational story told in the *Gorkhabijay* or *Mīnacetan*, where Mīnanāth, the *ādi* or original *guru* of the Nāths, hid in the womb of a fish that hovered underneath the boat in the middle of the Ocean of Milk where Śiv had taken his wife, Gaurī, to be absolutely alone in order to explain the secret of immortality, a conversation spurred by Gaurī's discovery that Śiv's garland of skulls were all her own skulls from previous lives. Because she was not immortal, she had repeatedly been reborn. During the explanation, Gaurī felt drowsy and fell asleep. When Śiv would ask if he should continue, Mīnanāth ventriloquized her assent, so Śiv proceeded to reveal the full secret to the eavesdropping Mīnanāth, while Gaurī remained oblivious. Here Ṣukdev, rather than Śiv, narrates. The manuscripts of the text of the *Gorkhabijay* or *Mīnacetan* attest three different authors—Phayajullā, Śyāmdās Sen, and Bhīmsen Rāy. See *Gorkhabijay*, edited by Pañcānan Maṇḍal, with an introduction by Sukumār Sen, and illustrations by Nandalāl Basu (Kalikātā: Viśvabhārati Granthālay, 1356 BS [ca. 1949 CE]); the story is found in the opening section of the text, pp. 5–8.

18. The language here conflates eating and love-making, one quite literal, the other alluded to, thereby protecting the young bride's modesty.

The suitor took off as soon as he heard, bubbling with expectation. "Now I shall snag this posturing lapwing by her own showy topknot."[19] When he arrived at her bridal chambers, he said, "Up to now, I have been playing a joke on you. Listen, love, my princess, to my description of what transpired. I played a game of dice with you and lost three times. I then grew ravenously hungry and you cooked for me, and I ate here in the flowered bridal chamber. We had no further conversations, my princess and darling of the king."

The young maiden thought to herself, "This is verbatim from the conversation I had with the garland-weaver." The young woman than said, "You have spoken with glib confidence. The two things you have told me are certainly true, but what exactly did you eat?"

Quickly racking his brain, this son of a ruler replied, "You made rice and curried vegetables, served on a plate made of gold."

This daughter of the king listened and then derided him, "There was no metal plate." And the suitors face fell in humiliation. In a similar manner she had countered the efforts of all one hundred suitors: not one had been able to satisfy the beautiful daughter of that king.

The next day Kuntalā made up her mind, "I will follow the banks of the Gaṅgā to find the lord of my life." Begging leave to do so from her father, the king, she said, "Not one of the hundred suitors could get the best of me. But I have heard that down along the banks of the Gaṅgā there is one Rājā Ratneśvar. He has a keen sense of discrimination and will be able to help determine which prince is the right one, my groom. So send the hundred prospective grooms to accompany me so that I might better make up my mind. As I move along the banks of the Gaṅgā, I will continue my own inquiries." When he heard this sensible proposal, the king had the royal flagship, the Madhukar, made ready so she could parley with the hundred suitors, each of whom would sail in his own ship. Two maidservants were assigned to accompany her, and

19. The bird is the *ṭiṭīr* or lapwing (alt. peewit, plover); the northern lapwing or *sobuj ṭiṭīr* (alt. green plover) is classified as *Vanellus vanellus* and is the only lapwing in Bengal to sport a distinctive crest or topknot. The image is especially apt because this lapwing will feign a broken wing, dragging it around, in order to distract predators from its nest, as apparently the suitors imagine Kuntalā to be dissembling regarding her marriage; and this suitor's attitude is consistent with the predatory sense of a hundred would-be-grooms pursuing a single bride.

tightly clutching the bridal sari, on whose edge her husband's particulars were inscribed, she took formal leave of her mother and father.

The boat quickly entered and skimmed along the waves of the main channel of the river and moved rapidly downstream. They navigated the various waterways, smoothly progressing along the banks of the Gaṅgā, heading toward Saptagrām, the reputed location of her husband. They put in at the landing ghat of Kīkaḍāpeli and moored their flagship, the Madhukar. The matchmakers hurried off to consult with the local ruler. "There is a kingdom along the banks of the Bhadrāvati River whose ruler is one Bhadrasil. The daughter of that king was given the freedom to choose her husband, so he assembled some hundred suitable prospects. From among that group, she was to select her marriage partner, but not a single one of the would-be grooms appealed to her. The one to whom she proffered the garland in the bridegroom choice was not to be found among those eligible hundred. She has come to your city in the company of the entire entourage of them so that you may help determine and identify who was the correct match."

The king immediately assembled all his advisors and ministers, and he summoned all the merchant traders of Saptagrām. Some arrived on horseback, others were carried in their litters, thick expensive braids of necklaces and garlands swaying around their necks. Watching, Madan queried them, "Where are you all going?" to which they replied, "There is a young girl, the daughter of the local ruler, who hails from the banks of the Bhadrāvati River. She hosted the ritual choosing of the groom, but she could find no one suitable enough to marry from those hundred possible suitors."

Madan recognized the story as his own, for he had climbed into that tree, ridden it to the wedding, and ended up himself getting married. "That young bride has come looking for me, so I shall go see how all of these merchants and advisors judge matters." He assumed the same guise as before, wearing a tattered dhoti. He went and secreted himself at the back of the public gathering. The ruler considered everyone in the assembly, but none of these princes was deemed to be the right one. *Can one just imagine what must have been going through the mind of that young beauty?* Then the chaste young woman said, "Was the content of the letter that brought me here all falsehoods? If my husband does indeed reside in this land, then why does my lord not remember me and greet me? How will I ever be able to return to the land of my mother and father if I can nowhere locate any trace of the lord of my life?" Harshly criticizing the assembly, she boarded her boat, prepared to dump her gifted gold wedding ornament into the waters of the Jānnavir River.[20]

Finally, Madansundar spoke up, "Listen, O king, I shall provide the correct answers to the bride's questions." When the ruler heard what Madansundar had to say, he called for the princess to return.

Śrī Kavi Vallabh sings a mellifluous song, his mind ever immersed in the presence of Satyanārāyaṇ.

All one hundred of the prospective grooms were astounded. As they stared hard at his face, they grumbled, "How will that pathetic son of a mere merchant win over this beautiful young woman?"

Madan ventured, "My darling, listen carefully. While the prospective grooms were all well dressed in their public procession, there was someone wearing a ragged garment, a mendicant standing behind the servants. After searching through the assembly, you placed the garland on that beggar. The women looking on began to laugh. Your mother was especially disheartened, and the king remonstrated with you, nonetheless the king gifted the traditional elegant and expensive dhoti to the groom; and you, his beautiful daughter, underwent all the preparatory rituals for the wedding. Later, you made your way to the nuptial chamber under the canopy of flowers, and there as bride and groom you played a game with silver dice. The groom grew suddenly famished, and you cooked for him. There was no proper plate to serve on, so you wept. The groom consoled you, saying, 'Do not cry, my beautiful woman, we have the two wedding canopy-veils.' You wove the two veils into a single piece, and with deep affection and tenderness, you fed the lord of your life. After eating his fill, the groom stretched out on the decorative divan. You then dug a trench in the northeast corner of the room and buried the makeshift plates. If you do not believe me, let us go there, and I will show you all the various items you buried."[21]

20. The Jānnavir is the Jāhnavī River, the Gaṅgā.

21. In the text, this last paragraph alternates between second- and third-person narration, which I have adjusted for clarity to reflect Madan speaking directly to Kuntalā about the events with her groom.

The young woman exclaimed, "I have found the Kṛṣṇa that I had lost. Alas, this is no joke, you really are my husband, my lord!" And for the second time she slipped the garland onto Madan's neck, which once again caused great embarrassment, indeed, humiliation, for the hundred suitors.

Śrī Kavi Vallabh sings of faith in Khodā: As the ranking saint among guides, may you grant prosperity!

Her father the king said, "What I have just heard, however unbelievable, is indeed a valid resolution, for Madan has preserved your honor and social standing." Bestowing a *jāigir* land settlement there in Saptagrām on the young merchant, he sent his daughter off in a palanquin to her new home.

Sumati and Kumati were heading to the Gaṅgā to bathe when they spotted the bride and groom some distance away. They recognized the young bride Kuntalā and their brother-in-law Madan. "What an incredible turn of events, sister, but what are we to do now? She is the bride we saw when we flew the tree to the wedding, so Madan must have hitched a ride in the tree's hollow. We shall have to explain everything to his brothers when they show up—and because of that *phakir*'s *mantra*, they will surely cut off our noses and ears, leaving us disfigured, to our utter humiliation!"

Kumati replied, "Sister, listen to my idea. Go and purchase some poison, then we will murder Madan and be rid of him."

As it turns out, the old shopkeeper would have charged a mere six cowries for the poison, but the watchful Satyanārāyaṇ reached her house first. "Listen carefully to what I'm telling you, you unscrupulous, conniving old crone. A woman posing as the servant of the king is going to come to purchase some poison. If you dare take her money and sell her the poison, Kālī, the great goddess, will decimate your lineage!" And with these warnings, he forbade all who were present to do so. As a direct result, Sumati was unable to procure the poison at the merchant's shop.

Stymied and distraught as she walked back along the road, she encountered the mendicant Khodā, Satyapīr, dressed in his patchwork cloak, directly blocking her path. He accosted her, "Listen, Kumati, where have you just been?"

She answered, "This predicament, this whole state of affairs, is the result of your *mantra*."

The Summoner, the *deoyān*, then replied, "It was you who violated the trust. How am I at fault when it was you who failed to go and search out your husband as promised? Now you would take this young man's life using a deadly poison—but if you succeeded in killing him, where would you dispose of the body? You will not be able to cover up the murder. Rather, take this potion of mine to transform him into a *saycān* falcon. Recall that when the merchant brothers departed for Pāṭan, Madan had requested them to bring him a falcon." So Sumati took the potion and headed home and this was how it came to pass that Khodā transformed Madan into a falcon.

She sped home and immediately began to cook. Listen, everyone, to Śrī Kavi Vallabh's song.

With her own hand Sumati took rice from her plate and mixed in the concoction as if she were feeding Madan *prasād*, the leftover food first offered to the gods. She mixed the potion into his food and then heaped the rice on a plate of gold. Like a growing boy, he devoured his food with gusto, then taking the spouted water pot, rinsed his mouth. The golden water pot dropped and lay where it fell. His ribs collapsed, imploded, and suddenly wings protruded. Transmogrified into a falcon, Madan flew up into the air, but, with a clap of lightning, Khodā sent him scurrying, driving him away. Eventually, Madan landed in a tree in the city of Pāṭan, the same Pāṭan where his two brother merchants were still held captive. In his bird form, Madan perched on a branch overhead as the Summoner, Deoyān, troubled that local king's dreams. "You are a ruler devoid of faith, so listen carefully to what I am saying to you. On what grounds have you incarcerated my servants? The seven thousand tenants from whom you collect rent, and the seven hundred dancers and actors who perform in your palace pavilions—when I merely utter the incantation 'Cut and slash! Shatter and kill!' they will all be exterminated and a river of blood will flow through your palace. After igniting a firestorm in your city, your wives and children, all of your merchandise, your worldly goods, will be consumed in the conflagration." After reckoning with that dream toward the end of the night, the king headed straight for the prison-house as soon as the dawn broke. He had the shackles of the two merchants removed and loaded their seven ships with cargo worth at least three times its original value.

Śrī Kavi Vallabh sings a mellifluous song, his mind ever immersed in the presence of Satyanārāyaṇ.

The two brothers made their way to their flagship, the Madhukar. The galley slaves were already in place, their oars in hand, at the ready. For Sumati they had collected a tiara made of gold, and for Kumati they had brought golden arm bracelets. When they looked in their ledger, they remembered that Madan had requested them to bring him a *saycān* falcon. They agreed to hand over one hundred *ṭākās* to several fowlers with instructions to bring them back a falcon. The fowlers accepted the merchants' proposal and quite pleased, began to fan out across Pāṭan.

About that time the *pīr*, in his patchwork cloak, showed up and said to the fowlers, "Come with me and you will catch your *saycān* bird. But you must give me *sirṇī* sweetmeats to a measure of one and one-quarter seers.[22] You must commit to me in good faith!"

They replied, "If we do catch a *saycān* falcon, then we promise to offer you one and a quarter weight of *sirni* sweetmeats."

The Summoner went ahead, and the fowlers followed behind. Pausing at the foot of a tree, he said, "Do you see that bird? Keep track of it lest it escape." The fowlers spotted the *saycān* falcon perched on a branch. Using a glue stick, they soon captured it.

As promised, the merchants paid the fowlers the one hundred *ṭākās* and deposited the falcon in a golden cage. With their seven ships fully laden, they began their homeward journey. The various ocean whirlpools and eddies now behind them, the merchants sailed past Setabanda, then soon pulled past Nilācal,[23] before entering the mouth of the Gaṅgā at Sagar. Safely skirting Magarā's hazards, they reached Digaṅga. They put in at the town of Hugli and celebrated for three days. The ships finally sailed into Saptagrām, where they moored at their own ghats. The merchants offloaded all of their precious cargoes onto wagons. Then the two brothers made their way to their respective

22. Satyapīr's preferred offering; see n. 8 above. Varying by region, the seer is about the same as a kilogram.

23. They are making their way up the coast, from Setubandha, the ancient link of the mainland with today's Sri Lanka, past Nilācal, the city of Puri in Odisha.

homes. Sumati and Kumati arrived with golden water pots in hand and ceremonially washed their husbands' feet, tendered welcoming gifts, and waved auspicious lamps.

Śrī Kavi Vallabh sings a pleasingly romantic song.

The items they had procured in Pāṭan, they gifted to the women, then they brought out the bird they had procured for Madan. "Listen to what I am asking, Sumati dear, tell me truthfully, where has Madan gone?"

When they heard this question, the two were suddenly all streams of tears. As they wept, they melodramatically smacked their foreheads in grief. Knowing they were mired in deception without end, they wept even harder. "Six months ago our brother-in-law Madan died. He had married the princess Kuntalā, a celebration on which one hundred thousand *ṭākā*s were lavished. The night of the auspicious wedding was passed in the flowered bridal chamber, and the next day that woman devoured our cherished brother-in-law. She ate him! For all those days that have passed since your little brother died, we two women have been unable to eat anything at all."

When they heard these words coming from Sumati's mouth, they could not have felt worse than Lakṣmāṇ shooting an arrow into his brother's, Śrī Rām's chest! "Alas, brother, where have you vanished, leaving the two of us behind? Mother and father died while you were still a small child. We were three brothers, but now you have passed away. In your absence, brother, it is senseless for us to hang onto life. Were one's father to die, at least an elder brother remains. The younger brother can look up to him the same as a father. Were one's mother to die, the elder daughter is there, and the younger brother can call her Mother just like his birth mother. But when a brother has died, O dear brother, there is no consolation, there is nothing more to be said. Our hearts are lacerated with sorrow for Madan."

Sumati submitted this for her husband's consideration: "Beware! There is no enemy, my lord, quite like a brother or close relative. When King Yudhiṣṭhir lost at dice, their cousins claimed possession and disrobed Dropadi in the middle of the assembly. Later, the five Pāṇḍav brothers were trapped in the house of lac and their cousins spread fire all around in order to kill them. I would like to suggest that when a brother is blind or lame and still covets a share of the wealth, you are under no obligation, my dear husband."[24] The two brothers were initially consoled by the seeming vigilance of the two women in looking after their interests. So they decided to take only the *saycān* falcon as a gift to the young bride.

As soon as they removed the bird from its golden cage, it began to chatter excitedly to Kuntalā. It blinked its eyes repeatedly and suggestively and pecked at her face, which only made the daughter of the king weep at the loss of the lord of her life. "My husband had requested this bird be brought, but bringing it now to my rooms only magnifies my anguish. Were the lord of my life present, he would have eaten your flesh—am I to understand that is why you are taking such delight in pecking my face? When my husband abandoned me I have been cruelly tortured, and now that torture is redoubled with the gift of this falcon!" With these words the moon-faced beauty mourned. But in the guise of a mendicant, Satyanārāyaṇ suddenly appeared there. Khoḍā called out, "I command you, bring some alms to feed this *phakir*, and be quick about it!"

The king's daughter spoke respectfully to the phakir *and at the command of that same* pīr, *Śrī Vallabh Kavi sings.*

Kuntalā said, "What have you given me, done for me? What is in my house that I can give to you? I only get about a seer of rice each day, and that is only enough to share with my two maidservants in the evening."

Khodā replied, "If you truly do not have anything at all in your house, then why don't you bring me a tiny palmful of broken rice. To give me that tiny helping of cracked rice will sate my desires, just as Govinda is always pleased with the meager offering I make to him each day. Proffer that small bit of broken rice with heartfelt respect and devotion and I will grant you the boon your heart desires." And so the princess fetched the pitiful helping of cracked rice in order to

24. The lessons of the treachery of close relatives seems to be an effort to lay the blame on Kuntalā for Madan's disappearance—they have already accused her of eating him, which they imply here must have been for his share of their future wealth. Without a husband, Kuntalā is no better off than a poor, blind, or lame relative.

present a *siriṇi* offering to Satyapīr with genuine attentiveness. Her maidservant rushed off to take that tiny portion of broken rice into town to sell it, like one who rushes a piece of found gold to the goldsmith in the jewelry market. Satyapīr then granted Kuntalā her desired boon, and the rice grains in the hand of the servant girl magically turned into pearls. The merchant gave her a fair price for the pearls and with the proceeds from selling the pearls, the maidservant bought *sirini*. She broadcast an invitation to all the inhabitants of the city: "Today, Kuntalā will worship Satyanārāyaṇ!" That evening, all the people in the city—*hindu* and *musalmān* alike—engaged in like-minded devotion. New pots were filled with *sirni* sweetmeats, which the exalted twice-born offered in the name of Satyanārāyaṇ. All the devout recited from the holy text of the *pīr*, then all the people present stood up and made formal greetings of salaam. Afterwards, they distributed *siriṇī* to everyone who had assembled. They ate, licking their hands, then running their hands over their heads in respect.[25] If some of the *sirni* fell on the ground and a bee were to come along and lick it up, that bee would certainly be drunk, giddy with pleasure. The fair woman, Kuntalā, distributed the *sirini* to everyone, and she kept back a single morsel for herself. Then she remembered the *saycān* and placed a tiny bit in its beak. The command was clear: no one was to be left out or deprived! So she lifted some of the *pīr*'s *sirnī* to the mouth of the bird. As soon as it was consumed, the golden cage shattered into a four pieces, and Madansundar shed the form of the bird, just as the young son of Nanda burst forth from the stone pillar.[26] And the chaste wife, who had a heart of pure devotion, magically regained her husband.

25. This is a common gesture when taking an offering of any sort, solid or liquid, consuming it, and then quickly rubbing the residue through one's head (or just above the head without touching) as a sign of humility and a symbolic statement of the relationship of the worshiper to the object of worship. In *pūjās*, this would also include the smoke and flame from waving lights, incense, etc. Once offered to God, the substance is in effect supercharged and its residue envelops the devotee in its power. The gesture is likewise seen when touching the feet of a superior.

26. The reference seems to be to Narasiṃha bursting forth from the pillar when Hiraṇyakāśipu mocks and insults Prahlāda who answered truthfully that yes, his God was indwelling in all things, including the pillar; famously repeated in numerous texts, see the source in *Bhāgavata purāṇa, Skandha* 7, ch. 8 .

The tale now comes to an end, but the song of the pīr's *exploits sails on.*

Śrī Kavi Vallabh sings a mellifluous song, his mind ever immersed in the presence of Satyanārāyaṇ.

The Madansundar pālā *is completed.*
18th of Baiśākh 1162 BS[27]

27. Thursday, 9 May 1755 CE.

Curbing the Hubris of Moses

Curbing the Hubris of Moses

Introduction to Khoyāj Khijir's Instruction to Musā in the Nabīvaṃśa of Saiyad Sultān

translated with Ayesha A. Irani

In a magnificent seventeenth-century Bengali poem titled the *Nabīvaṃśa* or the "Lineage of the Prophet," the Sufi polymath Saiyad Sultān tells the long history of Muhammad and his forebears.[1] He writes quite pointedly for what he characterized as a benighted local audience:

> "Listen, menfolk," cautions Saiyad Sultān, "pay heed
> to this story of the Prophet's lineage, the *Nabivaṃśa* of India.
> The locals cannot approach this tale through Persian,
> much less the Arabic of its original composition,
> so I have rendered it into a language of Hind,
> into the tongue native to Baṅga.
> When they hear it in their own Indic language,
> these morally ignorant peoples might well learn
> what it means to be truly righteous."
>
> Saiyad Sultān, *Nabīvaṃśa*, 1: 696

The larger tale begins with Adam and traces a multitude of major and minor prophets, creatively coopting popular Hindu gods in the process. After a lengthy account of Muhammad's life, the narrative closes at

1. Saiyad Sultān, *Nabīvaṃśa*, edited by Āhmād Śariph, 2 vols. (Ḍhākā: Bāṃlā Ekāḍemī, 1978). For a comprehensive study of the text, see Ayesha Irani, *The Muhammad Avatāra: Salvation History, Translation, and the Making of Bengali Islam* (New York: Oxford University Press, 2021).

the moment of his death. Saiyad Sultān drew from a number of literary works in Arabic, Persian, and languages closer to Bangla, such as Hindavi; yet master narrator that he was, he seamlessly wove this fabled history with a gentle instructional, but not hortatory, mode to make good on his promise to enlighten. The complete text totals something just short of thirty-five thousand lines. It is largely composed in rhymed fourteen-syllable couplets (*payār*), presented here as prose, and interspersed with emotionally charged triplets (*tripadi*) in free verse.

In our short translated passage, Saiyad Sultān produced an elegant rendition of the Qur'ānic story of al-Khiḍr—locally known in Bangla as Khoyāj Khijir or Khejer, a master of esoteric knowledge enlisted by Āllā to prick the Prophet Musā's ego and curb his impatience and hubris.[2] The original source of the tale's three enigmatic episodes is the synoptic version found in the Qur'ān (18:60–82), but the story was embellished as it moved through the varied languages of the expanded Islamic world. The particular story of Khijir and Musā that we have translated bears more than a passing resemblance to the Arabic version in the *Qiṣaṣ al-anbiyā'*, or *Tales of the Prophet,* of Muḥammad ibn 'Abd Allāh al-Kisā'ī,[3] but in details seems to have followed more closely the text of Juwayrī's Persian composition of the same title.[4] In the version that follows, God assigns Musā to the tutelage of Khoyāj Khijir, who does so on the condition that Musā is but to watch and learn, never to question his actions. Of course, Musā cannot restrain himself from asking for explanations about Khijir's puzzling actions: when Khijir knocks holes in the bottom of a perfectly good boat, or kills what appeared to be an innocent boy, or rebuilds a deteriorated stone wall without compensation. Their time together generates a compelling narrative of the mystical powers of the great Messengers as they undertake their inspired work, demonstrating Khijir's entertaining moral and theological discourse, whose mysteries challenge

2. Saiyad Sultān, *Nabīvaṃśa*, 1: 670–87.

3. Muḥammad ibn 'Abd Allāh al-Kisā'ī, *Qiṣaṣ al-anbiyā'*, edited by Isaac Eisenberg, Vita prophetarum, 2 vols. (Leiden: E. J. Brill, 1922–23), 230–33; see Muḥammad ibn 'Abd Allāh al-Kisā'i, *Tales of the Prophets* (*Qiṣaṣ al-anbiyā'*), translated by Wheeler M. Thackston Jr. (Chicago: Kazi Publications, 1997), 247–50.

4. Muḥammad Juwayrī, *Qiṣaṣ al-anbiyā'*, 4th ed. (Tehran, n.p., n.d.), 182–87.

ordinary people and confounds even the learned Musā himself. After the third breach of Musā's promise not to question, they part ways.

When Khoyāj Khijir, known as the "Green Man," began to appear in Bengal, his activities were often likened to and sometimes shared with those of the prophet Elias, with whom he has been on occasion depicted.[5] He was and still is associated with flowing waters, not only of the mangrove swamps of the Āṭhārobhāṭī that we know as the Sundarbans, but of all Bengal's rivers and the Bay of Bengal. Even today, it is a rare fisherman or boatman who does not turn to him for protection. On occasion he might be glimpsed surfing, riding the whitecaps of the expansive bay on his wooden sandals, or riding a fish as he goes about his mysterious business, and in this, his image and stories are often conflated with those of the legendary Badar Pīr of Chittagong, who reputedly floated across the Bay of Bengal on a boulder. For a figure that is widely known, Khoyāj Khijir has had precious few stories in Bangla to call his own; he has remained elusive and enigmatic, and when he has surfaced in one of our narratives, he has seldom appeared as himself, rather being invariably invisible or in a disguise that only the enlightened can discern.

In the longer narratives of the Bengali *pīrs*, Khijir tends to disappear as quickly as he mysteriously appears, usually at a critical juncture to aid the struggling protagonist. In Ābdul Ohab's telling of *Gāji kālu o cāmpāvatī kanyār puthi* translated as the second story above, he is ordered by Khodā, God, to help Gāji in the last of the all-but-impossible ordeals ordered by his father Śekandar, to find a needle thrown into the sea. First, he enlists the help of two giants celestials, Śura and Āśvari, to excavate and sift the sand, but without luck, then through meditation, he discover that the needle was used to pin up the hair of a princess in the underworld citadel of Pātāla, and he retrieves it. Later in his peregrinations, Gāji recognizes Khoyāj several times, though his half brother Kālu does not, the latter on the road when Khijir assumes the guise of a child. Later Khijir is found in a mosque where the queen of local king Śrī Rām is held captive, secured carefully in a separate room, by which Khijir ensures that her honor is in

5. Ananda K. Coomaraswamy, "Kwaja Khadir and the Fountain of Life in Persian and Mughal Art," in *"What Is Civilization" and Other Essays* (Cambridge: Golgosova Press, 1989), 157–67.

no way violated. On several occasions. Gāji publicly acknowledges him as his teacher.

In the lengthy saga devoted to the life of Satya Pīr, the closest thing to a fully developed hagiography in the fictional *pīr* literature, titled *Baḍa satya pīr o sandhyāvatī kanyār puthi* by the *darveś* Kṛṣṇahari Dās, it is Khijir who recognizes Satya Pīr immediately after his unusual birth. His birth is multi-staged, first from the womb of Sandhyāvatī as an unformed uterine mass, which she throws into the river, where it is swallowed by a turtle, who encases that mass in one of her leathery eggs and drops it onto a sandbank, where Satya Pīr soon hatches, undergoing a second birth, this time fully formed. Khijir is on watch and Satya Pīr instantly recognizes and acknowledges him for who he is. When Khijir confirms that the birth was a success and makes himself invisible, Satya Pīr follows the sounds of his anklets until they reach the Underworld, where Khijir initiates him as his student. For five years Khijir tutors Satya Pīr in the esoteric techniques necessary to wield that wonder-working power called *kerāmat*. It is during this instruction that he learns to control the elements of the natural world, and with those powers he is able to conjure storms, shape-shift into a giant or shrink to a fly, converse with the bears, tigers, serpents, and crocodiles, or bend the physical world to his needs, evidence of which abounds in that hagiography. Significantly, it is Khijir's initiation that grants Satya Pīr the exalted recognition of *jindā pīr*, the "living *pīr*," the superlative designation of rank among accomplished Sufis.[6]

The tale told by Saiyad Sultān is of special literary and historical import, because it is through the figure of Khijir that the Bangla stories of the *phakir*s began to integrate themselves into the narratives of the larger world of Islamic literature and history. It is al-Khiḍr who is the tutor and guide of Alexander the Great in his search for the fountain of immortality, which Alexander fails to find, while al-Khiḍr does. Being immortal, al-Khiḍr lives from age to age, becoming the *murśid*, or teacher, of all of the great Sufi saints of history, such as Abū Yazīd al-Bisṭāmī, Ḥusayn b. Manṣūr al-Ḥallāj, ʻAbd al-Qādir al-Jīlānī, Rūz-

6. Kṛṣṇahari Dās, *Baḍa satya pīr o sandhyāvatī kanyār puthi* (Kalikātā: Nūruddīn Āhmed at Gaosiyā Lāibrerī, n.d.). For more on these stories, including translations, see Stewart, *Witness to Marvels*, esp. ch. 1 and ch. 6

bihān Baqlī, and Muḥyī l-Dīn Ibn 'Arabī.[7] For at least three millennia, Khoyāj Khijir, or al-Khiḍr, is the teachers' teacher, as he clearly demonstrates in this retelling in the short tale that follows of the Qur'ānic episode of instruction to the learned Musā by Saiyad Sultān. Satya Pīr and Gāji Pīr, the heroes of other tales in this anthology, join these select few initiates, in so doing, making room for Bengali figures in the wider constellation of Sufi luminaries.

7. To understand the place of al-Khiḍr in Sufi traditions, see Hugh Talat Halman, *Where the Two Seas Meet: The Qur'ānic Story of al-Khiḍr and Moses in Sufi Commentaries as a Model of Spiritual Guidance* (Louisville: Fons Vitae, 2013); for a comprehensive study of al-Khiḍr in the literatures of the Middle East, see Patrick Franke, *Begegnung mit Khiḍr: Quellenstudien zum Imaginären im traditionellen Islam*, Beiruter Texte und Studien 79 (Stuttgart: Franz Steiner, 2000).

PRIMARY ACTORS, HUMAN AND DIVINE

Āllā, Nirañjan the Stainless – God

Iblis – the Devil, Śaytān, primordial rebel against Āllā

Iusā – companion of Musā

Jibrāil – the angel Gabriel

Kālut – exemplary *musalmān,* who attends to the welfare of the people

Khoyāj Khijir – teacher of all the greatest Sufi saints, and who drank from the fountain of life and so never dies

Musā, Son of Emrān – the biblical prophet or apostle Moses

Paygāmbar – Messengers, i.e., Khoyāj Khijir and Musā

Curbing the Hubris of Moses

Khoyāj Khijir's Instruction to Musā in the Nabīvaṃśa of Saiyad Sultān

translated by Ayesha A. Irani and Tony K. Stewart

THE COLLOQUY OF MUSĀ AND ĀLLĀ

It happened that the Messenger Musā wished to speak directly with Āllā, so he took himself to the enchanted reaches of Mount Sinai, for in that place Musā could converse freely with his Lord. At God's command, Jibrāil brought a golden throne to seat the Prophet. It was the throne that Musā always used in his conversations with Āllā. When he received the Lord's gracious answers to his queries, he returned to relay those conversations directly to the multitudes. Six or seven thousand men of distinction made the trek to Mount Sinai to greet Musā, and another seven thousand beautiful young women—the daughters of the prophets, all of noble lineage—went as well. They gathered to hear the words of the Lord directly from the Prophet Musā, the Messenger himself. Taking his high seat on the pulpit's lectern, he moved directly to the public reading of the Book of the Torah. Those good people listened to the Book of the Torah and when he left off, their minds rippled with the thrill of hearing the Lord's words. A wave of rapture raced through the Prophet Musā as he began to address the learned there among the assembled. "I spoke directly with Nirañjan, the Stainless. The Lord Nirañjan answered my queries and I in turn responded directly to the Stainless Lord regarding those questions he posed to me. There was no moderating intermediary between the Lord and me, nor did he see fit to summon the angel Jibrāil."

On a later day when the Prophet Musā had assembled his people, he read from the Torah to remind them of the principles of morality. "The Lord gave me special assurance: 'You shall not enter into sin.' The Creator made me understand my special dispensation, and he commanded me to express my concerns directly to him, the Lord."

At this, two men stood up in the assembly and began to question the Prophet. "Tell us, in all truth, is there any single person who knows more than you? Tell us, truly, whether or not there is a scholar anywhere greater than you, anyone more learned." Then Musā the Prophet said to them, "All that I utter is impelled by the Lord and Creator. I do not know whether anyone exists in the triple world who might know more than I."

MUSĀ'S HUBRIS AND KHOYĀJ KHIJIR'S INSTRUCTION

As soon as Musā uttered this self-aggrandizing praise, Nirañjan the Stainless was incensed and through Jibrāil fired off a rejoinder, "There are untold numbers of my servants and you certainly do not know nearly as much as they. Do not be so vain and boast about how great you are. You are not even aware that there are those who know more than you."

After he received this rebuke, Musā the high-minded Prophet respectfully addressed Jibrāil. "Tell me, brother Jibrāil, where do these meritorious and learned men dwell? Tell me, Sir, what are their names? Tell me precisely where I might be able to find them." Then the Lord responded again through the mouth of his emissary, "It is forbidden to speak openly of these matters." But he did say, "There are large numbers of the learned who are greater than you, nor are you equal to them in insight and erudition. You should go and become a disciple of one of those great scholars, only then will you attain their knowledge. Go and seek one of them."

When he heard this, the Prophet was ashamed, and bowing in obeisance to Nirañjan, the Stainless, he quickly replied, "Where shall I seek out a *guru* so replete with knowledge and insight? By what name is he called? Where should I search for him?" Again through the mouth of his emissary, Nirañjan sent instruction for him to search along the shores of the ocean. "He goes by the name of Khoyāj Khijir." He commanded him to go to his place and become his disciple. He ordered, "Go to the shore of the sea through whose waters dead beings pass over to the living. Along the shores of that sea will you meet him and you will honor him as your *guru*. Then those matters that leave you befuddled will disappear. When you gain that wisdom your mental bewilderment will dissipate."

As soon as he heard this, Musā, the esteemed Prophet, had Iusā fetch some flat breads, while he purchased a fish before setting out. Then the Apostle embarked with Iusā as company. The two men journeyed to the shores of the sea and began to search for sight of Khoyāj. There was a boulder perched on the banks of a river and the two men headed straight for it. The Prophet Musā instructed Iusā, "Stay here while I go to perform my ablutions." When Musā went to relieve himself, he was slow, taking his time. Meanwhile, Iusā waited patiently on top of the rock and from there spotted a bubbling spring close by. Iusā made for the fount and performed his own ablutions in the clean and clear waters he found there. Water from his hands splashed onto the fish, which had been previously seared and then kept in a clay pot. That spring was the legendary pool of immortality, the *amṛta kuṇḍa*. A single drop of its waters fell onto the fish and it sprang to life. Suddenly revivified, the fish plunged into the sea. Iusā personally watched this transpire, but it left his mind awhirl and, flummoxed, he was not clearheaded enough to tell Musā when the latter returned from relieving himself.

They walked on and when they had gone some distance from that place, the Apostle Musā addressed Iusā. "I am beginning to feel a gnawing in my belly," he groused, "so do give me some of that fish to eat." Iusā examined the pot, fully expecting to pull out the fish, but when he felt around inside he did not find the fish. Suddenly it all came back, so Iusā said to the Apostle, "That cooked fish is no longer here in the pot. When you left me to relieve yourself and told me to sit on that boulder, I saw a sparkling clear spring, so I went and performed my ablutions with its waters. When a drop of that water fell on the fish, the fish came back to life and dove into the sea. I witnessed this with my own eyes, but the memory of it escaped me. Confused and deluded by the devil Iblis, I failed to tell you."

As soon as he heard this, the high-minded Prophet Musā ran quickly back to the rock. He saw the waters gushing up from the rock's pool—rising up and falling back, the waters swirling into a vortex. As soon as he saw it, the Prophet Musā plunged straight into the waters. He dove in and then remained submerged deep under the waters, where he spotted a strange dome looming above him—it was the place where the two seas flowed together into one. Yet the waters of the one and of the other flowed without mixing together. Then he saw, situated within the dome where the two seas met, someone performing the ritual prayer, bowing in *nāmāj*. He had spread a mat of woven pearls there under the dome and was alternately rising and kneeling down in prayer. When he had returned to a sitting position after completing the full complement of prayers, the Prophet Musā stepped forward and made deep obeisance.

Khoyāj Khijir already knew that this was the Prophet Musā; he politely returned his gesture of obeisance and greeted him. Khijir asked, "Musā, why have you come? In truth, tell me."

Musā replied, "To become your disciple. The Creator has sent me to become your disciple."

Right then a bird came there to the sea and took up one drop of those waters. Watching it, Khoyāj then observed to Musā, "Previously you had considered yourself to be extremely learned. That bird you observed with your own senses just now sipped one drop of water through its beak—all the scholars there are in the world are unable to fathom even a drop of the knowledge of God and so are wretched. Those great scholars who went before and who will come after are equally worthless, because they failed to fathom even a drop of God's majesty. You brag that you know him. What hubris leads you to utter such sacrilegious words? There is no end to the glory and majesty of God. Neither you nor I have the power to comprehend. I know this fully, but how can I put it into words? I will never be able to fathom the full extent of God's majesties. The knowledge that you and I possess is like that single drop of water the bird sipped from the vast waters of the sea."

The Prophet Musā told the Khoyāj, "I have accepted you as *guru*. I will remain close in your company and serve you. I know intuitively that you will make me aware, enlighten me."

Khoyāj cut off the Prophet Musā and said, "You, my good man, will not be able to keep up with me. When you witness what things I do, you will be utterly bewildered. When you see me in action, you may call me 'stupid' or even 'bad.' You will find it impossible to remain with me when you see my actions. You will hurl vile imprecations at me, casting aspersions such as 'evil.'"

Musā replied, "I will maintain my equanimity and remain calm. No matter what you do, I will not intercede or object."

Khoyāj went on, "Listen, Prophet Musā, I have made up my mind firmly on this matter. You may come along with me only if you never question anything that I may do. If you question or doubt me about any action, then under no circumstances will I take you along. If you commit your mind to this and pledge before me, we'll get along famously." Hearing him out, the Prophet Musā confirmed his pledge, for only then could he accompany Khoyāj.

After they had travelled some distance, they came upon a large body of water, and the two *paygāmbar*s, Messengers, boarded a boat. A number of hands scrambled onto it, and it pushed off, taking them on their way. When the boat was at the midpoint of the waters, Khoyāj Khijir began to break it up. Taking his staff in hand, Khoyāj Paygāmbar set about punching out the bottom planks of the hull. Watching this take place, the Prophet Musā was dumbfounded. As he witnessed this bizarre action, he questioned Khoyāj. "Why have you dismantled the boat and scuttled it in the middle of the waters? Do you intend to drown all the boatmen?"

Khoyāj replied, "You have taken a firm pledge that you would not question me about anything. Now you have broken your pledge and challenge me. Go wherever you may, but you are not accompanying me."

Musā stammered, "I questioned you without thinking. Please find compassion in your heart and overlook my mistake. If I question you again, then you should dismiss me from your company." When the Prophet Musā put it this way, Khijir gave him permission to accompany him further.

They walked some distance and when a young boy crossed their path, Khoyāj grabbed him and instantly chopped him to pieces. The Prophet Musā looked on with horrified confusion. "Why did you just slay someone's child? Anyone who hears this will deem you a wicked man."

Khijir said, "Again you have broken your pledge. You continue to question me over and over. I know whether my actions are good or bad. Who are you to question me when perplexity rules your heart? You may accompany me no longer. It is no longer meet for you and I to remain together."

Musā pleaded, "I blundered, please again forgive this mistake. I unthinkingly questioned you, so please forgive this infraction. Graciously indulge me and take me along with you."

Khijir replied, "If you question me one more time, you and I will have to go our separate ways." Khoyāj Khijir, with Musā in tow, eventually landed up in the village of Turuki. Though the bellies of the pair were burning, not one among the people living there offered them anything to eat. Rather than feed the newly arrived, these sinful people ducked and hid. Sinners all, they did not even acknowledge the Prophets' presence. A treasure trove of priceless gems had fallen into the hands of those sinful people, but because of their perverted and unholy actions, that treasure slipped right through their fingers. Had they but satisfied the two by giving them food, an incalculable merit would have accrued to them in this world and the next. Those who fail to feed a guest meet with great suffering in this world and the next. So the two Messengers passed over that land without stopping.

When they had walked for some indeterminate distance, they ran across a massive wall that was listing and uneven. Khoyāj Khijir went over for a closer inspection. It spanned seventy-five cubits in height and one hundred-fifty cubits in length. The wall was in total disrepair, broken down and unsteady. It was leaning precipitously where its stonework was damaged.

Khoyāj said to the Prophet Musā, "We need to dance for our dinner. I have nothing with which we can buy food to eat. Come on, you and I together will go and find some work." The Prophet Musā then asked him, "Tell me, what sort of manual labor shall we do?" Khijir replied, "This wall is sound, but it is beginning to sag and list, so we shall shore it up and straighten it out. The owner of this fine wall will pay us for our labors." Musā applied himself to one side of the wall and Khijir to the other and they pushed and pulled, adjusting its structure. The two *paygāmbars*, strategically placed on either side of the wall, soon wrestled the wall back to its intended upright state. When they had repaired the wall to its original condition, Musā again began to question Khoyāj. "Who is going to pay us for the work we did? Why did we exert so much effort in vain on this job? Without taking money in advance, for whom have we exerted ourselves in hard labor? Our efforts have gone for naught. One settles on a wage in advance and only then does one undertake that work. If they had paid a little compensation, given even a little for the evening food, we would not have been laboring meaninglessly for free."

The moment the Prophet Musā uttered this reproach, Khoyāj Khijir lectured him. "You had given your word that you would not question me. You promised never to second-guess my actions. You have questioned me yet again and broken your solemn pledge. You have used up your opportunities to accompany me. Under no circumstance shall you accompany me further. You are no longer welcome to remain with me. Understand that you and I have parted ways."

The Prophet Musā took this very hard, and he clutched the hem of Khoyāj's robe, begging and pleading. In an act of contrition, Musā the Prophet petitioned Khoyāj over and again. Paygāmbar Musā then said, "If you will not take me with you, then please explain the meaning of these three incidents. For what purpose did you come to sink the boat of another person? To what end did you lay hold of some stranger's child and cut him to pieces? Why did you straighten up the wall of some unknown owner? Tell me the truth in a way I can comprehend." And when the son of Emrān begged him in this way, Khoyāj Khijir relented and began to explain.

KHOYĀJ'S EXPLANATION OF ESOTERIC TRUTHS

"The ruler of that first land
is the most wicked of men.
    He waylays and robs everyone.
When he spots a seaworthy vessel,
he steals it from them.
    He does not pay for it, but simply appropriates it.
Those people owned the boat that ferried us across the waters—
    they are good *musalmāns*.
Apart from that one vessel,
they possessed no other property—
    that boat alone was all they had.
Had that boat been confiscated,
they would not be able to come and go,

and they would not be able to sustain their trade.
If their vessel were kept shipshape,
there is no way they could retain it,
for some strongman would come and carry it off.
This is why I scuttled the boat,
for when those evil men see the boat damaged,
they will not bother to take it away.
Now do you understand why I was anxious,
concerned that the boat not be stolen?
But you judged this to be a mistaken, imprudent act.
Were the boat to remain with its owners—
even though damaged—
it could be repaired and made seaworthy.
But had the boat been stolen,
it would be difficult, if not impossible, to retrieve—
they could never pry it from the hands of the strongman."

"Later, I seized the young child,
I reasoned through the apparent reality,
which is why I put him to death.
He regularly thrashes his father;
that evil miscreant nags him
endlessly to become infidel.
Were he to remain alive,
he would continue his perverse ways
to confound his parents.
He would maneuver his mother and father unwillingly
to associate with clans of unbelievers
to turn both of them into infidels.
His mother and father both
are of exemplary conduct,
committed to righteous *musalmāni* acts.
But the son is of extremely vile character
with a mind bent on becoming a disbeliever;
He did not follow the *musalmānī* way.
The darling of his mother and father
he abandoned the principled *musalmānī* practice
to enter into the throngs of heretics.
His mother and father would advise him
not to run with infidel clans,
but he was set on doing as he pleased.

Had he been allowed to live
he would have committed so many wicked deeds
that he would have dragged his parents into hell with him.
Though born of a pure lineage
he confessed to the path of the unrighteous—
and that is the reason I killed him.
Had this child gone on living
continuing to commit his foul deeds,
he would have defiled his entire lineage.
By losing his life,
he gains residence in Paradise
and his manifold sins have now been completely effaced.
To console the horrible grief
of his mother and father,
the Lord will lavish on them many descendants.
Each and every one will be pure-minded,
they will engage in no untoward acts,
and they will perform pious acts of immense proportion.
The Lord and Creator will send
a solitary girl into their household—
a daughter in exchange for a son.
The Creator has decreed that
from this one girl's line, large numbers
of Prophets and Messengers will be produced.
The Lord, the Stainless Nirañjan, has ordered
that from this one girl's bloodline
seventy Apostles, *rasul*s, will spring forth.
Had I not slain the wicked boy,
they would never get the immaculate girl-child,
but would be stuck with the youngster who was evil.
Bad deeds had been placed among good,
now good has been vouchsafed through the bad.
You comprehended nothing of this."

Then Khoyāj Khijir
began step by step to explain
the business of the wall.
"The person who owns the wall
resides in Medina,
where he has lived permanently.
He is good-humored in heart,

possesses great wealth,
    and has given pious charity generously.
When he makes a loan to a man
he takes no profit whatsoever,
    nor does he take harsh measures to recover those loans.
He tells them to return the money
whenever it suits them;
    and he does not ask for settlement until then.
If the borrower wishes to settle his loan amicably,
he goes to collect it in a manner that is proper—
    only then does he accept the full payment.
But when the person is unable to repay the debt,
he explains he will not forcibly take the money,
    nor enlist the help of a debt collector.
His name is Kālut
and night and day he tirelessly
    works for the welfare of other people.
He has never harmed anyone,
nor has he ever uttered a lie;
    he abstains from all untoward behavior.
Kālut is always known
to have an agreeable temperament
    and he has never usurped another's property or land.
For this reason Nirañjan, the Stainless,
gave instruction to Jibrāil
    to look out for his welfare."
Says Saiyad Sultān,
Listen all you musalmāns*:*
    Good surely begets good.
He who commits wicked deeds,
will later be counted among the wicked,
    and for all eternity will suffer in hell.

KHIJIR'S FURTHER REFLECTIONS ON THE ESOTERIC

That Kālut had procured an exquisite emerald pendant, which he purchased for a staggering sum. On it he had inscribed five aphorisms, executed most diligently, then had it strung on a necklace of pearls. That noble man had secured an emerald of great value, and etched it with five aphorisms ever so carefully.

The first aphorism struck me as remarkably insightful:

In the distribution of wealth to any and every one, I accrue merit,
yet why do those recipients themselves shun the doing of virtuous deeds?
Why are they so heedlessly blasé about doing good?
These people seem unfailingly self-satisfied with the way things are;
not a single person gives a thought about dying.

Alas, the second was equally insightful:

Those men, without exception, are destined to die and enter the grave.
Why do those people build such towering mansions
and live in such grandeur, oblivious of looming death?

The third struck me as similarly astute.

When I know that death is inevitable, how can I remain unmindful?

The fourth observation was shrewd.

Why do those people, who know that hell holds punishments aplenty,
become so stupidly obtuse that they commit sin?
By being heedless, then, they are sure to reside in hell.

The fifth struck me as comparably insightful.

Everyone knows the truth that God is the Provider.
Why do those, whose innards are starved for something to eat,
not remember that it is God the Creator who will provide?

These are the five contemplative points he inscribed on the pendant and he wore it around his neck at all times. Whenever the pendant caught his eye, he pondered those five truisms, and that is why it was fixed around his neck at all times.

That Kālut was a noble man, a possessor of magnificent merit, and he owned enormous sums in treasures and jewels. And those riches he hid, secured beneath that wall, yet no other person had an inkling as to where to find that immense fortune. He had two sons, both still quite young at the time when he revealed to them where to find that treasure trove. But that honorable man has died, and the two small children are now orphaned by his passing. He provided explicit instructions about the wealth and told them to retrieve it when they had reached maturity. Without their father, the boys were certain to lose the treasure, for bereft of guidance they would not remember how to recover it. I knew that with their father dead, the boys would never retrieve the treasure, and I would be unable to preserve it were it to come to the attention of other people. The angels would have rightly chastised me: "Khoyāj Khijir, you did not do right by those orphaned children!" So for these reasons I rebuilt that wall, straightening it up, putting it back the way it had originally been. I explained to you that we needed to work to secure a little something to buy food to eat. You labored, then, for those two orphaned boys, and you received your wages in merit from Nirañjan, the Stainless. Not comprehending these actions, you found fault with me and, at the time, I was unable to reveal the secrets of these matters to you.

I have now revealed to you these three episodes, and I have divulged the esoteric meaning of all three. Henceforth you may not accompany me, but there are two significant issues I want you to consider, to hold dear. The first issue is this:

Just by remembering me, you will develop a conscientious discretion.
Never let anger crease your face, never hurl harsh words at anyone.

And the other piece of advice I hope you will take to heart:

Do not go anywhere without a purpose.
When some musalmāns *undertake a particular task,*
that they themselves cannot accomplish by any means,
only then should you go to assist them.
Otherwise, you should always stay within your own home.

When he had said this, Khoyāj Khijir went on his way.

The Prophet Musā then returned to Tihāt and all the Bani Isrāil came up to him. They began to question the Prophet Musā: "Reveal to us all that you have learned, so you may propagate that same wisdom in all of us, awaken us."

Musā the Prophet said to all those assembled, "You would not be able to fathom that which you heard. All of the Apostles, *rasul*s, understand these esoteric issues, but it would serve no purpose were you to hear of these inscrutable matters."

GLOSSARY

ābādī – a properly settled, well-functioning or cultivated community

abhimān – sensitivity to social snub or insult, esp. lover's pique, sometimes feigned

adhibās – preparatory and protective rituals for the bride to ensure a successful marriage

ādibāsī – term for indigenous inhabitants of the land who live more or less apart from the traditional social structures of both *hinduyāni* and *musalmāni* Bengal

ājān – call to prayer; from Persian *azān*

ākhon – instructor of traditional elementary school, *maktab* or *kuttāb*

ākṣārā – fundamental elements of existence

akṣauhiṇī – an army array composed of 109,350 foot soldiers; 65,610 cavalry on horseback; 21,870 on elephants, and 21,870 in chariots; *caturaṅga,* q.v.

amṛta kuṇḍa – legendary pool of immortality

apamān – offense at social snub or insult, pique

asura – a class of anti-gods who often engage the gods in battle over control of the universe

Āṭhārobhāṭī – low-lying lands of the eighteen tides, the Sundarbans

āuliyā – sainthood

avatār – a descent of God or appearing in the image of one *bāḍ* – somewhat derogatory term for an indigenous inhabitant of the land, or *ādibāsī*, q.v.

bādsā, bādśā, bādśāh – king, emperor, ruler

bāṅgāl, bāṅgālī – eastern portion of the Bangla-speaking region; a person from that region, with disrespectful overtones of inferiority; in early modern stories, nearly all of the boatmen were recruited from the east

baraka, barakat, bhaḍaka – a quality of saintly figures who receive this special blessing of charisma from God, but which also carries responsibilties for righting the world; often associated with and even confused with *kerāmat,* q.v.

bāramās – a poetic lament describing the pain one feels through each of the twelve months

bāṭā – a traditional first offering of food by a bride's father to the man who will be his son-in-law

bāulyā – traditional class of timber-cutters, haulers of wood, and escorts for workmen to ward off tigers

bechmellā – *bismillā,* q.v.

beg – honorable one

behest, bhest, bihisht – paradise, the citadel of heaven; *vaikuṇtha*, q.v.

bhābi, bhābī – sister-in-law, wife of the husband's elder brother

bhaḍaka – spiritual charisma bestowed by God on worthy Sufis; *baraka,* q.v.

bhagavān – standard epithet for God, especially among *vaiṣṇavs*

bhaṇitā – signature line often containing autobiographical information about the author or comments on the characters in the narrative

bhāratī – an elegant recitation form

bhāṭi – low-lying lands; cf. Āṭhārobhāṭī

bhest – paradise, God's realm, *behest,* q.v.

bhūt, bhut – hungry ghosts or ghouls

bibi, bibī – a respected *musalmāni* woman, sometimes a female Sufi of stature

bighā – roughly a third of an acre

bihisht – paradise; *behest,* q.v.

bismillā, bichmillā, bichimillā, bismilla, bechmellā – invocation "In the name of God"; often used in these stories as a kind of *mantra,* q.v.

brāhmaṇ – a priest, one who holds the highest rank in traditional *hindu* society, f., *brāhmaṇi,* the wife of a *brāhmaṇ caturaṅga* – a classical Indic array of soldiers on elephants, chariots, cavalry, and infantry, *akṣauhiṇī*, q.v.

caubāñc – Bengali version of the dice game called *caupaṛa* or Pachisi

caudhurī – chief revenue collector and headman of a region

cautriś – a poetic form that starts each verse with the succeeding letter of the alphabet, whose deployment allows the author to display his skill

chāheb – see *saheb, sāheb,* q.v.

chilimili – a Sufi's necklace that serves as a rosary for tracking recitation of the names of God

crore – ten million

ḍākinī – witch in the form of a virago

ḍāl – split pulses, especially lentils, dal

dānav, dānava – demon; offspring of Danu and Kaśyapa who became implacable foes of the gods

daṅka – the double-ended *dhol* drum, which has a bass end played with a wooden stick called a *dagga* or *daṅka*, the higher register end being played with a lighter *thili* stick

darbār – court, assembly hall, audience chamber

dargā – tomb of a Sufi saint; also the heavenly court of God

darśan – to glimpse, look, or see; as a ritual act to view an image of the god or goddess, or to see a prominent individual; reciprocally, the object of one's gaze shows itself and returns the gaze, which is to "give" *darśan*

darveś – generic name for a Sufi mendicant, dervish

deo – a demigod or spirit; extremely powerful and dangerous

deoyān, deoān – a "summoner" of people to join the community of practitioners of Islam, the *umma* or *ommā,* q.v.

dev, devatā – generic term for a traditional Indic god

devi, devī – generic term for a traditional Indic goddess

dharma – the traditional Indic regulatory principle of the universe, which dictates propriety and proper conduct according to one's social rank; morality; personal duty

ḍhol – a drum, often glossed as tomtom

dhuti, Eng. dhoti – the traditional pleated Indic cloth wrapped around the lower body of a man, always used on formal occasions

din, dīn – faith, religion

dobhāṣī – a register of the Bangla language that includes many words imported from Urdu, Persian, and Arabic; often simply called *musalmāni* Bangla.

dundubhi – small double-headed drum, each head being alternately struck with a ball on a string

dvija – twice-born; a *brāhmaṇ* priest

ejjat, ijjat – honor, prestige, stature; from Persian *izzat,* q.v.

ellālā, elellā, ellellāha – the first few syllables indexing the first pillar of the Islamic injunction "There is no God but God . . ."

emām – spiritual leader, *imām*

esk – passionate love, equated with *prem*; the experience that characterizes the burning love a Sufi has for God; from Persian *'ishq,* q.v.; cf. *prem*

gajamati – the largest size of pearls, styled "elephant" (*gaja*) pearl (*mati*), which in addition to size invokes the bulging gland on the temples of rutting elephants

gāji – a Sufi warrior saint

gandhabāṇik kul – the traditional community of spice-traders and perfumers

gandharva – celestial musician and image of celestial beauty

garbhapatra – guarantee letter issued by a man attesting to the pregnancy of his wife prior to his departure

gopī, gupī – cowherd girls, favorite objects of Kṛṣṇa's affections in his adolescent years

gosāñi, gosā̃i, gosāi, gõsāi, gosvāi, gosvāy – spiritual guide; protector, overlord

guru – traditional Indic spiritual teacher, but also a synonym for *murśid,* q.v.

hāḍi – low-caste wood-cutter, carpenter

hakikat – the third stage or step in Sufi practice, distinguishing the transient from the real; from Arabic *ḥaqīqa*

hakiki – divine beloved

hālāl – meat prepared according to Muslim prescription

hindu, hinduyān; adj. *hinduyāni* – individual following traditional Indic social norms; adj. traditional or Indic

homa – the traditional Vedic sacrificial fire still retained in brāhmaṇical rituals, such as weddings

Indrapuri – the heavenly citadel of the king of the gods, Indra

icchlām – Islam

ijjat, ejjat – honor, prestige; from Persian *izzat*

'ishq – pure love, *esk*, q.v.; cf., *prem*

īśvar – supreme lord, overlord

jabāi – ritual slaughter

jaban, jauban – foreigner, etymologically derived from "Ionian," to indicate a foreigner, who in these texts is nearly always a *musalmān*.

jāgaraṇ – an overnight vigil for reciting the story of a god or goddess

jahur, jahurā – fame, glory, acclamation

jāigir, jāygīr, jāgīr – a holding or assigned territory awarded for service by the governing agency

jāti – social standing by birth, often equated with the modern term "caste"

jikir – an act of remembrance through the recitation of the names and qualities of God, used for meditation; from Arabic *dhikr*, Persian *zikir*

jindā pīr – the "living" Sufi saint or teacher, signaling the highest spiritual achievement; from Persian *zinda*

jinn – genies, supernatural figures composed of flames, who shapeshift, and who mislead and create trouble for humans

jiyārat – a formal visit to the tomb of a prophet or saint, often for the sake of petition; from Persian *ziyarat*, pilgrimage

jñāti-kuṭumba – one's own relatives and one's relatives by marriage

jogi, jugi – practioner of yoga, ascetic

jogini, joginī – a female practitioner of yoga, but with the connotation of being a witch who uses her powers for nefarious ends

kāḍā – a small drum

kāji – judge; from Arabic *qāḍi*

kālām kitāb – the holy writ of the Korān

kālarātri – second night of a wedding, where bride and groom remain apart, recalling the legendary saga of Behulā, whose husband Lakhindār was killed by snakebite on their wedding night

kalemā – generally, the declaration that "there is no God but God," and in the greater South Asian context a sixfold declaration about the nature of the divine and the world

kaphar, kāphir – one who does not believe in God, an infidel; from Arabic *kafīr*

karma – action; the law of cause and effect, which is evaluated by its measure against proper conduct, *dharma*, q.v.

kartā, karttā – master, controller; epithet for God as the Creator

kathā – story

kāṭhā – a measure of land, one-twentieth of a *bighā*, which is approximately one-third of an acre, so about sixty-seven square meters

kāyastha, kāyesta, kāyet – caste group who served as scribes

kecchā – story or tale, from Arabic *qiṣṣā*

kerāmat, kerāmati – miracle-working power of accomplished Sufis, usually deployed to convince the unbeliever; from Arabic *karāmāt*

khilāphat, khelāphat – a realm established to cultivate the worship of God and to cultivate an ideal Islamic society or *ābādī*, q.v., related to, but not to be confused with, "caliphate"

kichaḍi – a colorful mishmash, usually of snack foods, but applied to other things

koś́, koṣ - a flat-bottom ship with a hundred oars

kroś́ – a land distance of about two miles

kul – family or clan, lineage, race; often paired with *jāti*

lakh – one hundred thousand

machalmān – *muchalmān, musalmān*, q.v.

machjed, machjid – mosque, *masjid*, q.v.

mahārāj – king, great king

mahārānī, mahārāni – queen consort of the *mahārāj*, q.v.

makar – a mythical creature, often described as part alligator and part goat, identified with Capricorn; the preferred vehicle of the goddess Gaṅgā

maktab – traditional elementary school teaching Qur'ānic recitation, reading, writing, and grammar, all laced with religious instruction

mān – sensitivity to social snub or insult, pique; *abhimān*, q.v.

maṅgal kāvya – genre of semi-epic poems about Bengali gods and goddesses

mandir – temple

mantra – short Sanskrit utterance that often has magical power (terms like *guru, mantra*, and *karma* are italicized in this book for their technical Indic meanings)

mārphat – the fourth and final stage or step of Sufi practice, gnosis; *makām*; from Arabic *maqām*

masjid, machjed, machjid – mosque

mātrikā – mother goddesses

maulvī – a learned scholar of Muslim law

maulyā – honey gatherer

maund – a measure of weight, approximately 25–28 pounds or ten pounds troy weight

māyā – the magic of creation and its illusory nature, often the source of confusion

miyā – sir, master, my good sir; affectionate for friend

mohāmmadi – Islamic, i.e., of Muhāmmad or Mohāmmad

mollā – leader of a mosque, ideally but not always with formal religious education; from the Arabic *mawlā*, master

mṛdaṅga – a large double-ended drum, resonant in the mid-ranges, with braces and blocks for tuning each head

muni – a traditional Indic sage, a seer

munśi, munśī, munsi, munsī – learned scholar and scribe

murid – student of a Sufi teacher, i.e., *murśid,* q.v.

murśid – Sufi teacher

musalmān, muchalmān, mochalmān; adj., *musalmāni, muchalmāni* – practitioner of Islam, oriented toward Islam

nabī – prophet, usually Muhāmmad as The Prophet

nāg, nāgā – serpent; underworld serpent deities that have their earliest roots in the Vedas

nāmā – book, chronicle

nāmāj – ritual prayer; from Persian *namāz*

naobata – kettledrum, which can vary in size

naphs – ego, self, spirit; but also the location of human frailty, desires, the animal nature of self that needs to be brought under control; from Arabic *nafs*

nasihat nāmā – a genre of didactic texts and tales, primarily to teach ethics and morality, in Bengal prolifically printed starting in the mid-nineteenth century

nāth – lord or master; follower of Gorakṣnāth, practitioner of *jog* or *yoga*

nur – the light of Āllā

nurnabī – lit., the Light of the Prophet, more often referred to in Arabic as the *nūr muḥammadī*, a preexisting entity in the formation of the cosmos that preceded the creation of Adam

oli – saint, guardian, friend; from Arabic *walliy* and Persian *walī omma* – community of the faithful, *ummā*, qv.

pākhoyāj – a barrel-shaped double-ended drum with deep sonorous tones

pālā – section of a composition

pāñcālī, pācāli – a metrical form that lends itself to song, usually in praise of a deity or heroic figure

paṇḍit – learned scholar or advisor, knowledgeable of scriptures and ritual processes

param puruṣ – supreme divinity

paris – færies

payār – early modern Bangla metrical form, a couplet of fourteen-syllable verses, with caesuras after syllables 8 and 14

paygambar, pekāmbar – messenger of God, usually referring to the Prophet Muhāmmad, and a generic term for special messengers other than Muhāmmad; in these texts, the term is also used as generic for prophet

phakir, phakīr; f., *phakirāni, phakirani* – Sufi practitioner, usually a mendicant

phānā – annihilation of the sense of self in the beloved; from Persian *fanā*

pharmān, pharamān – order, command, mandate; official decree

phārsī – Farsi or Persian

pīr – an advanced Sufi practitioner

pīr kathās – *pīr* stories

piśāc, piśaci – flesh-eating globlins

prāṇ – life, life-breath; beloved

prasād – food offerings made to deity and returned to worshiper as ingestible grace; also to show favor or be gracious toward someone

prem – pure love, equated with *'ishq, esk,* q.v.

pūjā – traditional worship of a deity, lit., to show honor or respect

purāṇ, adj., purāṇic – a genre of old tales, initially in Sanskrit, that tell the mythologies of gods, goddesses, and cultural heroes

purohit – presiding *brāhmaṇ* priest responsible for performing religious and life-cycle rituals

puthi, punthi, pūthi – a book or manuscript, but also the classification of inexpensive popular texts for *musalmāni* readers

rabāb – a lute-like stringed instrument

rachul, rasul – apostle, Mohāmmad as the Apostle

rāg, rāginī – often erroneously called a song, it is more of a melodic framework within which the musician improvises

rājā – king, ruler

rākṣas; f., *rākṣasi, rākkasi* – ghoul, demon

rānī – queen consort of a *rājā,* q.v.

ras – lit., juice or sap, semen; the essence of something; the experience of emotion

rati śāstra – classical texts devoted to the arts of love, which include the familiar *kāma sūtra*

ryot – peasant, tenant farmer

śā, sā, śāh, sāh, śāhā, sāhā – king; an honorific for any male in the royal line; an honorific for any accomplished Sufi

sadāgar – merchant, particularly long-haul oceangoing traders

saheb, sāheb, chāheb – honorific for someone of higher social rank; sir, gentleman, master, or king

sāi – a *phakir,* q.v., as an intimate associate and friend; more generally a good *musalmān,* q.v.

saiyad – honorific for those recognized or claiming descent from Muhāmmad

śākta – worshiper of the goddess, who frequently demands a blood sacrifice

sālām ālek – the greeting "May peace be upon you"; from Arabic *as-salāmu ʿalykum*

sandeś, sondeś – a quintessential bite-sized Bengali milk sweet, always available at festive occasions; made from sugar, paneer, and cardamom

saṅgam – confluence of rivers

sannyāsī; f., *sanyāsinī* – generic name for ascetic renouncer, or specifically a follower of the god Śiv; synonymous in these texts with *vairāgī, vairāginī,* q.v.

sarddār, saradār – leader, chieftain

śāriā – proper way of conduct for Muslims, religious law

sati, satī – virtuous woman or perfect wife, reference to Śiv's wife, daughter of Dakṣa

satya – true, real, pure, virtuous, valid

saycān – falcon

sekh, shekh – spiritual guide, village leader; from Arabic *shaykh sharīʿāh, śāriat* – the first stage or step in Sufi practice, following legal prescriptions

siddha – perfected mendicant of the *nāth*, q.v., tradition

śirṇi, śirṇī, sirṇī, sirni, siriṇī, sirini, śinni, śinnī – concoction of rice flour, sugar, milk, banana, and spices offered to Sufi *pīrs* and the favored food of Satya Pīr

śūdra – lowest of the four traditional Indic social groups or castes, the serving class

svayambhū – self manifested, applied to certain images of God, such as Jagannāth in Puri

ṭākā – rupee, basic unit of cash

tāl, tāla – rhythm of a musical *rāg*, q.v.

talwār – a single-edged sword with distinctive curved blade and generally a disc-shaped pommel

tāntrik – practitioners of esoteric, often transgressive, ritual practices

taohid – assertion of the oneness of God, which in Sufi terms suggests that all essences are divine and there is no absolute existence except God; from Arabic *tawḥīd*, "making one"

tapas – meditative penance through which ascetics gain salvific knowledge and through that, power over the created world

tarikat – the second stage or step of Sufi practice, overt spiritual exercises

tasbi – rosary or chaplet used for uttering the names of god

ṭhākur – ruling lord or master, god; f., *ṭhākurāṇī*, goddess

ṭiṭīr – lapwing or plover

tripadī – triplet, or three-foot meter, with the third line longer, normally 6–6–8 syllables or 8–8–10 syllables, but other even-numbered combinations that retain the symmetry are possible

turuk – Turk, used to indicate specific ethnicity, but also as a generic term for a *musalmān*, q.v.

ukil, wakil – a delegate who acts on behalf of a client, a lawyer

ummā – community of the faithful, *omma*, qv.

vaikuṇṭha – the traditional *vaiṣṇav* heaven, but also a generic name for heaven; *behest*, q.v.

vairāgī; f., *vairāginī* – *vaiṣṇav* ascetic

vaiṣṇav – worshiper of Viṣṇu, Nārāyaṇ, or Kṛṣṇa, and in Bengal, of the historical figure of Kṛṣṇa-Caitanya (1486–1533)

vasudhārā – preparatory wedding ritual that sanctifies the space by painting auspicious marks on the walls of the bridal chamber

Veda, adj., Vedic – earliest Sanskrit texts of revelation in ancient India; adj., from that early age

vidyādharī – a celestial nymph and heavenly musician

viraha – the exquisite agony of lovers' separation elevated to the sublime

vrat – a domestic ritual, usually performed by women, for domestic weal; the accompanying story, called *vrat kathā*

vṛddhiśrāddha – traditional Indic rituals honoring departed ancestors

yogī – practitioner of ascetic penance and meditation called *tapas,* q.v.

yūp (Skt., *yūpa*) – the ritual post on which the sacrificial animal is secured for beheading or dismembering

zamindar; (adj) zamindari – a Mogul-era collector of land revenue, or tax farmer

N.B. Flora and fauna are indicated in the notes ad loc.

ACKNOWLEDGMENTS

The myriad voices that crowd the head of any translator, story characters that intrude at the oddest moments and demand attention in the strangest ways, have a presence that is inevitably ephemeral, and I find the path we tread together sometimes a bit surreal, much as the author Kṛṣṇarām Dās did when he was waylaid on the road by the god Dakṣiṇ Rāy, who insisted he write the "correct" version of his tale that today is called the *Rāy maṅgal*. That I have inevitably engaged in conversations with the characters and the long-dead authors of these texts has engendered a curious and sustained interaction, a sense of intimacy, however imaginal, increasingly magnified in these past two years of Covid, when they were often my only source of social intercourse. But this communion has engendered a profound sense of privilege to bring their ideas, their literary impulses, to the attention of an English-speaking audience. While I may feel isolated amidst the crowds of characters I have conjured and with whom I commune, when I look back, I realize that I have not undertaken this task in quite the isolation it may sometimes seem, for I have leaned on others, on the their help and inspiration, many of whom may not even realize their rôle in the undertaking. These are some of those people I would like to acknowledge.

A little over a decade ago, Annu Jalais was visiting me at TeeKaySadan, my other home of six years in Baridhara, Dhaka, as I ran the Bangla Language Institute at Independent University, Bangladesh. As we sat in the living room that afternoon and talked about her ground-breaking work on Bonbibī,[1] she

1. Annu Jalais, *Forest of Tigers: People, Politics, and Environment in the Sundarbans* (London: Routledge, 2010).

pressed me rather earnestly to translate the full text of Mohāmmad Khater's *Bonbibī jahurānāmā*, a seemingly innocent suggestion on the surface that vacillated somewhere between a plaintive request and a quietly insistent imperative, both of which I took to heart. This anthology is the result. I have come to realize that what lurked behind Annu's entreaty was a concern that the stories of these Bengali Sufi *phakīrs* and *pīrs*, *bibīs*, and *pīrānīs* played a larger rôle in the cultural life of the Bangla-speaking world than has generally been recognized, that their stories were just as worthy of consideration as the well-known poets of Arabic and Persian who have dominated the world of Sufi translations, or the works of the myriad Hindu, especially *bhakti*, poets of early modern Bengal.

I first encountered many of the figures in this anthology in the early 1980s in Asim Roy's pioneering monograph *The Islamic Syncretistic Tradition in Bengal*,[2] a study that alerted me to the possibilities of this vast literature, which few seemed to recognize. Edward M. Yazijian, whom I first met in Bangladesh in the mid-1990s, and who is now teaching at Furman University, very graciously shared with me a draft of his translation of Ābdur Rahim's narrative of Gāji, Kālu, and the maiden Cāmpāvatī, which served as the basis for his master's thesis at the University of Chicago in 2001. While I chose to translate another version of that tale, it did confirm for me that there was a literature of no small proportion begging to be explored, prompting me to search for texts far beyond the considerable Satya Pīr material I had amassed, which resulted in the set of translations titled *Fabulous Females and Peerless Pīrs*.[3] A short while after that publication, I began a conversation about Bonbibī with Sufia Uddin, currently at Connecticut College, whose own early draft translation of the Bonbibī tale revealed that these texts were much more sophisticated undertakings than the term "folktale" would suggest. And since that time we have enjoyed many conversations revolving around these topics and the surprising worlds created in these texts.

When I presented my findings regarding these sophisticated and unusual narratives to different audiences around the globe and summarized the texts for them, they often had difficulty believing me. Why? Because these stories were unlike any Sufi compositions most had previously encountered. That repeated reception of incredulity settled the matter, so although I squeezed in as many translated excerpts as space allowed in my monograph *Witness to Marvels*,[4] I realized early on that audiences needed to be able to read

2. Asim Roy, *The Islamic Syncretistic Tradition in Bengal* (Princeton, NJ: Princeton University Press, 1983).

3. Tony K. Stewart, trans., *Fabulous Females and Peerless Pīrs: Tales of Mad Adventure in Old Bengal* (New York: Oxford University Press, 2004).

4. Tony K. Stewart, *Witness to Marvels: Sufism and Literary Imagination* (Berkeley: University of California Press, 2019), DOI: https://doi.org/10.1525/luminos.76.

the texts in complete unabridged translations. More recently, Amitav Ghosh enthusiastically added his encouragement to publish the translations, for as he succinctly put it to me late one night while sharing a glass of Johnny Drum Bourbon, people really need to hear these stories. I could not agree more.

In my search for texts, Robert Evans, my good friend and colleague since the late 1970s—whom I have affectionately dubbed "Bibliography Bob" since our book-buying jaunts together in Calcutta in 1981–82—not only conferred with me on text editions, but painstakingly photographed several rare texts from his personal collections, texts I could not locate in any repository, and which clarified differences among similarly titled works. Hena Basu, my long-time research assistant in Kolkata, has likewise consulted on a number of issues of bibliography and translation, and her dedicated work over the past four decades has forever endeared her to me. Farina Mir at the University of Michigan has been a strong supporter of this work and provided a much-needed boost when the anthology was lagging, though she probably didn't realize it at the time. Two wonderfully accomplished translators and skillful interpreters of Indic texts—Martha Ann Selby and Syed Akbar Hyder—both of the University of Texas at Austin, made fine-grained suggestions as readers of the manuscript, recommendations that in the end made it more legible and feel more natural to an English speaker. To them both I owe a debt of gratitude. And Cynthia Talbot, also of the University of Texas at Austin, in her rôle as chair of the Coomaraswamy Prize Committee, confirmed beyond doubt the rightness of the decision to make these texts available to a wider audience than our specialists' world might normally address.

Ayesha A. Irani, currently at the University of Massachusetts Boston, co-translated the last tale in the anthology, the story of Khoyāj Khijir's instruction to Musā. Her work on the *Nabīvaṃśa*, from which Musā's story is drawn, is a much welcomed addition to the analysis of early modern *musalmāni* literatures,[5] and I have and continue to draw on her considerable linguistic expertise in this project and others. Our many and varied conversations have had a salutary effect on all of the translations in this anthology. And of course, Dick Eaton's seminal work on Islam in Bengal has led to many conversations that contributed to my understanding of these texts, which I hope have opened new avenues of research that complement and expand his award-winning historical survey.[6]

5. Ayesha A. Irani, *The Muhammad Avatāra: Salvation History, Translation, and the Making of Bengali Islam* (New York: Oxford University Press, 2021).

6. Richard M. Eaton, *The Rise of Islam and the Bengal Frontier, 1204-1760* (Berkeley: University of California Press, 1996).

In an ongoing conversation with Max Stille that began just as he was finishing his master's thesis, "Metrik und Poetik der Josephsgeschichte Muhammad Sagirs,"[7] and who currently works with NETZ Bangladesch, Partnerschaft für Entwicklung and Gerechtigkeit, e.V., has over the past decade encouraged me to take seriously the literary value of these texts. Every time we have met since—in London, Nashville, Paris, Warsaw, Cairo, Lisbon, and Berlin—he has gently but firmly reminded me how important these texts are as literature and implored me to make them available to an English-speaking audience.

The late Professor M.R. Tarafdar of Dhaka University was among the first to encourage the research that led to both the monograph and these translations through his own work on the allegorical romance traditions of early modern Bengal.[8] His unexpected passing in 1997, just months after spending a half-academic year in residence with me in North Carolina, courtesy of the Rockefeller Foundation, was a crippling blow, which took a number of years for me to reconcile. I more recently mourned the loss of my long-term teacher and friend Anisuzzaman, distinguished professor of Bangla and Bangla Literature at Dhaka University, and Bangladeshi statesman, who in 2020 died of Covid-19 complications. We spent many evenings together, both in Dhaka and when he was resident in North Carolina, discussing issues related to his seminal book on Bengali Muslim intellectual history,[9] and more generally Bangla belles lettres, especially how best to present tales of this sort to both specialist and nonspecialist audiences. Professor Momin Chowdhury of Dhaka University and of the Asiatic Society of Bangladesh, a longtime colleague of mine, encouraged my work both in Dhaka and during the time he recently spent at Vanderbilt University; what started as a strong professional connection has now grown into a deeply personal one, for which I am grateful. Perween Hasan, long-standing art historian at Dhaka University and now Vice Chancellor of Central Women's University, was among the first to recognize how these texts change our perceptions of early modern Islam in Bengal and what it means to be both Bengali and Muslim; her encouragement to publish these tales has been productively insistent. Niaz Zaman, former Professor of English at Dhaka University and advisor to the English Department of Independent University, Bangladesh (IUB), always managed to pry open the uncanny in literatures both Bangla and English in ways that never failed to provoke new

7. Max Stille, "Metrik und Poetik der Josephsgeschichte Muhammad Sagirs," master's thesis, Ruprecht-Karls-Universität Heidelberg, 2011.

8. Mamtājur Rahmān Taraphdār, *Bāṃlā ramāṇṭik kāvyer āoyādhī-hindī paṭbhūmi* (Ḍhākā: Ḍhākā Viśvavidyālay, 1972).

9. Ānisujjāmān, *Muslim-mānas o bāṃlā sāhitya [1959-1918]* (Ḍhākā: Pyāpirās, 2001).